Clare Connelly w
among a family of
childhood up a tre
is married to her own real-life hero, and ~~~~~~~~
bungalow near the sea with their two children. She is
frequently found staring into space—a surefire sign
that she's in the world of her characters. She has a
penchant for French food and ice-cold champagne,
and Mills & Boon novels continue to be her favourite
ever books. Writing for Mills & Boon is a long-held
dream. Clare can be contacted via clareconnelly.com
or her Facebook page.

Rachael Stewart adores conjuring up stories, from
heartwarmingly romantic to wildly erotic. She's been
writing since she could put pen to paper—as the stacks
of scrawled-on pages in her loft will attest to. A Welsh
lass at heart, she now lives in Yorkshire, with her very
own hero and three awesome kids—and if she's not
tapping out a story she's wrapped up in one or enjoying
the great outdoors. Reach her on Facebook, Twitter
@rach_b52, or at rachaelstewartauthor.com.

NO STRINGS CHRISTMAS

CLARE CONNELLY

UNWRAPPING THE BEST MAN

RACHAEL STEWART

MILLS & BOON

First Published in Great Britain 2020
by Mills & Boon, an imprint of HarperCollins*Publishers*
1 London Bridge Street, London, SE1 9GF

No Strings Christmas © 2020 Clare Connelly

Unwrapping the Best Man © 2020 Rachael Stewart

ISBN: 978-0-263-27769-2

MIX
Paper from
responsible sources
FSC™ C007454

This book is produced from independently certified FSC™ paper
to ensure responsible forest management.
For more information visit www.harpercollins.co.uk/green.

Printed and bound in Spain
by CPI, Barcelona

NO STRINGS CHRISTMAS

CLARE CONNELLY

MILLS & BOON

PROLOGUE

CHRIST, HE LOOKS HAPPY. And 'happy' isn't generally a word that comes to mind when I describe my twin. Dedicated. Focussed. Intent. Determined.

But right now, looking at him with his bride and their son—a nephew I didn't even know I had until a week or so ago—I feel as though I'm seeing Dim for the first time.

And why?

Because he's married?

Jesus. I thought we were on the same side of the fence there.

Marriage is shit.

Love is shit.

There's no such thing as happily-ever-after.

I feel my smile dropping, a grim frown taking its place. It hardly says congratulations, and yet I can't help it.

We are both products of the same upbringing, and we've both always laughed—scorned, even—as our various friends took the plunge and dived into a life of matrimony. And we've met each other's eyes with a knowing look when, within eighteen months or so, divorce bells have rung.

Please. Marriage is for—what? Fools? Because Dimitrios is no fool and, looking at him and Annie, I feel—something. Not a change of heart, exactly, but a belief in hearts, and their power to open to each other. There's love between them, and there's love for their son.

Except love doesn't exist. My dad taught me that—taught both of us. It was a lesson I learned at a young age and it's stuck with me all my life. Love is a lie, and the flip side of believing yourself in love is inevitable pain. So what the hell is Dimitrios doing? Why would anyone walk into that willingly?

I force my smile back into place just as Annie's eyes slide towards me. She returns my smile, and then I look away again, guilty for the cynical direction of my thoughts. If Dimitrios is happy in this life—if marriage is for him—then I have no choice but to support him, even if I believe he's making a monumental mistake.

Give me a choice of lovers in every city in which we have business, and never more than two nights with each, and I'm the happiest I'll ever be.

CHAPTER ONE

'MACALLAN, ON THE ROCKS.' I tap my freshly mani-cured fingers against the top of the polished bar, slid-ing onto one of the stools, not daring to meet my own expression in the bevelled-edged mirror that hangs behind the service area.

I probably look exactly how I feel.

Frazzled and cross.

Fuck my fucking family.

I breathe out slowly, so my dark side-swept fringe lifts a little, landing with a soft thud against my brow. Why did I let my sister talk me into this?

'You can't not come home for Christmas, Jessica. It'll kill Mum.'

Yeah, yeah. I'm a sucker and it's Christmas—a time for family togetherness and all that schmaltzy warm, fuzzy crap that I usually love, but, ugh! This is the last place I want to be but, just like the good daughter I'm doing my best not to be, I stupidly boarded that plane and came back to Singapore. Except one hour with my parents, my perfect older sis-ter and my sister's creepy, sleazy, perfect-on-paper husband has reminded me exactly why I've made a life for myself in London. And despite the guilt trip my family tries to lay on me, London always will be home. It's where I spent the first ten years of my life, and it's where I feel most 'me'. Plus, when I'm on the other side of the world I only have to see my family a few times a year.

Like this—Christmas.

The bartender puts the Scotch down in front of me and I nod in thanks, lifting my phone to indicate I'll tap it as payment. He hands over the machine and without looking at the price I press my phone to the device. Several email notifications are sitting on my screen. I'll check those in a minute. Once I've calmed down and got some fresh air.

Well, as fresh as it can be in a bar. For the first time since walking in, I let my eyes drift around this place. It's long been a favourite of mine and as such is haunted with memories—good and bad. I've had a lot of important conversations here. Not to mention that time with sleaze ball Simon, aka my brother-in-law, when he calmly suggested we might like to have sex, you know, no big deal. And of course he did it in a way that almost sounded like a joke, because that's a skill serial philanderers have; but I knew he wasn't joking. Bastard. I grip my Scotch as though it's a life-line, lifting it to my lips.

The familiar pungency warms me immediately.

Heaven.

Relief.

I'm going to be okay. This is only two weeks.

Two weeks! Why did I come so early? Why didn't I just wait until December twenty-third?

Because of Dad's birthday—in a couple of days. It's a milestone—though he'll never admit that to anyone outside the family. I think my dad harbours some kind of fantasy that, despite having been at the helm of several blue-chip multinational corporations for the past four decades, and having a daughter who's thirty-two—Jemima—and me, twenty-eight, people might still believe he's only fifty.

'You're about to strangle that bloody glass, you know.' A deep, husky Australian accent has almost the same effect on my body as the Scotch. Warm and soothing, it reaches inside me, spreading warmth and pleasure like smoke.

I tilt my head slowly. I'm not sure what I'm expecting to see. This is a pretty prestigious institution so not exactly a beach bum, but the only Australian men I've ever known all boasted a certain air of salty, sandy dishevelment—just the way I like it. This man is not that.

In fact, this man is…

My eyes widen as realisation dawns.

'Zach Papandreo?'

His laugh is just as husky and sensual as his opening line would have suggested. His grin sends shards of awareness through me.

'Have we met?'

'No. Let's just say your reputation precedes you.'

'That doesn't seem fair.'

'You think there's something wrong with your reputation?'

His grin widens and he stands up so I get to appreciate the full six and a bit feet of him, his lean yet muscular frame in a dark grey suit with a blue and white striped shirt. No tie—the top two buttons are undone, revealing his neck and a hint of coarse chest hair. My stomach flips.

'Depends.' He lifts his shoulders as he moves to the stool opposite me, pointing at my drink then holding up a finger to indicate he'd like one of what I'm having. A quick glance shows me the bartender has seen and is already complying.

'So?'

I'm a sucker for male fragrance. I don't mean a department-store overly manufactured smell. I don't like men who are too fussy and vain. I like men who put a dab of something on in the morning, something masculine and woody, and then don't think of it again, so it mingles with their own hormones, and Zach Papandreo has got some kind of magical smell. I try not to breathe him in but there's some serious testosterone at play here. And is it any wonder?

Apart from being one half of a global media-mogul team—he and his twin brother own everything from television stations to radio networks to newspapers, magazines, websites, blogs and news apps all over the world—he is an undeniable playboy. Playboy? What am I, my mother? Try man whore. I don't mean that with even a hint of disapproval. He's renowned for his business nous and an aggressive investment strategy but, more than that, this half of the Papandreo brothers is renowned for the speed with which he goes through beautiful, glamorous lovers.

I'm not sure if he reads gossip blogs—I don't—but the app and online community I founded a few years back—She-Shakes—seems to get a lot of Zach Papandreo memes posted in there—shirtless ones get the most clicks. And I can see why.

Va-va-voom.

The bartender delivers Zach's drink; I lift mine towards it. 'Jessica Johnson.'

He grins again, clinking our glasses together. 'I feel like I'd remember meeting you, but your name's familiar.'

My smile briefly falters. 'You're probably thinking of my father—Clive Johnson?'

'Him I've heard of. I've met him a few times actually.'

No surprises there. Dad and this guy are cut from the same cloth and undoubtedly move in the same circles. I turn away, taking a drink of my Scotch until it burns all the way down.

'But no, I'm sure it's you I'm thinking of.'

I purse my lips. 'Really? Is that a line or are you being genuine?'

He laughs again and my whole body responds. My nipples tighten against the silk of my bra, my stomach clenches and heat fires in my veins.

'What do you do?'

I know he means for work, but I can't help flirting. I lean a little closer, my eyes locked to his in a way that is laced with suggestion. 'Do?' I sip my Scotch, not dropping my gaze.

His laugh is just a short sound now, husky and showing he has heard every hint of my suggestiveness and is returning it with his own.

I smile and lean back, more confident. 'I founded an online community, and a couple of years ago launched an app alongside it.'

He clicks his fingers. 'For women. The one that helps with job prospects and the like. She—She something.'

He's legitimately heard of me? 'She-Shakes,' I supply, surprised.

'Right. You're killing it.'

Pride hums inside me. It was a simple idea that kind of blew up into something much, much bigger. We're practically global now; the biggest hurdle is finding the support structures in each region.

'Thank you.'

'I'm serious. You work with women who are looking for jobs?'

I shake my head, brushing aside the over-simplification. 'It's so much more than that. We're an all-service programme for women. Yes, we offer job-prospect advice including how to rewrite CVs, pre-marital financial counselling, post-marriage financial counselling.' My lips twist cynically for a minute as I think of how many women use the latter service and how few the former. I see something spark in the depth of Zach's eyes, as though he understands the slight scepticism that colours my words. 'We help with salary negotiations and legal advice for all sorts of work-related situations.'

'Impressive. And your user base?'

'We have over five million clients worldwide.'

'On a subscription service?'

I nod. 'It's a modest fee for what we offer and we make sure we offer a percentage of our enrolment free every year. This isn't a money-making venture.' I frown. 'At least, it wasn't intended to be.'

He laughs. 'So what you're saying is you're making a shitload of money without meaning to?'

I sip my drink, not smiling. 'I reinvest almost all of the profits into building the community.'

His eyes are serious as they hold mine. 'You're an altruist.'

'And you're a capitalist.'

'You think you can't be both?'

I lift my shoulders. 'I'm not sure.'

He grins. 'Nor am I.' He chinks our glasses together once more, but this time he keeps his arm resting on the bar, creating a sort of frame around my body. I make no attempt to move away from him. I like being close—the intimacy warms me to the pit of my stomach.

'And now you're looking to sell?'

I lift a brow. 'How do you know that?'

'You're in my wheelhouse.' He wiggles his brows.

I'm not shy. Never have been, never will be. Shame briefly flashes in my belly because this is a trait I share with my father, and as much as possible I try to distance myself from the ways in which we're similar.

On autopilot and instinct, I lift a finger to Zach's chest, staring into the depths of his dark brown eyes. 'And what exactly does "being in your wheelhouse" entail?'

Heat sears me. I feel it erupt between us, as though a blowtorch is aimed right at me.

'I'm always looking for movers and shakers in the digital market.'

'And you like the way I move and shake?'

He stares at me for a second then bursts out laughing. 'You know how gross that would have sounded if I said it?'

I laugh right back. 'Yeah, true.'

He sobers. 'But you said it, so it was hot.'

'I'm flattered.'

'No, you're flirting, and you're very good at it.' More shame. So's my dad, if his string of affairs is anything to go by. I push those thoughts aside once and for all, wondering if one day his ghost will cease to haunt me.

Zach's other hand, the one that's not propped along the bar top, moves to my hip.

'You're sure we haven't met before,' he queries, moving so he can drink some Scotch. I smell a hint of it in the air between us, or maybe that's my own desire clouding all my senses.

'I think I'd remember that.'

'Likewise.' The word rumbles between us. 'What brings you to Singapore?'

'How do you know I don't live here?'

'Your accent.'

I lived in England for the first ten years of my life, then moved around depending on where Dad's latest corporate conquest required; his last job—and a long-term mistress—are both here in Singapore.

'You have an Australian accent but you live here.'

'I spend time here,' he says with a shrug. 'I live all over.'

'Ah. A man who refuses to be tied down. I hear that.'

He grins. 'Being tied down is highly overrated.'

Our eyes meet in a sign of solidarity. 'You're preaching to the choir.'

'Am I?'

My smile hides a multitude of hurts—hurts I've come to terms with over the years, but that doesn't mean they're not still lurking there. My father's philandering, the way it felt to discover how routinely unfaithful he'd been to my mother, my brother-in-law's attitudes to women—to think he could actually proposition me. The way I'd hurt the one man who'd ever loved me—I'd hurt Patrick so badly, just because I was careless. And the pain I've seen my mum and sister go through because of their marriages.

Who'd give up the freedom and independence of single life for the torment of a steady relationship?

I throw back the rest of my Scotch. 'Putting down roots is my idea of hell.'

It didn't used to be. As a kid dragged from one exclusive international private school to the next I used to desperately crave stability. I hated that Dad's job meant we had to move so often. I hated making new friends then losing them again almost as quickly; I hated needing to learn new systems, routines, rhythms, hang-outs, but now I feel completely blessed. Give me a rucksack, three bars of Internet access and a phone charger and I could disappear for weeks.

'So?' He leans forward and now his lips brush my cheek as he moves closer to my ear. My stomach feels as if I've just crested right over the top of a roller coaster. 'What brings you here?'

I bite down on my lower lip, massaging it with my teeth. For a second, I can barely think straight. 'To the bar?'

'To Singapore.'

'Family.' The word is grunted with all the feelings I have on that matter. He pulls back a bit and I suck in a sharp jab of breath, disappointed by the space between us. He grins as though he understands, but moves back further still. He's teasing me. Tormenting me. He's enjoying watching the effect he has on me.

Two can play that game. I take his bluff, sitting back in the seat myself, shifting a little so that the white silk blouse I wear strains across my bra. He's not a male with a pulse if he doesn't notice. I hold my position a moment then reach for my drink. It's empty.

He lifts a hand to the waiter then turns to me. 'Another?'

I shake my head. 'I'm feeling a little…light-headed.'

His lips flick into the hint of a grin. 'Something to eat?'

I shake my head again. I'm not hungry. At least, I'm not hungry yet.

'Are you staying in the hotel?'

I nod.

'What room?'

This is happening fast. I contemplate that for a second. Too fast? But hell, no. This is exactly what I need right now. A night of mind-blowing sex—meaningless, passionate sex—with someone like Zach Papandreo. It's the perfect distraction.

'The Orangery.' The suite I'm staying in was named for the enormous glass living space. Built in the early twentieth century, it's ornate and beautiful, and the glass gives it the feeling of being open to space and time.

His eyes don't flicker from my face.

'Have a bottle of Dom Perignon sent to The Orangery—charge it to me.' He stands, his hand brushing then curling around mine. 'And some oysters, chocolates and strawberries.' He grins, shrugs, and my stomach tightens. 'I'm a little hungry.'

I tilt my head back on a laugh, standing, but his arm whooshes me to his side and the laugh dies on my lips. My body melds to his, my slim curves pressed to his muscular hardness, and a bolt of adrenalin and desire splinters through me.

I'm going to do this and it's going to be fucking amazing. Because Zach Papandreo will definitely not disappoint.

'Well, Jessica Johnson, you've certainly brightened my night.'

I lift my eyes to his face, wondering if I'm not the only one who's come here to run away from something.

It's a question I don't ask, because I'm not sure I want—or need—to know the answer. This is just about sex, no secrets and soul-baring required.

'This way.' I nod towards the bank of elevators, certainty forming inside me. One night, no strings and a whole lot of pleasure. Yes, please…

CHAPTER TWO

I HADN'T COME here to hook up. I had a meeting with a network exec and I like the environment at the bar of this hotel. On a Friday evening there's a pianist who knocks out old jazz songs, and I'm recognised enough for my favourite bottle of wine to be brought to the table without any need to place an order. It's also somewhere that does the bare minimum of Christmas decorations and for a guy like me—who hates this time of year with a passion—that's a welcome relief. The crappy glittery abominations that line the streets right now almost make me want to gouge my eyes out. Here—it's muted, much more my taste.

Meeting Jessica Johnson was an unexpected bonus, but I've never been one to look a gift horse in the mouth. And she is some kind of gift. The elevator doors open, we step inside, they zoom shut. She presses her card against the panel then selects a button. The elevator begins to move, passing each floor with a little light buzzing above the door. I look down at her. She looks up at me.

Fuck.

I haven't felt this attracted to a woman I've just met in a *long* time. Jessica captivated me from the minute she strode to the bar wearing jeans that were like a second skin with fashionable holes in the knees, and a white silk blouse tucked in at the waist that high-lighted her curves in all the right ways. Watching her order a Scotch was another turn-on. She's a woman who knows what she wants and goes after it. There's no meekness in her manner, just pure confidence. She exudes intelligence and power.

And those are my biggest weaknesses when it comes to the opposite sex.

Her lips flicker into a smile. Not a normal smile. This one is pure promise. As if to underscore what she's thinking, her eyes drop lower, finding the open-ing of my shirt and lingering on the pulse point there, before sweeping even lower, as though mentally re-moving my clothes and assessing what she sees. Her eyes are huge and brown, glossy like liquid. Her lashes are long and as her gaze travels the length of my body her thick black eyelashes are like fans against her creamy skin.

Fuck it.

I reach behind her and press the 'stop' button on the elevator. It thuds to an abrupt halt—before that's complete I turn my body towards hers, sweeping her into my arms and pushing her back against the wall of the elevator. She gasps in surprise, her eyes like saucers.

'You shouldn't look at me like that.' The words emerge as a growl.

'Like what?' Innocent and sweet—my dick is already harder than a rock but somehow it tightens in my pants, making me shift my legs a bit.

'Like you want to fucking eat me.'

'But what if I do?' She purrs, lifting her brows in a silent challenge, one hand snaking to my waist and flicking the button of my pants open.

I suck in an uneven breath as she draws the zip down, her eyes showing amusement and promise all at once.

Pants unzipped, she slides her hand back to my navel then pushes it inside the cotton of my boxers, her fingertips curling around the length of my cock, her breath growing husky as she tilts her head back a little on a wave of something—pleasure, anticipation, triumph—I have no idea.

'Fu-u-u-ck.' Her touch is so good. Her fingertips brush the tip of my arousal and I make a throaty noise before dropping my head and nipping her shoulder with my teeth.

She responds with a groan, low in her throat, and suddenly I can't take it any longer. Her touch is inquisitive, too slow; I need more. I need everything and I need it now. But hell, we're in an elevator and I know there are security cameras in these things. Shifting my body and pushing her back into the corner, where she'll get maximum privacy, I kiss her, my lips ruthless in claiming hers, possessing her as an answer to her touch, showing her that the same madness runs rampant in my blood. She whimpers and I kiss her harder, pressing her head against the wall, my body hard to hers so her hand is flattened inside my pants. She moans, moving her fingers up and down, and I feel a hint of precum spill from my dick. I need to get her to a bedroom, or at least inside closed doors, and soon.

My hands pull her blouse from her waistband as though they've got a mind of their own, my fingers brushing the bare skin of her waist, pushing higher to the silk of her bra. I slide my fingers underneath, loosening it enough so that I can cup her breasts, feeling the sweet pucker of her nipples in the palms of my hands. She makes a mewing noise of pleasure right into my mouth; I grind my hips, pressing my cock harder into her hand. She flexes her fingers, rewarding me with a rhythmic movement that, while fantastic, completely threatens my equilibrium.

Without a slight buzz and definitely without our consent, the elevator begins to move again, continuing its upward trajectory. I don't want to stop what we're doing for even a second but the fact is somewhere deep inside me is a decent guy and I don't particularly want to expose Jessica to the kind of publicity she'd get if she were seen half naked in a lift with me.

I pull my hands loose of her bra, replacing it carefully, then straighten her shirt, dislodge her hand from my pants and step backwards. Jesus Christ, it must only take eleven seconds to reach her floor but they're the longest eleven seconds of my life.

She shoots me a look that is searingly hot as she

strides out of the lift, just as she strode into the bar downstairs—full of purpose.

The corridor has a high roof and windows that reveal a beautiful view of the city. There are only three doors, showing how few suites are on this level. At the end, she clicks her key card against a lock. The light flashes green and she pushes it inwards, holding the door open for me to follow. I step in as she flicks the lights on—dull, moody lighting, sensual and classy. I've been in quite a few of these rooms over the years but never this one. The furnishings match the décor of the hotel, playing up its late-nineteenth-century roots with colonial antiques, though hints of modernity abound too, in the classy lights and the enormous flat-screen television mounted across the room. It's a corner suite—one side is walls and doors, and the other two are open to the night sky, glass reaching over the city, creating an incredible sense of being out in the open.

'These rooms were added on in the fifties, when they did the extension,' she explains, as though I give a shit about the architecture.

'I know.' I shrug out of my suit jacket, moving deeper into the suite and draping it over the back of an armchair that's been upholstered in a floral material.

Her eyes drop to my chest, doing that thing again, as if she's mentally undressing me. I laugh, a husky sound of mirth that has her eyes gradually wrenching upwards. 'What?'

'You're doing it again.'

'What?'

'Looking at me like you want to eat me.'

'Didn't I already answer that?' she ponders, and now she doesn't stride towards me exactly. She glides, if that's possible, but there's the same look of purpose in her face, and her body's taut, poised for action. I stand exactly where I am, wondering at this slightly unexpected turn of events. I'm always in the box seat. When I take a woman to bed, *I* do the taking. I seduce and tease and flirt and tempt and pleasure—I pride myself on being able to deliver multiple orgasms—but Jessica seems to want to drive this and I don't find I have any issues with that whatsoever. She stands in front of me for a second, having to tilt her chin up to meet my eyes—she's probably almost a foot shorter than I am, but there's so much strength in her that she doesn't seem diminutive.

Her eyes stay locked to mine as she pushes my still-unbuttoned pants down to my knees where she lifts her foot and catches them, pushing them the rest of the way. I step out of them at the same time I kick off my shoes and socks, my eyes scanning her face as if to challenge her: what next?

She lets a slow smile cross her face in response, reaching to my chin and drawing my face down a little.

'Are the rumours about you true?'

I'm momentarily distracted, so I find it hard to respond. Her hands push into my boxer shorts, removing them in the same way she did my pants, until I step out of them.

'That depends on what rumour you've heard,' I somehow manage to reply.

Her smile is lopsided. 'You're a player.'

Something about that wedges inside me. 'Player' is one of those words that has negative connotations whereas my decision to avoid relationships is a gold-star choice, in my book. Nothing negative about it. 'Meaning?'

'That you like sex.'

'Who doesn't?'

'With a lot of different women.'

'Yeah.' I'm not ashamed of that. Fortunately, as a man, I haven't needed to be—that's a double standard I've never particularly appreciated.

'As in, you don't do girlfriends.'

A blade of panic slips into my chest. I don't do girlfriends. Haven't done since Emily and never will again, because of Emily. Once bitten, twice shy. But is that what Jessica's looking for? Does she think to-night is the precursor to something more between us?

I take a step back and she makes a throaty, laughing noise.

'Easy, tiger.' She steps my way, closing the distance between us, her eyes on mine in a way that pushes fire right into my soul. 'I'm not asking you to be my boyfriend.'

It's so absurd that I laugh, but even I can hear it's a shaky sound rent with relief.

'This is strictly a one-night thing, okay?'

I stare at her, relief flooding my veins. What is she? Some kind of creation from my fantasies? I don't think I've ever had a woman spell that out to me. I'm usually the one giving the 'boundaries' talk.

'You sure you'll be done with me in one night?' I tease, surprising myself because it almost sounds like *I* won't be done with her.

'Oh, I'm absolutely positive, but I do so admire your confidence.'

And on that zinger, she drops to her knees, batting her long black lashes up at me until I find that there's a stitch in my chest because of how hard she's made it to breathe.

'I must say, in this department, I can definitely see how you earned your reputation.' Her fingertip traces my cock from base to tip. I tilt my head back and stare up at the ornate chandelier overhead, my gaze shifting sideways to the glass ceiling across the room as she takes my arousal into her mouth, just the tip, just enough to make my whole body tighten, my balls firming up with the promise of what's to come. She moves slowly, as if she instinctively knows how much of a torment that is when I just want to dig my fingers into her hair and push her head forward to take me deep into her mouth. Fuck. Images of that roll through my mind as she flicks her tongue across me and then, as if she's read my innermost thoughts, she surges forward, taking my length in one sudden motion, so I connect with the back of her throat and have to rock on my heels a bit. My eyes fill with stars.

I dig my hands into my hips to stop from reaching for her—it takes every ounce of discipline I possess.

She works the length of my cock; her mouth is so wet and warm, I feel as if I could seriously lose myself right now—so much for one night, I might not even make it one hour... Christ.

She pulls back, looking up at me as she rolls her tongue over my tip and that's the final straw. I reach down, grabbing Jessica beneath her arms, lifting her in one urgent motion, kissing the delightful mouth that had, a second ago, been driving me beyond the point of sanity. I push her, or maybe she drags me, I can't tell because we're both moving with the same frantic, urgent, desperate hunger, until her back is against a wall and I'm pressing my body to hers, my cock at the seam of her jeans, the tightness of the denim a desperate, aching barrier to what I need.

'I want to fuck you so hard,' I groan, fisting a hand in her hair, its silky length reminding me of rope and blindfolds and all things good.

She bites down on my lower lip, lifting one leg around my waist, inviting me closer. 'Then fuck me. Fuck me now.'

I don't need to be asked twice. 'Bedroom?' I ask, swooping down and lifting her over one shoulder so she laughs—but it's an uneven sound, filled with a burst of emotion—and points down the hallway.

'So conservative? I'm almost disappointed.'

I grin, smacking her butt for good measure. 'I don't think anyone's ever called me conservative before.' I swipe my jacket as I pass, carrying it—and more importantly, my condom-holding wallet—into a massive bedroom with sweeping views over Esplanade

Park. I can just make out the lights of the cenotaph in the distance.

'There's a first time for everything.'

I drop her down on the edge of the bed, tossing my jacket beside her. She angles her face towards it with a hint of a frown, then looks back up at me. I'm already reaching for the buttons of her blouse, pushing at them quickly, until it opens to reveal the pale, creamy skin of her stomach, the white silk of her bra and the shape of her round breasts. I reach behind her, flicking the bra strap open; she sits up so I can disentangle the bra and shirt, tossing both to the ground beside me.

'Tsk-tsk, they'll rumple, Zach.'

I lift a brow. 'So we'll get Housekeeping.'

She rolls her eyes. 'So spoiled.' She reaches up, grabbing my arm, taking advantage of the fact I'm a little unsteady in the legs after the way she went down on me a moment ago, yanking me to the bed and rolling up over me at the same time. She holds herself above me, her naked breasts crushed to the cotton of my shirt, warm through the material, making me wish I had way fewer clothes—and that she did too. Even through the jeans she wears though, she begins to move as though I were inside her, rocking her hips, teasing me with how close we are. She bites down on her lip then sits up, arching her back so I have a perfect view of her breasts as she rolls her hips until her breathing is rushed. Jesus, she's going to come.

I shift my hands to her jeans, flicking the button open and pushing up, manoeuvring her to standing so she can get out of the damned things. When she's naked, I take a second, just staring at her, devouring her with my eyes, the dusky pink of her areolae fascinating me, demanding my attention, until my eyes travel lower to the hint of dark curls at the top of her thighs. I've never seen anything more beautiful. She is perfection. I reach for her wrist, my voice deep, 'Get back here.'

She laughs, that same off-kilter laugh, and I drop my head between her thighs, my tongue finding her most sensitive flesh and flicking her as I drive a finger into her moist core. She's already so turned on, she's so wet. I move my tongue harder, faster, and in a matter of seconds she's spiralling over the edge, her pussy tightening around me in spasms, her voice rough in the air as she cries out, over and over, calling my name to the stars above Singapore.

I've never felt more like some kind of fucking sex god.

CHAPTER THREE

HE'S A FUCKING sex god. Oh, my God. I don't think I've ever had a more intense orgasm in my life. I push up onto my elbows and he's not even taking a victory lap, looking at me waiting for praise like so many other guys I can think of. Zach Papandreo is way too self-assured for that. Didn't I peg him as an arrogant alpha CEO-type the second I met him? Even before that, I knew what he'd be like. Still, his overt self-confidence is refreshing.

He's kissing my inner thigh gently, slowly, as if he understands I need a minute to catch my breath. His fingers move to my stomach, drawing invisible little swirls there, and goosebumps lift my skin all over. I arch my back, making a low, soft moaning noise, writhing as warmth and pleasure spread through my whole body.

His mouth follows his fingers, his tongue tracing small circles over my stomach first then moving higher, running over the underside of one of my breasts so I groan, lifting my back; whatever hunger he appeased by making me come so damn hard is right back, building with unrelenting pressure, filling me with a deep, aching need. I roll my hips in a silent invitation, needing to feel his beautiful dick deep inside me.

'I need—'

But before I can finish the sentence, an unfamiliar noise peals through the suite. I stare at him blankly, but Zach is already pushing off me, reaching for his boxers.

'Room service,' he explains.

'Fuck the bloody oysters.' I groan. 'Tell them to leave it.'

He smirks—completely aware of how crazy I am for him. 'I'll be right back.'

I pout as he leaves, then fall back on the bed, staring up at the ceiling, a slow smile curving over my lips. I hadn't gone to the bar in the hope of company. In fact, I'd walked in pretty damned steamed up, just wanting to be alone with a Scotch for a half-hour or so before coming to my suite and running a bubble bath. Zach was a very unexpected bonus.

Exactly what I need to forget about my parents, my sister, my brother-in-law... I shudder, pushing them all from my mind. I don't want to focus on my family right now. Perfect from the outside, a red-hot mess on the inside. But lots of families are messy; it's not that. It's my inability to help. It's the reality of seeing your mum and sister hurt and disrespected every day—of seeing your dad be the instrument of your mother's pain. It's feeling as though two of the people you love most in the world are living in pain and not being able to help them.

I don't want to lose my buzz. I don't want to let reality intrude. I've grappled with my feelings about my mum, my dad, their marriage, for years and never made any headway. It just leaves me feeling heavy in the heart and, right now, I want to feel the opposite. I want a break from that.

I run my hand over my breasts, shivering at the sensations that his touch has aroused, that my fingers now echo. I move my hand lower, over my stomach and down to my sex, arching my back as sensations riot through my body.

'Uh-uh.' His voice is a deep growl from the door. I angle my face in that direction without moving my hand away. He's wearing just the cotton boxers, a very visible arousal making them tent in an obvious way.

I lift a single brow. 'Did you answer the door like that?'

He lifts his bare shoulders—they're very nice shoulders, and I'm a bit of a shoulder and arm aficionado, I have to say. His are rounded, muscular without being bulky, tanned in the way of someone who spends time outdoors, smooth and warm to the touch.

'Nothing they haven't seen before, I'm sure.'

He's carrying the bottle of champagne. His eyes hold mine as he strides across the room, placing it deliberately on the bedside table as he strips out of the shorts.

Swoon.

I move my fingers harder, waves of pleasure build-

ing inside me, an inexorable heat radiating through
my body demanding release. He watches with a look
on his face that makes my body throb, then reaches
for the champagne, curling his fingers over the cork
to avoid a loud noise.

My pleasure builds. I am riding a wave, my body
glowing with heat and desire. I watch as he removes
a condom from his wallet, his body taut, his concen-
tration all on me as he opens the foil and slides the
rubber over his length. My need grows. I groan, so
sure release is close at hand.

He hasn't brought any champagne glasses in. His
eyes hold mine as he lifts the bottle to his lips, taking a long drink—it's one of the sexiest things I've
ever seen. But when he brings his body over mine,
the weight of him on me combined with his masculine fragrance and the strength of his cock between
my legs, I feel as though I'm in complete free fall.
He kisses me, and it's only then I realise his mouth
is still full of champagne. He passes it to me; some
dribbles down my cheeks onto the bed, but the flavour is so erotic I don't care—I barely even notice.
I ache for him in a way that takes my breath away.

He pushes up on one elbow as though assessing me, but there's a look in his eyes of feverish desire that I completely understand. He reaches for the
champagne bottle, taking another drink, but this time
he brings his mouth to my breast, wrapping his lips
around my nipple so I have the strange sensation of
warmth and cool as the champagne dribbles over my
breast, fizzing as it slides towards the bed. I whimper.

Another sip of champagne and my other breast has the same treatment; I've never been so turned on in my life. His fingers pull at my nipples so that I cry out, because despite the anaesthesia of ice-cold champagne there's a pain in his touch, a beautiful, heady pain owing to how sensitised I am.

More champagne, this time he drinks it, then holds the bottle to my lips, tipping a small amount in. I savour the flavour, watching him. His eyes narrow, so I know he likes that—watching me drink, or seeing me follow his instructions?

'I want to fuck you hard.'

He's already said that and I want it as much now as I did then. 'So what's stopping you?'

His smile is dark. 'I don't want to hurt you.'

A shiver of something like hot anticipation radiates the length of my spine. 'Do you think I'm made of glass?'

Something zings between us, fierce and intense.

He laces his fingers through mine, pulling me up.

'I thought you wanted to fuck me?'

He nods, pulling me across the room to where an antique dressing table sits. 'I'm not really a missionary kind of guy.'

I meet his eyes in the mirror, excitement and adrenalin bursting through me. This night is blowing all my expectations right out of the water. 'That's good.'

'Yeah?'

He moves his hands to my hips, guiding me backwards, then presses a palm between my shoulder blades, encouraging me to bend forward.

'I want to watch you as I take you like this,' he grunts, and the command of his words is a heady aphrodisiac. I bite down on my lip and when I see the way his eyes cling to the gesture, the obvious arousal that moves across his face, I keep doing it, my eyes on his holding a silent challenge.

'You're so fucking hot.' He says it as if that's a complaint.

Warmth fills my veins. 'Fascinating. But I thought you wanted to fuck me?' I prompt with an attempt at impatience that I don't quite pull off. My voice is breathy.

His hands grip my hips, holding me still, and his knee separates my legs a little. I keep my teeth pressed to my lip and not a second later he drives his rock-hard arousal into me in one deep, powerful thrust, so I cry out, because his possession is so complete. I brace my palms on the glass top of the table, closing my eyes for a second, but his hands reach around and tweak my nipples hard. Startled, my eyes dart towards his in the reflection.

'I want to watch you and I want you to watch too.'

I don't even think of disagreeing. This is so goddamned hot.

He pulls at my nipples as he thrusts into me and every single fibre of my being is on fire, I feel as though I'm about to explode. He keeps one hand on my breast and moves the other to my clit, strumming me with his fingers as he drives himself into me and I orgasm in a way I didn't know possible, all of me splitting apart completely at the seams, so I feel as if my body is in a thousand and one different cells of stardust and pleasure.

I have never been made love to like this. I have never known any kind of pleasure even close to this. The hand on my clit eases off a little, slides around my hip to my butt, where he starts to knead the flesh there, radiating more intense pleasure that I can barely tolerate. It's almost too much.

Almost.

Many times I almost close my eyes, but his missive remains in my mind. And watching him— this—me—brings a new level of realness to what I'm feeling. It's the invocation of a different sense, one that layers extra urgency and intensity to the passion that's overcoming us. I cry his name as another orgasm begins to build. I say his name over and over again, as though I'm casting a spell, as though I'm begging, as though I'm mad. I say his name and when I come this time, he says my name too, just once, a guttural noise that burrows deep into my core and buries itself there. He grips my hips tightly and holds himself deep inside me, so I feel every flex and spasm of his cock as his own release wrenches him from this real world, makes him, for a moment, a being without consciousness. He stares at me though, his cheeks slashed with dark colour, his eyes vibrant with sexual triumph, his lips parted, his chest moving in rapid rises and falls as he sucks air into his lungs.

My own body is floating through space. I feel as if I'm being carried on a cloud, as though I'm suddenly weightless. Every part of me is alive. I mean that.

Every single cell in my body vibrates and trembles so I know they're there. I have never felt more alive and awake and fucking fantastic in my life. If this is a high then I could become an addict.

Addicted to great sex. Not Zach. I would never be so stupid as to let myself get addicted to any one man, let alone one like this. It's just enough of a sobering thought to have me distancing myself from the moment, pushing up a little, so he takes the cue and steps backward, removing himself from me in a way that I can only say makes my body ache with a sudden sense of emptiness.

I watch in the mirror as he turns his back on me and walks away, heading to the bathroom. A moment later he returns with a towel wrapped around his waist, meeting my eyes in the mirror for a moment before striding to the champagne bottle. He carries it towards me, a smile shifting over his lips, a question in his eyes.

'That was…amazing,' I surprise myself by saying. It's not my norm to praise men like him—as if his ego needs any more stroking.

'Just what I was thinking.' He kisses my shoulder from behind, his stubbly chin invoking more senses, different sensations, spreading goosebumps over me.

He puts a hand on my hip, encouraging me to turn to face him. I do, and our bodies brush, my oh-so-sensitive nipples pressing to his chest, sending little arrows darting through me. He lifts the champagne to my lips once more and I open, letting him pour a little into my mouth.

'I enjoyed that. A lot.'

'You're talking in the past tense,' I murmur—another surprise.

He lifts a brow. 'You mean you're not desperate for me to leave you now?'

'I thought we agreed on one night?'

He grins, taking a drink of the champagne before putting the bottle on the dressing table behind me then shifting his hands to my butt. His eyes are focussed over my shoulder, so I know he's watching the reflection in the mirror, watching as his fingers pummel the round curves of my butt, massaging me in a way that I desperately need, soothing aches, promising pleasure.

'Besides. That would be a waste of champagne. And oysters.'

He nods sagely. 'Indeed.' He moves away from me, holding a hand out for me to put mine in it.

I resist. 'You go ahead. I'll just be a minute.'

He doesn't push the point but nods, leaning forward and kissing my lips quickly before leaving the room. My stomach clenches. When I turn and look in the mirror I have a huge smile on my face.

'So, no missionary, huh?' I ask as I stroll into the living area ten minutes later, quickly showered and bundled up in one of the hotel robes.

He's set oysters, strawberries and chocolates out on the low-lying coffee table in the orangery area of the living room. I pad across to him, curling my legs beneath me as I sit on the sofa.

He shakes his head, eyes on me.

'What's that about?'

He lifts those broad shoulders again then reaches for a plate and arranges three oysters on it along with a wedge of lemon, then passes it to me. It's so like someone like him to just presume I'd like oysters when everyone knows they're an acquired taste.

'Just personal preference.' But the way he says it makes me think he's hiding something. I don't push him for more information—what's the point?

Instead, I smile, lifting an oyster to my lips and swallowing it, the flavour perfect—salty like the ocean.

He's watching me, and little blades of heat dance across my skin.

'So this is your thing?' I gesture to the oysters and champagne.

He comes to sit beside me, and in these close confines I feel how broad his frame is, how dwarfed I am by his physicality. Even that is a turn-on.

'What's "this"?'

'This sophisticated seduction.'

'I like oysters.' He lifts his shoulders. 'I've got to tell you, I don't have a "thing".'

'No?'

'I'm sorry if that disappoints you—if you think I'm some guy who's got some hard and fast routine or whatever—but that's not how I roll.'

'So how do you roll?' I push, reaching for the champagne bottle and lifting it to my lips, taking a couple of sips then handing it over to him.

'Jesus. I don't know, Jessica. However I feel like it.' He laughs, shakes his head a little. 'I will say I don't usually drink champagne from the bottle.'

I match his laugh. 'Hmm, that's new for me too.' I reach for the bottle, take a sip. 'I like it.'

He brushes a finger across my lips. 'Good.' His posture is relaxed, like a man who's had fantastic sex and is about to feast on his bodyweight in oysters and berries.

'So what was your beef tonight?'

'My beef? That's an interesting way to describe yourself.'

His laugh is baritone, immensely satisfying.

'You were clearly shitty when you got to the bar.'

My heart stammers. 'Well, I'm not now.'

He lifts his shoulders. 'I aim to please.' I watch as he reaches for an oyster, taking it straight from the silver platter and bringing it to his lips. When he's finished, he discards the shell back on the tray then homes his gaze on my face. 'Something with work?'

I shake my head. 'My work is the one thing in my life I feel almost one hundred per cent in control of.'

A small frown flickers across his brow, as if he doesn't believe me, or doesn't agree with me. Perhaps he's of the same mindset as me—that is, what's the point in asking uber-personal questions when this is just a one-night thing?—because he doesn't pursue it.

'So what, then?'

'Why are you so sure I was shitty?' That's not really a word in my vernacular but saying it, tasting it in my mouth, feels like him in a way that's pleasant and difficult to describe.

His face cracks into a sardonic smile. 'Your body language.'

'You noticed my body language?'

'I noticed the way you stormed up to the bar like you wanted to bust balls.'

I laugh at his description. He's not wrong. 'I didn't know I stormed.'

'It was actually a fucking sexy swagger, if I'm honest, but I could practically see steam coming out of your ears.'

My stomach swoops. I would usually hedge the question, but that's another 'why bother' because I don't really plan on seeing him again and it's not like it's a state secret. I'm not the only person who has issues with their family.

'Family dinner,' I say with a grimace, reaching for the champagne and taking a few big sips. There's only a third of the bottle left, but I don't feel even a little tipsy. My cheeks warm as I think how much was spilled on my breasts and down my cheeks. I replace the bottle and grab another oyster, thinking about dinner at my parents'.

'Not your favourite pastime?'

'Is it anyone's?'

'My family's not big,' he says, running his fingers through his hair. He's incredibly handsome. Not just hot, but beautiful in a way that would drive an artist to their canvas. 'It's just my brother and me. Mum, our stepmum. We don't do a lot of get-togethers.' Then, after a pause, he swears beneath his breath. 'And my brother's wife and kid.' He shakes his head. 'That's new. I keep forgetting.' An uneven laugh.

'That's right. A secret child or something?' News of Dimitrios Papandreo's sudden family had been in all the papers.

He shakes his head, clearly not keen to talk about it. 'I've known Annie—Dimitrios's wife—a long time. She's great.'

Defensive, ready to fight for her. I barely know the guy but I like that. I mean, I really like it—it shows integrity and class that he wouldn't open up to me about something that's been in all the papers. And nor should he. Despite our physical intimacy, we're virtually strangers.

I don't ask him anything else, respecting the boundary he's gently drawn. 'My family's not big either. It's my parents and my sister, Jemima. Her husband, *Simon*.' I can't help but add a layer of inflection to his name, a whisper of contempt. I smile in an attempt to cover it but even my smile feels awkward. 'They just drive me crazy.'

'In the usual "families can make you batshit crazy" way or for a particular reason?'

'A bit of both.'

'Plus it's Christmas,' he prompts gently, as though that might be adding to my situation, a type of seasonal malaise.

'Oh, I love Christmas. Are you kidding me? Give me a glass of eggnog, a blanket, some kind of cheesy holiday-romance movie and I'm the happiest girl in the world.' I'm pretty sure my expression reflects that. 'And every year I promise myself I'll organise to spend Christmas with some friends, get a cottage in some quaint little snowy village somewhere, or go skiing in Aspen, but every year I let my sister and my mum nag me back into coming here.' I shake my head. 'I really thought I was going to do it this year. I found the perfect village and everything—Fiamatina, in Italy.'

'But?' he prompts.

'But?'

'Well, you're not in Italy turning yourself into a paragon of cheesy Christmas. So?'

'It's my dad's seventieth in a couple of days.' I pull a face. 'I contemplated missing it but I'm pretty sure that's a bridge too far.'

'Uh-huh.'

'So I came and don't even get me started on how much I'm regretting that.'

'But you don't stay with them when you're here?'

'God, no. I know my limits and thankfully they do too. I just go spend some time through the day. Either breakfast or dinner usually.'

He frowns reflexively. 'You're not close to your sister?'

That's a tricky question, with so much behind it. 'We used to be.' Used to be, before Simon.

'Sounds like there's a story there.' He winks, leaning forward and grabbing a strawberry. I watch him eat it, surprised by a strong desire to confide in him.

'What about your parents?'

'What about them?'

'You live in London. They're here. Do you see each other often?'

I shake my head. 'A few times a year.'

More uneasiness. His eyes bore into mine, as though he's tempted to keep going, asking more questions—and to be honest, if he did, I'd answer them. Maybe he recognises that boundaries are normal for us to have, or maybe he's just lost interest, because he leans back in the chair and smiles, back to being a guy who looks as if he's had his cake and eaten it too.

'Well, I'm glad they pissed you off enough to drive you into the bar tonight. Their loss is definitely my gain.'

CHAPTER FOUR

I FEEL AS if I am King of the World. I kick my shoes off at the front door of my penthouse, wandering across the tiled foyer and down two steps into the lounge room. The pre-dawn light of the Singapore sky buoys me and makes me miss my native Sydney all at once. Lights twinkle in every direction, the floor-to-ceiling windows framing a picture-perfect view. The sky is an inky black but there's a whisper of grey building across it, with the first hint of colour—purple and a deep pink. I grab a beer from the fridge then make my way to the wraparound balcony, taking a seat on the edge of the infinity pool, cracking the top off the beer and throwing back a drink.

Well.

That was a decent night.

Decent?

Describing a night with Jessica Johnson as decent would be like calling the earth somewhat big. It was fucking awesome. When I'm an old man I'll be fantasising about her—everything about her. The way she went down on me just for starters. The way she met my eyes in the mirror, a challenge sizzling from her to me. Fuck. She was perfection.

I replay the night as I drink my beer, remembering the way we'd bored of eating once our immediate hunger was sated and had made love on the floor beneath the stars, then taken a spa bath together, me soaping her body from top to toe, finding all her most responsive spots and toying with them, driving her to the edge and over it so many times I lost count. I remember the way I carried her to bed wrapped in an enormous hotel bath sheet, laying her down in the middle and bringing the duvet over her body, the way she could barely hold her eyes open as she smiled up at me.

I remember whistling as I left, feeling a lightness in my step I haven't felt since the story broke about my brother's secret child.

I liked how she didn't keep digging there. It's been news all over the world—you'd need to have been living under a rock not to know that Dimitrios Papandreo just announced he's a father. Curiosity would have been normal, but Jessica Johnson didn't drill me for the juicy details.

Not that I particularly know them, anyway. Even if I'd wanted to spill state secrets I couldn't have; I don't know anything about the relationship except that they are, apparently, in love.

How is that possible?

Love is a construct of Hollywood, an invention to make us feel less lonely and sell Valentine's Day cards, but ultimately, we're all born on our own, we die on our own, and the truth is we're all motivated by our own self-interest at all times.

Another lesson my father taught me. Another lesson my ex, Emily, underscored.

A burst of self-disgust flares inside me. Emily is the biggest regret of my life and she's a mistake I don't intend to make ever again. I trusted her, I believed her, I thought I could 'rescue' her. I let myself care for her so much that even when she was actually just a lying bitch I couldn't see it.

It was all for the best anyway. I'm not the marrying kind.

Life's too short for commitment, and commitment, in any event, is a load of bullshit. A lie invented to fuel the wedding industry—a lie I'll never buy into.

'You should be selling now. You're at your peak. It's the time.'

Beneath the table, I dig my fingernails into my thigh, contemplating doing the same with a knife—if a visit to the emergency room is what it takes to get out of this dinner then I'd be seriously tempted. How can he look at me like this—as though we're just brother and sister-in-law—when at one time he leaned close and whispered that we should go and get a room together?

'Simon's right, Jess.' My dad's the only person who calls me Jess. I used to like it as a girl, back when I thought he was the best thing since sliced bread. But it's been a long time since I've felt that way and now the nickname is just another example of being infan-tilised. 'Your value is sky-high.'

'And growing all the time,' I point out with a tight smile, reaching for the champagne flute. My smile re-laxes as flashes of last night come back to me, spread-ing a heat through my veins that makes me kind of gooey.

'There's no guarantee that'll continue,' Simon pushes with his usual machismo know-it-all-ness. 'All bubbles burst.'

'She-Shakes isn't a bubble, it's a movement.' Simon makes a snorting noise of mirth. God, I hate him. I stare him down and continue in my iciest of voices. 'And there are a lot of potential clients out there who haven't engaged yet.'

'So you're waiting for every woman in the world to click before you sell?'

'On the contrary, I'm analysing my options,' I say coolly, then turn to my mum, desperate for a conver-sation change. 'The chicken is delicious.'

'Thank you, darling.'

One of the hardest things about growing up is real-ising your parents aren't perfect. God knows my dad is no saint—far from it—but it's when I look at my mum that my heart both breaks and grows hard. She is beautiful, intelligent, funny and yet she's let a man diminish her to the point I know she doesn't see those traits within herself. I feel a vulnerable, aching love for her, a desire to wake her up to the woman she is, but I know enough to know that kind of change has to come from within. I can't force it on her, but that doesn't make it any easier to see the way her confidence is battered on a daily basis. All I can do is firm my own resolve to never let a man disempower me.

'Who's interested?' Simon isn't going to let the conversation drop. That reminds me of Zach too. Of the easy way he took my cues and let conversations go when I wanted it. The contrast between them is one of many.

'I've had dozens of offers,' I say truthfully. My sister shoots me a look. Maybe she's afraid my success emasculates her husband. For my part, I think his behaviour does a good enough job of that all on its own.

'From anyone reputable?'

I fight an urge to roll my eyes. 'Yes, Simon. From the big guys. Obviously. She-Shakes is one of the top one hundred apps globally. It's prime to be snapped up. I'm aware of the commercial sense of that. But I'm also weighing up the future of the service. I don't want it to become something that's exploited purely for financial gain. This is a community, and I'm a part of it. If I were to sell—and that's a big "if"—it would need to be completely on my terms.'

'And what are your terms?' my father asks, leaning forward a little.

'I'd need to retain majority share,' I say matter-of-factly.

Simon snorts again. 'Jessica, that's naïve and foolish. None of the tech giants are going to agree.'

'Then I won't sell,' I say with a shrug.

'And they'll come up with a rival app.'

'Maybe.' I sip my champagne. 'And if it does everything I do, then I guess I'll have to put up with that. But for now my intention is to do it best, be the biggest, and to be a part of the community I've built—a community I would never betray by hastily selling out to the wrong corporate partner.' I put my cutlery down a little louder than intended. Perceiving the mood and the possibility that it might be about to sour, Mum smiles too brightly and scrapes her chair back. 'Jessica, why don't you help me with something in the kitchen?'

Three hours later, I feel as if I could weep. How can my mum stay married to him? My dad's affair is now an open secret in our family. We know when he checks his phone at night that it's highly likely to be from *her*. We know that the business meetings he 'travels' to once a fortnight are actually when he spends time with Ashwarya. We know he's cheating, as he has done for all of their marriage, and yet none of us confronts him. I would. I'd do that any day, but love for Mum keeps me silent. She's too proud, too old-fashioned, to want the hint of scandal, even within the family. The image she's created of a perfect family is very important to her and she deserves better than for me to tear down that façade so cruelly. Before Patrick, I might have followed my instincts and done what I wanted but my instincts would be wrong. Just because I think Mum should leave Dad, it doesn't mean it's best for her.

Just as Jemima stays with Simon even when he's clearly an arrogant, emotionally abusive prick who's undoubtedly sleeping around behind her back—after all, if he's willing to hit on her sister, what isn't he doing? I ache to help Jemima but she claims to love him. My experience with She-Shakes has shown me, time and again, that a woman can only ever truly extricate herself from a bad relationship if it's what she wants. I can't want it enough for her. The only power I have to effect change for Jemima—and Mum—is to show unwavering love and support, so that they know I'll have their backs when they need that.

My gaze is drawn to the hotel bar as I pass. I can't help it. My eyes sweep the elegant space, as though looking for Zach. My heart rate increases exponentially and I hold my breath. But the bar is empty except for an older couple sitting at one of the lower-set tables, and the barman from last night behind the counter. He looks up as I pass and our eyes meet. He taps his forehead in a silent greeting and I smile before looking away, ignoring the festering of disappointment in the pit of my stomach.

Even the elevator reminds me of Zach. I stand in the corner we made out in, remembering the way he surrendered to me, the way he seemed to be on edge as we made out. The way he felt in my hand, the thrill of power that came from knowing his arousal was all for me…

I make a muted groaning noise as I step out of the elevator, reaching for my phone as I make my way down the long corridor. I have a dozen or so emails to deal with once I've showered the night off me.

I wasn't exaggerating. I feel as if looking at potential purchase contracts is a huge part of my life now. I get legal advice too, but the control freak in me refuses to risk getting misinformation. I flag the three negotiation emails for later use and focus on the usual work emails. In order to provide the services we do, I have to have an array of professionals engaged in several countries. We have a network of legal teams who offer pro forma advice for free and more tailored advice for a massive discount, which is covered out of the subscription fees—that's the model of my business, and why it works so well. One flat fee covers a whole raft of services. Some you'll use, some you won't, but, just like insurance, they're there if and when you require them. The firms I use have a huge pro bono budget and they get a heap of advertising and extensive publicity in exchange. Keeping those networks in place and functioning means I can't ever get complacent. I also make sure my team of customer support agents is constantly running surveys with our clients to ensure their needs are being met and I pride myself on being responsive to suggestions.

I don't think my success is an accident.

I don't think I got lucky.

I think I had a great idea and I gave myself over to it completely for at least two years, leaving nothing to chance, micromanaging every single aspect. I criss-crossed the globe to meet with lawyers, accountants, therapists, personal trainers and dieticians, all to make sure we were putting the best offering possible out into the ether.

I wish my mum or sister would try the goddamned

app. I can only imagine what advice the community would give them.

With a grimace, I push the door to my suite open then press my back against it, allowing myself a minute to remember. I've been resisting these memories all day but now I let them seep into me, running a hand over the silky finish of my dress.

I move towards the orangery. Zach and my ghosts are on the sofa, where we sat and talked a bit like old friends. Strange that I felt so comfortable with him when I'm usually slow to relax my guard.

Twenty minutes later I'm showered and dressed in a pair of yoga pants and a singlet top. I have a large glass of pinot noir and a list of emails to respond to. I click my laptop open just as the bell peals into the apartment.

Frowning, I take a sip of the red wine as I stand, placing the glass on the dining table before crossing the suite towards the door. I lean forward so I can see through the peephole, then step back again immediately, as though there's a raging fire on the other side.

Oh, my God.

It's Zach.

My heart is going crazy fast. I press my hands to my belly in an attempt to stop it from swooping and swaying.

My mouth feels dry.

I reach up and disentangle my hair tie, loosening the messy bun and finger-combing my hair over one shoulder before I pull the door inward.

'Zach?' My voice is breathy, making it obvious that his appearance is not exactly unwelcome.

He eyes me with an emotion I can't understand. It's dark, and light. Impatient and euphoric. I stare back at him, trying to make sense of this random appearance.

'What are you doing here?'

His smile twists my stomach into knots and then he leans forward, just far enough to claim my lips, to move his mouth over mine, his kiss both a surprise and totally familiar, as if I'd been expecting it.

Without meaning to I step forward and he lifts a forearm to take the weight of the door so I no longer have to worry about holding it open. His kiss burns me to the tips of my toes.

But this isn't what we agreed. I force myself to pull back, to stare at him. I've learned my lesson about men who want more. I'll never be an instrument of hurt again.

My breath is burning in my lungs, my pulse thready.

His smile shows he remembers what he can do to me. Arrogant. Hot. Sublime.

'Aren't you going to ask me in?' It's a rumbly, sexy double entendre. I shake my head a little, to warn myself off how much I want that.

I'm so glad to see him, but I don't reveal that.

'I'm not sure.' Crossing my arms over my chest is a lapse in judgement. He makes no attempt to hide his appreciation for the silhouette of my bra-free breasts as he drops his gaze.

'I'm sure I could come up with a way to change your mind,' he suggests, but makes no attempt to move, and in the back of my mind I appreciate that. Because he's right, he could kiss me again and all my objections would melt away.

'We said one night, didn't we?'

'We did,' he agrees with a nod and a smile that show he understands my predicament. 'I thought we could revise the terms of our agreement.'

I consider that, noting how alike we are. Some people just let themselves get totally swept up in passion and the promise that's inherent in it, but not me, and not him. We both see it for what it is—an exchange. A contract. And contracts have terms that can be negotiated, just as I'm doing right now with the potential sale of a percentage of She-Shakes.

'Why don't you come in and we can discuss it?' He waits for me to step deeper into the suite before he follows, closing the door quietly behind him.

'I just got back,' I say, turning to face him.

'I know.'

'You know? How?'

'I had Ricky from the bar downstairs give me a call when you got to the hotel.'

I stare at him. 'But…why?'

'Because I wanted to see you again.'

My heart soars. I tamp down on it quickly. 'At the risk of repeating myself: why?'

'Because I had fun last night.'

'So did I.'

'And I want more.'

'Do you?'

'Yeah.'

I swallow past a lump in my throat, staring at him for a second before moving back to the sofa. I sit down, leaning forward and closing the laptop lid. He comes to join me, taking the seat beside me, just as he had the night before.

I don't tell him that my eyes had scoured the bar when I'd passed in the hope of seeing him again. I don't tell him that I had the same yearning for more time with him.

Just a bit more; another fix. Just to get me through the next two weeks.

'I'm not generally big on the idea of that.'

'No,' he agrees, but just stares at me as if to say, so what are we going to do?

'I'll go if you want me to,' he offers after a minute, leaning forward and reaching for my wine glass, taking a sip then handing it to me. It's a silent, unspoken challenge. If I take the glass I'm agreeing to so much more. I stare at him, then it, before reaching out and wrapping my fingers around the stem. Our eyes hold when I take a sip, and I'm right back where I was last night, the promise and lure of what we share driving all other considerations from my mind.

Knowing that there are bigger forces at play, and seeing that my agreement is a *fait accompli*, he visibly relaxes, as if the urgency is gone because we both know how this night is going to end. 'What've you been up to?'

'Tonight?' I lean back on the sofa and he surprises me by reaching for my legs and scooping them up, putting my feet on his lap. He begins to rub the soles of them, his thumb pressing into the tender flesh there.

'Let me guess. Family stuff.' He wiggles his brows in a way that makes me laugh.

'Are my ears still steaming?'

He holds his thumb and forefinger up, to gesture 'just a little'.

I sigh heavily. I was circumspect the night before but right now I feel as if I want to vent to someone. 'It's my brother-in-law,' I say carefully. 'He has a knack for driving me absolutely crazy.'

'In a bad way?'

'Is there a good way?'

He stares at me and I smile because of course there is—all the ways he drove me crazy last night.

'He's such an arrogant sod. Usually I can just grin and bear it but he's decided to take an overt interest in my business and believe me when I tell you I need his advice like I need a hole in the head.'

His lips flicker into a smile and then he nods slowly. 'What kind of advice is he trying to give you?'

'Well, you know I'm toying with the idea of selling She-Shakes.'

He dips his head in silent agreement.

'And while I'm gratified by the interest in it, a commercial objective was never really part of my model. Don't get me wrong, it's very rewarding, but I'm not someone who wants to perennially create tech start-ups. She-Shakes is my heart—that community exists because of my blood, sweat and tears. It was born out of—,' I stop for a second, aware I'd been about to veer off the marketing script for the business with a rant about ingrained misogyny and a need to break women free from the shackles of a patriarchal system that serves up benevolent—and malevolent— oppression as a daily meal.

'I did this because it's important,' I say instead, holding the wine glass in my fingertips, running my thumb up the stem thoughtfully. 'I can see the advantages to selling. But there are disadvantages too. My brother-in-law and father don't seem to understand that my goal isn't to make as much money as possible and move on.'

'And you care what they think?'

The question surprises me.

I jerk my eyes to his, a frown on my face. 'I wouldn't have said so.' I sigh. 'But maybe I do.' Then, I shake my head. 'No, I don't. It's just being here and having them go over and over the stock prospects of my "offering", reducing years and years of my work to commercial viability, it honestly makes me feel sick.'

'Your dad has made a fortune by taking companies and hyper-refining them to the point where their value when he leaves is considerably higher than when he came on board.'

I bristle a little. 'Is that admiration I hear in your voice?'

'I admire anyone who can do that,' he says frankly.

'But that's what you do. Albeit with media corporations but it's essentially the same thing.'

He lifts his shoulders and even though he's wearing a shirt, I visualise his naked flesh beneath. 'Which is probably why I admire that skill. In any event, my point wasn't that there's a right way or a wrong way, only that I can see why your father relates to your business in those terms.'

'Do you?'

He frowns. 'Honestly?'

I nod.

'I'd be lying if I said I hadn't looked into your company some more today.'

I make a small laughing sound then realise he's serious.

'I was curious,' he explains.

My heart rate picks up.

'Why?'

'It's what I do.'

Just like my dad and Simon. I straighten a little, uncomfortable at the idea of this man in particular trying to pull apart my business for his own commercial gain. 'And?' I say, though it's pushed through gritted teeth.

'And it's a solid offering,' he says. 'As you are no doubt aware.'

I wait, silently.

'Obviously there's a lot of potential to grow the app and the community, the services you provide; I imagine that's what you're focussing on in the next eighteen months.'

Eighteen months happens to be the exact timeline I have in mind.

'So you'd be looking for a partner rather than a wholesale buy off.'

I nod. 'I'll never relinquish control of She-Shakes. I know that having some of the biggest names in tech offering to buy me out is flattering and maybe I'll regret not just selling to them but, honestly, I can't imagine doing that. I can't imagine a world with She-Shakes where I'm not at the helm.'

'I get that too.'

'Do you? You don't think I'm crazy?'

One side of his lips lifts in a smile that is captivating and mesmerising. 'I think you're passionate and brilliant. I think you're the right person to run the business and if anyone wanted to buy it and not utilise you then *they'd* be crazy.'

His words are a support I hadn't realised I needed.

'If I were you, I'd be seeing it a bit differently.' He says it calmly, as if he's happy for that to be the end of it; he's leaving the conversation for me to pursue or not.

'Differently how?'

'You're not selling She-Shakes. Why would you?'

'Go on.'

'You're open to the possibility of an injection of capital—so you can expand.'

'Go on,' I prompt, moving my heel over his cock with a teasing smile. I feel safer discussing this with him. As if he gets what I'm doing with the app and why it matters to me. He's different from my dad and Simon. In this way, probably not in any others.

'In exchange, you hand over some of the app's shares.'

'But not the majority,' I say firmly.

He nods. 'And that's your sticking point.'

'Why?'

'Because once you get someone to buy in they're going to want to have control of it. That's just the way it's done. They'll be looking to keep you on in some capacity—'

'A figurehead?' I supply with a shake of my head.

'Perhaps a little more than that, but essentially.'

'And is that what you'd do? Hypothetically,' I insert quickly, not wanting him to think I'm hitting up for cash.

His demeanour doesn't change. 'No.'

'Why not?'

'Because from what I can see, it's your skill and talent that has turned She-Shakes into what it is. Only someone incredibly short-sighted would sideline you. Talk about a waste of talent.'

I feel as though my heart could burst right out of my chest. I know I'm great at what I do but hearing his succinct, businesslike appraisal of my skills, almost as though I'm one of the assets he's evaluated alongside the She-Shakes offering, makes me smile like an idiot.

He pulls a face. 'Don't look as though that's news to you.'

'It's just…in all the negotiations, no one's ever mentioned that. I feel as though I'm seen as an encumbrance.'

He shoots his brows up.

'And that's exactly the point of She-Shakes. Women should know their potential and proclaim it proudly. We need to demand a raise, push for the promotion, be aggressive about our skills. And I don't feel ready to just sell up and move on. I mean, I know I would eventually do something else, and God knows I wouldn't have to work in a long time but it's not really about that.'

'No,' he agrees with a small nod. 'Who are you negotiating with?'

I list a few of the principle tech companies. He lets out a whistle. 'Impressive. And they're offering a decent amount?'

I reach for my phone and pull up a contract, handing it over to him. He takes a few minutes to read it—I appreciate his thoroughness.

'You're getting a lawyer to consult on this?'

'Of course.'

'Because there's a few clauses I'd watch out for there.'

Again, he waits for me to ask the question rather than foisting the information on me. I appreciate that.

'Such as?'

He goes through the contract, flagging very similar concerns to the ones I had.

'Yep, that's my feeling too.'

'How'd you come up with this idea?'

That's easy, but the answer isn't one I'm willing to give over. Seeing my mum in such a harmful relationship fired me up—I had to do something. If I couldn't empower her, perhaps I could empower other women, whether they needed support in their private life or professional.

'I got sick of seeing women passed over for opportunities they are more than capable of.' I sip the wine, relaxing as he releases the tensions in my feet. 'We have this idea that we're this modern, egalitarian, enlightened society but it's still women who tend to do the bulk of the housework, women who tend to take career breaks to raise children, women who take jobs for which they're over-qualified but which offer flexible, school-friendly hours. Women who take a back seat in meetings, who hesitate to enumerate their skills because it might be seen as boastful. It's like we're conditioned from birth to accept that's just "the way it is" and I'm sick of it.'

He's looking at me with an expression that's half amusement and half—I think—admiration.

'To highlight my point, I could feel tempted to apologise for that outburst because, as a woman, I've been programmed to feel that speaking so frankly is somehow bossy or rude. And it's not. That's the damned truth. Sure, there are exceptions, and I'm not saying things are what they were in the eighties or nineties. But it's more dangerous now because we have this insidious idea that we're living in an "equal" society, but for the majority of women true equality is still a long way off.'

'And your app addresses that?'

'My community addresses it.'

I run my finger around the rim of my wine glass,

thinking about my sister and how she's the perfect example of a woman who could have been running the world instead of turning a blind eye as a matter of form to her husband's infidelity. A shiver of anger runs down my spine. And far be it from me to criticise *any* woman's choice in life. I believe feminism and equality bring with them an inherent right to choose—there is nothing 'wrong' with choosing to take a career break and raise children. In fact, I admire the hell out of women who do it. But it needs to be a choice—that is to say, a viable alternative has to exist in order for that to be a choice. Can women still have families without suffering financially?

'So don't sell, then,' he says with a lift of his shoulders.

I nod, considering that. 'But there's a risk in that too.'

'Oh?'

'There's a risk that I won't be able to grow my community to continue providing this level of support. There's a risk someone else will step into the breach and charge more, offer less, but still elbow me out of business with fancy advertising and media reach. I feel like I need to remain at the forefront of this and that's going to take an injection of capital. Selling a portion of the business is the smart thing to do, but, God, I hate having every man and his dog weigh in on it for me.'

'Sure,' he agrees sagely. 'So ignore every man and his dog.' He reaches into his back pocket. 'Call me. Any time.'

My heart stammers.

'Purely business.' He lifts his hands. 'We both know what we're looking for on a personal level. But if you want to discuss your options, bounce something off me, then just give me a call.'

I take the card, staring down at it. 'Why?'

'Because I know what I'm talking about.'

I shake my head impatiently. 'Why would you offer to help me?'

That's a great question. Why would I offer to help some woman I screwed last night? Just because she's amazing in bed, why am I—frankly—breaking all my usual rules? I'm here in her suite and I don't even really want to admit it to myself but I would have been pretty disappointed if she'd said no. Okay, it wouldn't have killed me. I'm pretty confident this infatuation will pass quickly but, yes, all day I've been infatuated with her. I've had a stupid smile on my face and I've been counting the minutes until I could be here with her again.

I had fun last night.

Lots of fun. And I want more.

The doorbell rings. She frowns, looking towards it.

'Room service,' I explain, gently easing her feet to the ground and standing up.

'You ordered room service? Isn't that a little presumptuous? What if I'd turned you away?'

I throw her a knowing grin over my shoulder as I walk off. 'I'm here, aren't I?'

CHAPTER FIVE

I'M NEVER GOING to get through this. I towel my body dry, staring out at the view towards the marina, mentally marking the dates off in my mind. Dad's birthday was yesterday. Cross that one off.

And I feel disloyal for thinking that way—this is my family and of course I love them. It's just *easier* to love them from a distance. I grimace, reaching for my coffee and taking a drink.

Okay. It's more than that.

The first time I had sex with Zach I had a fleeting thought that it was like riding the best high ever. Pleasure soaked my body. I felt as though I were flying and filled with stardust and rainbows. I felt—amazing.

And that high didn't go away. Not any of the times we had sex during our two nights together. And now I'm like a junkie in severe withdrawal because it's been too long since my body's known his. Without my permission, my eyes drift to a white rectangle placed against the pretty fruit bowl on the kitchen bench. Zach's business card stares at me.

Call him.

I bite down on my lower lip, reaching for the card and running my fingers over the cardboard edges. I slide it from hand to hand, feeling the corners, indecision rushing through me.

I can't call him. Neither of us wants more than what we've already shared. He's a total man whore, and we both made it abundantly clear we only wanted a night or two of passionate sex. Which we had. And it was amazing.

I was adamant about the limits of this and so was he.

I can't just go back on my word.

And what if I do and he rejects me?

Then he rejects me. Just like we tell women who want to ask for a raise—if you don't ask, you don't get.

This is a little different though.

It's a *lot* different.

I bite down on my lip, my fingers toying with the business card.

It's my indecision that finally pushes me into action. I'm not someone who hesitates. I like having sex with Zach, and God knows I could use the distraction.

A light bulb sparkles above my head.

That's it!

I just need him to get me through the rest of my time here! Just like that, all the pieces fall into place. I reach for my phone, butterflies I haven't felt in many years suddenly forming a busy kaleidoscope in my belly. I dial his number and press the green button before I can second-guess myself, putting it on speak-erphone out of habit.

I place the phone on the kitchen bench and grab my coffee cup instead. It rings once. Twice. Three times.

It stops ringing. I hear the crinkling of something. A thud. A curse that makes me smile. Then, 'Papandreo.'

His voice is deep and gruff. And ruffled. As if I've disturbed him. My stomach swoops in a way that's now completely familiar.

I stare at the phone, realising I was foolishly un-derprepared for this. He doesn't recognise my number. And why would he?

'Hey.'

A pause. 'Jessica?'

Oh, God. My name on his lips is... My insides clench hard. I sip my coffee, striving for any hint of normality.

'Yeah. Hey.'

'Good morning.' I hear a smile in his voice and my own lips answer it, twisting upwards in an in-stinctive response.

'Are you busy?'

'Just taking a run.'

I smile at that. Of course he's a runner. His phy-sique is proof of a dedication to physical activity. I hear beeping noises, as though he's turning off a treadmill.

'How are you?'

I nod, sipping my coffee. 'Yeah, good.' I clear my throat. Oh, God. I'm ridiculously nervous. What the hell? It's the fear of rejection, that's all. I know there's a risk here, because Zach isn't like anyone I've ever met before.

And if he says 'no'? Then no big deal. I get on with my life.

Except even as I think that I experience the whoosh of disappointment I'd feel if I never saw him again.

And just like that, I know this isn't a conversation for the phone. I'm more persuasive in person. I flick a glance at my watch, thinking of the activities I have lined up that morning. I'm due at my parents' in an hour, and I'll be there most of the day.

'Are you free this afternoon?'

The pause is long enough to give me serious concern.

'I can be.'

I expel a breath. I hear caution in his voice and I understand it. Neither of us wants anything serious. In fact, he's made an absolute art form of avoiding anything approaching a date.

'I have a proposition for you.'

'I'm intrigued.'

'You should be.'

A pause, and I imagine him smiling; warmth floods me.

'I'll come to you. What time?'

'Two o'clock?'

'Great.'

He gives me an address and a passcode to the building and just like that I feel the hint of my high surging forward.

I dress with care. As a teenager I adapted quickly to Singapore's climate but at twenty-nine, I find it a lot harder to process the humidity. I've come from a London winter after all, so the sultry heat makes me reach for a loose cotton dress, and no bra. I pull my hair into a topknot and do the bare minimum of make-up.

I go through the motions with my family and it's made all the more bearable because I have the secret knowledge that I'm going to see Zach again. And I'm excited. Excited in a way I haven't felt for a long time.

My naturally cautious temperament exerts itself, reminding me this isn't a done deal, that he might not agree to my terms, and then I need to walk away. Some things can't be negotiated.

Just before two, I step out of a cab in front of a huge steel monolith reaching high into the clear blue sky. My heart has begun to pound against my chest. My ribs feel every throb. I throw a glance down the street before crossing then enter large sliding glass doors. The foyer of the building is stunning. Modern but with lots of hints of Singapore's past and a huge Christmas tree right in its centre. I cross the highly polished tiles and my heels make a clickety-clack sound as I go. It breathes confidence in my body, but my fingers are still shaking slightly as I press the numbers he gave me into the elevator control panel. The doors open and when I get inside only one button is lit—the top floor. Of course.

I move to the back of the lift, wishing I could ascribe my loopy tummy to the lift's rapid ascent alone, but I know there's so much more at play. I'm nervous.

The doors whoosh open, straight into an entrance foyer. Like the foyer downstairs it has beautifully polished tiles that give it a sense of luxury—but it's not that alone. I step forward, my eyes catching hints of detail. The living space is double height with floor-to-ceiling windows, beautiful, sumptuous furnishings, an enormous crystal chandelier hangs centrally and there's a grand piano in the corner. But I only have a second to observe these things before a movement catches my eyes.

Zach.

My stomach hurts.

He looks so damned good. I wish I could have braced myself for that but I don't think there's any way to inure myself to his appeal. He's wearing dark grey suit pants and a pale blue shirt. His jacket is discarded, his hair is messed as if he's been running his fingers through it and his feet are bare. It's that last detail that draws a smile over my face. He walks towards me, and his manner is a little different—hard to read—which I understand. He's being cautious. He doesn't know why I'm here, and he's uncertain.

He has rules.

We both do.

He probably thinks I'm about to become a level-five clinger and beg him to marry me. I have to hold back a laugh at that thought.

'Come on in.' He sweeps his hand towards the living space. More details filter through to my mind.

Beautiful artwork—modern with splashes of colour in big black frames. White walls. High ceilings. A mezzanine. An enormous kitchen full of white and marble, a sweeping staircase.

'Would you like something? Water? Coffee? Wine?'

I shake my head. I need to get this over with.

'Take a seat.'

I fidget with my fingers at my side, moving to the chair he indicated and sliding into it. But the second I sit down I feel uneasy and stand back up again.

I shake my head in a silent apology, moving towards the window. This is crazy and yet it's not.

'I had an idea this morning,' I say, deciding I might as well cut right to the chase.

'Go on.' He looks as relaxed as anything, sitting in a black armchair with his legs kicked out in front of him.

'You know why I'm in Singapore and how I feel about being here.' I bite down on my lip. 'I do love my family but I find these trips incredibly stressful.'

'Yes,' he agrees with a small nod.

'I think I need some stress relief.'

His eyes give nothing away. Silence stretches. If he knows where I'm going with this then he's not going to make it easy for me.

I roll my eyes heavenwards. 'I have no plans on being here after Christmas. I'm booked to fly to London on the twenty-sixth and nothing will change that. I have things I need to get back for. I have a life in London. And apart from that, I have no intention of getting involved with anyone. I'm happily single and probably always will be.' I tilt my chin defiantly, daring him to disagree with me, as so many others have in the past.

Instead, he continues to look at me in that silently assessing way of his.

'But the thing is, I *am* here for another week and a half.'

He lifts a single brow, still silent, damn him. Well, in for a penny, in for a pound.

'And I quite like the idea of passing some of the time with you.'

It's a very lukewarm way to describe what I want to do with him, but I hold fast. Before he can speak, I rush on. 'If you're worried I'm going to want more from you, then don't. I can promise you I'm not interested in anything serious. In fact, that's the exact opposite of what I want. To be blunt, I like fucking you. And when we're together I feel happy and relaxed and I need that right now. So I'm suggesting that we extend the limits—but not the essential terms—of what we agreed to.'

'Are you saying you want me to be your fuck buddy, Jessica Johnson?' His voice is rich with amusement.

'Just while I'm here. Ten more days.'

He stands up, his face sombre, his body strong, and it's as if the world has stopped spinning and my breath no longer needs to escape my body. Everything grinds to a halt. I could hear a butterfly flapping its wings beyond the window, if there were such a creature at this height.

'You get what my limits are, right?'

'I just said that, didn't I?'

'I want to be clear.' He moves closer to me, toe to toe. Our bodies touch. Heat spirals through me. 'I don't want to hurt you. I don't want to hurt anyone.' He frowns. 'I'm as opposed to relationships as you claim to be.'

'Claim to be? Believe me—that's how I feel.'

'Fine. So we're in agreement. Nothing will change my mind there.'

'Good. I don't want to. Do you find it so hard to believe I could just be interested in you for a good time?'

He laughs. 'No. I totally get that.'

'Because it's all you want from me, right?'

A muscle throbs low in his jaw and then he nods.

'Great. So I'm not imagining that the chemistry between us is off the charts?'

He smirks. 'You could describe it that way.'

'I mean, I love having sex with you. So how about we just have sex and I blow off steam with you and at the end I'll fly to England and that's it? We won't call each other, we won't think about each other again. It's perfect.'

His nod is contemplative. 'Have you ever had a relationship like that?'

'I try to avoid relationships of any kind as though my life depends on it.'

He laughs, shaking his head a little.

'What?'

'You're just…too young to be so jaded.'

'I'm twenty-eight.'

'Yeah,' he growls, tapping a finger to my nose. 'But so, so cynical.'

'I'm not cynical. I'm just realistic. All that happily-ever-after crap might be great for some people but it's definitely not for me.'

'You don't want happily-ever-after?'

'I think my version of happily-ever-after just takes a different approach.'

'Yeah?'

I nod. 'But that doesn't matter. That's just the kind of thing we don't need to discuss.' I smile at him sweetly. 'In fact, the less discussion we have, the better.'

He laughs. 'So you're just going to use me for sex?'

He latches his hands behind my back, pulling me against his body. My heart forgets to beat.

'That's the plan.' My voice is husky.

'Starting now?'

Happiness blasts through me. 'Unless you've got something better to do?'

'Jessica, I can honestly say there's nothing I'd rather do right now than be with you.' He moves his hips so I can feel the hint of his arousal. Heat rushes my body. 'I'm glad you came up with this…proposal.'

'It's definitely one of my better ideas,' I agree, moving my hands to his waistband and undoing the button there. Now that he's agreed I feel a thousand and one things. Relief, anticipation, adrenalin, pleasure, relaxed. I feel as if the anxiety of the time with my family is completely offset by the pleasure of being with Zach. It's like the piece of the puzzle that was missing. Suddenly, the looming time until Christmas no longer fills me with a sense of dread.

Impatience zips through me. I'm an addict, I'll freely admit it, but now I've hooked myself up with a source of supply, I can relax. I'll wean myself, at some point.

I smile as I push his pants lower, pleasure at what's coming exploding through me. He pushes at the straps of my dress, his own needs making his movements jerky, his actions rushed. The straps slide lower, revealing my naked breasts; he swears and drops his head so our foreheads are pressed together, breath mingled. His hands find my hips and rest there, his fingertips beating a tattoo against my skin, his eyes shut for a second.

I don't think about the fact that if I hadn't come up with this idea I never would have seen him again. I don't think about the fact that I might be more addicted to him than he is me. In this moment, I'm certain nothing and no one will ever be able to hurt me.

CHAPTER SIX

I'M KING OF the world all over again. I push up onto my elbows so I can see her better, watching as her body shifts with each breath in and out, the movement of her breasts rapid as she struggles to regain her breath.

Fuck.

I love being with her.

I'm so freaking glad she came here this afternoon. I honestly thought she was going to pitch me her business, ask me to buy in, which is something I've been seriously considering anyway. I didn't expect, for even a second, that she'd pitch me this instead. But it's honestly exactly what I wanted. I'd been thinking the same thing—why can't we keep having sex? Why cap something so great at just a couple of nights?

We're both adults. We can play by the rules—so long as we both know what they are from the outset. And we do. We've been so clear. This is a foolproof situation.

I lift a finger to her nipple, tracing the areola, smiling as she slides her eyes towards mine. Her skin lifts into a delicate web of goosebumps. I lean forward and trace her other nipple with my tongue, delighting in the way she sucks in a sharp breath. We've been doing this for hours. The sun is low in the sky, the light outside fading, but here in my apartment time seems to have stopped. We could have been doing this for three days, for all I know.

There's a laziness to my touch now—relaxed and indolent, because I know there's no rush. It's the first time in a long time I've felt that. I'm always conscious of a ticking clock. When I'm with a woman, I know it will be just one night, possibly two, but definitely not more. Knowing I have the luxury of exploring her body is new and I relish the prospect of discovering everything I can about Jessica Johnson. In bed. She's made it clear discussion isn't what she's after, and thank God for that. If I thought any part of her wanted some kind of true intimacy, I'd run a mile—no matter how great she is in bed.

I hate that Emily still has the ability to reach into my life and influence me, even to this day, but the truth of the matter is she showed me how stupid it is to put your happiness in another person's hands.

My lips quirk in a smile as I move lower, kissing Jessica's flat stomach gently.

I prop my head up to find her watching me. She looks exhausted—and that makes me feel about ten feet tall, because I did that to her. The multiple orgasms and athletic sex have tired her completely. I have the opposite problem—I feel as if I'm just getting started. She is such a match for me, I want to keep exploring this. But there's no rush, I remind myself. We have days. A week and a half.

That's a very long time, even with someone like Jessica.

'How was your dad's birthday?'

She pulls a face. 'Fine.'

'Did he have a party?'

'Yeah.'

My laugh is a hoarse sound. 'You didn't enjoy it?'

'It was fine. Seventy of his "closest friends".' She looks away, but not before I see a spark of anger in her eyes.

Fascinated, I draw my body up, so my head is level with hers. 'You don't like his friends?'

She turns her face back to mine, looking up at me with an expression that can best be described as mutinous.

'They're fine, for the most part.'

'But?' I prompt, absolutely sure there's a story here.

She moves her hand to my hip, placing it there reflexively, distracted, tentative.

I feel as though she's weighing something up, working out what she wants to say. Eventually, she lets out a slow sigh. 'Things like that are always... strange.'

'You don't like birthdays? Parties?' She shakes her head. I feel as if this is the most serious I've seen Jessica. She's choosing her words with care. 'Champagne?' I tease, and she flicks me a smile but it's tight, as if it costs her a mammoth effort.

'No, it's—' She blows air out of her lips, so they vibrate quickly. 'It's my dad's mistress.' She shifts a little, moving away from me, sitting up in my bed, her body language screaming tension.

'Your dad's mistress?'

'Ashwarya.' She rolls her beautifully expressive eyes. 'They've been together a long time. She's always at our family parties. I don't know how she stands it.' Her laugh is hollow and short. 'I don't know how my mother stands it.'

'Your mother knows?'

'I think she's probably known about all of them.' Her eyes are tortured, awash with emotions that make something primal inside me roar to life. It takes me a second to realise it's a defensive instinct, a desire to protect her.

'Not his first affair?'

'No.'

I consider that, feeling pretty ill-equipped to hazard a comment on someone's marriage given my feelings on love and commitment. 'So, why does she stay?'

Her voice is strained. 'That kind of thing has an insidious way of undermining a person. My mum's used to the fact he cheats, maybe even believes she's not good enough for him.'

I consider that. 'Perhaps fidelity isn't important to her.'

Jessica's eyes widen. 'Seriously?'

'All relationships are contracts, of a sort. Perhaps their contract has other clauses she considers more important.'

Jessica looks at me as though I'm an alien. 'I don't think anyone would get married if that were their expectation. Would they?'

'I'm the last person to answer questions on why people get married. None of it makes any sense to me.'

'No,' she agrees after a beat. 'Me either. The thing is, it's the saddest situation. She loves him. And I know his affairs hurt her, never mind the fact he makes no attempt to hide what he's doing from her. He's such a sadist.'

She pushes the sheet off and stands, striding towards the window completely naked and uncaring. I'm at the top of one of the tallest buildings in the city—no one could ever see in. She stares down at the street below, a frown on her beautiful face.

'I used to idolise my dad. He was my hero. He's very smart and dynamic.' She turns to face me. 'I'm sure you're familiar with the prototype.'

I have an uneasy sense that she's comparing me to her father in this way. Having seen what my own dad put my mother through I can safely say I would never do something like cheat on my wife. Then again, I'd never be stupid enough to get married.

'And then one day I heard him on the phone to someone—in what was clearly a romantic conversation. I was old enough to know what was happening straight away.' She shakes her head. 'My mum was in the kitchen; it wasn't her. I hedged around the subject for a few years and then, as more evidence came to light, eventually spoke to Mum about it. I was so nervous, terrified of devastating her but convinced she should have the facts.'

'Of course.'

She rocks back on her heels a little, then nods, as though being swallowed by the past. 'She told me relationships are complicated and that I should remember we're a family, that our business is private.' Her eyes slice me with her grief. 'That was it. That was the extent of it. She knew about the affairs; she made it seem like she didn't care. I was so angry that day, I blamed Mum. How could someone put up with that? How could she disrespect herself in that way? But then—'

I wait, watching as she rallies her thoughts. Her smile is tight, lacking humour.

'Then, I grew up. I realised that life isn't black and white and relationships *are* complicated, just like she said. I realised she did care, deeply, but that she was trying to protect me and the fragile construct of our family—because it means so much to her. I realised she didn't feel she had any options or power, and that Dad was the reason for that.' She sucks in a furious breath. 'I stopped being angry with Mum and began to feel that solely for Dad. He betrays Mum every day. He undermines her confidence and damages her every day.' Her eyes flick to mine.

'Something I imagine you had at the forefront of your mind when you came up with the idea for She-Shakes?'

Her eyes find mine, surprise evident in their depths. She nods slowly.

'My mum doesn't have a lot of close female friends. We moved around a lot and that was very isolating—for her, and us. It meant she didn't have any girlfriends supporting her, telling her how great she is and that she doesn't need to stand for what Dad does.' She swallows, her throat moving softly. 'The app is that for millions of women around the world. A voice of support, a show of faith.'

'That's very important.'

'I know.' Her brow crinkles as though she's trying to remember what we were talking about. Her laugh is uneasy. 'Anyway, it was stressful. The party, I mean. I respect Mum's decision to stay with Dad, and I love her so much, Zach. But I hate watching it all play out in front of me. I hate seeing how he treats her.'

It's something we have in common. I too witnessed the pain one parent could inflict on another—with absence rather than presence and cruelty, but the hurts and resultant wounds were just as deep.

'And that's before you get into my brother-in-law,' she says with a grimace and a shake of her head.

I open my mouth to ask her about that but she stands up on tiptoes and presses a finger to my lips. 'Nope. Don't want to talk about him. I've made myself all bitter and stressed already.'

But something about her worry bleeds into me. I drop my head, kissing her gently, wanting to ease her worries. 'Why don't you come see the rest of my place?'

'You mean, there's more than this?' she teases, gesturing to the bedroom.

I grin. 'Just a bit.'

* * *

An hour later, I've seen every room of his palatial penthouse and I have to say, even though I expected something pretty grand, this has blown me away. It's three stories and each level takes up the whole floor of the high-rise. To call it a sky mansion would be an understatement. When I make some throwaway comment about being terrified if there was a fire—how would you escape?—he shows me to the roof where there's an extensive garden, a second infinity pool and a helipad complete with a sleek black helicopter. His apartment has its own private lift, though we use the sweeping staircase. There's a basketball court on the top floor with panoramic views of the bay, and a library that looks as if it has just about every book ever printed.

There are only three bedrooms, four bathrooms. When I mention how unusual that is for a place of this size he agrees, explaining, 'I had several of the bedrooms joined to make the study.'

'The study' is a misnomer. The space he's referring to is half of one level of the apartment, and when you step inside it's like being in any corporate high-rise. His corner office is huge but there's also a boardroom, and two ancillary offices for his assistants. The design of his penthouse means they can access the office space directly from the foyer, without coming through his living area.

'It's incredible,' I say sincerely as he walks towards me with a glass of champagne, shirtless, just the way I like him. The living space opens out onto a large balcony. The floor has terracotta tiles and large vibrant pots house bougainvillea that climbs rampant across the pillars, making it feel as though we're in a garden high up in the clouds. There's a beautiful pool here too, and in the warmth of the evening I contemplate a swim.

'Yeah, I was lucky to snap it up when it became available.'

I pull a droll face. 'I can't imagine there'd be too many people with the cash available to "snap it up".'

'You'd be surprised.'

'No, I don't think I would be.' I know he's wealthy—the Papandreo name is synonymous with money, and lots of it—but this is different. This is a level almost unto himself.

'You don't have any domestics?'

'Nah.' He shakes his head. 'I have Mrs Amaro, who comes and cleans for me once a week. She leaves some meals if she thinks my fridge is looking bare—she doesn't approve of my habit of ordering in,' he says with a laugh that sends flickers of pleasure spreading through me. 'I send my shirts out for laundering. But don't tell my mum.'

He winks—a joke. I'm not going to meet his mum and he's not going to meet mine—obviously.

'She wouldn't approve?' I respond in kind, moving towards the swimming pool as I sip the champagne, sitting on the edge and running my fingers through the water.

'Hell, no. Even the fact Mrs Amaro drops food off

88 NO STRINGS CHRISTMAS

would offend Mum's sensibilities. "I didn't raise you boys to be waited on hand and foot."'

'Your parents weren't together?'

'No.' His smile is easy but I feel a hint of tension behind his response. Curious, I watch him for a moment, waiting to see if he'll expand, but he doesn't. He sits beside me and presses a kiss to my shoulder, the feeling of his mouth against my warm skin sending little darts of pleasure spinning through me.

'Divorced?'

'Never married.' He moves his hand to the strap of my dress—I pulled it back on before we toured his apartment. He pushes it down so he can cover a little more skin real estate. I tilt my head back, looking at the dark sky above. I can make out the dull twinkling of stars in the distance, their faraway beauty slightly dimmed by the light display of the city.

'You were raised by your mum?'

'Until we were ten.'

His other hand pushes my other strap down so the dress falls once more, showcasing a lot of cleavage.

'I like you like this,' he says seriously, then draws a line across my breasts. 'I like being able to look at you. In fact, next time you're here, I think you should just be naked the whole time.'

I lift a brow. 'And you?'

'I'll think about it.'

'That doesn't seem fair.' I pout.

'My house, my rules.'

'I see. So when you're at my suite, it's my rules?'

'That seems equitable.'

'Okay, then.' I flutter my eyelashes at him. 'Then seeing as you call the shots, what next?'

'That's easy.' He moves forward and removes my champagne, placing it on the edge of the pool behind him. 'How about a swim?'

'You read my mind.'

'Fancy that.'

I move closer, so my dress falls lower and my breasts brush his torso. 'Only, I didn't bring any bathers.'

'What a shame.' His grin is pure wicked.

'I suppose I could go naked?' I suggest, standing, holding the top of my dress and slowly guiding it down my body, heat gathering in my cheeks as his eyes follow its progress. A sense of my own power throbs through me.

I have never wanted someone in such an inexhaustible way. Comparing Zach to an addiction is perfect—I am addicted to him in myriad ways. No, I correct swiftly. I'm addicted to him in precisely one way. And that addiction will end just as quickly as it began, because I'm nothing if not disciplined.

I let the dress fall all the way to the ground then move languidly towards the pool. 'How deep is it?' I ask, eyeing the glistening water.

'Two metres.'

'Perfect.'

Before he can respond I lift my arms like an arrow above my head and dive in, years of swim training coming back to me like riding a bike. Bliss erupts as I slice into the water, the feeling on a hot, sultry day like manna from heaven. The water shifts as he dives in behind me, the subtle change in current appreciable as I stroke through the water. But he's fast and powerful, his arms cutting through the water. I look behind me as he reaches my feet, then he pulls equal, pausing to smile at me for a second before he reaches out and tries to grab my waist. I laugh and kick harder, pushing myself forward with a spurt of speed. A second later his hand connects with my waist and he's drawing me back through the water, pulling my body to his. Naked, wet, hot, cool.

We tread water together, our eyes locked, mine lined with thick, clumped lashes, my dark hair like a pelt against my head.

'You're a fish,' he murmurs. He's still wearing his boxers but somehow even that is sexy—the feel of wet cotton against my naked flesh is an insane turn-on. 'Or a mermaid.' He pulls back a bit, looking at me through eyes that see everything.

'Or perhaps a siren, designed to lure men to their death at sea.'

'We're not at sea.'

'The principle is the same.'

'Am I luring you to your death?'

His smile is sardonic. 'You're luring me to do something I've never done before.'

'Ah.' I nod. 'But not really. Does it matter if it's two nights or two weeks? Sex is still just sex.'

'Yes,' he agrees, but I feel a hint of indecision. Or perhaps I imagined it. A moment later he smiles at me brightly then lets me go, tossing a look over his shoulder as he torpedoes through the water, swimming towards the edge. I watch him for a few seconds and then duck dive beneath the surface, turning back and going the way I came.

I don't chase anyone, ever, and I've definitely done enough chasing of Zach for the day.

When I surface, he's nowhere to be seen, but a few moments later I feel his fingers curve around my ankles, roaming the length of my legs before he emerges beside me.

'You changed direction,' he accuses, drawing me with him through the water, towards the corner. There's a step there. I feel it beneath my feet and press down on it.

'I didn't want to chase you,' I say seriously, wondering if he understands how unprecedented this situation is for me. I came out on a limb today. I pushed myself way out of my comfort zone by asking him to make the next week and a half easier.

'Well, now you know that if you don't chase me I'll chase you,' he says simply. 'I wanted to see you again too, Jessica. But I've had enough experience to know that repeat performances can lead to disappointment. It's easy to get hurt, to build things up in your mind. And I didn't want to hurt you.'

'I'm not going to get hurt by you.' Or any man, I tack on silently; the pledge I made not to find myself in Mum's shoes is one I hold dear to my heart.

'I know that.' He moves closer, pushing me up another step, his body coming over mine. I sit there, underwater to my breasts, his body pressed to mine, and I feel desire warring with a drugging sense of relief. Because he did want me—the only thing that stopped him from reaching out was a desire to protect me, which is actually kind of sweet.

He kisses me and I wrap my legs around his waist beneath the water, holding him there, sensations exploding beneath my skin, an ache low in my abdomen as I feel desire stretch my nerves taut as if I haven't been with him several times today already.

'How can I want you again?' I complain with a shake of my head.

He responds with a grin against my lips, moving his hand between my legs. 'Because you're perfect.'

His fingers move over my clit, slowly at first, until I'm moaning his name and begging for him, needing to feel him inside me.

'No condom,' he murmurs, but he slides a finger inside me and then another, until I'm writhing on the step of the pool, an orgasm tearing through me at this man's touch. I stare up at the stars as I come, and I feel as though I've died and gone to heaven.

She arouses caveman instincts in me that I didn't know existed. I lift her from the pool, carrying her wet, naked, beautiful body to the shelves and pulling out a large towel. I drape it over her and she smiles up at me, her eyelashes all clumpy from the water, her skin beaded in moisture.

I've lost all concept of the time, but we've been doing this for hours—since she arrived mid-afternoon—and I know I'm hungry as all hell. I'm going to guess she is too. I ease her feet to the floor in the lounge room, brushing my lips over her forehead. 'I'm going to make some dinner.'

'Make dinner?' she teases with a wiggle of her brows.

'Well,' I acknowledge, 'reheat something Mrs Amaro made.'

'Perfect.' She adjusts her towel, wrapping it around her shoulders like a cape, clutching it at the neck, her dark hair brushed over one shoulder, wet and glossy, so I can't help but reach out and run my fingers over the ends. 'I'll be right back.'

I watch her walk through the hallway of my apartment, disappearing into the first bathroom she passes. A minute later the sound of running water fills the apartment and I move into the kitchen, lifting a container from the fridge. It's labelled in Mrs Amaro's precise handwriting, 'Lasagne'.

Mrs Amaro has been very clear about the use of microwaves—strictly forbidden for her meals. I slide the meal onto a tray and place it in the oven accordingly, grabbing some lettuce from the fridge and tearing it into a bowl. I put on an NFL game in the background as I work, grabbing a beer with a grin I can't shake.

Hot sex. American football. Great food. Ice-cold beer. What more could I want in life?

CHAPTER SEVEN

'THIS IS DELICIOUS.'

Zach's right; it is. I lift one of the *arancini* balls to my mouth, taking a bite so that the gooey cheese dribbles down my chin. I wipe it with my fingertips then realise he's watching with a look that is unmistakably sensual. I dip my eyes forward, but heat burns through me. I honestly thought this might have fizzled out by now. I've never been with someone like him but I just presumed a purely sexual connection would fade as we indulged ourselves at every opportunity we had. And we've done that—a lot. When I showed up today it was with an arm of groceries. Of course, I didn't actually get around to cooking for hours after I'd arrived. Zach had been waiting for me, naked and in bed, so what was I meant to do?

'Where'd you learn to cook?'

'When I lived in Paris.' I reach for a lemon wedge, squeezing it over the other half of my *arancini* before sipping the wine. I lift one foot onto the seat, resting my chin to my knee. 'I was fifteen, and didn't speak

a word of French.' I shake my head. 'That's a lie. I
could say *vin blanc sec*.'

'Tsk-tsk. Drinking at fifteen?'

'What can I say? I was a rebellious teen.'

'I'm surprised.'

'Are you? Why?'

'You strike me as a rule follower.'

'What gives you that impression? My desire to
crush the patriarchy and set the world on fire behind
me?' I angle my head to show him I'm half joking.

He grins. 'As a member of the male sex, should I
be threatened?'

'Oh, I'd keep you around for...amusement. When
it suited me.'

'Naturally.'

I grin. 'We lived in a big, old apartment on Av-
enue Montaigne. It was so beautiful, but I was miserable. We moved around a lot—I was starting my
fourth school in five years—and I'd left behind a best
friend and a boyfriend in Tokyo. I was so unhappy
and hated my parents, like all self-respecting fifteen-
year-olds, I guess.'

He's quiet, watchful and intent. I think this must
be how he operates in the corporate world, micro-
focussing and extracting what information he wants
from a conversation.

'So you weren't always averse to the idea of boyfriends, then?'

I wrinkle my nose. 'I was young and idealistic
once, what can I say?'

He flashes a smile; my blood simmers.

'What happened to him?'

'Distance. Boredom.' I lift my shoulders. 'I've always had a short attention span.'

He lifts his brows. 'Always? So no boyfriends since him?'

Out of nowhere I feel a blade of pain that I haven't felt for a long time. I jerk my face away from his, surprised by the intensity. 'I—was seeing a guy, a few years ago.'

'It didn't work out?' His question is quiet and again I have that feeling that I'm under the microscope, being carefully examined by him.

'No.' I bite down on my lower lip. 'It was a mistake.'

He's quiet, waiting, and somehow that drags the words out of me. 'When I first found out about Dad, it kind of cured me of the idea of relationships. I know that might sound silly but—'

'It doesn't sound silly,' he promises. 'You had a prime example of why men aren't to be trusted. Seeing a man you idolised behave like that would have shaped your view of the world. That's only natural.' His words sound as though they're dredged from the depths of his soul.

'I held that viewpoint for a long time. Then I met Patrick.'

'And fell in love?' he prompts thoughtfully.

'No. I don't know. I liked him, but not as much as he liked me. He fell in love and I liked having him around. I should have ended it way sooner but I kept leading him on.' I drop my head forward, shame at that selfishness eating through me. My voice is raw as I continue, 'Then one day Patrick proposed and I freaked out. I'd been stringing him along for two years, Zach. Two years. Because he was easy to get along with and I liked his company. Can you believe that?'

His frown is instantaneous. 'He could have left. Asked you how you felt sooner.'

I shake my head. 'I think he knew. I think he was afraid that if he asked he'd get an answer he didn't want. But that doesn't excuse my behaviour. I'd been hating on my dad all these years and, in a way, I was just as bad.'

'How does your behaviour compare to his?'

'I was using Patrick—every day I didn't tell him that I was nowhere near as serious about him as he was me.' I shudder. 'I swore to myself after that never to get involved with a guy again. I don't like the person I turn into when I'm in a relationship. I don't want to be my father.'

'I still don't understand how you think you compare to him.'

'Because I knew I was hurting Patrick—or that he was bound to get hurt—and I didn't care. I used him, Zach. I used him for convenience and because I liked being with him marginally more than I liked being on my own. How awful is that? Because of such lukewarm, selfish feelings I strung this poor guy along then broke his sweet heart.' Remorse sweeps through me. 'The thing is…' searching for words '… I just don't have a healthy perspective on relationships. I made a decision, after Patrick, that casual sex is fine, because no one ends up falling in love. Relationships are—a disaster.'

His eyes hold mine and something sparks in the air that hovers between us.

'I get that.'

I shake my head, clearing the memories of that time, aim for a bright smile. 'What about you? No girlfriends in your past?'

'One.' Jesus. Where did that come from? I never talk about Emily, not with anyone. Except Dimitrios, who's been subjected to a few messy, drunken ramblings about the woman I thought I loved—back when I was stupid enough to believe in love. I don't talk about Emily because she messed me up, and for a long time, and even now I don't like to open that wound. But something about Jessica's confession has stirred truths within me.

'Really?'

Having started on this path, I realise I don't hate it. Talking to Jessica is easy. Maybe because we're so similar, both completely independent and self-contained, refusing to rely on anyone else for emotional satisfaction.

'More recently?' She leans forward, clearly fascinated. I don't blame her. My reputation is as incontrovertible as the day is long. I'm not a relationship guy. I'm a 'bachelor'. 'Party boy'. All the tags the tabloid press can come up with, I wear.

'A few years ago.'

'Seriously?'

'Mmm.'

'What happened? Who was she?'

'She's a friend of my stepmother's. I've known her since I was a teenager.'

'So she's older than you.'

I dip my head in silent agreement. 'My stepmother is considerably younger than my father was. Emily's twelve years older than me.'

'So what happened? Don't spare the gory details. Make me feel better about the way I screwed up Patrick's life.'

Her supposition that I was the guilty party is natural. But she's wrong. 'I'd had a crush on her for years. A totally inappropriate, forbidden crush—perhaps that was part of the appeal. She's beautiful, intelligent and off-limits. What teenager wouldn't be drawn to that?'

Jessica nods, her eyes holding mine without reaction. Had I been hoping for jealousy? Jessica's way too self-assured to feel something so petty.

'She was married. *Is* married.' Disgust runs through me.

'So you had an affair?' she prompts, after a while, a note of something hard to hear in her voice. Something that sounds a lot like judgement.

That we had an affair isn't an entirely accurate description—at least, it's not from my perspective, but I nod grimly. 'We ran into each other a few summers ago, in New York. What are the chances, right? It was such a strange coincidence, I invited her for a drink. To catch up. I was older. No longer a teenager in awe of her, not sure what to do.'

'Right. You'd had years of screwing your way through the women of the world,' she asserts evenly. It's the truth but there's that tone in her voice again and it ignites a spark of shame inside me.

'My approach with women had improved,' I concede.

'So you hit on her?'

'Harmless flirtation,' I amend, shaking my head.

'Even though she was married?'

'Yes.' My eyes meet hers and I feel it again. Guilt. Now it's impossible not to see the recrimination in her features. I guess the situation with her parents makes her see this through a unique veil.

'I see.' Her disapproval surprises me. She's so liberal with sex, I didn't expect this. Then again, infidelity and sex are two different ball games.

'But it was just flirtation—I had no intention on acting on it. I don't want to get married but I still respect the idea of it. I'm not a home-wrecker.'

It's so important to me that she believes that, but her expression is impossible to read. 'Then she told me she and her husband were separated.'

Her eyes narrowed. Jessica, clearly, is smarter than I, because the explanation is met with the cynicism I should have felt at the time.

'We spent the weekend together. I thought I'd got her out of my system. I was done. But she called me the next week, wanting to see me again. What was the harm? They were getting divorced, or so she said.'

She's very still, waiting for me to continue.

'They didn't divorce; she lied to me. I spent over two years supporting her, falling in love with her—or believing I loved her—' I shake my head impatiently, taking a swig of beer.

'So you left her?'

I grimace. 'I gave her an ultimatum. I can't believe I stuck around as long as I did.' I replace the beer on the table slowly, wiping condensation from the body of the bottle. 'I figured she'd had enough time to work out what she wanted. She chose him. To be honest, she never had any intention of leaving him. She was bored—he worked a lot. I adored her and she liked having her ego stroked by a younger guy.'

'Jesus. I'm sorry, Zach.'

'Don't be. It was a valuable learning experience.'

'Oh? And what did it teach you?'

'That love is a crock of shit. Though I already knew that—or should have.'

'It sounds pretty rough.'

'At the time, yeah. I was surprised at how quickly love turned to hate. She's a well-known actress, her husband's a director. I think a big part of it for Emily is that she liked the image they had. They're one of those perfect Hollywood couples. A divorce would have ruined it. Marriage to me would have dimmed the brilliance of the image she'd constructed.'

'You wanted to *marry* her?' Jessica's voice is a little squeaky.

I tilt a glance at her. 'I was stupid, remember?'

'Wow. I just can't imagine any world in which you get married to anyone.'

It makes me laugh. 'How do you know me so well after not even a week?'

'I've known men like you before,' she reminds me with a twisty smile that makes a dimple form in her cheek.

She's teasing, but for some reason I don't really like her assertion.

'Have you?'

'Mmm. Though you're the first one I've actually liked.' Her eyes widen. 'I just mean "liked" as in, enjoyed spending time with beyond the bedroom.' She dips her head forward, her cheeks flashing pink. I don't think I've ever seen Jessica embarrassed. Fascinating. 'I don't mean "like, like".'

'As in you don't harbour a secret romantic crush on me?'

She lifts her eyes and glares through me. 'As if.'

I laugh. 'Jeez, thanks.'

'Well, don't say I didn't warn you. That's not who I am. And it's not who you are.' She gives up the glare and smiles instead. 'That's why this all works so well.'

She's right. We've both had relationships that should serve as cautionary tales. Problems only arise when one person gets out of step with the other—when expectations get built and then crushed. Sex—just sex—is best.

'Emily and I broke up a week before Christmas. I was never a huge fan of this time of year but that kind of cemented it. I can't hear a Christmas carol without thinking about that disastrous night.'

'You're still hung up on her?'

'I'm hung up on how I let her affect me,' I correct. 'I was an absolute idiot not to see what was going on. After two years I should have realised she had no intention of divorcing him. After two weeks I should have damned well seen that she was lying to me.' I push my fingers through my hair with irritation. 'I don't believe in regrets, but I'm…disappointed in myself for the whole sordid chapter.'

Jessica reaches over, puts her hand on mine and squeezes it. I'm surprised by the gesture, and kind of touched by it as well. 'We all make mistakes. At least you learned from yours.'

'Yeah, no married women.'

'And no love,' she tacks on.

'Right. No love.' Our eyes lock and it's as if we're making a pact or something. Satisfaction shifts through me.

I take his hard cock deep in my mouth, my body over his, my breasts brushing his waist as his mouth torments my clit, his tongue running over my sensitive cluster of nerves until I can barely breathe, much less focus on what I'm doing. I move instinctively though, his primal noises groaned against my sex driving me wild—more wild than I've ever felt in my life.

I taste him in my mouth—just a hint—and I feel heat flood my veins, the animalistic passion of this almost tipping me over the edge. His stubble brushes between my legs, his fingers digging into my butt, massaging me there as I try to keep hold of my sanity, but pleasure is carrying me away, lifting me on a wave, extracting me from this world, this life, from Zach. I grip the base of his cock with one hand, flicking his tip with my tongue but I'm coming, so hard, against his face, his mouth relentless, skilled, perfect.

I groan, my mouth around his tip, but then he's moving, pulling away from me at the same time he reaches for my hips and lifts me, holding me on all fours. I hear the crinkling of foil and then he pushes into my still-trembling body, pushing me back onto the wave of pleasure, so that it's almost painful because every nerve ending in my body is throbbing with euphoria.

'Don't stop,' I groan again, pressing my face into the bedding.

'I won't.' He moves faster, his fingers still kneading my butt, and I feel every single touch deep in my soul. He holds me close as he drives into me and as my orgasm builds his own releases, his hand coming around to stroke my clit and tip me over the edge with him. His other hand reaches for my breasts, lifting me up, so my back is pressed to his chest, our bodies glued together, his hands roaming my body as though I am a part of him, his cock buried inside me as if it's a part of me. I whimper in pleasure, biting down on my lip, heat like lava coursing through me.

He drops his head and bites my shoulder, just lightly, but my whole body jerks in response. His fingers tweak an overly sensitive nipple and then drop back to my clit, lightly sensitising me, gently buzzing my flesh as though to remind me that he can make me come again and again and again so easily.

So easily.

I am putty in his hands. And I don't even care. I collapse forward, rolling onto my back, and as if to prove his point he brings his mouth to my sex once more, his tongue whispering promises to my throbbing, indulged flesh. I feel worshipped. I feel as though his purpose in life is to pleasure me. I lift my arms over my head, digging my fingers into the bedsheet, staring up at the ceiling as he catches me high on the wave and holds me there, my orgasm so intense I can barely breathe. My lungs burn with the sting of this, my body is on fire, my soul eternally trapped in this moment. And then I'm crashing and flying, a thousand shards of me splintering into the atmosphere as I break apart cell by cell, lightning striking me into pieces that no one can ever catch. I collapse against the sheets, my breath the only sound in the room, each a torment, a battle, my lungs fighting my brain, my instincts to simply shut down and process this.

I sweep my eyes shut, needing to block out everything and everyone—even Zach. I moan softly and stretch, a slow smile spreading over my face as bit by bit my feet come back to earth.

It isn't just that he's great in bed, it's that he's thoughtful as anything. He's the least selfish lover I've ever had. Most guys would be done after they've come, but not Zach. I can't believe how much he loves making me come. I push up onto elbows that feel like jelly, my eyes hooded as they meet his.

'I feel like I've died and gone to heaven,' I say honestly.

'And you're a perfect angel.' He grins, climbing up my body and kissing me hard, so I can taste myself on his lips. It's so erotic. I run my fingernails down his back to the dip at the base of his spine, trailing them across his skin, our eyes linked.

'Thank you.' I don't know why I say it, it just feels appropriate.

'Thank you right back.' He runs his hand over my cheek. My heart twists. Something shifts inside me. I remember his assertion that he doesn't do missionary. I was baffled by that at first but with his body on top of mine, our eyes linked, I get it. It's too intimate. Too close. It takes a purely physical act and turns it into something more.

Strange that I've never seen it that way. For me, sex is an exchange and it doesn't matter what form that takes, nothing changes the parameters of what I want from it. But…with Zach…maybe because this has already lasted longer than I expected, I feel as if imitating true intimacy could be really dangerous.

Dangerous? That's just being paranoid.

Nonetheless, I push at his chest with both hands, surprising him and rolling him onto his back. I lift up, straddling his waist, somehow changing the sense of intimacy when I'm on top and in control.

As tends to happen with Zach, I've lost all sense of time and place, but a quick glance at the digital clock on his bedside table shows it's the early hours of the morning.

'I have to go,' I say with true remorse.

He catches my hands in his, lacing our fingers together. 'Why?'

'Because I'm having breakfast with my mother and sister tomorrow,' I say with a lift of my eyes heavenward. 'Then shopping on Orchard Road.'

'Shopping?'

'Christmas shopping,' I explain. 'It's a tradition. We try to do at least one day together every year. Get our hair done, you know, all that kind of thing.'

'That sounds…sweet.'

I pull a face, but at the same time I'm sort of looking forward to it. 'It is actually kind of nice. Away from Dad and Simon, we seem to have an easier time.'

He lifts a hand to my hair. 'What will you get done?'

I bite down on my lip. 'Maybe a yellow Mohawk?'

He grins. 'I was thinking more blue. Dreadlocks?'

'Ooh, tempting.'

'You'd suit dreadlocks.'

'Would I?'

'Hell, yeah.'

I laugh. 'Thanks for the suggestion. I'll take it under advisement.'

'You do that.'

He lifts his hands to my face and runs them through my hair. It cascades around my face like a waterfall. 'Don't change it. This suits you.'

'This? This is the *I've-been-too-busy-to-sleep* style I've been rocking for about fifteen months…'

'I like it. I like the way it falls around your face when you're on top of me. I like the way it's long enough for me to grab hold of while I'm inside you. I like watching it fall down your back, like a black waterfall, as I thrust into you.'

I shiver at the vivid imagery his erotic words evoke. 'You know that asking me to keep it like this makes me all the more likely to change it?'

'Because you're contrary?'

'Because I only listen to my own good judgement.' I wink. 'Though you're definitely currying favour with me.'

'How am I doing that?'

'By giving me more orgasms than I knew possible in a single night?'

'Ah. That old chestnut.' His grin, though, is pure ego. Damn it, I hadn't intended to enlarge that but I'm honest to a fault and always have been. I lean forward and kiss his lips hastily.

'I have to go.'

'Stay.'

I shake my head, but his request flatters and pleases me in a way that should, perhaps, serve as a warning. Maybe he's not the only one whose ego's getting stretched out by this.

'I can't.' I go to pull away from him but he holds me where I am.

'Why not?'

'Because I don't have any clothes, for one. Or a toothbrush.'

'I have spare toothbrushes.'

'Clothes?'

'You were wearing clothes when you arrived, weren't you?'

'Yes, but I came straight from my parents' place. If I arrive to breakfast in those same things, my mum and sister are going to know exactly how I've spent my night.'

'I don't think they'll know *exactly* how we've spent it,' he teases, reaching around and slapping my bottom lightly. I laugh.

'Well, that's true. And thank God for that.'

'Mummy wouldn't approve?'

'Please, I don't think I've ever called her Mummy in my life.' I brush a finger over his lower lip, my heart throbbing. 'And she'd be thrilled if she knew I was with you. I mean, so long as she thought there was the prospect of marriage, of course.'

'She's old-fashioned?'

'She would think you're a catch,' I respond with a shake of my head.

'And you disagree?' His expression shows mock hurt.

'Well, I guess it depends on your definition of a catch,' I point out. 'For me, being a fantastic lover would never compensate for the fact you're completely emotionally unavailable.' I'm surprised by the words I've just said, surprised because they're not what I actually think. Are they? I mean, whether he's emotionally available or not is beside the point—I'm not interested in emotions. So why does it sound like I even give a toss about that?

His eyes hold mine for a second too long and my breath catches in my throat as I briefly contemplate that I've hurt him in some way. But then he smiles and releases his grip on my hips.

'That's because you're a smart cookie.' He flops back onto the bed, staring at the ceiling. 'Now get out of here before I chain you to the bed and never let you leave again.'

CHAPTER EIGHT

'So? WHAT DO you think of it?'

'What do I think of it?' Dimitrios scans the papers then puts them aside. 'Obviously it's a good deal. Why are you even asking me?'

I reach across his desk and lift the analysis I've had our international finance firm conduct.

'This is the kind of app you buy for breakfast,' he continues. 'It's not going to take much capital, relatively speaking. Why haven't you acted on it?'

I thumb the pages distractedly. 'I've met the owner. Jessica Johnson.'

'And?' Dimitrios stares at me for a few seconds then throws his head back and laughs. 'Let me guess. You slept with her?'

Despite the veracity of his assessment, something like anger snakes in my gut. I compress my lips, tapping my fingers on my knee. 'I don't mean that.' It's not, exactly, a denial. 'I just mean I've spoken to her, got to know her. And I know how important this is to her. If we bought it—any part of it—the investment would need to be purely passive.'

'No input?' Dimitrios frowns at that. 'It's not generally how we do business.'

I dip my head in agreement.

'Christ. What'd she do to you?'

I fix him with a stare that's pure businesslike. 'If I thought there was anyone better to run the operations of She-Shakes I'd be putting them forward. Jessica Johnson is the best person for the job. She's the reason it's become such a phenomenal success, and I think she's the person who needs to keep managing it. What she needs is capital, and quickly. Other players with more financial backing are already stepping into her sphere. In order to grow, she needs cash.'

'I've already said I agree.'

I nod, not sure why I'm hesitating. Yes, I'm completely sure why I haven't already made her the offer. Everything's complicated by our physical relationship. I don't want her to think I'm offering to buy into the business just because she's hotter than Hades— because I'd never do anything so stupid. This is just good business sense.

'But I've read the full report,' Dimitrios says after a minute. 'The evaluation at the back—with a full one hundred per cent buyout—is pretty compelling. With our existing media network, the app could be grown exponentially.'

Something closes around my chest like a vice. 'She won't sell the whole thing.'

'Everyone will sell for the right price.'

I shake my head. 'Jessica Johnson is the rare creature who's completely unmotivated by money.' A small smile shifts my face. 'She seemed almost… annoyed with how successful the app's become.'

Dimitrios is watching me as though I've sprouted two heads. 'Seriously, what's going on with you?'

'Nothing. I'm just amused by her.' Amused? Yeah, that works. I'm fucking amused—turned on—going out of my mind with lust for her.

'You are unbelievable.' He shakes his head but there's a smile on his face—Dimitrios knows me better than anyone. He might not agree with my life decisions but he never gives me grief for them. 'Just don't fuck it up by—fucking.'

A thread of disloyalty runs through me. Dimitrios and I don't ever really talk about my social life. He doesn't ask questions, I don't volunteer information. But he knows that I'm not exactly lonely. I know if he'd asked about anyone else, I wouldn't have shied away from the conversation. Not the details, just confirming that, yeah, in fact, we are, in a sense, seeing each other.

But there's no vernacular to adequately describe what Jessica and I are doing. 'Seeing each other' sounds too formal. 'Fuck buddies' isn't right either. I know that's what we agreed to but it's not just fucking. I like her.

Even thinking that makes me smile because I remember the way she was last night, blushing when she inadvertently admitted that she liked me too. And now I'm grinning like some kind of adolescent.

Jesus.

I sober, standing up, pacing to the windows of Dimitrios's office. 'I don't want to fuck it up,' I say, seriously. 'Her business is hugely important to her. I want to buy it because if we don't, I'm not sure what will happen.'

'So you're doing this purely out of a sense of altruism?'

'No.' She'd hate that. 'It's a good investment.'

'I agree.'

'But I'd be lying if I said I didn't have some personal agenda.'

'Just—'

I turn to face Dimitrios, waiting for the rest of the sentence. He rubs a hand over his chin in a gesture that I do so often it feels familiar. 'Yes?'

He looks frustrated. 'Who am I to talk? Just use your head.'

'You seem different.' Jemima frowns as she studies me, her fork poised halfway to her mouth. I feel Mum's eyes burning me from the left.

'Different?' I flick my fingers through my hair. 'Could it be this?'

She grimaces as she eyes the hint of pink I had foiled into the ends. I couldn't resist a chance to tease Zach—and to show him I'll do whatever I want with my hair. It had the unexpected bonus of appalling Jemima and Mum. *'I suppose you can tuck it into a bun,' Mum had said with a watery smile.*

'No. I noticed it at breakfast too. What's going on with you?'

'What do you mean?'

'We've hardly seen you this week.'

My jaw drops. 'Hardly' seen me? I feel as though I've spent hours of my life at my parents' place. I quickly turn my surprised expression into a smile. 'I'm sorry you feel that way. I've had a lot going on with work.'

'You work too hard, darling. How are you ever going to meet anyone if you're always in the office?'

'I don't want to meet anyone,' I say reflexively, my insides tightening as I think of Zach. A sense of longing creeps over me, flooding my veins. It's a visceral sense of need—a need to see him, to touch him, taste him, smell him, to wrap my arms around his warm body and feel his arms around me, to step up onto the tips of my toes and kiss him slowly, kiss him hard. It's a need to see him smile, to watch the way it spreads slowly over his face as if every muscle is being gently prodded to life until even his eyes appear to smile. It's a need to hear him laugh and watch him move, his lithe athleticism always captivating. It's a desire to ask him the thousand and one questions I forgot when I was with him, because he's too mesmerising for my brain to fully function.

'I'm serious, Jessica. You're *grinning*. What's got into you?'

I flatten my smile. 'I told you—it's work.'

'I take it it's going well, then?' Mum asks, trying hard to keep her tone light even when I know she disapproves of how much emphasis I put on my career.

'Yes, very.'

'Have you decided which of the offers you're going to take?'

I turn my attention back to Jemima. 'I know Simon thinks I should sell, but I really don't know that I will.'

'He's looked into it a bit. He really does know what he's talking about.'

I know she's trying to be kind, to look out for me, but I wouldn't trust Simon even with choosing a logo for my business. I shake my head. 'I've got some great advisors weighing in.'

'Let Simon help you,' she insists. Her eyes hold a challenge and it infuriates me. She knows what happened between us. I told her—because how could I not? I'm a firm believer that a woman should know if her husband's messing around behind her back. Jemima simply told me I must have misunderstood, that he'd never cheat on her and certainly not with her own sister.

I don't know how I'm supposed to have misunderstood his slurred voice whispering that we should get a hotel room together.

'I'll think about it,' I offer, placatingly. I suppose her desire to see the best in her husband is only natural.

'Now, Christmas lunch…' Mum changes the subject with her usual panache for avoiding conflict. 'Martha's planning a turkey this year.'

'It's going to be so hot,' I point out, then compress my lips because it sounds petulant. 'But of course there's air conditioning and we can go for a swim.'

'It's not Christmas without turkey and trimmings,' Jemima agrees. 'I'll make the pudding. You know, Si's family one?'

'Yep.' I wonder what Zach does for Christmas. His brother lives here, doesn't he? And his new wife and nephew? Will he spend it with them? Or his mum? More questions. I'll ask him tonight.

I frown. Tonight? Am I seeing him tonight? I've seen him every night since we agreed to this. But we haven't made any arrangement that we'll hook up each night, it's sort of just happened. I've gone to his place simply because it made sense to do so. A feeling of unease creeps through me, a feeling of resistance because I don't want to be so easy. I don't want to be so…enamoured of him.

'Let's get shopping, ladies,' I say a little hastily, pushing my plate away. Mum finished her salad earlier and Jemima's been picking for the last ten minutes. I signal for the bill, impatient now to do something else. I don't want to think about Zach any more—I have a sinking suspicion I've already given him way too much of my time.

How was shopping?

I read his text message and my tummy goes all loopy.

I slide my hand through the water of my bath, a smile lifting my cheeks. It's just past eight o'clock. I've been for a run in the hotel gym, done some work, eaten some sushi. That is to say, I've kept busy and ignored the fact I hadn't heard from him and that my body is in overdrive with wanting him.

Which is all the more reason to lie low. Just for tonight. Just to prove to myself that I can.

I write back.

I think we bought half of Singapore. I got you a Christmas-themed tie.

Anyone who claims to hate Christmas should have a Christmas tie. I saw it and couldn't resist—the garish colours and Santa motif will be *perfect* for Zach.

I know exactly what I'd like to do with that.

Oh?

I include a little 'shrug' emoji.

It involves you, and my bed.

My heart thumps.

I can't imagine what you mean.

Then you need a demonstration.

Perhaps that can be arranged. Tomorrow night?

There's a pause. My heart soars.

Or in an hour?

I smile until my cheeks hurt.

Tomorrow.

Even as I type the word I regret it, but I force myself to hit 'send'. We both came into this with boundaries and rules. I'm just reminding us of them.

So you had a good day?

I settle back into the bath, smiling as I reply.

It was…better than expected. Yours?

Interesting.

I wait, as three little dots bobble on the bottom of the screen to indicate he's still typing.

Your name came up.

My breath turns shallow.

With whom? And in what context?

I'll explain tomorrow night.

That's not fair.

Isn't it?

I shake my head. His message zips in before I can reply.

You're pouting, aren't you?

I might be.

What else are you doing?

I bite down on my smile.

I'm in the bath.

Ah…

I smile, waiting for him to send something else. He doesn't. Disappointed, I put my phone down. Ten minutes later, the doorbell rings.

It can't be him. Can it? I climb out of the bath and grab a bathrobe, pulling it on and practically running towards the door, my heart pounding overtime.

'Room service, madam.'

'I didn't order any—'

The waiter dips his head. 'The order was phoned in. There's a card.'

'Oh.' I eye the tray with a smile then nod towards the table. 'Thank you.'

He moves into the suite, depositing the tray then leaving again. Once I'm alone, I move to the table with a sensation of butterflies in my tummy.

A bottle of champagne, which I recognise as the same label we shared the first night he came here. The night we met. I finger the neck with a rush of pleasure and a strange apprehensiveness. I lift the silver lid. Chocolates. Strawberries. My stomach squeezes. Sure enough, there's a white envelope with my name on it.

I peel the back and lift a crisp white piece of cardboard out.

Thinking of you...

I smile, lifting the tray and carrying it into the bathroom, where I place it on the side of the marble vanity. I half fill a glass of champagne and grab the bowl of strawberries, carrying them to the edge of the bath. Back in the warm water, I reach for my phone once more and call him.

'Well, that was a nice surprise.'

'You should always have a glass of champagne to hand. Or breast.'

Heat fills my cheeks.

'Only when you're around to distribute it.'

I can hear him laughing.

'I did offer...'

'Well, now I'm tempted,' I joke.

'I'm happy to come over...'

God, he's persistent. Like I'm not completely flattered by that. Still, this is about proving a point to myself. I shake my head with true regret. 'Tomorrow. I have to catch up on work.'

'You can't see me right now but my face is very sad.'

'Your poor face. I'll kiss it better tomorrow.'

'Other parts of me are wounded too.'

I laugh, sipping the champagne. 'I'll kiss them too. Maybe while your hands are tied to the bed with the Christmas tie.'

'My hands? That's not quite what I had in mind…'

'Trust me. You'll enjoy it.'

'I do trust you.'

I pause, something zapping through me. I stare at the screen, a dryness forming in my mouth. I don't know how to reply.

I put the phone down and reach for a strawberry. It's sweet, perfectly ripe. Juice dribbles down my chin. I imagine how Zach would be staring at it if he were here and a strange lurching sensation rolls through my gut. I arrange the bubbles of my bath around my breasts so that only a hint of cleavage can be seen and reach for my phone. As an afterthought, I lift the champagne to my lips then take a selfie.

I send it to him with the caption: Cheers!

You're killing me, Jessica Johnson.

A second later.

Is that pink in your hair?

I can't stop smiling. I smooth some of the bubbles away so considerably more of my cleavage is on display and a little more of my hair then snap another photo. I don't caption it, just hit 'send'.

A second later, my phone rings. I swipe it before realising it's a video call, but then Zach's face is staring back at me. 'What are you trying to do to me?' he complains.

I stare at the screen for several beats, trying to rally my brain into sensible action.

'I'm just having a bath,' I say with mock innocence.

'You're tormenting me.'

'Am I?' I bat my lashes.

'As you're fully aware.'

I laugh, reclining against the back of the bath, just my face filling the screen. 'How was your day?'

'It got better about two minutes ago.'

I smile.

'You do realise I'm going to have to print and frame that photo.'

I pull a face.

'Or have it turned into a coffee cup so I can look at you every morning.'

I laugh. 'I think I could get you a better picture.'

'No such thing.'

I roll my eyes. 'Your flattery is not necessary, Zachary. You've already got me into bed.'

'Mmm…' A gruff noise. 'So tell me about shopping.'

'What do you want to know?'

'Whatever you want to tell me.'

My heart skips. He's being sweet. He knows I was a little anxious about it and he's giving me a chance to vent. I take a sip of champagne, focussing on the screen. 'Like I said, it was better than I expected. I actually really like spending time with Jemima and

Mum, when it's just the three of us. We're all very different but we're family.' I lean forward a little, inadvertently angling the screen lower. His grin alerts me to the fact he can see a fair amount of my body.

'Eyes up, mister.'

He holds his free hand up in a silent plea. 'That was way too tempting.'

'I'll be more careful.'

'Don't.'

I laugh.

'What do you do for Christmas?'

He frowns, surprised by the question. 'Me?'

'No, the guy behind you,' I tease. 'Yeah, you. We were talking about it today, our traditions and what we do, what we'll eat. I know you're not particularly a fan but you must have some plans?'

'Not really.'

'Do you see your mum? Your brother?'

'This year will be a bit different, given my brother's just got married. I'm not really sure.'

'What about your mum?'

'She's in Sydney.'

'Alone?'

'She's remarried. He has kids. They do a big family thing.'

'That's so sad.'

'Why?' He looks genuinely perplexed. 'It's just another day, Jessica.'

'How can you say that? It's Christmas.'

'And I hate it.' He uses the same tone I did. 'Now, loosen your grip a bit.'

I make an exaggerated sighing noise but drop the camera a bit lower. He groans in frustration. 'You're really choosing a bath and work over me?'

I blow him a kiss. 'Yep. I'm sure you're not used to hearing "no" very often but I'm afraid that's what I'm saying.'

He clutches his chest in a wounded gesture.

'What about when you were a kid?' I push. 'What did you do for Christmas then?'

He sighs. 'You really want to hear about this?'

'Sure. Why not?'

'Give me a second.' I watch as he walks through his place. The night sky appears above his head and then the phone is placed down so the sky is all I can see. A short while later he's back in shot, his torso naked, a glass of something that looks like Scotch in hand. I watch as he steps in the water.

'That's better. Now we're both all wet.'

I feel jealous. Now I feel as if I'd give just about anything to be in the pool with him. His double entendre does what he clearly intended and sends a zing of need spiralling through me.

'Christmas, when I was a kid.' He props the phone against something so his hands are free. I have a full view of his face and torso. I watch the movement of his chest muscles as he shifts, running his fingertips over the water's surface. 'Money was tight for us, so it wasn't like we were spoiled with gifts or anything.'

I lean forward a little, the sincerity in his voice pulling at something in my chest.

'But Mum tried really hard to make it special. She

always made sure we had something beneath the tree, not to mention the gift Father Christmas would bring.' He grins and my heart twists—he's way too gorgeous. 'We'd go to church, have lunch together, then a phone conversation with my grandparents—they lived in another state and we didn't see them often. There were little traditions, things I took for granted because I was just a kid.' He grimaces.

I search for something to say, reaching for the champagne and taking a sip.

'And at ten we came to live with Dad and his wife, Chao-Xing.' Something tightens in his face, his smile looks a little heavier. 'She wanted to make Christmas magical for us, like something out of a movie, so really went to town with decorations and presents.' He shakes his head.

'The dichotomy of that must have been unnerving.'

'We were ten—and the living epitome of not looking a gift horse in the mouth. We just loved the presents.' But I can see more in his eyes, even like this, separated by two screens and miles of sky.

'As you got older, then?' I prompt, instinctively knowing there's more to it.

'Yeah, as we got older, we found it hard. I mean, before that our mum struggled. She could barely make ends meet, and we grew like weeds, always needed new shoes and clothes. We did a thousand and one sports and she never told us it was too expensive, that she couldn't afford the equipment. She worked hard to be able to give us what we needed and we just...took it for granted.'

'That's very normal for kids, Zach.'

'Yeah.' His voice is gruff. I hear the self-condemnation there.

'Your dad didn't...'

'Support her?' He finishes for me, his voice darkening. 'No.'

I feel everything he's not saying. I tell myself not to ask, that knowing this isn't part of our contract, it's not part of our deal. But despite that, I say, 'Why not?'

If he's surprised by the question he doesn't show it. 'He just didn't think about her. My dad was selfish. Mum was just some woman he'd banged years ago. We were her kids, not his.'

'So he wasn't in your life?'

'Before the age of ten, not really. He used to fly in and out from time to time. Take us on ridiculously expensive holidays—always with a nanny, who we'd spend a lot more time with than him—then bring us back to Mum where we'd never have quite enough to eat.' He shakes his head with clear disapproval. 'He was a selfish asshole. At least, he was where she was concerned.'

My voice is a little husky when I say, 'Families are complicated.'

His eyes meet mine in the camera. My heart flips. 'Yeah.'

'You can love someone and still disapprove of their actions.'

He grimaces. 'When he got married, we suddenly took on a new value for him. Chao-Xing couldn't have children and really wanted to be a mother so he brought us over to Singapore to live with them. I thought it was us he wanted. I thought that for years but it was never about us, just what he could give his new wife.'

I can't help my indignant intake of breath. 'You're kidding?'

He shakes his head slowly.

'And your mum?'

'She stayed in Sydney, consoling herself that at least now we could have the things we needed. I'm ashamed to say I didn't realise—for a long time—how much she sacrificed so that we could live a better life.'

'Oh, my God, Zach.' Tears fill my eyes and I am not someone who cries easily or often at all. I stare at him, momentarily lost for words.

His laugh is deep but I hear the bitterness to it. I hear the pain he's trying to cover. And he does a good job but somehow, for some reason, I just know him better than that. I see inside his soul and my heart aches for the ten-year-old boy he'd been then.

'It was fine, Jessica. We were spoiled. We were happy. It was all good.'

I see it's important for him that I believe that, but I shake my head, wishing I could reach through the screen and touch him, wrap my arms around him, cup his cheek, draw him close and kiss him gently.

'We went home and saw her a few times a year.'

My throat thickens at that. I can't imagine how hard that must have been for his mum. As Zach said, perhaps the thought that at least her children were

happy was enough to dull that pain. But I doubt it—
and I'm not even remotely maternal.

'And now?'

'She still lives in Sydney. I split my time between
there and here. She comes over often. It's different.'

'You must feel—'

He flashes me a smile, but I see behind it. 'What
must I feel, Jessica Johnson?'

'A thousand things.'

'I don't.' He drinks his Scotch, then moves closer
to the camera. 'I'm a pretty simple guy, really.'

I believed that about him. I really did. But now
I don't. I feel as though the veil has been lifted and
there's no stopping it now. What would that experience do to a person? Being pulled away from your
mum and the only home you've ever known at that
age, thrust into a world of unimaginable wealth only
to know your mum was still struggling to pay the
bills? I shake my head in silent condemnation.

'I'll never forget that first year though.' His voice
is serious; his eyes are focussed beyond the phone,
as if he's both talking to me and not. 'It was right
before Christmas that we came here. Mum sent the
presents she'd bought for us in our suitcases. They
were already wrapped in this cheap, thin wrapping
paper she used to get. It got holes punched in it during the trip.' His voice is deep and rumbled, but quiet
too. 'We forgot all about them because of the deluge
of presents that were under the tree when we arrived.
We didn't even thank her for them. At ten, I knew
enough to feel guilty.'

Tears thicken the back of my throat.

'She sounds like a great mum.'

'Yeah.' His smile is tight. 'I wondered about how she spent that first Christmas. If she still went to church, spoke to her parents. She must have hated it.'

I nod in agreement. What can I say?

'The thing is, Dad never cared about Mum. He never really cared about us.' His voice is thick.

'He must have, Zach, to bring you to live with him.'

'Nah, that was all for his new wife.' He shakes his head and, before I can ask him to clarify, continues, 'He never saw Mum as a person of worth and it took me a long time to realise that—to understand what that must have been like for her.' He compresses his lips and the veil lifts further because I see the anger contained in that small gesture.

'It must have been hard for you to see that.'

'I didn't get it at the time. But yes, Jessica, when I was old enough to understand, it was hard. It taught me a lot about my dad, and about relationships.'

'I'm sorry.'

He shakes his head, brushing away the apology.

His tone brightens, as though sweeping aside our conversation. 'The saving grace is that my stepmum's really great. She's a beautiful person. Kind, sweet, and she loved us like her own kids. So in the end, we got two mums, and a father who was, as it turns out, a total bastard.'

My heart throbs painfully. 'I'm glad she was good to you, Zach.'

I want to be there with him more than anything—which terrifies me. This deep and meaningful conversation isn't what I signed on for. He's not meant to be someone who makes my heart hurt with his stories. He's not meant to be someone who brings tears of sympathy to my eyes.

'Do you see her for Christmas?'

'Yeah. She's actually away this year, visiting friends in Switzerland, but usually we have lunch with her.'

'So you do celebrate it?'

He pulls a face. 'I have lunch with her like I would on any other day she invites me for lunch.'

His cynicism makes me smile and I'm desperate to lighten the mood, to move back to safer, more familiar ground. 'I don't know. I think I could bring you around to the Christmas side.'

'Oh, really?' He moves closer to the camera. 'What's so good about it?'

I sigh, trying to work out where to start. 'So many things. The food, the decorations, the music, I love it all. Fruit mince pies, shortbread, eggnog, pudding.'

'Ah, see, that's not really the kind of Christmas I grew up with. We're more prawns and mangoes at the beach people.'

'But that's still Christmas food—your Christmas food.' I pause. 'Though it's not quite the same, you're right. Why don't we have Christmas dinner together?' I stare at him, shocked at the words that flew out of my mouth. 'Obviously I don't mean actual Christmas dinner. I meant, the food. I mean another night, not

Christmas, and just some of the yummiest Christmas things.' I glare at him, annoyed I sound so stupid, embarrassed at what I've just offered.

'I'd like that.' His voice is low, dipping through me, reassuring me, warming me, fixing me.

I ease my glare.

'Okay.'

'But not tomorrow. Tomorrow I have plans for you.'

'Oh?'

'Though I guess they're a little festive.'

'In what way?'

'The Christmas blindfold?'

I stare at him blankly for a second and then laugh. 'It's a tie, Zach…'

'Potato, potahto.'

CHAPTER NINE

'YOU'RE WEARING CLOTHES,' I complain as I walk into Zach's penthouse the following evening, the sun dipping low in the sky.

His grin is slow and sexy as he prowls towards me, his stride long. 'Am I not meant to be?'

I reach into my bag and pull out the silk tie, lifting it around his neck when he's close enough to reach. 'On the contrary,' I murmur, folding it into a knot at his neck, concentrating on the job so I almost don't feel the burn of his gaze on me as I work. I pat it in place when I'm done then pull back a little to observe my handiwork. It's absolutely ludicrous—so cheesy and festive—and yet, of course, on Zac it totally works.

'Clothes means I can get this on you right now.'

'I couldn't have worn it naked?'

'Now there's a thought.' I bat my eyelids and he laughs, a low growl, as he pulls me towards him and kisses my lips. I surrender to the kiss, my body flooding with happy endorphins and adrenalin, desire energising me at the same time it relaxes me.

'I want to talk to you about something.'

'Oh?' I pout. 'It can't wait?'

He grins. 'It has waited. It won't take long.' He links his fingers through mine, directing me into the kitchen. He pours two glasses of white wine and removes a tray from the fridge. There's a block of cheese, some crackers, a dip and carrot sticks.

'No strawberries?' I murmur teasingly.

He meets my eyes and heat sparks between us like a live volt of electricity. I feel it hum through my entire body.

'Strawberries are reserved for special occasions. Like when you're naked.'

'So if I strip down I'd get some?'

'Would you like some?'

I reach for the bottom of my shirt and lift it over my head. He watches, his expression assessing, and then he laughs, shaking his head as he turns and walks back to the fridge, pulling out a container of fruit. He picks one from the bowl, and carries it towards me, placing it to my lips. I hold his gaze as I open my mouth and take a bite. A little juice runs down my chin. He catches it with his thumb then lifts it to his lips, tasting it.

My stomach flips.

'That's just made it about a thousand times harder to concentrate,' he says with a grimace.

'Do you need to concentrate?'

He groans. 'You're incorrigible.'

'Because I want to fuck my fuck buddy?'

His expression is serious. He steps back, putting

the kitchen bench between us, gesturing towards the wine. I panic.

'Oh, God.' He's going to say he wants more from me. That no-strings sex isn't enough. I stare at him, trying to work out how to defuse that, how to not let him become another Patrick, but I have no idea what to say. Words won't come to me. I just know that if I hurt Zach in some way I will never recover. I can't hurt him. I'm not my dad.

'What?' His expression shows concern.

I have to say something, to explain my reaction. 'It's just—I thought you might be—wanting to change the parameters of our relationship.'

He nods. 'In a sense, I do.' I grip the stem of the wine glass tightly, my insides vibrating and quivering in response. I can't work out what I'm feeling but given my opinion on relationships, it must be fear, right?

'I'm not—'

I'm not, what? Why can't I say it? I stare at him and the objection won't come.

'I've been thinking about your business.'

Something whooshes through me. Relief?

'Oh?'

'I'd heard of it before I met you. I was mildly interested in the proposition, or in attempting to recreate what you're doing. But having met you, and looking into it further, I realise there's no sense in that. So I want to come on board.'

I stare at him, my mind scrambling to make sense of his statement. 'You want to invest in She-Shakes?'

He nods. 'Yes.'

My eyes feel enormous. 'I can't let you do that.'

'This is purely business,' he explains quietly. 'Like any other investment I make. I'll have lawyers handle the contracts, the payments. I'll be as hands-off as you want. In fact, you won't even know I'm there. The money will be real though, and you can start using it immediately to expand your objectives. Isn't that what you want?'

It's everything I want and he knows it, but damn it! 'Why are you doing this?'

'Because I think you're sitting on a gold mine and unlike you I *am* motivated by commercial success.'

Something bristles. He's reminding me so much of Dad right now, talking to me in a way that has me instantly revolting. I shake my head, turning away from him, my hands pulling my shirt back on quickly—this does not feel like a conversation I want to have while I'm wearing just a bra.

'Jessica, I know you seem to find the idea of profiting from your initiative distasteful but, like it or not, that's the situation you're in. Anyone who buys the app will have those expectations. The difference is, I have no interest in asserting any directional control over the day-to-day operations—or the big-picture operations, for that matter—of what you're doing. I would leave it to you, completely.'

'I'm not even going to talk to you about this,' I say, feeling a sudden burst of inexplicable anger. 'I feel completely ambushed.' And I do, but that's not why I'm so angry. I can't put my finger on it but dark emotions whirl through me.

'That wasn't my intention.'

'You should have warned me.'

'Did it really not occur to you that I would be thinking about this?'

'Of course it didn't! We're two people who are having sex. I don't care that you have all *this*.' I gesture around his palatial penthouse. 'All this goddamned money and power. I just like sleeping with you. I definitely don't want you feeling like you have to sweep in and come to my rescue, like I can't make a good decision unless you come to the party and help me.'

'I don't think that. How can you hear what I'm saying and extrapolate a lack of faith from it?' He stalks back into the kitchen and pulls a thick pile of papers from a drawer, then carries it to me. 'Look at this.'

I flick the first page angrily then pause as I see my company's name, and corporate information—profits for the last three years are listed, countries of operation, tax details.

The name of a well-known finance firm is printed on the bottom.

'You had an analysis done?'

'As would anyone who's seriously looking to buy.'

He's right but that doesn't make this feel any less weird. I push the papers towards him.

'This is too bizarre. It's mixing everything up. We're not about business. And we're not about anything beyond Christmas. If we're business partners I'd have to see you again—'

'And you think we wouldn't be able to control our-selves?'

'I didn't say that.'

'We're two adults, aren't we? Are you really incapable of separating the business from the personal?'

He's making me feel about an inch tall. He's making me feel...like my dad does, like Simon does, like every bloody alpha male like him always does. He's taking my business, my blood, sweat and tears, and taking over completely. And seeing him in the damned Santa tie makes me feel like I want to cry because I came here in such a great mood, I was so looking forward to seeing him, and now I just want to disappear and pretend the last ten minutes never happened.

'I need to think about this.' Ice drips from my words.

He expels a breath then smiles. 'Okay. What would you like to do while you think?' He wiggles his brows. 'Because I have some ideas.'

'No.' My voice is cutting. His smile drops. 'I need to think about this alone.'

His own face assumes a mask of businesslike resolve. 'Did you want to have your wine on the balcony while I organise dinner?'

I'm pretty sure he's not misunderstanding me. He's just going to make me say it aloud. 'I'm going to go back to my place to look at my options.'

His own tone is quiet and calm, non-threatening and reasonable. 'You don't even know what I'm offering.'

'The amount doesn't matter.'

'Of course it matters.'

I fix him with a level stare. 'You know what I've already been offered. I presume you're offering more, to make it attractive, without offering so much more as to make you foolish.'

He compresses his lips, obviously getting pissed off, and I'm glad about that—because I want to fight with him. I'm angry, and fighting feels like the best way to deal with that emotion. I want him to be angry too.

'And on what terms?' he says flatly. 'Over what period of time, how much cash now, what control do I want of which assets in which markets, what can I bring to the table other than liquid cash? What components of my multi-media empire would I be able to put at your disposal? Which talents—actors, financial advisors, in-house lawyers—could we make available to you?'

I drop my gaze to the kitchen bench because he's right—there are many things beyond cash that require consideration, and yet I'm just too steamed up to think straight.

'Don't you get it? I wouldn't ever think you'd done this because it's a good investment. You're sleeping with me and now you're trying to—use your considerable wealth to help me—and I have spent my adult life being independent from that, and I have run so hard from any kind of relationship that could be translated as a quid pro quo. I am never going to sell my business to a man who might think that means I owe him something.'

'For fuck's sake!' His eyes show fury, and I know I've gone too far, but, God, it felt good. 'How dare you?'

I stick to my guns. 'You think you won't want to sleep with me again, maybe in a year's time? That the fact you're propping me up with over a hundred million dollars might not make me feel beholden to you?'

'I think that if we have sex in a year's time it will be because you want me as much then as you do now.'

'I don't want that!' I grind my teeth together, my body shaking, my emotions rioting. 'I don't want to see you again after Christmas. That's the only reason this works—the boundaries we've put in place. I can't believe you thought I wouldn't be angry about this. I can't believe you thought I might actually see this as good news.'

'You're absolutely crazy not to,' he snaps, slamming his palm down on the bench then putting his hands on his hips, making a visible effort to get himself under control.

'Oh, well, thank you for telling me how I should feel,' I snap back, turning away from him and moving to the door.

A second later he's right behind me, his fingers curling around my wrist, slowing me down. 'Jessica.' His voice is calm but loaded with reproach.

That's even worse. I wish he'd release his temper. Snap at me. I want to claw him. I have no idea what's made me feel this way but I'm angrier than I've been in ages.

'You're overreacting.'

I flinch. It's exactly the kind of thing my father says to my mother. I've heard him gaslight her my whole life and I won't have it happen to me. Especially not by some guy who's meant to just be a bit of fun. I suck in a deep breath, preparing my tirade, but Zach presses a finger to my chin, lifting my face to his, and I see then that he's not calm, only his voice is. His eyes are glittering with purpose and his face is tight with the effort of his control.

'Business is business and I know a great investment when I see one. Pleasure is separate.'

'You can't just draw a line in the sand—'

'I can.' He presses a kiss to my lips, a kiss that halts every emotion rioting through me and tosses them around, putting new ones in their place. 'I can,' he assures me again, kissing me longer, slower, but I shake my head, feeling as if I need to fight this with all that I am, and again, nothing about that makes sense but I'm drowning all of a sudden.

I don't know if he's a lifeline I need or a current from which I must swim but my body has taken over and I'm kissing him back, but so angrily, so hard, my hands at his chest pushing and pulling, ripping his shirt from his pants, desperate for something that makes sense, that I can make sense of.

'I can't believe you didn't tell me this,' I say, pushing his chest, but I'm right behind him, kissing him, and he's lifting me, wrapping my legs around his waist, carrying me through the apartment.

'I just fucking did.' He drops me down on the

bed, his eyes challenging me, as if to say, *What else you got?*

'After you've already had a finance firm put together a two-hundred-page buy-in proposal.'

He finishes the job of removing his shirt, tossing it and the Christmas tie hard to the ground at his feet.

'That's standard goddamned practice for any asset I'm interested in acquiring.'

Anger floods my veins.

'I'm not a fucking asset.'

A frown briefly mars his face and I realise I've made a tactical error. I've shown too much of my hand, way too much of my neuroses and weaknesses.

'Of course you're not an asset, Jessica. You're a woman. But your business is very much a piece of commercial value.'

I glare at him, my breathing rushed. 'It's *my* business.'

He growls. 'You are unbelievable.' Then he's kissing me again, pushing me back on the bed, his hands finding the elastic waist of my skirt and pushing it down, taking my silk G-string with it, still kissing me while he dispenses with his own pants. His kiss is everything I need in that moment because it's so real, so tangible, so filled with everything I feel.

He grabs my hands, holding them to my sides and pushing up to stare at me, a muscle throbbing low in his jaw.

'This is just sex. Is that what you want to hear?' He thrusts into me, and I stare at him, my chest in a state of turmoil.

'Meaningless, fantastic fucking sex.' He drives into me again and now I bite down on my lip to stop from crying; emotions are bursting through me—intense pleasure at his body's possession of mine, and an ache deep in my soul that seems to have come at me from nowhere.

He groans, shaking his head and kissing me, and I taste the tang of tears in my mouth as he slows his speed, taking me gently, each movement speaking to me, calming me while still driving me to the edge of sanity. But I don't want gentleness. I want the fervour of passion, the anger of it, the sheer ecstasy of those emotions.

I lift my hips in a rapid rhythm and he responds, answering my silent demands, until I'm tumbling into a state of physical pleasure, white lights blinding my eyes for a moment as all of my body suspends its operations to process what's unfolding. I feel starlight in my skin. He holds me as I come and then I feel him following, his cock pulsing inside me, spilling from his body, his own breathing harsh but silent as he binds his orgasm to mine for the first time.

Usually I come several times before him; tonight is different.

Everything's different and I can't even say why, just that something's shifted.

He rolls off me afterwards, lying on his back, staring up at the ceiling. I do the same, mirroring his position and expression. I thought I'd feel better but I don't. I'm completely jumbled.

It's in the wasteland of time that passes next, the

immediate aftermath of our passion, that I realise two things. He somehow managed to remember a condom—which is impressive. I didn't have that presence of mind. And we broke his first rule—we made love with him on top of me, looking into my eyes.

I stand up, restless, frustrated and just…sad. I don't look at him.

'Forget the offer, Jessica. I thought it would solve all your problems. I thought in offering to buy forty per cent of your business I'd be freeing you up to realise all your dreams with it. I thought that in buying forty per cent you'd understand that I'm probably the one corporate partner who will never—wouldn't ever dream of—interfering in your operations.'

I nod, his explanation clarifying several points for me. 'You thought I needed you to rescue me,' I say quietly. 'You thought I wouldn't be able to make the right decision, or negotiate the best deal myself, so you offered me the best one yourself. Would you have ever made me such an advantageous offer if we weren't sleeping together?'

He sits up, turning away from me and striding to the bathroom, disposing of the condom and returning a second later wearing a towel slung low around his waist.

'I wouldn't have known you like I do,' he concedes. 'So I might have wanted more control. And you would have responded by saying all the things you already said to me—about the reasons you developed this community and what it means to you—and then, sex or no sex, I would have seen what I see now:

that the only person running your business should be you. That to empower anyone else to do what you're doing would be criminal. The fact we're sleeping together is beside the point and you have to know that I'm the last person who would ever let a personal relationship play into my business movements.'

My chest tightens because I know he's right—of course that's true. His reputation is established there. You don't get to be the kind of success he is without having strong commercial instincts and adhering to them strictly.

'Obviously this was a misstep.' He moves towards me but stops about a metre away. I look at him and it's as if my chest has been opened up. I feel vulnerable. I feel different. I feel as if he's seeing everything I usually keep so well hidden. 'You're right. I was arrogant to think you'd even welcome my offer. Arrogant to think you'd need it. I'm sorry.'

I flinch, because he's wrong—he did nothing wrong and doesn't need to apologise. I know what my blind spots are; I know my own weaknesses. I know I'm so determined to be alone that I push away anyone who wants to be close, and that the possibility of having Zach in my life in any kind of ongoing capacity is too much to bear. Fear made me lash out, but that wasn't his fault.

He's being the bigger person and apologising and I hate that I can't make myself do the same.

'It's my life,' I say, devastated when my voice cracks a little. I spin away from him, looking for my skirt. My shirt is still on—another first for us.

'I know.' He's behind me, the skirt in his hands. He crouches down, holding it for me step into. I put my hand on his shoulder as I do so, dipping my head forward, closing my eyes.

'I'm sorry.' I whisper the apology he deserves. 'It just caught me off guard.'

He slides the skirt into position then stands, catching my hands and holding them in front of me. He's smiling in a way that's encouraging, wanting me to smile back at him, but I can't.

'I meant what I said before. This is just sex. You don't need to worry that anything has—or will—change for me.'

I feel as if I'm being stretched on the rack. I nod, forcing a smile to my face, squeezing his hands right back. 'Let's just forget it.'

He scans my face and then nods, putting an arm around my waist and pulling me closer. 'I'm really sorry that I upset you.'

The more he apologises, the more kind he is, the more perfect he is, the more the feeling in my chest worsens. The more I feel as though I'm being tortured in some awful, primitive way. I nod jerkily, assuming the face I have thousands of times in my life, a face that tells the world I'm completely fine— better than fine. I'm Jessica Johnson and no one can fuck with me.

'Let's eat, Zach. I'm starving.'

CHAPTER TEN

It doesn't take a rocket scientist to realise I hit a big fucking nerve. I watch as she eats a piece of sushi, noticing the small details. The way her newly cut bangs come across her brow, hiding her eyes when she dips her head so I find my fingers itching to reach across and pin it out of her way. The sweep of her lower lip as she pauses and thinks—no doubt about the argument we just had. This is all new territory for me. With the exception of Emily, I've never been with a woman long enough to argue with her.

I've never got close to having any kind of conversation that would even lead to an argument.

Hadn't I predicted that something like this could happen? When I was talking to Dimitrios I foreshadowed that it wasn't as straightforward as a usual business proposition, and this is why. Except with Jessica, nothing would ever be as straightforward as a normal business transaction because she's singularly uninterested in financial gain.

I frown, reaching for a piece of sashimi, dipping it heavily in soy and wasabi before eating it, my eyes still resting on her face. She lifts her gaze to me and something throbs low in my gut. I smile, and it's a smile laced with a question. She returns it, her lips a little tight, her expression hard to read.

I swallow, wishing we hadn't argued. Wishing I hadn't offered to buy her fucking business. Wishing I'd just kept in my lane.

But isn't her business my lane? Not *her* business, per se, but business in general. I'm the opposite of Jessica. I do what I do because I'm good at it. Dimitrios and I inherited our father's media empire, but we didn't rest on our laurels. We took what was already a successful global enterprise and turned it into the major player in all forms of media. We invested heavily in online news distribution, buying up any trending website particularly as pertained to news and opinion blogs, we invested in infrastructure early, recognising that fast and reliable Internet access only bolstered our business model. We did all this because we like to win. I like to win. I see a problem and have to work out the solution; I see an opportunity and am always compelled to act on it.

Jessica Johnson's business model is a massive opportunity.

But she doesn't want to make the most of that. I lift another piece of sushi, dipping it in soy sauce then placing it over my plate.

'Jessica?'

She looks at me again and all I can see is her eyes as they'd been when we made love earlier, tears in them, recrimination, hurt. Jesus. My stomach feels as though it's filled with rocks. She's not the only one afraid of hurting someone she cares about. When I was seventeen, on one of our trips back to Sydney, I walked into Mum's room to find her crying. She was looking at a photo of us in a frame she kept beside the bed—both of us smiling on the deck of Dad's yacht. She'd dashed the tears away and smiled weakly, but it had left a hole in my heart because finally I'd seen for myself the grief she'd been living with for so many years, a grief that our absence had caused. A grief our father had forced on her with his selfish, thoughtless actions. I am not the kind of man who puts women through that. I won't hurt Jessica; and yet I have. Fear kicks me in the gut.

'Mmm?' Her voice is normal, but I see beyond what she's projecting. I see the effort she's making to look like always, even when she's still making sense of what happened between us. But she's here. She didn't bolt. She didn't storm out and tell me she never wanted to see me again. That's something.

'The night we met, you said something I found really interesting.'

'I should hope so.'

I smile—it's a hint of normality, of the way we always interact, sparking off one another quickly and easily. I could take the easy way out and roll with it, turn the conversation to something non-controversial and easy, but I don't.

'You said that She-Shakes wasn't intended to be a money-making venture.'

She bristles slightly, and I feel her uncertainty. To

discuss her app is to revisit everything that's just happened. But Jessica Johnson is brave; she's someone who faces things head-on, rather than shirking from anything unpleasant. She nods, sipping her glass of wine before responding.

'Yes. I said that.'

'I didn't think much about it at the time. But I've wondered about it since. It was almost like you were annoyed at the acclaim you've received.'

'The success of She-Shakes is the only reason I'm able to help so many women,' she contradicts carefully.

'Mmm, and that makes sense. I definitely felt there was a level of irritation though.'

She eats a piece of avocado sushi, then reclines back in her chair a little, her gaze locking to mine. 'You're right.'

I knew I was, but having her admit it does something strange to my chest. Puffs it up and weighs it down. 'Why?'

Her smile is sardonic, laced with self-mockery. 'That's hard to explain.'

I wait, my eyes holding hers, challenging her to try.

After a moment, she nods once, then lifts her foot to the seat, bending her leg so her knee is beneath her chin.

'I'm gratified by its success. How can I not be, right?'

I nod, waiting for her to continue.

She sighs after a moment, then reaches for another piece of sushi. Silence stretches between us and I begin to wonder if she's not going to give me any more information. Impatience zips through me.

Finally, she speaks. 'When I was a kid, I freaking idolised my dad. I grew up thinking he was just the greatest. Everything he did I wanted to do, but better, so he'd be proud of me. He used to bring me to his office, let me sit in on board meetings. I'm talking when I was young, like six or seven. And I'd sit there and take notes, and ask him questions on the drive home—God knows what his colleagues and staff thought.' She laughs, a sweet sound that adds to the weight on my chest.

'It's not like I ever consciously decided I wanted to be a CEO. I just knew I wanted to be like him. I knew what university I'd apply to, what I'd study, everything.'

'Which was?'

'Economics and Law at Harvard. Just as he did.' She rolls her eyes as she says it, her voice a little saccharine.

'We spent a lot of time together. The older I got, the more he involved me, letting me shadow him during school holidays. I learned heaps.' She appears to lose her train of thought for a second, taking a sip of her drink before continuing.

'And then I found out he was cheating on Mum. That he had been for a long time. I found out that the man I had idolised basically since birth had been treating my mum like dirt for most of their marriage. And I couldn't reconcile the two versions of him I had. There was nothing about his incredible business instincts that made me okay with his personal behaviour. I wish my mum had left him, I wish she'd stood up to him more, but none of this is her fault. She gave up everything for their marriage, she had children with him, she wanted, more than anything, to keep our family intact. He's my father, and I love him, but there are parts of him I hate too, parts of him I'll always hate.'

I feel the ice in her voice, the determination, and I want to move to her, to draw her into my arms and comfort her.

You think I need your help. I've already made the mistake of underestimating her once tonight. I won't do it again. I sit where I am, listening.

'I got offered a place at Harvard on a scholarship and my dad was so proud of me. You should have seen the fuss he made.' Anger tinges her words. I bite back on the observation that that's only natural—I can sense how unwelcome her dad's actions were.

'This guy was screwing around behind my mum's back, cheating on her and all of us, and then he was proud of me? I felt dirty. I didn't want his approval, his pride. Suddenly I wanted to do everything I could to piss him off, so I turned down the offer.'

'And was he pissed off?'

'He was disappointed,' she says with a tilt of her chin, showing that's exactly what she wanted. 'He kept trying to push me on what I was going to do, how I couldn't waste my intelligence, and that made it even worse.'

'Why?' I push, leaning forward.

'Because mum is incredibly smart. Before they got married she was studying law—that's how they met—and she dropped out to become his perfect wife.' She shakes her head scathingly. 'And he never encouraged her to finish, never encouraged her to continue with her studies, never encouraged her in any damned thing.'

I nod, understanding the source of Jessica's anger. And yet... 'Is it possible your mum's ambitions changed? That what she wanted most in the world was to be married, and to live a happy domestic life?'

Her eyes widen, something shifting from her to me that I don't comprehend. 'Yes. I'm sure that's true. It's the same with my sister—she followed in Mum's footsteps precisely, getting married young to some guy who—' She shakes her head and I remember something else about Jessica, the way she shied away from talking about her sister and brother-in-law. 'Some guy who doesn't respect her,' she finishes awkwardly.

I shelve my questions on that score for later.

'But that's what they wanted,' she says with a nod. 'And if I've learned anything in running She-Shakes it's that there's no one blueprint for happiness. What is someone else's idea of "life goals" isn't necessarily mine, or anyone else's. I understand what Mum wanted—but it wasn't to watch my dad have affairs. It wasn't to know that when he said he was working late he was actually banging his secretary or the wife of one of his colleagues or whatever.' She shakes her head scathingly.

'So you wanted to piss him off and you wanted to hurt him for hurting your mum.'

She nods.

'And let me guess.' My voice is low, like a growl. 'He's proud of you anyway.'

'What do you think?' Anger fills her words. 'The app took off into the stratosphere fourteen months after I launched it. I was being written about in all the finance papers. Dad's friends were calling him up to congratulate him, so even She-Shakes was tainted.'

I run a hand through my hair, feeling her frustration.

'But the thing is, it's also its own beast, and it's too important to sacrifice at the altar of childish revenge. Mum made her bed and she's lying in it. I'll never respect my dad with the same wholehearted devotion I did as a kid, but also, I've learned that nothing is simple. I can respect his business acumen and admire him for the judgement there without condoning his private actions. I'm trying to make my peace with it, Zach.'

I nod, reaching across the table and weaving our fingers together. I feel as though I'm standing over a bottomless pit. She squeezes my hand back and relief surges through me, because our argument is a part of this fortnight now, but it's just one thread in a fabric of many—something that neither of us wishes to let derail what we've got, this perfect, temporary fling.

'Not everyone has the courage of your convictions,' I say quietly, stroking the base of her thumb.

'No.' Her smile is wry. 'The thing is, I'm the epitome of someone who cuts off their nose to spite their face.'

'In what way?'

'I would have loved studying at Harvard.' She rolls her eyes again. '*I* wanted that. Maybe because of Dad, or maybe because that's just who I am. But I shut the door on it because I wanted to hurt him. What if She-Shakes hadn't worked out? There was no guarantee I'd ever find something else about which I was passionate.'

'I disagree,' I say, squeezing her hand for emphasis. 'You are someone who was always destined to set the world on fire. Whether with your online community or something else, you would always have made magic.'

She drops her head forward, her sleek dark hair with its little highlights of pink covering her eyes.

'You said something I found interesting that first night, too.'

It takes me a second to focus on what she's saying. 'Yeah?'

She nods, pulling her hand away to reach for her wine. 'You told me I was in your wheelhouse.'

I had said that. And Jessica had used it as a way to make it abundantly clear that she was interested in me. The conversation had branched in an entirely different direction.

'You were already interested in my business?'

'You'd crossed my desk,' I agree. 'I have a team actively researching good investment prospects. Your company was mentioned.'

She nods slowly. 'So you probably would have made me an offer regardless of the fact we've been sleeping together.'

I lean back in my chair, watching her carefully. 'Your name was one of a dozen that was flagged for my attention that week. I hadn't got around to analysing your company data but, yeah, I'd like to think that if I'd seen your subscription model and services I would always have realised what a good fit you'd be to come under our umbrella.'

She winces a bit, rejecting the very idea. Fiercely independent, determined to prove herself, not wanting praise. Jessica is a thousand contradictions all wrapped into one beautiful package.

'So I shouldn't have been so surprised tonight. I was blindsided by everything going on between us but you basically told me right from the start. I just wasn't paying attention.'

I expel a long, slow breath. 'It's not like I've been fucking you to get the inside track on the investment opportunity.' I regret my choice of words once I've said them—too harsh, making this sound too… I don't know. I make a noise of frustration and push to standing, moving around to her side of the table and sitting with my butt on the edge of the timber surface, right beside her.

'Look, Jessica, I'm not going to buy into your community. Even if you wanted to sell a percentage of it, there's no way I'd do it now. So let me give you some impartial advice. From a friend.'

She bristles and I know exactly why. Her dad and her brother-in-law and God knows who else ram advice down her throat—advice she clearly doesn't need if the success of her business is anything to go by. But she nods, just a shift of her head, and I realise what that concession has cost her.

'As a...friend, and an outsider to your operations, you *are* vulnerable.' I push away from the table, moving to the kitchen and removing the financial appraisal from the drawer. I stride across the room and hold it towards her. She stares at it for several seconds before lifting a hand and gingerly accepting it.

'Read it. See how the market is appraising you. See the advice a completely objective third party gives for your acquisition.'

She nods again, a tight movement, then places the file down beside her. The air between us is charged with energy—emotion and frustration—but it's not anger any more. There's sadness. There's too much of everything.

I suspect Jessica feels it too, because a second later and she's standing, looking at me with eyes that tell me exactly what she needs to push all this away, to get it out of her head.

But I'm not done yet. I need to make sure she understands what I'm saying and then I'll back off.

'A minute ago you said you cut off your nose to spite your face when you backed out of Harvard.'

Her eyes stay locked to mine. 'Zach—' She's about to shut me down. I can feel it.

So I shake my head, holding up a hand. 'Just let me say this, then we'll never talk about your business again, okay?'

She hesitates before nodding once.

'Don't cut off your nose to spite your face with

your business decisions now. Don't self-sabotage. Don't let someone else come in and do what you're doing—with all the resources and backing of being a huge player in tech—just because you feel like you have something to prove. You'll never forgive yourself for it, Jessica, and honestly, nor will I.'

I stare at the shadows and light as they dance across his bedroom wall. It's still early, a time before the sun will make its appearance above the horizon, the sky dark grey, the lights of the city never dulled, not even when we sleep. Zach is behind me, his body still, his breathing rhythmic. I stare at the patterns and I replay our conversations, our fight, the angry sex we had, the way he looked into my eyes, the way my heart practically stopped beating.

His warning not to self-sabotage.

His understanding that I do that.

Everything feels so difficult suddenly. Zach was my escape from the situation with my family and yet he's become something else. This isn't just hedonistic sex now. There's something more here, something dangerous. He's different from what I expected, or maybe I'm different from what I thought. But for whatever reason, I'm still here, lying in his bed, knowing I have no intention of leaving before he wakes up, knowing that I'll see him again, that I'll keep seeing him until this ends, on Christmas Day.

He was right about regrets. If I mess up the next step with She-Shakes I'll regret it for ever. And if I mess this up with Zach, if I sabotage what we've got just because suddenly there's something more going on than I bargained for, then I will live with those regrets for a long time to come. I told myself we'd have two weeks and then I'd forget him.

I'll never forget Zach.

I'll leave him, at the end of this, and I won't let myself look back, but he'll always be in my rear-vision mirror and I know why. He's the first person I've let under my skin in a long time—probably ever. I know that when he talks to me it's because he understands me. He sees me. Earlier tonight I had that same feeling, and it made me feel vulnerable. It still does, but I'm not running away. We agreed to what this is, and there's security in that, because I know we're both too stubborn to let anything change our plans. Sex is what we have and it's all we'll ever have.

Reassured, I let my eyes drift shut and I fall asleep, conscious in my last moments of wakefulness that Zach moves closer, putting an arm around me and holding me tight to his body. We fit together perfectly.

CHAPTER ELEVEN

HE WAS RIGHT. There is an intimacy that comes from having made love to someone while looking into their eyes, seeing every emotion that flickers across their face, kissing as bodies entwine, lacing fingers, nipples against hair-roughened chest. It is the closest two people can be, and having experienced that with Zach I feel a shift inside me. Or perhaps it was arguing with him and making up with him. Perhaps it was the way he made it easy to forgive him even when I can't say with any definitive certainty that he was wrong and I was right.

I flick through the financial document he gave me last night, one hand on the corners of the pages so that I can turn them quickly and another on my coffee cup. The morning light dances above Singapore, promising a hazy, hot day. For a moment my eyes skim longingly to the infinity pool.

Later. Zach is still asleep. I woke early, when it was still dark, unable to get this document out of my head, his warning something I didn't—don't—take lightly.

The first thirty or so pages are standard. I've seen

the figures often enough. The evaluation of She-Shakes' potential is familiar to me because I also engage a top financial appraiser to work with me— it's one of the ways I've raised capital to this point.

'I'll lend you money, Jess. Or become an investor. You know it's no problem.'

Dad's offer set me on a fierce path of independence early on. I've had bank loans, and now the company's liquidity is such that I don't need financing for day-to-day operations. My staff's salaries are well covered by the revenue raised from subscriptions.

But growth takes money and I definitely want the whole business to grow.

As I flick through the pages, moving nearer to the back, my heart begins to rush faster, until I stop flicking and stare at one page in particular.

41.1—Complete Buyout Option

It's all there, detailed in black and white. The comparison of quick profits if I'm removed completely, or installed as an interim CEO, but the app is completely brought under the umbrella of Papandreo Holdings. My heart is hammering into my ribs, because this is an argument for splitting the app up and, worse, leveraging it to mine user data and on-sell that information.

I feel physically sick. I close the document for a moment, lifting my eyes to the view of the high-rises beyond the window, barely seeing their twinkly morning lights against the backdrop of dawn.

I push back my chair, carrying the coffee cup with me as I move to the large sliding glass doors. I push one open, stepping into the morning air. It's warm and humid outside, the air already thick with heat. I sit on the edge of his pool, running my fingertips through the water as I sip my coffee.

He warned me.

He told me that there was risk to holding out. And he's right.

Anyone big is going to want to exploit She-Shakes for what they can get out of it. They'll want a return on their investment—it's Finance for Beginners.

So what do I do?

'You're up early.' His voice sends my pulse haywire, and I almost spill my coffee as I spin to face him.

'Hey.' Perhaps my smile doesn't quite ring true because his lips quirk downwards as he paces towards me, wearing only a pair of grey boxer shorts low on his hips. An arrow of dark hair spirals into the waistband.

'You read it?'

I can't meet his eyes. 'Yes.'

'And?' He sits beside me, his legs spread wide, hands clasped between his knees.

'And…' I contemplate that '… I don't know.' I look at him quizzically, then put a hand on his knee, a weight I've been feeling since we argued still pressing on me. 'I know that your offer came from a good place.' I lean closer, nudging him with my shoulder. 'I was just very surprised.'

'I should have told you sooner.' He puts his hand over mine.

We're quiet for several moments. It's comfortable and comforting.

'I just don't know what I'm going to do.'

He returns my gesture, nudging me with his shoulder. 'It's a good problem to have.'

'You think?'

'You've made an incredible, amazing business—this is what happens with tech start-ups that take off.'

'The thing is, there's so much more I want to do. The idea of diluting my vision, of having to kowtow to a board of directors is just…so not what I want.'

'What do you want?'

I pull a face. 'That's easy.'

He lifts his brows, silently encouraging me to continue.

My smile is tinged with melancholy. 'I want to have my cake and eat it too.'

'Ah.' He returns my grin. 'That old chestnut.'

'Yep.'

'What else do you want to do? What's your five-year plan?'

I sigh. 'So much, Zach. It's like, literally, the size of this balcony.'

He laughs. 'Should I get a coffee first?'

I offer him mine instead. He takes a sip.

And then, I start to tell him something I've never told another soul, something that has felt so big it's almost impossible, something that got me thinking about taking on capital in the first place. 'I mean, I want to expand all of my offerings, to really make as much difference as I can in the existing countries we service.'

I take the coffee and have another sip. 'But what I really want to do is—and I know how fanciful this might sound—expand into developing countries in a meaningful way. Most of the women I want to help in those countries don't have access to iPads, phones, they're not worried about protecting their asset base if they get divorced. Their needs are more immediate. What I want to do is build schools, universities, vocational training. I want to be able to fund education programmes and as part of that to partner with someone who can provide technology for ongoing support and assistance. I can't stand the disparity between how I live and how women in some countries live. I want to create opportunity and change.

'That's why I'm doing this. Not because I want to get rich. Not because I want to see my bank balance getting bigger. God, do you have any idea how much I hate that? We're already way too wealthy—where's the equity, Zach? Look at this place!' I gesture towards his penthouse. 'Look at what we have and there are women out there not eating for days just to make sure their children have enough—and they don't, they don't have anywhere near enough. I'm talking about access to education, vaccinations, self-defence classes, food; I'm talking about giving women the tools to seek higher-paid work, to earn more to provide more, to change their lives.'

The sun crests higher, piercing the sky, forming

a perfect light ray between two high-rises, reaching across the deck like an arrow made of gold.

'It will cost a lot. And it will mean juggling a lot of different balls—I can't have the services we offer suffer because I'm over-committing resources to my charitable branch. And I don't think any corporate partner, including you, would give me the latitude to funnel so much money towards this.' I bite down on my lip, searching his eyes for something. 'I know there'd be the lump-sum payment when I'm bought out, but that's a one-time injection of cash and for this to work it needs to be funded by an ongoing business. I think. I don't know. What do you think?'

He reaches to my chin, moving my face closer to his, his eyes probing mine, his expression impossible to understand. 'I think you're incredible.'

My heart soars, and I smile, a smile that stretches my cheeks and reaches all the way to my eyes. 'Thanks.'

'I think you're going to change the world and that there's nothing fanciful about what you're suggesting.' He slides his thumb across my lower lip then leans back, putting space between us. I feel cool instantly.

'I think you're right about how a potential investment could affect your plans. You're right to be taking your time and working out what's best.'

'But at the same time—' I move to playing devil's advocate '—I could miss my window. Right?'

He dips his head. 'Yes.'

'See why it's not such a good problem to have?'

He nods thoughtfully, contemplatively. 'I have complete confidence in you, Jessica. If anyone can work this out, it's you.'

His words are everything I need to hear. Maybe I'd been expecting him to reiterate his offer—maybe I'd even been hoping he would—but this is better. He's putting the ball in my court, telling me that I can do this, and I can.

I smile again, and I'm still smiling a second later when he leans closer and kisses me.

'So we're not buying it?'

I cross one ankle over my knee, assuming a look of nonchalance when all I can think about is the way Jessica spoke to me yesterday morning, revealing her innermost thoughts for the direction she wants to take her business in.

'Not for now.'

'Why not?'

'I'm not sure she actually wants to sell.'

'So?' Dimitrios reaches for his mineral water. 'Since when has that ever stopped you? Make the offer better.'

I dig my heels in. 'Nah. I'm just going to wait and see.'

'Wait and see? What the hell's got into you?'

I stand up, frustrated, uncertain, because Dimitrios is right. A month ago I would have simply gone in for the kill. Everyone has a price—even Jessica Johnson. But pressuring her in any way is something I'm not willing to do. This is her decision and it should be on her terms. And if that means she accepts an offer from someone else?

I ignore the sense of panic.

I know it would be the wrong decision for her business. I know anyone else is going to want to have a say in her operations.

But it's *her* business, her decision. In less than a week, she'll be out of my life. For good.

It's what we agreed, so why does the prospect of that fill me with an ache in my chest now? Why does the idea of never seeing her again make it seem as though I'm drowning?

Because she's not like anyone I've ever known.

The answer comes to me quickly. It's obvious.

Jessica is—so easy to be with. She's fun, smart, sexy, different. I just like spending time with her. My lips form a grim line, because I see the difficulties in reaching that decision. I see the difficulties before me.

Liking spending time with someone is only a very short step away from *liking* someone. And I do mean in the '*like* like' sense. I mean in the halfway to 'love' sense, and, Jesus Christ, not for a billion dollars would I even think about going down that hellhole again. I learned a lesson I shouldn't have even needed to be taught.

I focus on the building across from us, the highly tinted windows making it impossible to see in, the sun glinting off one of the sides in a dazzling display of golden light.

Besides. It's the last thing Jessica wants. I think back to the first night we met, when we were both so scathing of love and commitment, both so completely on the same page when it comes to relationships. I think about a few nights ago when we fought and then made love and I told her in no uncertain terms that what we were doing was meaningless sex.

My gut twists uncomfortably.

I said it because I knew she wanted to hear it— she needed reassurance that nothing between us had changed, that I wasn't trying to buy her into my life by buying into her business. Because she doesn't want to be in my life beyond Christmas.

I expel a long, slow breath, telling myself I feel reassured by that. Placated. Because she'll go back to London and I'll get on with my life and things will be as they always were. After Emily, I found the best way to get on with things was to fuck around. I have a reputation for being a playboy and, hell, I've earned it. I have enough women's numbers in my phone to last me a lifetime.

Jessica will leave and I'll get back to my normal routine.

Why does that feel so strange to contemplate?

'Anything else?' I turn around to see Dimitrios has packed up and is standing by his office door.

'You're in a rush.'

He lifts his left hand, showing me his wedding band. 'Newly-wed, remember?'

'Right.' I contemplate that—how he's managed to shake off the impressions of our childhood and take the leap into marriage when the very idea leaves me ice cold.

And I come back to the same conclusion I reached at their wedding: he met the right person. And for the right person, you change everything you ever thought you felt. For the right person, you move heaven and earth to be together.

If you believe in all that shit—which I don't.

It's all the reminder—and insurance—I need. There's no danger here. No risk. I know who I am and why. I know the forces that shaped me into this man, and they were strong—too strong to ever resist or ignore. Even if Jessica begged me to turn this into something more, I'd say 'no'—albeit gently—because I know I'll never want a relationship. So I can let go of the worry and just surrender to the pleasure of what we're doing. Just as we agreed.

'You come here often?'

She fits perfectly into my side, her body so sensational that I've struggled to take my eyes off her since I picked her up half an hour ago. I'd told her we were going to a bar and she's dressed in a silk dress with thin straps and a draped sort of neckline that hangs low enough to show more than a hint of her rounded breasts. It's cut in a way that sits firm on her body without being skintight, and it stops mid-thigh. In strappy high heels and with her hair out and waved, she looks good enough to eat. And I can't wait to do just that.

Why did I even suggest we go out?

To prove to yourself you can, a voice reminds me. To do the normal stuff I do with other women. I don't usually chain a woman to my bed for the whole time we're together, so why am I guarding my time with Jessica so fiercely, as though she means too much to share?

More stupidity from me.

'From time to time.'

'I just thought the doorman seemed to know you?' She has to lean closer to be heard above the low, bass-heavy music. She smells like vanilla and honey.

'Maybe.' I don't point out he probably recognised me from the newspapers, because it seems unnecessarily arrogant, but a second later her grin shows me she's jumped to the same conclusion.

'You're such a big shot.'

I laugh, low and soft. 'And don't you forget it. Champagne?'

She wrinkles her nose as she considers that. 'No. A cocktail.'

I run my fingers over her hip—the dress is silky and soft to touch. My dick jerks in response to her warmth, her proximity and the feeling of silk beneath my palm.

At the bar, I reach for a menu. She scans it and, when a barman approaches, leans forward to place her order. I see the way his eyes drop to her cleavage and every masculine instinct I possess fires to life, my hand forming a fist at my side before I realise what I'm doing.

Since when is that in my repertoire?

Jessica is a big girl, she can look after herself. One thing's for certain—she's been hit on by a lot of men in her life and she's more than capable of deciding for herself if she's interested or not.

I add my order to hers then loop my hands behind her back, drawing her closer to my body, letting one hand inch lower to the top of her butt, brushing her there, aching to have her home and naked. Her breasts against my shirt are soft—she's not wearing a bra, and that makes my head thud, close to exploding.

'Seriously, though, do you come here often?'

I look around the bar, my eyes taking in the opulent setting, rich with details that evoke the glamour of the twenties. The décor is distinctly art deco, the carpet a rich burgundy, the tables a mix of banquettes that look as if they'd be at home in a mob hang-out, seats with green leather and table tops heavily glossed timber, and high tables with gold seats. The bar throngs with well-heeled patrons, many of whom I recognise—some as people I've done business with, others because they're personalities. Anonymity comes from the fact it's busy, and busy with the kind of people who value privacy.

'I like it,' I say.

'So it's somewhere you'd come to hook up?' she prompts as the waiter slides our drinks across the bar. I hand over my black credit card with its distinctive gladiator logo and silver edge.

'Hook up?'

Her eyes lift heavenwards. 'You know, meet women.'

I wonder why I shy away from the conversation when Jessica apparently has no issues with it.

'I've met women here.'

Her eyes narrow inquisitively. 'And you do that a lot.'

I can't say why but this conversation is one I really don't want to have.

'Why do you ask?'

'I'm just interested.'

'Why?'

She laughs. 'Is it a crime to wonder?'

'What about you, then?' I flip the tables, drinking my soda. 'Do you hook up with men you meet in bars?'

She shrugs her beautiful, slender shoulders and my eyes flick to her cleavage. 'Sometimes.'

That answer is just as unsatisfying. I wonder at the curiosity that flares inside me even as I want to talk about *anything* else. 'What kind of men do you usually go for?'

'I don't really have a type,' she says.

'I guess when you're just looking for a one-night stand, you don't need to consider a lot of factors.'

'You're one to talk.'

'I wasn't judging you,' I say, lifting my hand.

'Weren't you?' She stares at me for a minute and then smiles mysteriously, sipping her drink, her pink lips forming a perfect 'o' around the straw.

'I don't generally meet women in bars,' I say after a moment. 'I mean, from time to time, but usually if I'm with a woman it's someone I've known a while, perhaps met through a mutual acquaintance. Flirtation might develop slowly.' I shrug. 'I've never done anything like this.' I gesture from her to me.

She captures my hand, lifting it to her lips. 'And you never will again. I'm irreplaceable.' She's teasing me, making light of what I've said, keeping things fun and frivolous, just as we've agreed.

'So the newspapers have you all wrong?' she pushes, placing her drink on the bar between us, moving her body closer to mine so I can feel every soft undulation of her frame, every whisper of her breath, and I'm certain she can feel me growing harder by the second.

'Not completely.'

She nods slowly. 'I thought not.'

Something like dissatisfaction snakes through me. I'm about to clarify when a couple approaches us—too close to be an accident. I turn to look at them with obvious impatience. Something about the woman is vaguely familiar.

'Jess?'

Jessica angles her head, her swan-like neck drawing my attention back before I put a bit of space between us, accepting that she's going to have a conversation with whoever this is.

'Jemima. Hi.' Her voice isn't exactly bursting with enthusiasm. Jemima? This must be her sister and brother-in-law. That's why the other woman looks familiar—there's something in their features that's similar. Eyes and smiles.

Jessica disentangles herself from me to lean forward and kiss her sister's cheek, then the man behind Jemima leans forward, bringing himself against Jessica and kissing her on the other cheek.

Jessica springs back, right against my side. 'Guys, this is a friend of mine, Zach Papandreo,' she murmurs, gesturing to me in some misguided belief they haven't just seen us getting up close and personal right here at the bar. 'My sister, Jemima, and her husband, Simon.'

'Jesus, Jess, you've been keeping this quiet,' Jemima says with a grin. I've heard enough from Jessica to make me interested to observe their interaction. I contemplate asking them to join us in a booth but I honestly think Jessica would hate that.

'Kept what quiet?' Jessica asks with a face that's sheer innocence.

'You two.' She points from me to Jessica. I feel Jessica bristle.

'It's nothing.' She looks to me for help. 'Right?'

'Oh, absolutely nothing,' but I grin and wink conspiratorially at Jemima, I can't say why, before reaching out and extending a hand to her. 'Nice to meet you.' I follow the action for Simon, shaking his hand, remembering belatedly that there was some particular beef with him and Jessica.

'We have a table booked. Why don't you join us for a drink?' Simon suggests, gesturing to a booth in the corner.

I wait, leaving it in Jessica's hands. 'Oh, we were just here for one drink.'

'Then have it with us!' Jemima enthuses, reaching out and squeezing Jessica's hands. 'Come on. Just ten minutes.'

Jessica looks at me as if she's drowning, but her

words ring clearly in my ear. *Don't rescue me. I don't need your help.*

'Fine,' she says with a tight smile. 'Just quickly. We do have plans after this.'

Yeah, we absolutely do, and it's going to start with me stripping that dress from her body as quickly as I damned well can.

'Oh, my God. Why didn't you tell me? This is amazing.'

'Calm down, Jem. There's nothing, really, really nothing, to get excited about,' I mutter, squeezing her wrist.

'Like hell. Do you even know what a big deal this is?'

'Oh, it's so not.' I look towards the bar where Simon and Zach are in conversation, waiting for Simon to order their drinks. Jemima and I slide into the booth, and I feel a thousand and one things. I'm tied up in knots and I can't say why, but seeing Jemima and Simon definitely hasn't helped. 'I didn't know you were coming here tonight,' I segue the conversation slightly. 'You didn't mention—'

'Uh-uh, don't change the topic. Mum is going to flip. How come you didn't tell either of us? How long has this been going on?'

I need to put an end to this or, God help me, Jemima's going to tell Mum and Mum's going to be planning the whole damned wedding. 'Jemima, I know who he is and so do you. Zach Papandreo fucks around, okay? That's what we're doing. Sex. There's no big romance here. I just wanted to have a bit of fun while I'm in Singapore and he's hot and single and that's the end of it. Please, please, *please*, don't mention it to Mum and don't get a single idea in your head that either of us actually means anything to the other. Okay?'

She visibly pales, shocked at my approach to this. 'Jessica…'

I grimace. I definitely didn't pull any punches but desperate times and all that. 'Please, Jemima. Just…' I turn towards the bar in time to see Zach look at me and my heart skids to a halt in my chest. 'Just let it go, okay?'

Simon and Zach begin to walk towards us and I assume a polite smile, turning back to Jemima. 'Okay?'

'Okay.' She lifts a hand in surrender, but I can tell she's not happy about it.

'We were just having an interesting conversation about She-Shakes,' Simon says as he slides into the booth, his knees brushing mine as he passes. I shudder. Zach takes the seat beside me, draping an arm around my shoulders comfortably, naturally, and, despite my assertion to Jemima, I do feel better the second he joins us, relaxing into his frame, glad for his proximity.

'Oh?'

'You know, there'd be no better investor than Zach here,' Simon says with a jolly laugh that makes me want to slap him. I feel Zach stiffen beside me—and no wonder. I tilt a glance at him, wondering if he's mentioned anything to Simon about our 'negotiations' and decide quickly that he hasn't. He wouldn't.

'Jessica's already told you, she'll make her own mind up about that, Si,' Jemima surprises me by interjecting. It surprises Simon, too, going from the look he shoots her.

'Though I guess if you two are sleeping together that could be awkward,' Simon continues, and Jemima's jaw practically drops to the table. Even I'm surprised by Simon and I don't have a particularly high opinion of him at all.

Zach, beside me, tenses. I put my hand on his leg beneath the table, looking up at him reassuringly. 'Yes, well, that's one of many reasons it wouldn't work,' I offer breezily. 'Jem, how's the pudding going? Fruit all soaked?'

It's a relief to pivot conversation to something easier, and Jemima and I manage to hold things together for the next fifteen minutes or so, before Zach murmurs in my ear, 'Is it time to go yet?'

I smile gratefully up at him, and he stands. 'It was a pleasure to meet you, Jemima,' he says with his charming, lovely voice. 'Simon.' He nods curtly in Simon's direction and I notice he doesn't extend a hand either.

'I'll see you tomorrow,' I murmur, leaning down to kiss Jemima's cheek. 'Remember, not a word.'

We emerge into the warm night air and a flash goes off, startling me—I'd forgotten about this. Zach, however, draws me closer to him, shielding me from the lens as we approach his car. He holds the door open and I slide in; a second later he's right beside me, taking the driver's seat. He floors the engine, pulling away from the hotel and pointing the car towards his place.

We're almost there before either of us speaks.

'About your brother-in-law.'

I turn to face him, the cocktail having turned my blood to liquid. 'Mmm?'

'Do you have a history with him?'

'A *history*?'

'As in, did you date him before your sister? Is he one of the reasons you're so anti-relationships?'

I stare at him, shocked firstly by his perception and secondly by his interpretation.

'No, I never dated Simon.'

He slides the car into the undercover car park then kills the engine and turns to look at me with eyes that are appraising. Not suspicious, but...something. As if he doesn't quite believe me.

Indignation fires in my blood.

'You honestly think I'd ever be interested in a creep like him?'

He continues to stare at me for several seconds then shakes his head. 'I have no idea.'

'God, no. Simon is—he's just—Simon.'

'What does that mean?'

I don't answer.

'Something happened between the two of you. You hinted at it a while ago.'

'I didn't hint,' I correct matter-of-factly.

He lifts a brow, challenging me wordlessly.

'Okay, fine. I don't really…know how to talk about it. It's quite…hard to explain.'

He looks at me for several seconds then nods. 'It's your personal business.' The words are calmly said, as though he doesn't care, but beneath them I'm almost sure I detect an undercurrent of something.

'He hit on me.' I blurt it out and then wince. 'A bit over a year ago. He was really drunk. He suggested we get a room together. It was—icky. I was appalled.' Heat stings my cheeks and a raw ache throbs in my throat.

'I see.' When I look at Zach his jaw is tight, his face giving little away. 'What did you do?'

'What do you think I did?' I ask with a hollow laugh. 'I left. I felt physically ill. That's my sister's husband. And he did it so casually, he was so cavalier, I could tell it's something he must do all the time. Just like Dad. He's just the same.'

Zach is silent but strong waves of emotion emanate from him. 'And your sister has no idea?'

'On the contrary, I told her straight away. I felt awful doing it but obviously she deserved to know.'

'And?'

'She made it clear he was just "drunk", just "being a guy".' I bristle at that, the low expectation so insulting to the male sex. 'And that I shouldn't bring it up again. So I haven't, but I don't really love spending time with him, or them, even though I adore Jemima. I just feel so angry that she can even be with someone like that. He's such a creep and she deserves *way* better.'

'Yeah, he is. He looks at you like he's possessive of you.'

Heat flares through me: angry, indignant heat. If he was, I didn't notice because I was focussed solely on Jemima.

'That's not being a guy,' he says quietly, leaning across and putting a hand on my cheek, angling my face to his. 'It's being a dickhead.'

My heart stammers. My stomach squeezes. 'Real men don't need to sleep around behind their partner's back to feel good about themselves.'

I stare at him for several seconds, something shifting inside my belly. His words run through me, so simple, so truthful.

Real men *don't* do that. There's some kind of inadequacy in any man who needs to bolster his masculinity by being a creep.

'Real men don't make a commitment if they don't intend to keep it.'

I stare at him in awe for a second, because I know Zach would never make a commitment to a woman and break it. He's just not cut out that way.

I lift a little in the seat, kissing him gently, slowly, sliding my tongue into his mouth and duelling with his, lifting my hand to the nape of his neck and running my fingers into his hair, drawing him closer, holding him there. One of us moans but I don't know if it's him or me. I just know I want to hold him right there, like this, breathing him in, tasting him, losing myself to him. Just for now.

CHAPTER TWELVE

'YOU COULD COME, if you want.' The second I make the offer I wonder what the hell I was thinking. Inviting Zach Papandreo to a Christmas Eve lunch at my parents'? It would be like throwing him to the piranhas. My dad's friends would swarm him, for sure.

'I think I'd like that.' He grins, that sexy, dishevelled grin of his, and my heart skips a beat. Steam from the shower envelops his body, and my eyes follow his hands as he soaps his shoulders. 'But I've got plans.'

'Oh?' I push my robe apart and let it drop to the ground, then step into the shower with him. His grin widens as he pulls me closer, holding me to his muscled frame.

'Mmm.'

'What have you got to do today, hmm?'

He drops his head and nips at my lips, his hands on my hips possessive and familiar. In the back of my mind, there's an oppressive darkness I try to ignore.

Two nights.

In two nights this will be over. A trip I was dreading has gone so ridiculously fast. I can't actually believe that we have fewer than forty-eight hours left.

I push the thoughts away, not wanting to focus on them.

'I'm meeting Dimitrios and Max.'

It takes me a second to join the dots. 'Your nephew?'

'Yeah.' He lifts the bottle of fragranced body gel from the shelf and puts some in his hands, then begins to lather it over my body.

'That sounds…like…fun…' My words emerge breathy as his hands move lower, curving the roundedness of my butt, then lower, so he has to crouch to wash my legs, trailing his fingers over my thighs, my ankles, then back up to my hips, still with him crouching at my feet. He looks up at me, the shower water making his head a dark pelt, his eyes swirling with things I can't interpret and a second later his mouth comes to my sex, his tongue flicking my clit so that I whimper at the sensual touch. His hands push my hips wider and I take a step backwards, my back pressing against the cool tiles, my eyes squeezing shut as water douses me, running over me.

Two more nights of this—senseless orgasms, mind-blowing sex, pleasure that explodes through me. I don't think about the fact that most of my time is going to be taken up by my family now. I don't think about anything except how good Zach is at this, and how much I love being with him.

* * *

'What about clothes?' I suggest, feeling as if I'm the worst person in the world to help my brother choose a Christmas present for his wife. I'm not exactly a 'present giving' kind of guy. I don't think I even bought anything for Emily and we were—in love? It wasn't love. I know that now.

'Mummy has tons of clothes,' Max says with a shake of his head.

'Sounds like you've got all the help you need,' I point out with a grin and Dimitrios chuckles.

'Oh, Max has got lots of ideas.'

We walk in silence a little way, with the exception of the occasional slurp of hot chocolate as Max drinks.

'She's mad about Christmas,' Dimitrios says after a while, seeming a little distracted. 'And you know that's not really my—our—thing. I know we need to get her something but I've no idea what.'

Honestly, I'm fascinated by this. I've never seen Dimitrios into a woman before. He's like ice man, completely focussed on business. Annie's under his skin though, and his frustration at not knowing what to buy her is evidence of how much he cares.

'Well, what if it's not a gift so much as an experience.'

'What does that even mean?'

I think about that. 'You guys have just got married. You're a family. What about a new family tradition, something you can share each Christmas after this one? Maybe you buy a puzzle and do that together each Christmas day.' I think about Jessica and the stories she's told me about her family and the baking they do, the way that reminds them of their extended family each Christmas. 'Or what about a Christmas pudding? Does she have a recipe she makes each year?'

'Nope,' Max chimes in. 'We sometimes get a bit of pudding from our neighbours upstairs.'

Beside me, Dimitrios stills, and when I look at him I see something in his expression that haunts me. Torment. He looks guilty as fuck. I nudge him with my shoulder, understanding as no one else can.

Our mother was dirt poor and so were we, until Dad swept in and took us away. Now Dimitrios finds out that the mother of his child was raising Max in similar circumstances to our mother.

His guilt is understandable but, given that he had no clue about Max, it's hardly his fault.

'You don't make a pudding?' Dimitrios asks Max thoughtfully.

'Nope.'

'Maybe that's what we should do.'

'With raisins and dates? I like that one. Mrs Appleby upstairs makes it like that. And she puts cinnamin—cinnamum—a nice spice all through it.'

'Whatever you want,' Dimitrios agrees. 'We'll find a recipe with Mummy.'

Some time later, we pass a playground and Max goes in for a run around. Dimitrios and I stand with takeaway coffees, watching him.

'I've been seeing someone.'

I have no idea why I blurt that out.

Dimitrios tilts a brow at me. 'Aren't you always?'

I acknowledge his remark with a bland smile. 'I mean, for a couple of weeks.'

He's been in a strange mood all morning, dark and heavy without giving me any explanation. He glowers when he responds. 'That's practically a lifetime for you.'

'I'm serious.' I frown, wondering why I'm pushing this conversation. 'I mean, it's not serious or anything.'

'Obviously.'

I grind my teeth, his bad mood leaching into me.

'She's leaving Singapore the day after Christmas, so it's, you know, temporary.'

'Plus you have the attention span of a bumblebee so there's that, too.'

'Stop,' I say, more harshly than I intended. I grimace in apology. 'It's not like that.'

Dimitrios frowns, as if he's just starting to realise something more is going on, though God knows what. 'I thought you'd sworn off relationships after Emily?'

'I have. I did. This isn't… God, I don't know what we're doing.' I turn to face him, knowing I need to be honest. With him, myself, and eventually with Jessica. 'I just know that we agreed we'd do this for two weeks, while she was in Singapore. But she leaves the day after tomorrow and I'm fucked if I know how to say goodbye to her.'

Dimitrios's eyes narrow thoughtfully and then he nods. 'So don't.'

As if it's that simple.

I am never going to be able to escape.

I read her text message with a growing sense of frustration. It's almost midnight on Christmas Eve and she was due at my place hours ago.

What's going on?

My dad's playing carols now. Everyone's singing along.

The image opens something up in my chest. Despite the image she's painted and the reservations I know she has about her family, that sounds kind of…nice.

It sounds like family and it sounds like why she's here in Singapore. She came to spend time with them. Not see me. From the beginning, Jessica said this was a distraction and if she's having fun with her family then I just need to let that be.

Fuck.

I pace into my room, staring at the bed with a strange throb low inside me.

This has got out of hand.

I need her to go back to London so I can get back to my normal life. I need to forget she exists because Jessica is something like kryptonite to me. And just like that, I get it.

I don't want her to go. I don't want this to be over. I like what we're doing and I think she probably feels the same way.

I dig my phone out of my pocket.

Take your time. I'll wait up.

It's almost two when I let myself into the lift of his building and crest all the way to the penthouse. My head is swimming with carols, hymns and eggnog. In my hands I have a little Christmas smorgasbord all for Zach, and plans of setting it out for him in the morning. Pudding, fruit mince pies, shortbread, everything festive, the perfect way to wake up on Christmas morning. And despite the fact I'll have to be back at my parents' in time for lunch tomorrow, I'm glad I'm spending the night here. I'm glad I'll get to wake up with him on Christmas morning.

He's the only present I could ask for, and definitely the thing I'll most look forward to unwrapping, I think with a smile.

The dull ache is still there. The knowledge that our time is almost finished, that soon I'll be leaving and that will be the end. But I refuse to think about it. I refuse to focus on that now.

He's awake, just as he promised, sitting at the table with a laptop set up, wearing only boxer shorts and looking impossibly gorgeous.

'You're still awake.' I smile, carrying the package of Christmas treats to the kitchen island bench then moving towards him. He stands as I approach, his smile somehow hesitant. Or maybe it's not. Perhaps it's just that I know him now, so well, that I understand every nuance that crosses his face.

'I said I would be,' he murmurs, putting a hand out. I ignore it and walk into his arms instead, lifting up onto tiptoes and kissing him.

'Let's go to bed.'

He frowns. 'Are you tired?'

I shake my head, impatient for him—all of him that I can possibly get in the few hours we have left. 'Not even a little bit.'

His laugh is throaty but he shakes his head. 'Have a drink with me. I want to talk to you.'

'Oh?' I pull back, looking up into his face. 'Is everything okay?'

'Yeah.' He nods, but I have a feeling that it's not. Something's wrong. 'Tea? Coffee? Port? Wine?'

I've had enough eggnog to make my head spin. 'A tea would be perfect.'

I watch as he makes two cups and carries both to the lounge room. As an afterthought, I pull out some fruit mince pies and put them on a small plate, bringing them with us. 'My secret recipe,' I say as I place them down. 'Lots of rum.'

He nods in acknowledgement—no smile.

'What is it, Zach? You're starting to freak me out.'

He laughs uneasily. 'Sorry.' He shakes his head. 'This is no big deal.' He frowns. 'I just wanted to take your temperature on something.'

Is he going to talk about my business again? I brace for that, knowing that I still haven't made up my mind—it's impossible to get clarity with Zach in my life. He overpowers everything, all my senses. I'll be able to breathe again in a day or so. Won't I? I ignore the dull ache low in my chest.

'I like being with you.'

The statement draws me back to the present, back to him.

'I think we've established that.'

'I mean, I really like it. And I like you.' He clears his throat. 'Fuck. As it turns out, I'm not good at this.'

'Good at what?' My heart is going crazy for no reason I can think of. Hope—an impossible to define, all-consuming hope—fills me. 'Zach?'

Suddenly I wish I had a wine, rather than a tea.

'I *like* you. Like you like you. And I don't want you to go back to London.'

He stares at me for several seconds then runs a hand through his hair. 'Say something.'

I shake my head, numb and electrified all at once. I don't know what to say but I know that pieces of me are clicking into place in a way I didn't realise I needed them to. I do know that my own feelings are starting to make more sense. I do know that I 'like like' him too. And that's only the beginning of how I feel. I'm terrified by that but as soon as I realise it I know I can't run from this—from him. I stare at him blankly as finally everything starts to make sense, and I mean *everything*.

'You don't need to look so panicked. I'm not of-fering marriage. I'm not saying that I love you or can't live without you. I'm just suggesting you extend your trip a bit. Until this thing has really run its course.'

My heart swoops. My stomach feels hollowed out. Crushing disappointment follows the strange realisation of what I've been feeling.

'Nothing more than what we've got now.' He leans closer, brushing his lips to mine, perhaps misunderstanding my silence. 'Just a few weeks more of this. Meaningless, amazing sex.'

My heart almost grinds to a halt.

I ache all over. It's the champagne and eggnog, right? Making me woozy and confused? Making me think I feel something I've never ever felt in my whole life? This can't be happening.

'Because that's what this is,' I say uncertainly, but he must think I'm being emphatic, reminding him of the terms of our agreement.

'Scout's honour.' He nods.

Crap.

I shake my head, standing up, rejecting his words, rejecting this.

'I know it's not what we said.' He speaks quietly, gently trying to convince me. 'But are you really ready to go?'

I stare out over Singapore.

'Think about it, Jessica. The day after Christmas was just some arbitrary date—the date you happen to be leaving. Do you really feel like this is over between us? Are you ready to not see me again?'

My heart squeezes and I make a strange, strangling noise as I try to suck in enough air to sustain me. Oh,

God. I'm such an idiot. How could I let this happen? I turn to face him, the drowning sensation not abating.

'No.' The word is just a whisper. 'But that's why I have to go.'

He stands up, his frustration obvious.

'That doesn't make any sense.'

'Yes, it does.'

'You don't want to leave me.'

'No.'

Tears fill my throat. I swallow hard, refusing to give into them.

'So stay. Just another week. Stay here, not at the hotel. Be here, in my life, my bed. Nothing has to change—we both know what we want from each other. This is so perfect, Jessica. I've never been with anyone who had the same outlook on life and relationships as me.'

I feel like the biggest fraud in the world. I feel as if I've duped him completely, but, in my defence, I duped myself too. I didn't see any of this coming. I'm completely blindsided to realise how I feel about him, but there's no avoiding it.

'This is just sex?' I say quietly, my eyes locked to his, my heart needing to hear the truth of how he feels.

'Absolutely.' He frowns. 'I mean, I really like you, so no, I guess there's something more there too, but it's nothing serious. It's just fun, like we said.'

I stare at him, wondering if he has any idea what he's doing to me.

'I can one hundred per cent promise I'm not going

to be like Patrick—there will be no declarations of love at the end of this. No marriage proposals.'

Apparently not. I swallow a sob. I feel as though my heart is being disconnected with a scalpel.

I stare at the fruit mince pies on the table, remembering how excited I was to prepare them, remembering how ridiculously excited I was to bring them to Zach. My heart had been bursting then. Sharing things with him, being with him…how could this have taken so long for me to understand?

'I—' I search for words and draw a blank. 'I can't—'

'It's just more of what we're doing,' he insists, no idea he's making this worse with every 'assurance' he gives. 'Sex, fun, you and me.'

'No.' I shout the word then wince, shaking my head. 'I can't. I have to—I have to go.'

'Why? What's in London that needs you the day after Christmas? Stay for New Year's, at least.'

I'm going to start crying if I don't get out of here. 'No, I have to go now. Right now.'

'What?' I move to the bench where I'd put my handbag and scoop it up, tucking it under my arm. A flash of lightning makes me jump—I look towards the windows just as the sky opens up and begins to dump the torrential rain it had been threatening all day down on the city.

'I have to go.'

I know my very survival depends on it. If I don't get out now I know I'm going to fall into a thousand pieces and I won't let him see that.

'Don't. If you don't want to extend your trip, then fine. But don't ruin the time we've got left.' He reaches for my hand, catching it in his. 'Stay.'

'No, I really can't, Zach. I can't.'

I bite down onto my lower lip to stop from crying then pull my hand free. I can't see him again. I can't.

I jab my finger into the elevator call button, standing there with my arms wrapped over my torso, conscious of him watching me the whole time. The doors ping open and I step in, pressing the button for the ground.

'You're seriously just going to leave now?' He looks hurt.

'I can't stay.' I feel as if my head is about to explode. I don't know what to say to him, what to tell him, I just know I can't breathe right now and that if I get away from him maybe the world will stop spinning like this.

'You just can't handle the idea of anything blurring the lines, can you?' he says, the words tinged with frustration. 'I want to buy a share of your business and you shut me down because heaven forbid our circumstances change even in the slightest. You're doing that thing you do, Jessica, and you just can't help yourself.'

'What thing?'

'Cutting off your beautiful damned nose to spite your face. Can't you see that? You like being with me too but instead of showing even a hint of flexibility you're sticking to some stupid agreement we made way back when we didn't even know each other.'

I flinch, the hurt of having him throw that accusation at me deeper than he could possibly realise. He has his hand thrust against the elevator doors so I can't escape as I wanted to.

'This isn't that.' The words are weak, watery.

'So what is it? Why not just roll with this a bit longer?'

My stomach hurts. I feel as if I'm being badgered into telling him something it will destroy me to admit.

'Just let me go, Zach. I don't want to be here any more. I don't want to be with you now. Okay?'

'That's a blatant lie. You walked in tonight eager to jump straight into my bed. I'm just asking you to stay there a week or two longer. Is that a hanging offence?'

I press my back to the wall of the elevator.

'I'm playing by all your rules otherwise.' He lifts a finger to enumerate. 'No talking about your business. No developing actual feelings for you. Nothing beyond the sex we both love so much. And you're running away from me?'

'That's not why I'm running away from you,' I growl, moving away from the wall and pushing at his chest, everything finally burning into flames within me. 'I'm leaving because if I stay another second I'm terrified I'll tell you that I've fallen so fucking in love with you that the idea of being with you even a minute longer knowing you feel absolutely nothing for me is killing me. Okay? Are you satisfied?' I jab at his chest again and this time he steps backwards, his eyes round, shock obvious on his handsome features.

I move deeper into the lift, pressing my finger on the button a few times, my jaw locked.

'So let me go and forget all about me. I'm sure it won't be long before you've found someone else to have meaningless, amazing sex with.'

I try my hardest not to cry but I know he must see the tears that fall down my face right before the door slams shut.

CHAPTER THIRTEEN

WHAT THE HELL?

I stare at the closed doors for all of ten seconds before anger surges through my veins. She throws that at my feet and then expects to just waltz away? My heart drops because she wasn't waltzing anywhere.

She was hurting.

Jessica Johnson was hurting and that's because of me.

My stomach feels hollowed out. I run to the staff elevator, stepping inside as soon as the doors open. It's not as fast as mine. By the time it reaches the ground floor she's out of the foyer of the building. I run after her, emerging onto the streets barefoot, bare-chested, rain lashing me.

'Jessica?' I see her stop walking and turn around, disbelief on her pale face, her hair wet, her clothes wet, sticking to her body.

I run up to her, no idea what I want to say, no idea what I feel except for anger. So much anger. This isn't what we agreed but, God help me, I don't want her to go, not now!

So what? I say I love her when I don't believe in love? Just to get her to stop hurting? To stop her from crying? I refuse to hurt Jessica Johnson; I can't let this happen.

But I can't lie to her, either. I won't. Not even if they're the only words I can offer that will make her feel better.

'Don't run away from me like this,' I say instead. 'Come inside.'

She shakes her head, staring at me as though I'm the devil incarnate. 'What for, Zach? What do you want from me?'

Great question. But she knows the answer—I gave it to her a thousand times before I knew how she felt. I close my eyes as I remember the firm insistence with which I'd told her I don't want anything other than sex. That what we're doing is meaningless.

'I like you,' I say, aware as soon as I do that it's just making everything so much worse.

'I know. You like being with me. That's sweet, Zach, but it's not enough. None of this is enough.'

I stare at her, aching to pull her into my arms, aching to kiss her and make this all better.

'It's not your fault.' She has to shout above the sound of the lashing rain. 'I knew exactly what you are. I knew what I was getting into. I just didn't expect to feel this. It's not your fault.'

She takes a step away from me. I have the sense I'm trying to catch water in my bare hands. I don't know how to fix this.

'I should have realised sooner.' She's shaking. 'The

night you offered to buy into She-Shakes, I was so upset and I've just realised why. I thought you were going to tell me you wanted more then. And instead, it was all about money. Business. Nothing personal.'

I grind my teeth together, not wanting to point out that we had an agreement on that score.

'I was devastated and it was easy to think your offer was the reason but it was never that. When we had sex, you kept telling me that it meant nothing, over and over again, and honestly, Zach, I felt like you'd scraped out my heart.' Her voice cracks and my arms are heavy with being useless by my side. I want to draw her closer, to hug her, but I don't. What an ass I was that night, all in thinking I was reassuring her.

'Just go back upstairs and forget about me, like I said. I don't blame you. It's okay. This isn't your fault.'

She keeps saying that over and over and I wish she wouldn't because it feels as if this is completely my fault. I hurt her, and right now I hate myself for that, but I can't say what she needs to hear because I don't feel it. I thought asking her to extend her trip was a huge step, but it wasn't anywhere near enough.

'I'm sorry. I wish I could give you what you want.'

She looks away from me, but I see it. Pain.

'It's fine. I'll be fine.'

God, so fiercely independent. My stomach twists.

'Please just let me go now.'

I was wrong. There is a way I can make this better for her—or at least stop making it worse. I can leave her alone, just as she wants. I'm making it worse by trying to talk to her.

'Okay.' I lift my hands in the air, knowing I need to respect her boundaries here. 'I'll go. I just want to say again that I'm sorry. I wish I could feel—'

She nods jerkily. 'I understand. It's okay.'

It's not okay. I broke my own damned rule and Jessica got burned. I should have known better than to go along with this. Two nights work, two weeks are a whole different ball game.

'Goodbye, Zach.'

I stare at her, my lungs barely able to function, but then I nod. 'Goodbye, Jessica.'

Her shoulders slump as she walks away and it takes every ounce of willpower I possess not to chase after her, but I don't. I stand there in the pouring rain and watch until she's out of sight and, when she is, I feel only a consuming sense of emptiness.

'I still don't understand why you had to bring your flight forward.'

'I have an urgent meeting with my team.'

'On Boxing Day?' Jemima says sceptically.

'I can't help it,' I lie, zipping my suitcase shut with an emphatic sweep of my arm.

I have never found anything harder than I did today and, for once, my family wasn't to blame. The hardest part of the day was acting like my normal self when my heart has been shattered into ten billion tiny pieces.

'Maybe I can come see you in a month or so?' she suggests, surprising me. I turn to face her, frowning. Jemima has only been to London a few times since

I've lived there, and usually when Simon has business. 'A girls' trip,' she insists and I nod, because if it's just Jemima, then the idea has infinitely more appeal. Though right now, it's hard to muster enthusiasm for anything.

An hour later and I'm in a cab on my way to the airport, completely numb. I wasn't able to stay for the family lunch, in the end. I couldn't hold it together. I need time and space and I need to be by myself. I keep my phone switched off as the car powers through the streets of Singapore, desperately trying not to think of Zach. That's easier said than done though—I fear he has become a part of my soul, and I will never liberate myself from him again.

'You're drunk?' Dimitrios is looking at me as though he doesn't know what to make of me.

'Merry Christmas to you too.'

He frowns. 'It's almost midnight. What's going on?'

'Nothing.'

Behind him, Annie appears, her features showing worry. 'Zach? Don't just stand there, come in.' She steps to the side, gesturing into Dimitrios's home. It's like something from Santa's grotto in here—trees, lights, music, the works. He's pulled out all the stops for Annie, just because she likes Christmas.

And because he loves her.

Because they're married.

Because that's what you do when you're married and in love.

Fuck love.

I move into the living room without being invited, making my way to the bar and pouring a measure of Scotch. Before I take a drink I catch the look Annie and Dimitrios throw one another, a look of total confusion.

Fuck.

'Zach, what's going on?'

'Nothing.' I hear the word slur from my mouth and inwardly groan. 'Can't I come to wish you a Merry Christmas?'

'Of course you can,' Annie soothes, moving across to me, putting a hand around the Scotch glass and holding it. 'How about a coffee?'

If it were anyone else, I might snap that I don't want a damned coffee, but Annie is so sweet and I've known her so long, and she is clearly worried about me, so I nod once. 'Fine.' Dimitrios clears his throat, his expression stern. 'Thank you,' I add, closing my eyes.

Why did I come here?

Annie smiles at me, putting a hand on my shoulder. 'I'll just be a minute.'

She leaves the room so Dimitrios and I are alone. 'Out with it.'

Just the two of us, he doesn't pull any punches. I stare at him, lost for words. All day—all fucking day—I've tried to see my way through this. Knowing Jessica is across the city and I can't see her—for her sake—has been like a knife in the gut. This isn't about sex. I'm not that much of an idiot. If I felt less for her then I'd just, I don't know, either forget about her as she said or try my hardest to seduce her back into my bed where all of this fades into nothing, because nothing matters when we're together.

But she deserves so much better than that. And I know I can't forget her. Not easily.

'You said you were seeing someone,' he prompts, coming to stand beside me.

I grunt my agreement.

'And something's happened with her?' he asks again, staring at me as though he can find the answers in my face.

I keep my mouth shut.

'Zach,' he sighs heavily. 'You're my brother and I love you, but if you've come here drunk as all hell on Christmas night just to stand there mute and brooding I'm going to have to kick your ass out of here.'

My first reaction is anger but then I look around his perfect living room and feel a twinge of guilt. I know how important it was for him to get this Christmas right. His first with Annie and Max. And here I am, torpedoing his Christmas night. 'Shit, you're right. I'm sorry, man. I shouldn't have come.'

'Don't be stupid. You know you can *always* come here, but just tell me what's bothering you. I can't help you if I don't know what's going on.'

I feel something groan to a halt inside me, a sense of disbelief. I haven't needed anyone's help in a long time but he's not wrong now. I need help. I don't understand what to do but I know I can't leave things like this with Jessica.

'I've been seeing this girl.'

He's quiet, just nodding softly.

'We agreed from the outset that it was just going to be casual, just...'

'Physical,' he supplies gently.

'Yes.' I grind my teeth. 'But two weeks is a long time. And we spent a *lot* of time together.'

'Jesus. Are you trying to tell me you fell in love with her?' His disbelief is warranted.

'God, no. Of course not.' I shake the idea off quickly.

'Ah.' He nods thoughtfully. 'But she has feelings for you. She wants more from you.'

I've had too much to drink to think straight. 'I wanted more from her. I wanted to extend our arrangement but keep it the same. I like the way things were with us, I just wanted more time.'

'And she didn't?'

I compress my lips. 'She wanted the impossible.'

Dimitrios scans my face expectantly.

'She says she's in love with me.' I spit the words with derision but inside I feel bleak.

'And you don't love her.'

I pull a face, looking at him dolefully. 'Come on, man. I know you've got all this—' I gesture around his lounge room '—but you know me. You know me better than just about anyone. What do you think?'

He sighs. 'I think you and I don't know shit about love.'

I wait for him to continue, but Dimitrios is mulling it over. Annie emerges with a cup of coffee and places it on the bar. She smiles up at me gently. 'It's good to see you, Zach. I hope you won't be offended if I go to bed?'

'No, of course not.' I force a smile. 'Merry Christmas, Annie.' I dip my head down and kiss her cheek.

She turns to Dimitrios. 'Goodnight.'

Heat sparks between them; I look away, but the image of them together stays in my mind. It creates the exact same impression I had on their wedding day—that they just make sense. Seeing them together isn't a question of 'love' or 'commitment', it's just that it's right for them to be together. Something fuzzy moves through my brain; a thought I can't quite grasp.

When we're alone, Dimitrios props an elbow on the bar and continues as though we were never interrupted. 'I think you've told me about a woman you're seeing for the first time since Emily. I think you've had a fight with her and you've come here after having more than enough to drink because you're upset, and that if you didn't care about her you wouldn't feel like that.'

'I don't care about her. I care about hurting her. I didn't want to do that.'

He frowns. 'I'm sure that's a part of it. But you're hurting too, Zach.'

I stare at him in total confusion.

'You're hurting. Take it from someone who knows you.' He shrugs his shoulders ruefully. 'And knows what he's talking about. You're hurting. I don't know if you love her but I do know things aren't as straight-forward as you're trying to pretend.'

I stare at him, feeling a thousand things.

'You know what I think?'

'What?'

'I think pushing people away is easy. I think you and I both get gold stars for that. Loving someone and letting them love you—with all the risk that entails—is a shitload harder.'

'I've loved someone before. I loved Emily,' I lie belligerently.

'Bullshit. You went after the impossible woman. You self-sabotaged your own happiness with that relationship and then you've used it as an excuse to avoid a meaningful connection with anyone since.'

I glare at him but can't disagree.

'I can't tell you what you're feeling but I can tell you that you need to dig deeper. There's obviously more going on with her than you're admitting to yourself.'

My throat feels raw. I stare at him, bereft and lost, then nod. I throw back the coffee, wincing as the heat scalds my mouth.

'You don't regret it?' I murmur, looking around the lounge room.

'Regret what?'

'All this. Marrying Annie.'

'What do you think?'

I think I've never seen my brother happier. Great for Dimitrios but it doesn't mean Jessica and I are in the same boat.

'Thanks for hearing me out.'

'Any time.' At the door, he reaches for my arm, stopping me from leaving. 'I mean that. Any time, bro.'

The next morning, I wake up with a banging hangover and a swirling torrent of thoughts. How do I feel? What do I want? What can I give her? I don't have any answers but I do know this: Jessica is leaving Singapore today and if I don't see her before she goes I'm going to hate myself. I don't know what I want to say to her, just that I need to see her. I need to see her smile. I need to know she's going to be okay.

I hail a cab to her hotel rather than drive—I'm pretty sure I'd be over the limit. It's not even eight o'clock when I get there. I take the lift to her room and knock on the door.

No answer.

I press the doorbell and wait.

Nothing. I press an ear to the door and ring the bell again, expecting to hear something—her moving around the suite, anything.

But there's silence. A sense of unease shifts through me. Maybe she stayed at her parents' place last night? That would make sense, wouldn't it? That's what families do around Christmas and Jessica is all about Christmas, right?

I pull out my phone and dial her number; it rings several times then goes to message bank.

For God's sake. I know she's pissed off, but she can't seriously be dodging my calls? Of course she can be. Just like that I remember how she was that night in the rain, her beautiful face scrunched up with hurt and sadness. I'm in free fall.

I phone my executive assistant next. I know it's the day after Christmas but there's a reason I pay twice the going rate. 'I need the address for Clive Johnson. Immediately.'

Five minutes later I have it and I'm in another cab, cutting across town.

Jemima answers the door.

'Hi.' I nod curtly, looking beyond her. I can see the kind of Christmas scene Jessica has described to me—the enormous tree, halls decorated, twinkling lights. 'Is Jessica here?'

Jemima frowns, shaking her head. 'I thought she would have told you.'

'Told me what?'

'Something happened with her business. She had to fly out yesterday.'

I feel as if a stone has dropped through my gut.

'Fly out to where?'

Jemima looks at me quizzically. 'Back home. To London.'

Home. London. My skin feels feverish. 'Right.' I swallow. 'You said she left yesterday?'

'Yeah. At lunchtime. She didn't tell you she was going?'

I shake my head.

Jemima's eyes narrow. 'I guess that makes sense.' She frowns though, looking over her shoulder. 'Did you want to come in?'

I feel a hollow, deranged laugh fill my oesophagus. I shake my head. 'Thanks. Another time. I've got somewhere I have to be.'

London is my favourite city in the world. At any time of year, I love it, but at Christmas, it shimmers. The streets are decorated with wreaths and garlands, the nights come early, the mornings are slow, there's magic and snow in every bit of air I breathe.

From the window of my Mayfair apartment I can see the corner of Hyde Park, the trees lightly dusted in white from a heavy fall of snow we received overnight, and the streets are buzzing with cars beetling around, many undoubtedly on their way to the famous Boxing Day sales. I'm only a block away from Oxford Street and I know if I ventured out that way I'd be surrounded by more heaving humanity than I can handle.

I don't want to be surrounded by people though. Even though crowds bring anonymity, they still bring contact and I desperately need to be alone.

Even the idea of spending lunch with my family filled me with a cloying sense of grief.

It isn't just that I fell in love with Zach. It's that I was *stupid* enough to fall in love with him. Stupid enough to let my guard down, to let him in, to look inside his soul and become addicted to what he is. I feel like an idiot. I feel as if I've let myself down. I feel so angry with myself and I feel so helpless and hopeless.

The day drags.

I pull some work out and try to focus on it, but by four o'clock in the afternoon my brain is fried. I pull on my jacket and beanie, make a hot chocolate in a takeaway cup and step out of my apartment. It's bitterly cold, the wind freezing my cheeks; the night's snow has turned into an ice wind and a hint of sleet. I drop my head forward and walk fast, sipping my hot chocolate as I go, ignoring the buzzing of the world. Hyde Park is better—quieter, especially at this time of day. There's a man selling chestnuts near Speakers' Corner. I nod in his general direction as I pass, then keep walking. I don't have a destination in mind, I just need to stretch my legs and put my mind into abeyance.

At the Knightsbridge entrance I pause, looking at the wide horse paths here, then back towards the rose gardens. In a few months, the bracken shrubs will be covered with new growth, fresh green buds and promise. The desolation of winter always gives way to spring, doesn't it? I walk back towards the rose garden, reaching out and brushing my fingertip over one of the branches. I'm almost disappointed when a thorn doesn't jab me.

I don't know if spring will come for me.

I really don't.

I know that I've lived my life so confident that I don't want a relationship, that I sure as hell don't want a man, and now I realise I've been generalising. I've put all men into one box, lumping them in with Dad's sins, Simon's sins, my lukewarm feelings for Patrick. I've avoided relationships but it turns out you can't avoid love, no matter how hard you try. It's part of the human condition, hardwired into our brains.

A tear escapes from the corner of my eye. I dab at it with a gloved thumb then start to walk again, back through the middle of the park this time, taking the path that cuts at a diagonal angle towards Oxford Street.

It's not a long walk and I move quickly, cold now and exhausted. I tell myself it's jet lag but I know it's more than that—it's heartsickness. Weariness from grief and the sting of rejection.

I replay the things he said on that last night, late on Christmas Eve, as I walk. The way he trivialised the idea of a relationship, assuring me he doesn't care about me beyond sex. I think about the way he took such pains to make sure I understood that, and my heart breaks all over again, because it took hearing him say those things for me to finally understand how I feel, and what I want.

I want the dream.

I want everything he'll never give me.

I want everything I've always derided.

Tears sting my eyes. Impatiently, I wipe them away, angrier still that I can't get a grip of my emotions. It's not like me. Before I reach the corner I cut through the park, to the gate nearest my street. There's a pedestrian crossing with lights here. I wait until they turn green then zip across. The sky is now dark, the headlights taking on that streaky red light they get. At the steps to my building, I reach into my pocket, pulling out my keys then dropping them to the ground by accident. I bend down to pick them up as someone approaches me, presumably walking past. I stand, looking automatically in their direction only to have my heart squeezed tight, my whole body frozen in shock.

'Zach?' I can't quite believe what I'm seeing. I take a step back and blink, ascertaining he's not a figment of my imagination.

'Hey.' His hands are shoved in his pockets and his expression is impossible to read. My heart is twisting and thumping, my tummy is in knots and my eyes are still wet with tears. I swallow hard and look down the street. There's no one around. It's the day after Christmas and it's dark out. Shoppers will have gone home.

'What are you doing here?'

He nods, as if I've asked a 'yes' or 'no' question. I stare at him, waiting, my throat raw.

'You're in London,' I prompt, with a hint of disbelief.

'I came to talk to you.' He frowns, shakes his head. 'This morning, in Singapore, I came to talk to you. But you were gone.'

Something trembles in my chest; I recognise it as a relic of hope. 'I left yesterday.'

'Jemima told me.'

I'm freezing, but I don't want to go inside. More than that, I don't want to invite him inside. I can't be alone with him—it's asking too much.

'Why did you want to talk to me?'

His Adam's apple jerks as he swallows. 'I guess I wanted to make sure you were okay,' he says gently. Sympathy will be my undoing.

'I'm fine.'

'Really? Because I'm not.' His lips twist into a grimace. 'Except when I realised you were gone, I had this feeling in my chest that I can't describe. I couldn't breathe, Jessica. I felt like… I felt like all the light had gone out of my world. I felt like I still thought, up until that moment, you might change your mind. I thought things weren't over between us. And then you were gone, and it was all so final, and I realised something I should have seen much sooner.'

My stomach is in loops. 'What?' Just a whisper— barely a sound.

'The idea of going a day without seeing you is unbearable.' He moves closer and I freak out, flinching away from him, because I'm *definitely* not strong enough to be that close to him *and* to hear him say lovely things. 'The idea of you being in London and me being in Singapore is anathema to me. It runs contrary to everything I want.'

He's offering me more than he did before, but it's still not enough. I refuse to be damned with faint praise, faint affection. I won't settle.

I tilt my chin angrily, glaring up at him, glad to have that emotion to rely on.

'You want two more weeks of meaningless, hot sex. I remember.'

He winces as though I'm the one hurting him with that description.

'I thought that's what *you* wanted, and yeah, honestly, I thought it was how I felt too.'

I look away from him, my heart in shreds.

'I never let myself think beyond that because I thought it wasn't even a possibility.'

I grind my teeth together, not willing to listen. I can't. It's too dangerous. I feel as if everything is at risk. 'Don't pretend you feel something you don't.'

His face is imploring. 'I just don't know where to begin.'

Something wells inside me—frustration and impatience. Why has he come here if only to say he doesn't know what to say? 'I don't want to do this.'

It seems to shake him. His voice becomes more authoritative.

'Listen to me, Jessica, please. From the first day I met you I have wanted more from you than I ever have another soul. I have been obsessed with you, fascinated by you. I have wanted you in a way that is new and different. I have wanted to send you flowers and scream it from the rooftops that we're together. Remember the night you stayed home and we talked for hours over videocall? I couldn't *not* call you. I couldn't go a night without seeing you. That wasn't about sex, it was about you and your ideas and your beautiful smile and your stories and your feelings.'

I suck in a deep breath. 'I just—' The words fall into nothing.

He pushes on, my inability to form words not something he's experiencing. 'When I suggested buying into She-Shakes it wasn't because I wanted to rescue you. It was because I wanted to be your partner. Your ideas excite me; you excite me. I wanted to work with you, to be near you while you work, and

I wanted to see all your dreams come true. And yes, I know you'll hate this because you're independent as fuck, but if I could have one small part in making your dreams come true then I wanted that too. I have spent a long time telling myself that I don't want a relationship, that I don't want love, but the truth is, I've had no idea what love is. It turns out, it's nothing like I thought.'

I turn back to face him, my heart beating wildly.

'You don't get it. You've already told me how you feel. I don't believe you'd lie to me, Zach. I don't believe you'd pretend you just wanted sex if deep down you were madly in love with me.'

'I was stupid, Jessica. I didn't have a fucking clue how I felt. I just knew I didn't want you to go. I knew I didn't want to go a day without you.'

'Yeah, yeah, until this thing between us burned out.'

'It's not going to burn out. That's what I'm saying. I was stupid and naïve and too messed up by Emily to realise that this is the real deal. Nothing I've ever known compares to this. This isn't just love. This isn't something anyone else has ever felt, right? I mean, this is just you and me, and whatever we are together. I just know that you complete me. You literally fit into all the places that are empty inside me, and you make me feel—' He pauses, looking down at me, searching for words. 'You make me feel like the best version of myself, and you make me want to be that for ever, to make you proud, and make you happy. You make me happy, Jessica. And I think I can make you happy too. I think I can complete you.' He holds a hand up to forestall what he anticipates will be my likely response. 'Not that you need a man to complete you.'

Despite myself I feel a hint of amusement flicker inside me. I'm a raging feminist and I appreciate that he gets that and—more so—respects it.

'Zach...'

Again, I fail to find words, and again, he has more than enough. 'I get it. I get what I've never understood before now. Love is an abstract fucking concept until you meet the right person. For the right person, you change, everything changes, because there's no viable alternative. Love isn't abstract now. It's here, right here.' He bangs his hand into his chest, staring at me. 'Because of you.'

I make a noise that is half sob, half something else.

His voice softens. 'I'm not asking you to hang up your heels and be my trophy wife or whatever; I'm not that kind of guy and I think you know that. I don't want you to change. I don't want you to give up on any of your dreams. I want to be beside you while you chase them. I want to be the guy you come home to and enthuse with, I want to be your sounding board, I want to be your best friend, your lover, everything you'll let me be in your life. I want to be your biggest supporter—not because you need it but because supporting you is the best, most meaningful thing I will ever do. Just let me back in your life. Please.'

The ice wind has stirred itself into a frenzy and a dust of snow begins to fall, landing like little white kisses against his dark coat. I stare at them for a moment, my heart beating so fast I fear it might burst out of my body.

'You told me you'd never give me a declaration of love,' I say quietly, needing to remind him of the things he'd said, needing him to understand how badly he hurt me.

He moves closer, and his masculine aroma teases me and makes my stomach clench. 'Yeah, well, I also said I'd never propose to you yet here I am like some lovesick idiot asking you to kindly put me out of my misery and promise I won't ever have to spend another night without you.'

Okay. Shit just got real.

'Did you just…ask me to marry you?'

'No.' He gets down on one knee in front of me. 'I'm *begging* you to marry me. And not to put too fine a point on it, but I'll be pretty inconsolable if you say "no" so please take me at my word that I will never hurt you again and remember that you love me too.'

I stare at him, too shocked to speak.

'And that I'm new to this and I'm going to make mistakes but that one thing neither of us will ever doubt again is how much you mean to me and how much I love you. Okay?'

I nod, not even sure what I'm nodding for, but then something cold touches my hand and I realise he's pulled off my glove and is pushing a ring onto my finger, a big fat diamond ring that glistens in the evening snowfall.

'Zach.' I expel his name on a sigh. 'This is too much.'

He stands up, pulling me into his arms. 'What's too much?'

'You showing up here with a ring? Like you planned to do this?'

'I made a tiny stop on the way from the airport,' he says gently. 'I needed you to know that I'm serious. I made a mistake the other night but I'm a quick learner and, it has to be said, there was no more effective teaching technique than realising I might have lost you for ever. I don't want to live that reality.'

I grip his cheeks in my hands, holding his face steady. 'You don't have to. I was miserable the whole way back. I felt like I'd left so much of myself in Singapore and I didn't know if I'd ever get it back again. I love you, Zach Papandreo, and I always will.'

EPILOGUE

Two years later, a week before Christmas.

'I'M SO PROUD of you.'

I stare at the still-empty building with a sense of bursting pleasure. 'Me too.' Zach squeezes my hand then turns to Dimitrios. 'What do you think?'

Annie answers. 'I think Max gives it his seal of approval.' We turn in unison to the brightly coloured playground, where Max is running over the equipment, testing it all out.

My first school is due to open in January—a joint venture between She-Shakes Global and The Papandreo Initiative—and three more are in the works. That's on top of the work we're doing for the children of single parents, making it easier for these kids to access books, clothes and technology to relieve the burden on their parents.

Annie and I work together often, our passion for these projects one of the many interests we've bonded over. Strange to think that two years ago I had a prickly relationship with my own sister and now Jemima and I have become so much closer and I've gained Annie as another sister.

'The twins are finding it a bit harder.' Dimitrios grins, as his daughters attempt to climb up onto the slippery slide.

'Oh, dear.' Annie smiles as she moves towards them and a moment later Dimitrios follows, each parent scooping a happy little bundle into their arms.

'It's perfect,' I say honestly, looking up at Zach.

'You had a vision.'

'Yep.'

'And you made it happen.'

'It hasn't happened yet. I want twenty more of these schools.'

'And then twenty more,' he agrees, pressing a kiss to the top of my head.

'For now.'

'Things might get a little harder for a while,' he reminds me, pressing a hand to my rather rounded stomach.

I put mine over his, certainty filling my heart. 'That's okay. We'll make it work.'

And we will. Because we're a team, and with Zach by my side and me at his, there's nothing we can't do. That, I have learned, is the power that comes from loving someone—strength, confidence and knowing that there's one person out there who always, without fail, has your back. And Zach has mine, and always will.

* * * * *

UNWRAPPING
THE BEST MAN

RACHAEL STEWART

For Natalie.
Your love of *Getting Dirty* knows no bounds.
Here is your festive sequel...
Merry Christmas!
Rachael x

CHAPTER ONE

You are cordially invited to the wedding of
Lady Coco Lauren
and
Mr Ash Livingston
August 1st
Livingston Castle, Scottish Highlands

YOU KNOW WHEN you feel like you're dreaming...not because you remember falling asleep, but because what's happening before your eyes, within your grasp, is too good to be true?

That's me right now.

I feel like a million dollars—I'm English, but pounds just doesn't have the same ring—and it's not the hefty price tag associated with my emerald silk floor-length dress making me feel that way, or the diamonds that sparkle in my ears. It's the way my dance partner is looking at me as he sweeps me across the ballroom floor.

My dance partner, *Jackson Black*. Even my brain says his name all breathy and hitched.

Today he's the Best Man to my Maid of Honour status, and the same man I've lusted after since the day we met six years ago. Six years of unrequited, mind-losing, toe-curling desire, without so much as a kiss to the lips… Oh, I've given him a fair few to the cheek, I've leaned in slightly longer than could be considered platonic, hugged him tighter than perhaps I should, all in an attempt to have him lower his guard, to see me as more than just a client. More than just a friend of his best friend's girl.

But he doesn't bite.

He has rules.

Rules he won't break.

You see, as a client of his club, of Blacks—a sex club protected by non-disclosure agreements, and catering to the British elite—my membership status brands me as *off-limits*.

Only I don't feel off-limits now. Not when we are hundreds of miles from the London club itself, celebrating the marriage of our best friends in the Highlands of Scotland with champagne swimming in my blood and his cologne swirling through my senses.

I could say it's the drink going to my head, the seductive music that floats around us, but I swear his need is pressing between us, beneath the shield of his sporran. I want to make a joke of it, a tease— *is that your sporran talking or are you just pleased to see me?*

If I was myself, I would…hell, I'd even make it into a serious come-on.

But Jackson isn't just any guy I have a crush on;

he's Jackson and he's made it clear we can never be. It doesn't stop me wanting it though.

It doesn't stop me curving into him ever closer, tighter, head to toe. Forgetting how to breathe, or speak, or do anything other than follow his expert lead. He can dance, really dance, and I'm wrapped up in his hypnotic rhythm, following him step for step, sway for sway, arse grope for arse grope...*almost*.

A little giggle rises up within me. It's nervous, ridiculous, but he only holds me closer, his hard, muscular warmth seeping into my sensitised skin, the delicate silk of my dress doing nothing to hinder its penetration. Nothing to ease his effect on me.

Tradition dictates that we have this dance—or rather it dictates that we have *one* dance, but that was three songs ago, after the Bride and Groom had shared their first. The fact that he hasn't stepped away, that neither of us have ended this sudden intimacy, isn't lost on me and hope swells.

I tilt my head back, intending to say something, anything, but my lips merely part, words lost in the darkness of his eyes way above mine. His impressive height and brawn make my petite frame feel all the more so.

I know his eyes are grey, steely grey and swoon-worthy, but right now they are as dark as the night outside and glittering with so much... I want to say passion, but I know my hope is soaring past the realms of possibility. I tell myself it's the low light of the room, the ambient lighting from the low-hung chandeliers sparkling in their depths, giving the impression of it, rather than its existence. But the wild state of his dark, overlong hair only adds to the dizzying effect, convincing me, pushing me to believe he wants just as I do.

I wet my lips. His eyes flicker again and his fingers on my lower back flex.

'Jackson?'

I'm not sure what the question is on the tip of my tongue, I only know one exists.

One I couldn't ask of him in London.

One that has the power to end this night doing what I've dreamed of since I accidentally fell into his lap that first night at Blacks, six years ago.

His lips quirk to one side—strong, masculine, full, and so perfectly edible I can almost taste them.

'Caitlin?'

His voice is low, husky, as unrecognisable as his jawline is, devoid of its usual stubble. I want him to say my name again, in that exact same tone, with that exact same fire burning in his gaze. He's never looked at me this way, never given me this much of himself in a simple look, a simple word—my name.

A tiny tremor runs down my spine as my brain replays it, inserting all the meaning I believe exists within it and I lean into him closer, stroking my hands up his chest to entwine them behind his neck.

'I never knew a kilt could be so sexy,' I say, my smile all sultry as I toy with the hair at his nape.

His laugh is gruff, the cock of one eyebrow so sexy and sure, and my stomach somersaults, my every response to him magnified this close.

'You know, it's polite to offer a compliment in return…'

Another chuckle rumbles through him and he looks away with a shake of his head. 'You don't give up, do you?'

'Oh, I gave up ages ago, Jackson.' I see no reason to lie. 'But now we're hundreds of miles from London, your argument has lost its hold.'

'My argument?'

I tilt my head to the side and wait for him to meet my eye. He does so, eventually, and I don't miss the betraying little pulse that ticks away in his gritted jaw. He doesn't want to want me…but he does.

'That you won't sleep with the clientele.' I run my teeth over my bottom lip, savouring how his eyes darken over the gesture, his arms tensing around me. 'Club rules and all that frustrating jazz.'

He scoffs. 'You're still a client, Cait. That hasn't changed.'

'Well…' I stroke a hand into the hair at his nape as I bring us to a pause on the dancefloor. 'There's a simple fix to that.'

He doesn't prompt me. I sense he's holding his breath, waiting, wanting. I'm so close I can almost taste victory. I wet my lips, swallow past the need choking up my throat and blink up at him. 'I can revoke my membership, Jackson, effective immediately.'

'It's not that simple,' he rasps.

'And why not?'

'It's just not.' I hear the strain, the desperation

even, and start to smile anew. 'You have to give notice, Cait, and there are payments, arrangements...'

'Excuses, excuses, Jackson. Surely those things
only apply when one has behaved well and stuck to
the pesky rules...' I catch the rising heat in his gaze
and victory pumps hot and fast in my veins. 'You
see, I have no intention of being good...' I reach up
on tiptoe, brush my lips beside his ear, all breathy.
'In fact, I have every intention of being bad, Jackson.
Very. Very. Bad.'

'*Jesus*, Cait.'

His hands are on my hips so fast, their grip flexing and pulsing as he forces me down and spins us
back into the music.

'What, Jackson?'

He shakes his head, diverts his gaze, but I see
enough to realise this isn't about the club at all. It
hits me, winds me, makes me frown. Something else
is coming between us, something so profound he's
tormented by it.

'What's going on, Jackson?'

'It's not just the club, Cait.' He shakes his head like
he doesn't want to be saying any of this. 'There are
other reasons I won't...that we shouldn't.'

'Then tell me. Explain it to me, because right now
I have a thousand wants and every one of them involves you and a shitload of debauched fun.'

His eyes spear me; they flash wild with hunger,
fringed with panic. 'Don't do this.'

But I'm past putting the brakes on. I'm too close,
we're too close to acting on this heat that's plagued

us for so long. 'What? Don't push you into admitting what's there between us? Don't make you dance another track up close and personal? Because believe me when I say it's not just my desire that has us dancing long after our duty is done.'

'It will never end well.'

'The dance?' I tease, but he doesn't laugh and his eyes don't sparkle with amusement. They're still plagued and hot with a desire I can feel right down to my toes.

'Or...' I rise up, his hands on my hips failing to restrain me now as I pause close enough to feel his breath brush over my lips, to see his own part '...do you mean the sex, Jackson? Because I beg to differ: sex *always* ends well when the spark is as powerful as this.'

I lift my lashes, my eyes lock with his and the truth sears me to the bone: no one has ever triggered a spark in me as powerful as this. No one but him.

And that realisation should have me running, not pushing for more. Because this will never have a future. I know that as much as I know he wants me now.

Whatever the demons that haunt him, they will always put a stop to anything more. He's a self-professed bachelor and I may be confident in my appeal, but I'm not so naive as to think I can break him.

No matter how much I long to.

Do you mean the sex, Jackson?
Sex—sex with Cait.
Fuck.

She's wicked. Wicked, seductive and too damned attractive for her own good.

A tiny bundle of carefree fun… Only Cait's eyes have lost their usual carefree sheen, their striking ring of blue as they darken and intensify, projecting a wildness that my body is only too willing to respond to.

I should have ended this after the very first song. The proximity, the closeness, the whole fucking dance. All I had to do was one track. A tick in the dutiful Best Man box.

And run.

Hell, the second I caught sight of her at the entrance to the aisle this morning I should have shut my body down and *mentally* run, because I *knew* what trouble lay ahead.

Yes, the bride was stunning, Coco was perfect in every way, but Caitlin—*fucking Caitlin*. I couldn't breathe. I couldn't tear my eyes away. She is my every fantasy. The reason I fuck my fist too often to admit and why I don't ever go there. Not with her. *Never* with her.

But there she was. Her flaming red hair, usually free and wild, tied back at her nape, exposing her shoulders and the flimsy shoestring straps that hold her dress in place. The presence of a bra, something to debate, to torment myself over. I do it now, just as I did this morning, my body overheating as she stepped ever closer, provoking me with all her grace and poise. The delicate green silk of her floor-length dress sets off her auburn hair and clinging to her every curve, the split to her thigh teasing with a hint of leg. The dipped V meets with a slash of tartan at her waist, unveiling the freckles that run a teasing path down. Freckles that I stared at for far too long as she walked up the aisle, but snapping my eyes up only led me straight into hers.

And that look.

I close my eyes and squeeze the image out. I switch direction on the dancefloor out of time and cause her to stumble. She leans into me further and I tighten my grip.

Like that's going to help.

'Come on, Jackson,' she coos softly. 'You know I'm talking sense.'

I refuse to answer. I refuse to even look at her as I scan the room, desperately seeking distraction. But the challenge in her eyes across the aisle and in my arms now, the want, desire, need—the sight is burned into my brain. I continue to see it. I continue to feel the effect of it all the way to my disobeying dick, which wants nothing more than to seek satisfaction for the last six years of denial.

Around us I take in people dancing, talking, laughing but all I really see is her: her body and eyes aglow, enhanced by the intimate lighting of the room, the amber strands that have escaped the twisted knot at her nape and fall over her flushed cheeks. The combination makes me think of a thousand different reasons she could look like that. Every one of them as debauched as me. More debauched than any fun she has offered…

There's the sex she's accustomed to, and then there's sex with me.

Dark, twisted and fucked up.

Never going to happen.

It's not just how she looks either. It's how she feels. Her warmth beneath my palms and the way she curves into me, her thighs, her stomach, her breasts gently touching.

She tilts her head back and I can't resist a glimpse.

Fuck, she's perfect.

Her cupid's bow lips flush their own shade of pink and I see the tiny gap between her two front teeth that I've wanted to probe with my tongue for so long. Then there's the easy smile that lights up her face, the room, me. She gives it to me now as she eases herself up my body.

Her lips brush against my ear again and I have to stiffen to stop the teasing tremor that threatens to run through me. Worse still, I know the only reason she can reach so high is because I've bowed my head, my body defying my every intent to resist.

'Come on, Jackson, live a little.' Her mouth caresses my ear, her breath sweeps inside—*fuck*. She may as well have tongued the sensitised flesh for what it does to me and now I'm actually relieved that her body is pressed against me, the sporran too. Anything to stop the way my unrestricted erection is free to set up camp under the kilt.

'What happens in the Highlands stays in the Highlands,' she murmurs.

Yes, fuck, yes. Listen to her. Screw your con-

science. She wants you. You've never been a saint, so why now? Why with her?

But I know why.

I take her hand and fling her out, encouraging her to twirl beneath our fingers above her head and re-member too late my predicament down below. Panic, a surge of colour to my cheeks, and I'm yanking her back just as swiftly. Her length comes up hard against my body, her palms too, as she gives a flirtatious giggle.

'Miss me?'

'You could say that,' I grind out, relieved that my kilt is back in place, not so relieved that she's over-powering me anew.

Christ, if you do it, maybe you can move on from this impossible attraction.

Hell, maybe she'll move on and then it will no lon-ger be an issue.

Yes, take her to bed, give her a glimpse of the real you, and it should see her run a mile.

Because if she knew me—the real *me*—if she knew what had gone before, this wouldn't be up for debate. Not that I'll tell her. That's my cross to bear and mine alone.

But a night, one night so far away from home—

'Excuse me, Black, may I have this dance?'

I still at the plummy-toned intrusion. It's Philip. Philip Lauren, Coco's brother. I flick him a look that takes in his hand on my shoulder and he snaps it back.

'I think you'll find it's the Best Man's duty, Lauren.'

I struggle to hide the contempt in my voice, but

loyalty is everything to me and he has yet to earn any of mine. Coco may have forgiven him. Hell, Ash too. But me… I'm not so easily won around. Not when the guy tried to destroy his own sister's reputation less than two years ago and managed to tap a hole in the protective shield I have in place over my club, Blacks. He crossed too big a line for me.

I release Caitlin but my arm wraps around her waist—merely a protective gesture, of course, nothing more—and I'm grateful that Philip's presence works its magic below my waist.

'Of course.' Caitlin speaks before I can respond, and I lift my brow as I look down at her. He can't have won her around too. There's no way. Caitlin is as fiercely protective of Coco as I am. 'I was clearly wasting my time here,' she murmurs, and then a hardness creeps into her gaze. 'I know when I'm not wanted… Come on, Philip, let's show them how it's really done.'

Philip sends me a questioning look, his hesitation clear. He wants to know if he's stepped in, if I'm real competition.

My lips quirk up. I should make it clear I'm not. But it seems my body's less eager to let her go and I want to make him nervous. I tower over him three or four inches at least, and I train daily; I know I'd make light work of him. He knows it too, judging by the way he wriggles his cravat and clears his throat. *Good*.

But then Cait hooks her arm into his and moves out of my hold.

I watch Philip take my place, watch his hands fall to her hips and I clench my jaw tight. I don't do jealousy, nothing close. It was carved into me from the ripe old age of sixteen not to bother with the idiotic sentiment. But as I burn a hole into the dancefloor beneath their feet, I acknowledge I feel far more than I should. I also know it has nothing to do with Philip's shady past and everything to do with my feelings for her.

Hell, even with Philip's past, he's better for her than me.

I spin away and head to the bar.

You're dark and twisted. She's light and kind. You don't belong together.

Maybe she and Philip…

My fists ball at my sides.

Over my dead body.

CHAPTER TWO

DANCING WITH PHILIP is a blur. I almost feel sorry for him. If not for his questionable past, I likely would do.

But I can't stay on task, I can't focus on him when my mind and eyes constantly wander to Jackson, standing on the sidelines. His presence, dark, brooding, calls to me even though I should know better.

A cheer ripples through the guests and wakes my mind from the stupor that is all Jackson.

Philip and I stop dancing, as do many others, all craning their necks to see what the commotion is, and then I spy the cause. My lips lift, my heart too. There's Ash and Coco making for the exit as the guests around them cheer and toast. A blushing bride swept up in the arms of her husband, their eyes for one another alone, their grins so full of love, of passion.

Philip gently nudges me. 'No need to guess where they're heading, hey?'

I shake my head as I watch them and give a cheer of my own, but I feel it catch, feel a hollowness in my chest, the same empty weight that gripped me during the ceremony. My happiness for them is dampened by a sudden pang of…envy? A wistful longing for something I hadn't known was missing.

Yet the only man I can imagine wanting it with is the one man who's put himself so out of reach…until now, until the glimpse of what I saw in his face as I walked down the aisle this morning.

And, as I did then, I force my smile to widen, my thoughts to quit and I throw my focus into the moment. The celebration. Having fun. It's what I'm good at—*fun*. I'm the life and soul. I don't let things cut too deep. Jackson included.

The band starts up again, a quick number I'm more than happy to get lost in. I throw my focus back into Philip, pull him along with me. *Dance. Have fun. Dance.* It's a mantra in my head, but the more I try and force it, the less it works. The less I'm able to push Jackson out.

His eyes are on me, on us, I know it without looking. I dance faster, I laugh as Philip does the same, I feed off his obvious enjoyment, the mantra building to a crescendo in my head as I twirl—and then I feel it. Nothing.

He's gone.

I come to a halt, my eyes landing on a couple who have taken his place.

I turn on the spot, scanning the crowd, trying not to look bothered, but my stilted movements tell Philip exactly what's amiss. He tries to gather me up in the dance, gain my attention but I shake my head. I can't see Jackson anywhere.

For a brief second I wonder if he's left the castle altogether, such is the sense of loss, and then I realise how foolish that is. We're miles from the nearest village; we might as well be in the middle of nowhere when it comes to sourcing alternative rooms for the night. The small number of holiday cottages and B&Bs in the area are already full to the brim with wedding guests. There is nowhere else for him to go.

No, Jackson, just like me and the rest of the bridal party, have been given rooms in the newly renovated east wing of the castle and, if I remember rightly, he's only two doors down from me.

Two doors…hardly a walk at all.

'Can I get you a drink?' Philip asks, vying for my attention.

I give him a weak smile, part gratitude, part apology. 'I'm good, thanks though.'

'You're good, but you have somewhere else you'd rather be.' He gives me a grin to soften his words and rakes a hand through his blow-dried hair that's just too perfect for me to find attractive. I prefer it darker, longer, untamed… 'Prefer a bit of rough, hey?'

I laugh. I can't believe he's vocalised my exact thoughts and I'm too stunned to try for a lie. 'You could say that.'

'And I'd say I couldn't blame you. Ash and Coco certainly like the guy.' He scans the crowd now too, looking for the topic of our conversation. 'I struggle to see the appeal myself. He looks like he could kill by look alone.'

I laugh even harder. 'True.'

He gives a mock shudder. 'Putting that quality aside though, he quite obviously has a thing for you, so I guess the feeling is mutual.'

I still, my eyes narrowing on him. 'You think?'

'You don't?'

'Yes, no, yes— *Hell*, I don't know.' I smooth an unsteady hand over my hair. I don't like being un-sure. I pride myself on being able to read people. I run a PR firm, for Pete's sake, a very successful PR firm; I *know* people. But Jackson...

I feel my head shake. Why does he do this to me?

You know why... You like that he puts you on edge. You like the challenge. You like him...and you want a whole lot more.

And if Philip, a total outsider whose opinion isn't tainted by his own feelings, thinks it's mutual, then I'm not imagining it.

I just need Jackson to get over whatever's stop-ping him.

Maybe it's some weird big brother stance. He's been my agony aunt more times than I can count. Not that he looks the part, but he is. He listens. He's let me drown my sorrows at the bar, rant and rave about my over-protective family, celebrated my latest PR win, teased me over my outfits, my cheek, my flir-tatious exploits.

But never has his facade cracked. Never has he hinted that he wants the same.

Until today...and it's an opportunity I can't let slip away.

'Sorry, Philip, I just need to...'

I'm already walking in the direction of the exit and working out where to try first.

Where would I go if I were sexually frustrated to the extreme?

I smile. The idea of him being so hot for me that he's had to take himself off is an aphrodisiac in itself.

If it were me, I'd go outside for air, to cool down. But then I'd be no more satisfied. The bedroom, however—there I'd be able to tend to my needs privately. The image of Jackson taking himself in hand has my smile widening, my lower body pulsating with carnal heat, and I realise, regardless of which way he's gone, *I'm* the one needing air now. Because when I find him I want to be in control of this.

I want to be able to walk away with my head held high if he rejects me again.

And if he surrenders himself to it… *Oh, yes*, I want him to be the one who closes the deal. Who kisses me and seals our fate. I will seduce to a point, but I need to know both his body and mind are in the driving seat. I have no interest in regrets that come later, in backing him into a corner and having his body do all the talking.

I want him to *want* me, unreservedly.

I break out into the grand entrance hall and slow my stride, not wanting to draw attention or appear too eager in case he's there.

Calm, collected, in control, I scan the vast room. A few guests stand before the fire burning in the hearth sipping drinks and a couple are canoodling up against one of the ornate pillars supporting the imperial staircase above. Another couple are leaning precariously close to a freestanding floral arrangement that has three lit candles at its heart. I consider interrupting their full-on snog-fest before the lady's hair catches fire, but I doubt they'd even hear me.

Wedding fever, it seems, is contagious. Maybe I've caught it too and that's why I'm so on heat. *Yeah, right.* I want to laugh at the very idea as I scan the twin staircases and what I can see of the landing above. I know I'm like this because of the change in Jackson, the change that tells me I'm *this* close to getting what I've wanted for so long.

If only I can find him…

Rooms, or outside? My gut says the latter. I cross the entrance hall, my heels click-clacking against the gleaming parquet floor and drawing the eye of the doorman standing beside the impressive doorway.

'Ma'am.' He gives me a smile and I contemplate asking if he's seen Jackson, but when I run through my description of him in my head it's enough to keep me tongue-tied.

I'll just go outside and look for myself.

I return his smile. 'It's rather warm in here. I think I need some air.'

'Do you have a coat I can get for you?'

'No need.'

It's August and not exactly balmy this far north, not when you're used to the city heat, but either Jackson isn't out there, in which case I'll be back soon, or he is, and I won't be needing a coat to warm me.

He gives me a nod as he pulls open the door and

the cool night air greets me, sweeping over my skin and causing goose bumps to instantly prickle. I breathe it in, feel it soothe and calm. The air is so different here, so clear and crisp. I realise the door-man is waiting for me to move off before closing the door and I'm letting all the chill in by standing there. I shoot him another smile and promptly move off, my eyes sweeping over the grounds.

It really is beautiful, an idyllic retreat surrounded by nothing but rolling hillside strewn with heather that now gives off a dusky purple hew in the moon-light. The moat that runs around the four-turreted cas-tle glistens black, white and grey. The clear sky above twinkles with a zillion stars that you wouldn't be able to see in London. And straight ahead the stone-built bridge joining the castle to the mainland sparkles with fairy lights, the same fairy lights that have been used in the potted plants that mark out the driveway and were brought in especially for the wedding. There's no way their delicate foliage would survive long in a Scottish summer, let alone winter.

And, in truth, I'm not sure I would either in noth-ing but this bridesmaid dress.

I shiver. But it's not just the cold. It's an awareness of him. He's here, I know he is.

I don't realise I've stopped walking until I sense movement to my left and that's when I see him. I can only make out his silhouette leaning against the trunk of a very old tree, but I know it's him. No one else has the same imposing frame, the same assured stance. He rakes a hand through the wildness of his hair and stares out at the water. Pensive. Reflective.

Have I driven him here? Or is there something else that's sent him seeking the quiet solitude? Either way, I now feel like I'm trespassing, intruding.

I go to turn back and stumble on the gravel beneath my heel. 'Oopsie.'

I clamp my hand over my mouth.

Oh, God, did I really say that out loud?

'Caitlin?'

Busted.

Too late to go back now.

I straighten and turn towards him, tentative, sheepish. 'Sorry, I didn't mean to disturb you.'

'No?' Even across the distance I can imagine the amused spark in his eye, the one-sided slant to his lips that triggers a ripple of warmth through my lower belly. 'Then what exactly are you doing?'

'I… I thought I'd get some air.' I raise my chin, shake out my hair—a force of habit since it's pinned back—and close the distance between us. My smile is small, my pulse racing with every step. How can one man be this good-looking? This distracting? This overpowering?

I'm grateful for the chilling wind now as it suddenly picks up around us, blowing strands free from the twisted knot at my nape and staving off the inner heat.

'You know the saying,' I continue. 'Great minds think alike.'

'And you didn't think to put on a coat?'

I take a leisurely tour of his body, his loosely knotted cravat, the navy waistcoat and Argyll jacket that strain over his frame and yet fit him perfectly. My journey slows as I take in the black sporran hanging low over his front, concealing, disguising…the navy and green tartan of his kilt that coordinates with his cravat and ends above the knee. Slower still, I take in the exposed knees, the black socks with the sheathed knife, and swallow before meeting his eye again.

'I think we're fairly even on the clothing stakes.' I'm proud of how steady I sound.

He laughs, the surprising roar gruff and seductive as his smile spreads, the shake of his head sending a lock of hair curling over his forehead. 'Fair point. So, you bored of Lauren already?'

I pause before him, close enough that if I were to reach out I could touch him, and I flutter my fingers against my hips. Oh, how I want to touch him.

'Bored, no.' I toy with what to say next. I don't want to push him away, scare him off like I sensed I did in the ballroom, but… His scent travels on the breeze, flooding me with another rush of warmth, another hit of what I so desperately want, and I forget caution. 'He's not the man I'd rather be with.'

He pushes off the tree. 'And I shouldn't be the one you do.'

Damn it. He goes to move past me and I reach out, my hand gentle on his arm, the heat of his body seeping into my palm as he pauses, eyeing my hand. I can feel the ongoing debate in the tension under my fingers, see it in the pulse ticking away in his jaw, but I can't stop this any more than I can stop my eyes from feasting on him.

'I'm twenty-six, Jackson. I think I can decide that for myself.'

His eyes lift to mine, and I see it all. The darkness, the same torment I witnessed on the dancefloor...

'What is it, Jackson?' I squeeze his arm softly. 'Just tell me.'

He's quiet, still, and I frown as I lose myself in his eyes, desperate to understand. I've never seen Jackson pensive, troubled, torn between taking what he wants and...well, walking away. He's all fun and games in the club, *his* club. He teases, he provokes, but there he has his rules.

Is he hiding behind them? Are they some kind of crutch for whatever this is?

Regardless, I hate the idea that I've done this to him and I'm damned if I'll leave him hanging with it now.

'If you don't want me, you only have to say the word and I'll leave you alone, I promise. My ego can take it.' I add the last for good measure, hoping to tease out a smile at least and reassure him all is okay between us. That we'll always have this, our friendship.

He takes a breath and looks away from me, his laugh small, more of a sigh.

'If only it were that simple.'

He lifts my hand from his arm but doesn't release it.

'I don't *want* to want you, Caitlin...' I can hear the

vehemence in his tone, see it in his eyes as they come back to me hard and soft all at once. 'I want you far enough away from me that you are safe.'

My laugh is startled, unnaturally high, but his choice of words is extreme, ridiculous even. I've never felt safer than I do when he is near.

'In case you've forgotten, you saved me the very first night we met.'

'That was different.'

'No, that was a man taking advantage and one word from you and I was released... Granted, it was your club and granted, I did land in your lap, but you see, you're like my knight in shining armour. How can I possibly be anything but safe with you?'

He's silent again and his hesitation is driving me crazy. Crazier than six years of living with this undercurrent. His eyes blaze into mine and a sudden shiver ripples through me in time with the breeze.

'You're cold.' Before I can deny it, he's releasing me and shrugging off his jacket, flicking it out to wrap it around my shoulders. I'm cocooned in his residual warmth, his scent, his... Oh, God, my lashes flutter closed and my nostrils flare as I breathe him in. When I open them again he's there, so close.

So fucking close.

'Cait...'

It's a groan and his eyes fall to my lips, burn into them. *Yes, kiss me.* I'm pleading, begging, my lips parting, ready, so ready. I slowly run my teeth over my lower lip and he snaps, his growl fierce, a split second before his mouth claims mine.

Yes, God, yes.

It's desperate, urgent, his tongue delving deep as his grip tightens over my upper arms, holding the jacket in place, or holding me closer, or trying to fight it. I don't know but I'm dizzy. Dizzy on an explosion of sensation that starts with the taste of whisky, the roughness of his tongue as it grazes mine, and ends with the delicious tension coiling through my body. The pooling heat and the pulsing ache between my legs demand satisfaction.

He spins me against the tree, another growl low in his throat, and I feel his frustration, his anger at himself as he tears his mouth away. I suck in a breath and open my eyes to look up into his. They're still tormented, plagued by a fire that's not all desire, and I want it to be. I want the pain, the battle, the barrier—whatever it is, gone.

'What are you doing to me?' His breath rasps over my lips as he strains ever closer, but not close enough.

He shakes his head and presses his forehead to mine, his ragged breath bursting over my front, down the valley between my breasts, teasing at the goose bumps still alive. He squeezes his eyes shut and the second he opens them again I sense the shift, his surrender and resignation, but it doesn't make me as relieved as it should.

'If we do this…it's for tonight only, Cait. There can be no repeats, no playing around when we go back to our lives in London.'

'But—'

'But nothing, Cait, this is it.'

'If you *just* let me finish, I never said I wanted more…' I say it confidently, more confidently than I feel because hell, I know I'm going to want more. I've wanted him for six years; returning to London won't suddenly change that. Neither will one roll in the bedsheets—or the heather even. 'Did I?'

'No.'

'This is just sex, Jackson,' I say, forking my fingers through his hair. 'You know, that thing people do in your club to let off steam? I'm sure we can manage it here without any strings.'

'I'm sure we can manage a great many things.'

I laugh softly. 'Anything in particular spring to mind?'

I feel the tension in his body start to ease, feel the battle continue in my favour.

'Too many.' It's so gruff, so husky, so fucking sexy. 'The things I've wanted…the things I've fantasised about doing…'

Whoa, whoa, whoa.

'Rewind!' I press my palm into his chest. 'You've *fantasised* about me?'

His swallow is confession enough, the tension returning to his body, cording his neck, creating lines either side of his mouth.

'And you're only just admitting it to me now?' A spark of anger hits. 'Do you *know* how I've driven myself crazy fantasising about *you*? But no, you have to stick to your no-shagging-the-clients rule.'

'You're angry?'

'Hell, yeah!' I shove against him, forcing him back

a step. 'We could have had this done and dusted years ago and had it put to bed.'

His eyes flash. 'In the literal sense?'

'*Fuck*, Jackson! Is this some weird game you're playing?'

'No.'

And I believe him. That one simple word is so raw, and I know he means everything he has said.

'So why now? What's changed?'

'I'm listening to you and you can be very persuasive when you want to be.'

'But I'm still a member of your club?'

He rakes his hand through his hair, breathes in deeply and looks to the heavens before looking back to me.

'Hell, Cait, the club is so far from my mind right now.' He palms the trunk above my head, leans over me. 'But it's true—you shouldn't shit where you eat.'

I choke out a laugh. '*Shit?* Really?'

There's a spark of humour in his eyes, a glimmer of the Jackson I'm used to. Fun, teasing, easy-going. 'Sorry PR lady, would you prefer I said you shouldn't dip your pen in the company ink?'

Another laugh. 'Better.'

His eyes scan my face, softening and serious all at once.

'But it's more than that with you…' His hand falls to my cheek as he cups my jaw, the delicate touch stalling my breath. 'I don't want to hurt you.'

'You won't,' I manage to whisper.

'You can't know that.'

'I do.' I nod in his hold, fighting the urge to kiss his palm—too sentimental. 'I trust you, Jackson. I trust you enough for this one night, or...'

My brain is racing ahead. We're here for three days. There are activities planned. A timetable with various gaps, night-time hours. 'Why not make it three?'

I watch his jaw pulse. 'Three?'

'We're here for a few more days.' I shrug with the nonchalance I know I need to convey. 'Why not make it a holiday fling?'

I look down at his sporran and toy with its flap. I seriously do have the hots for his attire. I wonder if I can get someone to wear something similar down south when the mood suits.

Yeah, right. I shoot the idea down. It leaves me cold. Not even the Groom himself—the tall, dark and ruggedly handsome Ash—can beat the appeal that is all Jackson.

And again, I'm back to the same conclusion. It's him. Not wedding fever, not his clothing, not his no-sex-with-clients rule that I'd love to flout, but him. Purely him.

The tiny sense of foreboding that has threatened to creep in since I started this merry dance perks up, but I refuse to listen. I fill my mind with the various 'things' he has hinted at and let the heat take over.

'A holiday fling?' he repeats back at me.

I raise my fingers to his cravat and toy with it as I lift my eyes to his and project every carnal thought.

'While we are here anything goes, and then we go back to life as it was, just friends.'

'Just friends. Agreed. And no one will know, not even Ash, Coco?'

'Well, Coco kind of has a way of—' I stop talking as he shakes his head.

'Not even Coco, Cait.'

'Okay.' I look at him and the sense of foreboding swells. Is this about his rules still, or is it something more? And hell, why do I care if it means I can finally have him? Why am I overthinking this?

I just need to keep in mind it's just sex. Incredible mind-obliterating sex. Nothing that runs deeper, no feelings, no future…

But what if this changes things?

What if we're putting our friendship at risk?

Panic clambers up my throat and I swallow it back before he sees it. I can keep this under control. I've lived with this dogged attraction for six years; at least now I'll have the memories when we move on, and he's agreed the same.

If he can do it, I sure as hell can.

'Agreed, Cait?'

I give a harried nod and yank his cravat to bring him closer. 'Now hurry up and kiss me before I'm forced to climb you.'

His laugh is so fucking sexy, the flash of desire on his face seconds before he crushes me to the tree and claims my lips sexier still.

There's no foreboding now. I feel like I'm dream-

ing again, and this isn't a dream I want to wake up
from any time soon. Not now.

Not ever.

No feelings... Really?

CHAPTER THREE

My control is slipping into the moat behind me. All I can hear are her panted breaths, her moans trapped low in her throat, and I want more of them. More of her. But we're outside, it's cold, and the goose bumps that I witnessed over her skin the second before covering her in my jacket tell me she feels it.

I try to tear my mouth away, to usher her inside, but her hands are in my hair, refusing to release me. And then she arches and my jacket opens up around her, her breasts pressing into my chest, and there's no stopping this now. My hands are there, desperate, hungry, my growl fierce. She's really not wearing a bra. Their warmth is too acute, their softness too pliable and her nipples—*fuck*—their pebble-like nubs press into my palm, daring me on.

I bite at her lip, punishment for teasing me all day, punishment for teasing me all these years—and she moans, claws at my shoulders, giving as good as she gets.

Fuck, I'm in too deep. I know it, but it's not enough to stop.

From the second she fell into my lap six years ago and gave me a glimpse of her every curve, her melodic voice, her easy smile, I've dreamed of this. Spent too long conjuring up her sounds, sounds I've heard in the club enough times, their effect as visceral as if she'd uttered them, and now she is under *my* touch, *my* caress, *my* attention.

'I want you,' she says against my lips, lifting her leg and causing the split to part as she wraps it around me, drawing me up against her, only the blasted sporran gets in the way and she laughs as I curse.

'I made a joke about that earlier,' she pants before tongue-fucking me deeper, distracting me from asking what it was. I'm too busy tasting her, exploring her, feeling her skin prickling beneath my palms— *she's cold, remember.*

'We should go inside.'

'This is too much fun.'

'You're cold.'

She laughs. 'You're kidding, right?'

I bow to her neck, taste her skin, her perfume. 'You have goose bumps.'

'And they're for you, Jackson, not the chill.'

I smile into her throat, into her collarbone. I roll my thumbs over each tautened peak and listen to her breath hitch. 'You like that?'

Her laugh is trapped in her throat now. 'Not obvious enough?'

I capture one nub in my thumb and forefinger and pinch: *Dare to mock.*

She bucks against me. It's another carnal punishment and I have so many more under my belt. So many more that I need to cage. Because this is Caitlin, and I'll never take her down my twisted path.

'More Jackson, *more*.'

I raise my head to look down at her. Even in the moonlight I can see her cheeks are streaked pink, her skin flushed with desire, eyes glassy and wanton. I repeat the move, only harder, and she bites her lip.

'Don't push me,' I say.

A little crease forms between her brows. 'Why not?'

Her question cuts right through me, to my inner battle, my torment, my darkness.

'You might not like what you find.'

She has the audacity to laugh and I frown. My erection is pressing painfully between us. The heat is too much to bear. And she…she laughs?

'This isn't funny.'

She bites her bottom lip, the move so damn seductive I have to run my thumb over the trapped flesh, force her to release it so I can breathe.

'Tell me it's not funny.'

Her lustful eyes dance and the crease between her brows deepens.

'*Say it*, Caitlin.' I hold her chin steady, my stare hard.

Her lashes flutter as she breathes in deeply, her eyes searching mine for answers she doesn't even know the questions to, and then with her outward breath comes her obedience. 'It's not funny.'

My cock pulses, loving her compliance.

'Say it again.'

The crease eases between her brows as her eyes relax and blaze in one. She's a swift learner. 'It's. Not. Funny.'

I lift her chin higher. 'Better. Again.'

She tilts her head back under her own steam now and says it again, stronger, and my cock bucks beneath the kilt as the power I'm addicted to rushes my veins.

'*Again.*'

'It's.' She drags her hand down my front.

'Not.' She slips between the sporran and my kilt— *you should stop her*.

'Funny.' She takes a hold of me through the fabric and *fuck*, I squeeze my eyes shut against the intense rush of pleasure, grab her wrist and pull her away.

'*No.*' I take up her other wrist, forcing them both above her head. 'You don't touch me until I say.'

I'm the one in charge. I'm the one in control. *Always*.

'If we do this, there are rules…' I tower over her, staring into her darkened gaze that reflects the moon back at me, and try to forget that by my own reasoning she is forbidden to me. That we shouldn't be crossing this line. That she is Caitlin. Fun, flirty, spirited, a candle to my dark. I don't want to taint her, break her, but I know no other way.

'I thought we'd put those aside, left them at the club door, so to speak.'

'I'm not talking about the club.' This is about me. My shit. But I can't say that.

'Oh?' Her eyes light up. 'You mean you have rules in the bedroom?'

She practically purrs it out and I almost grind against her, so desperate am I to take her. Desperate *and* scared at the same time. It's a complete headfuck but I can't go back, not now I've tasted her, felt her... but she needs to know what she's letting herself in for.

I force a nod. 'You do as I say at all times.'

'*All* times?'

She's looking up at me, wide-eyed, curious, so fucking turned on.

'If you can't deal with that, this ends now.'

She wets her lips, looks to where I have her hands pinned to the tree trunk and nods.

It's not enough. I need her verbal affirmation.

'Okay?' I push, my fingers flexing around her wrists. They're so small in my grasp, dainty, just like the rest of her. She's all strawberries and cream, freckles and ivory skin, and me... I couldn't be more different, inside and out.

She nods again, her eyes falling to mine.

'Say it.'

'O-okay.'

I take a ragged breath, pulling on my reserves just to speak; I've never needed my control more and the way she's looking at me, the way she's captive to my spell...

'Leave your hands above your head until I say otherwise.'

She nods, the pulse working wildly in her throat as it bobs. 'Okay.'

'Good.'

I release my hold over her to trail my fingers down her arms, my eyes never once leaving hers. My jacket is wedged between her back and the tree, but it offers her no protection now; it's fallen away from her shoulders, leaving them bare save for the slender shoestring straps. I run my finger beneath one, aware of her every response, how her breath catches and her lips part.

'Bring this arm down,' I instruct, continuing to run my finger beneath the strap, and slowly she does as I ask. 'Good girl.'

I tease the strap to the side, let it fall in a low loop at her elbow, and even though I know I'm unveiling her as I encourage the cup of her dress away and slip her arm through the strap, I'm still not prepared for the rush that assaults me as her breast is exposed. The milky skin prickles with goose bumps, the tiny rose-tipped nub is small and puckered and so ripe for touching.

'Now this one.'

She lets me slide the other strap away and I can scarcely breathe for the tension drawing my body tight.

'Raise them again.'

She does as I ask, her arms forming a diamond above her head, her breasts lifting with the move and offering up her tautened nipples. *Sweet Jesus.* I drag in a breath, fighting the urge to cup them. They're perfect, not quite a handful but perfect in their small, sweet roundness, and exactly how I imagined her to be.

I've not let myself catch more than a glimpse of her in the club. Not because I didn't want to. *Christ*, how I wanted to; I wanted to see every last inch of her exposed to my gaze.

And that's just it—*my* gaze, nobody else's.

I wanted her for me.

And now I can have her; for a finite time she's mine and the control that I depend on, the control that I *insist* on and have done for the last twenty years, is sliding away so swiftly I think I'm falling. Or maybe I already have, and this is my punishment, to have her once—or thrice—and have to walk away?

It's why I don't touch her naked skin, not yet. It's a test—a test I have to pass.

I bow my head and seek out her mouth with mine, a single taste—and groan as my body aches for more, as her mouth opens and seeks more too. *No*. I lift my head just enough to stop her and stroke my fingers up her arms, her soft skin teasing my fingertips, her tiny tremors pleasing, oh, so pleasing.

'I want you to touch yourself,' I murmur.

She shivers, her hum a nonsensical response, and I step back, creating enough distance so that I can see all of her. Her skin glows pearlescent in the moonlight; her head is angled back, exposing the delicate arc of her neck, the line of collarbone. Her bare breasts rise and fall with her harried breaths, an eye-catching dance, and then there's her dress. It's held up by the tartan sash at her waist and the moonlight creates slashes of green against black that run to the floor, save for where the split parts over her thigh. She has her leg angled just so, a seductive pose. A vision that I want to imprint on my memory and recall over and over again.

Her throat bobs as she wets her sweet cupid's bow lips and I recall my instruction that she has yet to follow. 'Not shy, are you, Cait?'

She looks it; she suddenly looks coy and all manner of lovely things I want to provoke.

'Here?'

I nod.

She glances towards the entrance of the castle, soft strands of escaped hair fluttering over her flushed cheeks. The faint sound of music steadily flows on the breeze towards us, broken up by the odd cheer from the guests, the drunken revelry. She spies a light turning on in a room upstairs and runs her teeth over her lower lip. I know she does this—she's done it enough times today alone—but it's a habit. A thing she does when she's excited, nervous or outright flirting. And being the target of it… I swallow against the surge of lust and address her sudden hesitation.

'They can't see us from this angle; it's too dark…' My voice is so tight I hardly recognise it. 'But imagine if they could, what a sight you'd make.'

Her eyes come back to me wide, so full of want, of need. *Fuck*. What a sight she's making, right now, for me…

But then she frowns. 'Do you truly find me sexy, Jackson?'

I almost choke on my tongue; it feels too big for my mouth. 'What?'

'I've often wondered, often hoped,' she says softly, 'but never…you've never once hinted…'

'Yes.' It's abrupt, definite. *Jesus*, how could she doubt it? Standing before me, brazen in the semi-clothed state I've left her, her arms raised above her head, vulnerable and exposed, because I asked it of her.

'Yes, I find you sexy, Caitlin.' I let my gaze linger on her exposed skin, feeding the desire that's burning a path all the way to my groin, testing my control, and the truth is out: 'I find you sexier than is safe.'

'Safe?' Her eyes sparkle, amused, curious now. 'There's that word again—though I'm not sure whether you mean safe for you, or for me…'

I can't answer her, and thank fuck I don't need to because she's already moving, her hands trailing down the tree trunk, over her shoulders and down the valley between her breasts. She shudders, her lower lip catching in her teeth, baring that alluring gap as she stares at me all heavy-lidded now.

'You are…exquisite.' It's the only word I can think of to describe how she looks right now, and still it's not enough. The moonlight makes her look ethereal, magical, and I could almost believe this isn't real. That it's a dream, and we can be safe in a dream. I'm still denying myself a touch, a caress, something which would make it *feel* more real, and I fist my hands at my sides. *Not yet.*

I follow the path of her fingers as she trails them

around each flushed peak, not quite brushing against their pleading hearts.

'Tweak them,' I grind out, 'like I did.'

She does it. Fuck, she does it and it's everything. Her eyes are languid, her whimpers carnal and wanton as she brazenly pinches and rolls. I drink her in, all that is familiar and new. Her delicate fingers doing what I've only ever imagined before. The bands of twisted gold that she wears on several fingers glint in the white light, and oh, how I want to run my mouth over them, tongue them, toy with them.

'Feel good?'

She parts her lips, her, '*Yes,*' so quiet, so breathy.

I reach out and start to gather up the skirt of her dress, more blood rushing south as I imagine what colour her underwear will be. It's invisible through her dress; she could be as naked as me beneath.

'Don't stop,' I say as she lowers her hands to help. 'I've got this.'

'Fuck, Jackson.' I love how she says my name, her voice thick with lust, her hands returning to her breasts, more frantic, almost ruthless in their exploration now. I'm driving her crazy but she's driving me crazier, not that she can know it. My control serves many a purpose and that's one. I *need* the upper hand.

But *Christ*, I swear she's my Achilles' heel.

As I listen to the crazed whimpers she utters, watch her skin pink up where she's marked it with her own nails, her own fingers, I'm losing it. The urge to sink my teeth into every indent, every line, to tease her nipples between my teeth—*soon, very soon.* I fight the carnal haze that's descending, thick and fast; only when I'm ready, when my sanity dictates, will I let go.

'Pluck them harder…that's it, baby, let go.'

The hypocrisy of what I'm asking isn't lost on me and I bury the judgement in another power trip as she does exactly that, her uninhibited cry rippling through me, provoking one of my own. I touch upon lace at her hip and sweep my other hand beneath her dress, parting her legs to cup her. I feel her wetness, her pleasing warmth through the lace, and grit my teeth to stave off the heat.

She moves against me, her moan wild, and my cock literally weeps for it all.

'Easy,' I say through my teeth, but my smile when I can manage one is full of satisfaction that she's losing it so completely while I remain in control. I lean back and look down over her; she's not tall but with the gold stilettos adding inches to her she is the perfect height for me, for us. Here. Now.

My cock bucks against the sporran and I feel the cold air sweep beneath my lifted kilt, the pre-cum at my tip tantalisingly warm. It's an alien feeling. I've never worn a kilt before, but now, here, watching her and having the freedom to stiffen up, no restrictive underwear to get in the way, to feel myself so eager, so ready…

I smooth my hands around her hips, hooking them inside the lacy waistband of her thong, and slide them down her thighs, her calves, her ankles. 'Step out.'

Carefully, she does.

'Thank you,' I murmur, looking up at her from this fresh angle and wishing her dress was still raised so I could see her in all her wet glory.

She looks down at me, her smile hot and needy. 'Shouldn't I be thanking you?'

I stand and open up the sporran, slipping the warm lace inside and making the reason for my gratitude clear.

Her lips make the perfect 'O' as the soft sound escapes and I want to tongue it. I want to kiss her so deeply the only sound she can make will come from deep within. But I daren't. Not until I trust I'm still in control. That I've still got this.

'Call it a gift of sorts.'

'Do I get one in return?'

'Hate to break it to you, baby.' I lean close to her ear. 'I'm not wearing any to give.'

When I step back, her eyes aren't on mine; they are below my waist and the obvious effect she has on me. Her turn. I want the evidence of her need. I want to see it glisten in the moonlight, as obvious as the high colour in her cheeks, the fire in her eyes.

'Lift your dress,' I command. She does exactly as I ask.

'Good.' *So good,* my brain repeats for me. 'Step wider. I want to see that sweet pussy of yours, all wet for me.'

My voice breaks and it's so revealing. The way her eyes flash, her skin flushing anew, I know she's heard it too. I curse the vulnerability, the exposure, even as I acknowledge that it turns her on more.

I wet my lips, imagine tongue fucking her, her hands clawing at my hair as I take her to heights she's never seen before, heights I'm scared I haven't been to either.

'Show me what you'd like me to do to you,' I say, blotting out the sudden fear.

Focus on the way this feels, not what it means to you, the fact that this is Caitlin, the only woman who has ever made you crave more and wish you were different.

Not true. The denial is fierce, memories trying to claw their way back to the surface that younger me failed to eradicate. But I'm not the teenager or the man I once was. And she's not Eliza.

She's Caitlin. *Caitlin.* I watch as she holds the dress in place with one hand and trails the fingers of the other lower. My mouth dries, my body pulses; my cock nags me to fist over it, but I refuse to.

I fold my arms, lock my stance and focus on her pleasure.

I keep my control locked in place.

Control which starts with her coming first…and only under my command.

CHAPTER FOUR

I'M HOOKED ON Jackson's gleaming gaze. It's so much more than I ever imagined, being here like this, with his need, his desire so obvious, and all for me.

I'm not just the Caitlin he teases at the bar, the little redhead who always brings out the protective big brother in him. He wants me.

Me.

With one hand gripping my dress in place, I trail my other lower, smoothing over the wrinkled fabric. I know what I'll find as soon as I brush over my curls: the dampness, the need…

God, I want it to be him, his fingers, his caress, but seeing the way his eyes darken, his jaw pulses, power swamps me.

It doesn't matter that he's giving the demands, the instruction, the effect I have on him is as powerful as any command he issues.

'I want you to part me…' I watch his eyes flare at my directness and fall to the V I create with my fingers, separating my folds, exposing my slick, wet heat to his burning gaze. Christ, if the cold wind doesn't sweep over my throbbing clit and tease as much as a physical caress from his fingers would.

I keep the dress in place with my arm, freeing my other hand to lower…

'I want you to stroke me…'

My words break as I do just that and my hips buck into my caress, needing the friction, the tantalising roll.

'I want you…'

His jaw pulses; his eyes flick up to mine. 'You want?'

I bite my lip. This is too much—too much force, too much sensitivity. The icy air adds to the thrill as it sweeps over my naked extremities. My nipples, my pussy, my clit.

I shake my head as the tell-tale heat swirls through me, tightening up my limbs, my lungs, my breath.

'Tell me, Caitlin.'

'I want you… I want you.'

'Not enough. You need to *tell* me exactly what you want.'

Through the lusty fog, the whipping heat, I catch something raw, something honest in his voice and I force my eyes open, force them to connect with his, to see through whatever this game is. Because it's more than just sex. Of that I am sure.

Oh, I'll tell him everything, deliver every detailed demand, if that's what he wants, what he needs. Christ, I'll beg if I have to. I'll do anything to see this need sated but the severity, the almost desperate need I see in his gaze, feel in his words, has me sobering just enough to question it, but not enough to douse the heat.

And I know if I question it openly I'll push him away, just as I see the tightrope on which we currently walk. That, regardless of my vulnerability, my partial nakedness, my surrender, he will walk away from this.

What I don't understand is why.

Jackson is always so sure, so in control, so in command of every situation, but I sense a shift in him. A shift that has me reaching out for his hand and drawing him against my breast, my other hand working myself harder, faster, higher.

'Please,' I say, coaxing his fingers over my skin. As much as I love getting off with him watching, I want him a part of this—my undoing, my loss of control.

I want to know he's losing it too.

'What, Caitlin?'

'I want you to be the one doing this, the one cupping my breasts, caressing, teasing, pinching...' I arch back against the tree, thrusting them into his touch as I manipulate his hand into doing as I say. 'I want you to bury your fingers in my...my...'

'Your?' His voice is rough, thick, and his eyes blaze into mine, the colour high in his cheeks, telling me he's on fire with me. He strokes his free hand down my arm, follows its path to the apex of my thighs and hovers.

'Your?' he repeats, more steady, controlled.

'My pussy.' It erupts out of me and the approval I see in his face is almost my undoing.

'I'll do it…on one condition.'

'Anything.' I'm not sure I say it aloud. The blood is whirring in my ears, my body, the pleasure-filled ache fierce and building.

'You cannot come.'

I gasp as my body bucks uncontrollably, my eyes widening into his, dark and stormy, and what the actual fuck?

'Not until I say.'

'What?'

'You heard me.'

I shake my head. 'I never…' pant '…took you…' pant '…for a sadist!'

His eyes flash, his smile darkens. 'Don't worry, baby, I'll let you come, just not yet.'

I rock with the thrill of it, of him getting off on the idea as much as I am.

I nod. It's hurried and pleading and oh, my fucking God, if his hand doesn't drop to my pussy right now I think I'm going to scream, regardless of any unsuspecting audience I may draw, the panic I might spark in him. But he does it. He takes hold of my dress in one hand and nudges both of mine out of the way.

'As you were…' He nods to the tree trunk stretching out high above our heads and I know exactly what he's asking. I raise one arm, then the other, and bite into my lip as he gathers the skirt of my dress in his fist and presses it into the tree beside my head, leaning over me. 'I'm going to stroke you…slow and sure…and you will stay still…*very* still.'

I frown into his eyes. Is he for real?

'One movement and I'll take it away.'

He *is* for real and I nod. God help me, I nod.

I'm not sure I'm even capable of staying still. Hell, I've been going to Blacks for six years; I've lived out many fantasies ten, twenty times over, but prolonged, delayed pleasure like this? Never.

'Good girl.' It's a husky whisper that teases down my spine, making me squirm and wriggle and—

'I said, stay still.'

I bite my lip harder as I stare up at him and clutch my hands together, pressing them back into the cold, harsh wood.

'Better.'

Yes. His gruff approval is enough to make me want to whimper and please him and make this game last. He lifts his hand to my neck, his fingers soft, delicate, a frustrating tease.

'So long as you let me reciprocate later.'

His eyes flick to mine, his fingers pause as they trail over my collarbone. 'That's not how this works.'

I choke back a laugh but I know he senses it, his eyes flashing ever more dangerously.

'I mean it, Cait.'

He's so serious that I want to laugh all the more.

Then I remember his rules—his bedroom rules.

'This is how sex is in my world. If you don't like it then…'

I shake my head. *God, no.* 'Don't stop.'

I clamp my lips together as I breathe in deeply through my nose and let it out slowly, his fingers tracking the movement of my chest as they trail down my skin. His cock juts, lifting his sporran between us, the strength of his need undeniable. He wants me. *Really* wants me. And I've never known a man to want like Jackson does right now and walk away. Would he? Truly?

I stay still, perfectly still; I'm not about to test it. I'm happy drowning in his gaze as he watches his fingers explore my every inch. He barely touches me, his fingers almost hovering rather than caressing, as though it's his body heat, the shift in the air between my skin and his that I feel and it's driving me crazy, making me want to beg, to move, to thrust myself closer.

But I don't.

'So you *can* follow instructions…' I hear the hint of bemusement in his desire-laden voice, wrapped up in that intoxicating approval, and I bite back the retort I want to give. When you're the youngest of five, being told what to do is a life hazard and I hate it. *Hate* it. It brings out my rebellious streak and if he's not careful—*I'm* not careful—it will out and this… whatever this is…will be over. Just as he warned.

He cups one breast, his palm hot and soothing to the intense ache beneath, then his thumb rolls over my nipple and I whimper, fighting the need to move, to beg.

He repeats the caress, again and again, each time the shot of pleasure ups and the battle to remain still intensifies, the mix taking me higher and higher and—he tweaks the sensitised nub, a sudden pinch between his thumb and forefinger, and my body thrashes, my clit pulses.

'Jackson!'

He stops and his hand falls away.

'What did I say?'

I shake my head at him, heaving in a breath. He can't be serious. How can I...? As I look up into his dark, oppressive gaze I quit the mental ramble and realise the battle I have already lost. I wet my lips and soften my voice, all acquiescing and hopeful. 'Sorry, I'll do better.'

It pleases him; the approval is back in his eyes, and, God, does it please me in turn. It shouldn't, it really shouldn't; I'm my own woman, I do what *I* want. But the squirming heat low in my abdomen tells me otherwise.

'Maybe I should take pity on you.'

I want to tell him *yes*, I want to nod, but I'm still too stunned by this turnaround in what makes me tick that I rely on my eyes to do it all and as if he can read them he lowers his hand to the back of my thigh, his palm smoothing upwards, cupping my bare arse, stroking, squeezing.

'I've often wondered what you'd feel like. The curve of your arse has teased me one too many times, Caitlin.'

I want to scold him again for not telling me before, for making me wait for this, but I'm obedient, docile...eager to hear what else he might say.

'Your cheeks are so perfect, so small and round, the perfect shape and size to fill my palm.'

They do, as he squeezes. I feel his fingers delve between them, a second's brush against my puckered opening that has my body wanting to gyrate.

'I could feel you like this, explore you like this for ever.'

For ever. Oh, yes.

He sweeps around to my front, his fingers curving around my thigh, his thumb brushing over my dampened curls, the briefest touch. I bite into my lip harder and tense my body head to toe—*Do not move. Do not end this.*

He rewards me with a deeper sweep, a deeper caress that teases at my swollen clit—*yes.*

'Tell me, do you want to move?'

'Yes.' It comes out strained, needy, desperate, and he grins, his thumb probing and making my nostrils flare, my eyes widen, but I stop my body from bucking just in time.

'Do you want to come?'

'*Yes.*'

'Are you wet for me?'

'*Yes.*'

'Let's find out how wet.'

I don't speak. I swallow. I force down the lump of desire that's wedged my throat closed, and then he rotates his hand, slipping it between my legs. His fingers are hot and teasing as they dip inside me and my pussy clenches around him, desperate to keep him.

He drags in another ragged breath, withdraws his

fingers and raises them between us. He eyes them in the moonlight, all slick with my need. And then he licks them, *fucking licks them*, slow, unhurried. He lets out a hum—no, a *growl*—of appreciation and the heat inside me flares.

'You taste so good, Cait,' he murmurs. 'So fucking good.'

'Wanna share?'

The question surprises him; his eyes flash, his jaw pulses. And I'm so fucking turned on to this game that I fear one more brush over my clit and I'll be gone, regardless of whether he permits me to come or not.

I hold myself stiff as his hand lowers and he slides his fingers between my thighs, only the slightest touch against my throbbing clit as he coats himself in me, and then he's back.

'Lick them clean...' His voice is gruff, his eyes burning into my lips as he presses his slickened fingers against them 'Taste yourself.'

I flick my tongue out, separating his fingers in my eagerness as I loop around each and then I take two in whole, sucking along their length and staring into his eyes that tell me exactly how much he enjoys it. His swallow is audible, his groan too.

'Fuck, Cait, I knew you'd be trouble, always trouble.'

His words penetrate my lust-hazed mind—*trouble*. Why? If this is just sex, why am I trouble?

But I have no time to think about it further as his hand returns to my pussy and slowly, too bloody slowly, he parts me and slides against my clit, back and forth, back and forth, while I remain still. His lazy pace makes my hips want to roll, my body pleading for release as the ache turns painful, persistent and so bloody desperate.

'*Please*,' I beg him.

'Shh.'

I almost want to cry—hell, my eyes are pricking. It's punishing, cruel to keep me in this heightened state. To keep his touch so steady, so measured, so fucking controlled.

He keeps doing it, slipping in and out, in and out, in and out. He doesn't change the tempo, just keeps going as his eyes stare down into mine, almost daring me to move, to plead.

'Such a good girl, such a pleasingly, good girl,' he teases into my eyes. 'What is it? Are you desperate? Am I driving you crazy?'

I let my eyes do all the talking because, I swear to God, I'm going to come any moment. It doesn't matter that his rhythm doesn't alter, that his pressure doesn't vary; every muscle in my body is drawn up tight as it savours as much as it can, using it to feed the spiralling warmth, the delicious tension.

'That's it, baby, can you feel it?'

In. Out. In. Out. *Oh, yes.*

'Bet you wish it was my tongue flicking over your clit. My cock buried deep inside your pussy. My teeth tight around your nipple.'

A whimper escapes, a moan, a cry of pleading.

'Let me come.' It rushes out of me and he chuckles low in his throat, the sound broken by the heavy doors to the castle swinging shut. I hear voices. A man and a woman's laugh. I start to lower my arms and Jackson steps forward swiftly, one hand taking hold of my wrists above my head, his other staying buried within me as his body covers me head to toe and the tree shields us from view.

'Who is it?' I whisper as footsteps approach, the steady crunch of gravel ringing through the night feeling so much louder than it truly is with the fear of being caught like this.

'No idea.' He is so close his mouth brushes against my forehead, his cologne assails my senses, his fingers flex between my thighs, calling me to their presence, the immediacy of what had been my climax. He resumes his intimate caress and my eyes shoot to his in question: *Are we doing this? Still?*

His answer is a grin so full of daring and I resume my obedience; I do not move against his fingers, I do not speak. I listen to the couple talk, the man's soft murmur and the woman's flirtatious laugh. I let the risk rise with the ebb and flow of my own pleasure.

He releases my wrists to cup my chin and drags his thumb over my lips. I want to take it inside my mouth but I daren't. My arms ache above my head, urging me to lower them, but I daren't. My body wants me to whimper, wants me to beg, but I daren't.

My eyes sting more—the denied climax, the crazed battle of wills…it's too much, all too much.

He slips his thumb inside my open mouth, over my tongue, and drags it out, spreading my saliva over my lips as he watches. And then I feel it, the pressure, the ache, coiling up through my toes, my calves, my thighs, my arse, my pussy and I'm going to come. My eyes widen, I give a tiny shake of my head; I hear a twig snap, so close, too close, the guy's chuckle—*Fuck*.

I shake my head more, my eyes pleading into Jackson's warning him, telling him I can't stop this.

He shakes his head back at me. *No.*

I nod and pant, my nails clawing into my hands as I grip them tighter above my head, and I can't hold on, I can't—*fuck!* The explosion inside me is fierce, unrelenting, my body thrashes against his. His mouth crushes mine and I realise I've cursed aloud, but hell, I don't care, I'm delirious on this. On us. It's still within me, pulsing hot, every wave, sharp, incessant, rolling.

His tongue is fierce as he delves inside my mouth, his head slanting over me as he goes in deep, punishingly deep. I hear the woman smother a giggle, hear their footsteps retreat, but they might as well be as far away as England for all I care.

'I told you not to come,' he rasps against my lips. I can hear his displeasure, feel it in the roughness of his kiss. 'They could have heard you.'

I look up into his blazing gaze. 'If you were so worried about that you should have stopped.'

His throat bobs, the crease between his brows severe. 'Hell, I couldn't stop.'

He couldn't stop and it bothers him. Really bothers him. Power floods my veins. I did that to him.

And now I want nothing more than to see him lose it so completely at my hand, my mouth.

'Lucky I like to live on the edge; let's see if you can keep quiet while I do the same to you…'

I go to lift his kilt and he moves lightning-fast, crushing me to him as he forks one hand through my knotted hair and tugs my head back.

'I told you, that's not how this works.'

'Ah, yes,' I say softly, the tug of his hand shooting pleasure straight to my clit. 'Your bedroom rules.'

'Don't test me, Caitlin.'

He thinks I'm making light of them…

'What if I like testing you? What if I want to see the stoic Jackson crack?'

I think about all he has said—*don't push me, don't test me, I want you to be safe*. The thrill of what it can all mean pulses through my body.

He heaves in a breath. 'No, you don't.'

I wet my lips slowly, surely. 'Oh, yes, I do.'

He yanks my head back further, his kiss rough, controlling, and when he pulls away this time my legs are like jelly, my head's dizzy, my pussy's aching with reawakened need.

'Go back inside.'

My stomach plummets. 'But—'

'Go to your room.'

'Like hell—'

He presses a finger to my lips and I frown against it.

'When I come to you, I want you naked and standing before your bed.'

My eyes widen as my frown lifts and I pull his finger from my lips. 'What if someone else walks in?'

'Are you expecting someone?'

My heart gives an excited little squeeze. 'No.'

'Good.'

He steps back and my body instantly pines for the heat of his. I concentrate on righting my dress and he comes to my aid, his hands gentle and contradicting everything else about him.

'Now go.'

He breaks away, turns his back to me, but not before I catch a glimpse of his very real need still thrusting beneath his kilt and I smile as I walk away. I smooth out my dress, my hair—I'm sure I look truly ravaged, but the excited buzz in my veins stops me from caring.

I'm already fantasising about what's to come. Tonight, tomorrow, the day after. What fun we can have in three days…

So much fun that maybe he'll realise we could have so much more.

If he'll give us a chance, a real chance at a future.

No feelings, Cait, remember. This is nothing more than sex. A finite arrangement.

Unless, of course, we both decide otherwise…

CHAPTER FIVE

I DIDN'T TELL her how long I'd be and as I glance at my watch for the umpteenth time I know it's been half an hour, but walking back into a wedding reception teeming with people didn't appeal. Not when I'm in this torrid state of limbo. Between running and staying.

And hell, if I'm honest, the idea of her standing as I commanded, naked and waiting...

I'm the master of building anticipation; my lovers come back to me for just that. But, with Caitlin, she's not just another lover, and I'm also not naive enough to put this entirely down to building her sexual thrill. It's my own too, wrapped up in fear.

Fear of crossing a line we can't come back from.

I try to bury the thought as I scan the landing outside her room. It's deserted save for the eyes that follow me from the antique portraits lining the walls—I run a finger through the inside of my shirt collar. People from years gone by, all seeming to add to my own threatening judgement, telling me that this is a bad idea, that I should keep on walking. That I should get to my own room, lock the door and stay there until this fire inside me subsides.

I blow out a breath and rake my fingers through my hair. There's no calming this fire though, not now I've let her in, *seen* her, felt her come around my fingers, witnessed her all doe-eyed and languid in my arms.

Caitlin. Fun and flirty Caitlin. All *mine*.

I conjure her up, naked and waiting. I plan out what will happen. It's part of my control: no surprises.

I live my life to the full—I've been told, recklessly. But, when it comes to sex, I'm careful. I keep a close leash on everything: my need, what I'll permit, what I'll do, and what I'll let them do in return.

That way it never blurs into something more.

Something that can't be contained. Something that has the power to hurt. I've been there, done that, and I'll never be that weak again.

Yet my hand still trembles as I reach out for the door handle to her room. *Trembles. Fucking trembles.* I don't shake, I don't get edgy, I don't let anything bother me that deeply. But this...

The power of anticipation isn't over her, it's over me right now, a thrill that far surpasses anything I've ever known. I take a second to calm the fuck down and strain to listen through her door.

Nothing.

Will she even be there? Or will she have taken the opportunity to run while she still can? As she should. As I should *want* her to.

Only I don't.

Footsteps down the hall, voices approaching,

spur me into moving and I swing open the door, step straight in and—

I freeze. Hell, the whole world freezes.

I'm barely aware of flicking my wrist to swing the door closed again. Barely aware of the noise of the party still underway downstairs, barely aware of anything but her. My ears fill with the rapid beat of my pulse as it pounds in my head, the words *stupid* and *naive* pounding with it. What the hell am I doing? How did I ever think I could keep *this* under my control?

I try to take in air; I try to steady the vibration that runs through my rigid body and do what I can to ease the strange stuttering in my chest, the instant punch of heat, desire and a far more emotional response that would have me running for the hills if I was capable of it.

She's naked. Just as I instructed. All brazen and coy at once, her arm hooked around a footpost of the four-poster bed behind her, her body entwined with it as she stares at me. And then she moves, a smile lifting her lips as she raises one hand to her mouth and hooks her French-tipped thumbnail in the gap between her teeth.

Is it a nervous gesture on her part or a seductive one? Damned if I know, but the effect it's having below the waist tells me how I see it and I wonder if she knows it too. Knows that for six years I've fantasised about that gap, of probing it while I fuck her and go wild with her, and only her.

My breath shudders out of me as I do my utmost

to regain control but, hell, I can't stop drinking her in. The soft light cast by the bedside lamps plays over her skin, creating a captivating contrast of dancing shadows and gold.

She's freed her hair from its knot and it's wild once more, blazing like a true fire. Her breasts are teasingly concealed beneath her arms as she keeps herself attached to the post, one foot crossing in front of the other, enhancing the slender curve to her waist, the pop of her hip and partially concealing the teasing strip of hair I glimpsed outside.

She's like a painting. A truly magnificent, emotive painting. Pure temptation, all seductive and warm, and the sense of something tender, something alien, grips me. I snap my eyes away, to the bed behind her, but it's no less evocative. The sheets are all ruffled, as though she's lain in it already and writhed, her hands fisted in the deep-red satin, pulling at them as her pleasure builds.

'You took your time,' she says, tugging my eyes back to her.

'Miss me?'

I throw the question back at her, the same teasing line she delivered on the dance floor, and her smile is answer enough.

Fuck this. I throw off the conflicting sense of right and wrong, what's good and bad. What I should want for her, from her, and what I actually do. Six years of keeping this caged only to lose it now, in her bed, at Ash and Coco's wedding of all places.

And I know Coco will crucify me, Ash too, if

they think I've fucked with her, dragged her into my twisted world.

But hell, they've found their happiness; they have it all. Surely I can have one night of insanity.

She asked for three though...

I move before the point registers, before my debate can take hold further, and shuck my jacket. I head for the grand mahogany dressing table that's likely as old as the bed, as old as the castle even, and focus on the mundane, the antiquated beauty of the room. Not her. Anything but her.

I keep every movement slow and steady. I hang my jacket over the back of the dressing table chair, test its sturdiness, assess its anchor points... Yes, many a play routine could be satisfied here. But then I look to the four-poster; it's the real deal.

It's perfect.

The posts have an intricate pattern carved into the wood, weaving in and out progressively, providing sections slender enough for what I have in mind. Especially with her wrapped around it like she is now, all resplendent and waiting. Anticipating.

I pop open the buttons of my waistcoat and watch her tongue brush the back of her thumb as she keeps that nail hooked teasingly between her teeth, her eyes fixed on me.

'Saving me a job?' she murmurs against it.

'You could say that.'

Though the truth goes much deeper and she doesn't need to know it. No one does. Save for the woman who instilled the need in the first place and

I dismiss her as readily as I strip the waistcoat from my shirt. I feel my eyes go to the mirror before me, wanting to see what she sees, what puts that glint of need there, but I don't dare.

I don't want to see my reflection looking back at me.

I don't want to see the judgement, telling me to leave.

I don't want to see the carnal longing that exists either, driving me to do this.

I'm twenty-six, Jackson, I think I can decide that for myself.

Her words, not mine. And I know she said it to reassure me, to draw attention to the fact that she's a woman, not some child who doesn't know her own mind. But I feel so much older—jaded, more like. Ten years and it might as well be an eternity. And she'd laugh if she knew how I feel, I know she would.

In the club I'm Jackson. The easy-going, easy smiling, easy teasing, hell, even easy listening Jackson. Everything is as light and as fun as you need it to be. Me included.

But we're not in the club now; we're in the real world and my façade, if you can call it that, is gone. This is me.

And I know this is Cait. She's always been real, open, honest—my total opposite. Perhaps that's why I'm so drawn to her, why I'm so vulnerable around her…and why I don't deserve her.

I lay the waistcoat over the top of my jacket as the wave of doubt takes over. Doubt I don't want to listen to, and as though she can sense my hesitancy she moves towards me.

'Jackson?'

I drag my eyes to her…and become ensnared by her wide, captivating blues, and the gentle smile that is all the more captivating for the soft hesitation I can read there. I turn my body to face her completely and the sight of her unveiled, no longer half hidden by her stance, makes me drag in air that is filled with her floral scent and I'm almost lost to it, to her.

I shake my head and go for a last-ditch attempt. 'You're playing with fire, Cait.'

Her smile lifts to one side. 'Glad to hear it. I've been getting kind of cold waiting for you.'

I shake my head even more. 'I'm serious.'

'So am I.' She pouts, her eyes raking over me as she stops walking.

'Not everything's a joke, a tease, a bit of fun…'

Please understand me, please run the other way…

'No?' Her eyes flick to mine, her frown as seductive as it is serious. 'I thought sex was fun. Isn't that the point of it? To enjoy it, to go wild…to let go.'

My eyes sweep over her—the delicate breadth of her shoulders, the gentle swell of her breasts, her slender waist curving out to her hips, the smallest strip of hair that protects her modesty and that tender force is back, deep inside, spreading.

'Am I wrong?' she whispers.

'No.' Hell, she's not. It's just sex. Forget the guilt, the worry. I dredge the confidence I need from the darkest depths of my soul and hold her eyes as I remove one cufflink then the other, tossing them on the table. 'You're not wrong.'

I dare to look in the mirror and my stare is hard, determined. It's just sex. A fuck. Nothing more.

I fold one sleeve back then the other, feeling her eyes on me, watching, and when I turn to her I'm in control. I'm ready for this. She'd better be too. I move towards her, untying my cravat as I approach and watch the pulse dance in her throat.

Oh, Cait, you have no idea...

'Hold out your hand.'

I pull the strip of tartan from my collar as she does as I ask, the plump flesh of her bottom lip caught once more in her teeth. I twist the fabric in my hands, fashioning it into a rope, and all the while she watches and waits—obedient, subservient...perfect.

I slip it around one wrist and she sucks in a breath, her eyes flaring into mine. I use it to pull her towards me and she presses her soft, pliant body up against me.

'You sure you want this?'

Her nod is quick, certain. I want to kiss her parted lips but, the moment I do, this becomes something else, something I've not planned...

'You're happy for me to tie you up?'

Another nod.

'I'm not gentle.'

'I don't need gentle, Jackson. I just need you.'

I breathe in deeply, needing it to calm me as she wets her lips and smiles. 'I want you to make love to me.'

My breath catches, icy shards piercing my skin with the cold sweat that spreads instantly. 'I don't make love, Cait, I *fuck*.'

There's a flicker of something in her gaze before the shutter falls and it's gone too quickly for me to read, but I'm backing away when she grips the silk still connecting us and tugs. 'Then *fuck* me, Jackson.'

Heat consumes me, her demand seeing off the hesitation, and I'm striding forward, forcing her back to the bedpost as I crush my lips to hers. To hell with my perfect plan. I kiss her to force out any stray doubt, I kiss her to remember how she tastes, I kiss her to coax out her sultry little moans in the hope I can get enough.

It's her hands lifting to my hair that brings me back a second's clarity, a reminder of the cravat caught between us and why it's there. I tug it down, her hand with it as I tear my mouth away.

'What's your safe word, Cait?'

She blinks up at me all dazed, but I know she'll have one—hell, most members of Blacks do.

'My...my safe word?'

I study her face, see the high colour in her cheeks and the widening of her eyes.

'Yes.' *Please tell me she has one. I can't be the first to ask, the first to need...*

'Would *red* suffice?' She swallows hard, a confident smile quick to follow. 'Or is that a little common?'

I'm thrown. First by her hesitation, her obvious inexperience, next by her flippant remark, and hell, those eyes, those big blue orbs that I can feel myself getting lost in. They scare me and I spin her away to face the post, her body hot beneath my fingers at her hips and I breathe in the scent of her hair, close my eyes tight as I press my lips to the blazing mass. *Get it under control.*

'No, red is perfect.' I sweep her hair over one shoulder and kiss the tip of her ear, then lower as I scrape my teeth along her lobe and feel her shudder as she gives a breathy little moan. 'Red matches your fire.'

I stroke my free hand down her front, tracing a delicate path between her breasts and brush my arm, only very slightly, against her nipple. It's enough to make her rock and I smile as I flatten my palm over her stomach, smoothing it down further.

'Are you wet for me again?'

I press a kiss to her shoulder as she nods, her stomach contracting beneath my palm.

'Do you want me to touch you?'

'*Yes*,' she whispers, her hands reaching back to claw at my kilt.

'No.' I step back. 'Not until I say.'

She looks at me over her shoulder, all mutinous and wanton in one. 'Not fair.'

I can't help but grin. 'I want you to hold onto the post.'

Her eyes narrow but she does as I ask, and I sweep my hand lower, brushing over her curls. My intent is simply to tease but she tilts her pelvis into my touch, the impatient move forcing my fingers deeper. And *fuck,* I'm too turned on by the evidence of her need surrounding my fingers to rebuke her for taking what she wants.

I pull back and she makes a panicked whimper, the sound turning into a pleasing moan as I roll over her clit, make the move more deliberate and she bucks, one hand flying to cover mine as she tries to ride me, to take over and I nip her shoulder in punishment.

'I told you to hold the post.'

'But you're driving me crazy.'

'And I'm about to drive you crazier...' I take hold of her hand, place it back on the post and squeeze her fingers around the wood. 'I'll make it worth your while.'

Her eyes blaze into mine. 'You promise?'

I chuckle deep within my throat. 'I promise. But this time you won't come until I say. Understood?'

Her eyes flash, the colour in her cheeks deepens, and I know she's reliving her forbidden climax against the tree.

'Yes.'

'Good.' I reach around her to take up the free end of the cravat. 'Lower your hands down the post.'

I watch her trail her fingers down the wood, her eyes still fixed on me.

'Lower.' I press a kiss to her shoulder, another nip. 'Lower still.'

The move forces her to bend forward, her arse pushing me back and nudging at my hardness. I clench my jaw as the heat rushes to greet her, my cock so grateful for the sweeping touch. And I know the force of it, of every touch, every caress, every sound is amplified because it's her. Caitlin. Surrendering to me.

I walk around her, a safe distance, as I wrap the silk around the bedpost and bind it to her other wrist, my eyes averted as she watches me tie her down and test the binding. There's a little give, but not enough to free herself.

'Perfect.'

I say it in reference to the bond but as my eyes trail over her I know I'm talking about her.

I deliberately chose to position her this way, to have her body facing away in an attempt to keep the hunger under control and my eyes out of hers. But I realise the error I've made, because now she's bent over, her arse thrusting up, her breasts falling free and she's all mine.

She's all mine for the taking.

The image and idea merge and send the blasted sporran lifting parallel to the floor. She cocks one eyebrow at the sight and wets her lips, ever brazen. I know she likes that she can see how much I want her, but it's my turn; I want the same from her.

I trail my fingers down her back as I walk away and turn to eye her salaciously upturned rear from a safe distance—the perfect vantage point. 'Step wider.'

She does it.

'More.' The hint of her pussy, her wetness grips me, winds me, and I drag in a breath.

'Again.'

She does it, turning her head to look at me. 'Better?'

Fuck, yes.

'I'll take that as a yes,' she says, eyeing my need, goading me.

My lips quirk. Goading me, she's fucking goading me, even when she's at my mercy. I shouldn't love it but I do. It's so her.

I step forward and palm her arse cheeks, so soft and warm as I circle over them, gripping and kneading, exploring and spreading, eyeing her tightly puckered opening and knowing what it is I want, what I have planned.

'Admiring your handiwork,' she murmurs.

'I'm admiring you…' I spread her arse wide to emphasise my point '…before I take you.'

Her breath is a hiss in, her head lifting as she rocks back, telling me how much she likes it, how much more she wants. I dip one hand to her pussy, fingerfuck her deep and she tightens around me, her, '*Yes,*' loud enough to echo around the room, but I don't care if anyone else hears. Not now. I'm too lost to this. To her.

My fingers are saturated by her need and I drag them up, between her crack, and tease them against her opening, easing the tip of one finger inside as she moans and thrashes, and I have to use my other hand to grip her steady.

In and out, I ease. Sweat beads over her skin, along her spine as she starts to mewl, mewl like a fucking kitten, begging as her head falls forward, her eyes on the floor as she forces me deeper inside her. Thank fuck she can't see my face. I know how unguarded I am in this moment but hell, Caitlin like this, for me, her wrists bound, her body mine; it's more than hot, it's…it's…

I quit my mind, I quit the motion and spin away. I'm shaken. Torn inside.

It's just sex, Jackson—sex.

'*Jackson.*' My name is a plea. Hell, she thinks I'm doing this to tease her. What would she say if she knew the truth? That I'm too shaken up by her.

I unbutton the collar of my shirt and several more, desperate to ease the tightness in my throat, my chest, but it's all a placebo effect. I know it has nothing to do with the shirt and everything to do with what this is doing to me, to her, to us.

I unfasten the sporran as I head to the chest of drawers and tug it away from my waist with more force than it requires and the straps whip against the antique wood.

'You'd think you were uptight about something,' she says, always with the teasing, and it only serves to highlight how very different this is. How very different *she* is. No other lover would dare to tease me now. They play a role, a submissive role to all intents and purposes. Though I'm no Dom. I'm just a control freak in bed.

But her confidence, her knowledge of me, her ease around me…not even Eliza projected this kind of… *this kind of what?*

Vibrancy, relaxed arrogance, easy appeal…

I flick open the sporran and take out a condom, feeling her eyes on me, inquisitive, searching.

'I'm clean,' she says into the quiet. 'We have to be, don't we?'

She means for Blacks. Testing is a must. My mind tries to torture me with all the partners Cait may have had… *May?* Okay, *has* had. And it's a healthy reminder that this is all it is for her too—more sex. A bit of fun. Nothing serious, nothing more.

I look to her, still bent forward, her breasts waiting for me to cup, her upturned arse daring me to return and I swallow. 'What about birth control?'

She nods, her eyes below my waist again as she takes in my dogged need beneath the kilt. I should strip the rest of my clothing away, but I'm used to being clothed while my lovers are stripped bare. It's another piece of my control, my delayed gratification, and I've never needed it more than I do right now.

I toss the condom back on the side and stalk towards her.

She traps her lip in her teeth once more and her arse gives a little wriggle of its own. Like she knows that's exactly where I'll start. That it wasn't an empty promise. I plan to fill her from behind while my fingers take her from the front; I want her filled to the brim with me. Only me.

'You're not going to strip?' she asks as I come up behind her.

My one-sided grin gives her my answer. 'I think you like me in a skirt.'

Her laugh is a flirtatious lilt and as I trail one finger down her spine I feel it ripple through her, the next coming from her in a breathy whisper. 'You should wear it back home.'

My cock beats its own answer, desperate to thrust inside her. I use it to block out the reference to home, to where this cannot happen, and flick the kilt up. My erection lands against the warm skin of her arse and she rocks to caress it, trying to take some control and tease.

'Not so fast.' I press her away and widen my stance, bend my legs as I force my cock to slide along her seam. She gives a breathy little, '*Yes,*' and arches her spine, her legs straightening up and locking in place as she tries to draw the sensation out.

'You're so responsive,' I murmur.

'And you're a tease.'

Her fight has my cock jerking up, pre-cum already escaping, and I take a controlled breath, gripping her hips to raise her that little bit more. Better. I angle myself and rock, catching her clit with the head of my dick and smothering myself in her liquid heat. Each move coaxes out a whimper, a whimper that's building in its desperation and, together with her slick warmth surrounding me, it's pushing me to the brink.

It's that worry that has my hand tightening around the base of my cock, my other easing around to her front, seeking out her clit, needing her to be as far gone as I am. I circle over the hard nub and she writhes, moans. I step back, freeing my cock to palm her arse again. To knead and grope before I dip my fingers inside her molten wet heat. One finger, two, three. Christ, she's so hot for me they slide in with ease and my cock is bucking, ready to jack off all by itself—*fuck*.

'*Please,* Jackson, *please...*'

'What is it, baby?'

'I need to... I want to...'

Her words are barely audible, her body barely moving now as she tightens every limb in an attempt to stave it off: the climax I haven't yet permitted.

'Not yet.'

Her eyes are glazed with lust as she looks to me over her shoulder.

I ease my fingers out and run them between the cheeks of her arse and her lashes flutter, her lips parting with a breathy moan.

'I want to be inside you, here...' I finger her tight opening, lubricated with her own dampness '...when you come.'

Christ, I do. I want to fuck her every which way she'll have me and never have to face the question of what this means for us going forward.

'Stay still.'

I caress her arse cheeks, exploring like I did before, only this time my cock is buried between her legs, easing back and forth, lubricating itself on her. I ease the tip of my finger inside her tight opening and she lets out a strained cry, her body trembling as she works to hold herself still, and I grip her hip to keep her there as I ease in further.

'That's it, baby...push out, take me in.'

She opens to me as I delve deeper, the sheen of

sweat on her skin builds, my own too. I reach around her and stroke over her clit, pressing until she begs.

'Fuck me, Jackson, fuck me now.'

She's ready, I can feel it. And hell, I am. But I need to keep this slow, I need to keep it in tune with her. I slip my cock from between her legs, position my moist head where my fingers once were and push slowly.

She stills; her breathing quiets.

'Relax, baby, relax.' I stand straighter, one hand low on her back, the other guiding myself inside her. The sight of my head pressing inside her arse is enough to tip me over and I clench my jaw, feeling my body pulse. *Not yet.*

The master of delayed gratification—like hell!

It's taking every last shred of control not to come like some inexperienced fool.

'You feel so good, Jackson.'

Her arse opens around me as she pushes out and moves back and *fuck*, I'm stretching her wide, going in deep. I grind my teeth, keep my movements slow, steady. Talk is impossible now.

'So fucking good,' she moans, the blissful sound echoing through me, melding with my own cries that I'm barely aware of making.

I reach around her front, my cock half buried inside her as I seek out her clit. I need to… I want her to… I need her on the precipice. She bucks back with a moan, a plea. 'Now, Jackson, now… I need to… *please.*'

'Yes, come for me, baby, come for me.'

It's like turning on a switch. She writhes against my finger, my cock, her whole body pulsing and then she arches, her cry guttural as she lets go and my cock sinks inside her, deep, closed in, squeezed. I try to back out, scared to hurt her, but she pulses around me, her muscles clenching and holding me there and, *Jesus,* I can't hold back any more.

Pleasure rips through me and I throw my head back and let go. The world spins, my head filled with her pleasure-charged moans as I call out her name again and again. And then my head falls forward, my eyes take in my cock buried so deep within her, and I take a sucker punch straight to the heart. I know it.

I fear it, but I know it.

I may be arse-deep in Caitlin, but I'm the one who's well and truly fucked.

I bend over and ease her up against me as I move us forward and slide her hands up the post. She's all breathless and warm, her soft little noises doing a merry dance over my writhing gut.

Silently, I untie her wrists and scoop her up. She looks up at me, but I can't meet her gaze. I'm too exposed, too fucking vulnerable. I fucked her like I promised—we had sex, just sex. So why the hell do I feel like I've just used the most important person in my life and ruined her in one fell swoop? Worse, why do I want to keep her in my arms and never let her go?

I swore this would never happen again. That I would never want to keep a woman in my life. Ever. I fuck and go.

I use like I was once used, always with full consent.

But Cait…*fuck*, Cait.

She rubs her head into my shoulder, snuggles down, and my heart clenches in my chest. I flick away the covers on the bed and lie her down before drawing them back up to her chin.

She blinks up at me and pats the space next to her, her eyes sleepy, her smile sultry and warm and everything I could ever want is looking at me right now.

No.

I look away. Drag in air.

'Come to bed?'

I force my eyes back to her. And when I do my chest swells fit to burst. She's all soft and inviting, big eyes and wild hair, and I swallow. Hell, I can hardly leave now. We've already made a pact: a holiday fling.

But getting into bed is almost as bad as vanilla sex. Vanilla sex while looking into Cait's captivating blues. I shake my head to clear the dangerous vision so strong in its possibility, its near reality, and swallow down the swell of emotion it sparks.

Never going to happen.

But to fuck and run would make me a callous chicken shit, and I'm neither.

Or so I thought.

CHAPTER SIX

Four months later

'SLOW DOWN, CAIT, you're making me dizzy!'

I spin around and practically dance backwards on the pavement as I grin at Coco, my arms laden with shopping bags. 'I want to do Hamleys before closing; I love it there this time of year, with their cute little window displays and the excitement of the kids.'

'*Seriously*, I'd rather be doing Harrods.'

'Well, I need to get Jake something and Harrods ain't going to work.'

'Jake—your nephew?'

'Yup, and the twins, Annie and Alice. I can also see if they have anything for Joe's kids, although they're older and a royal pain in the whatsit to buy for, and it needs to be something cool. I am the young, funky aunt after all.'

She laughs. 'Oh, there's no risk of you losing that crown.'

'There really is.' I cringe at her as I continue to bounce backwards. 'I have no idea what to get them, and my brother is about as helpful as a chocolate fireguard—ah, now there's an idea!' I press a finger to my lips, crushing half my shopping bags to my chest. 'Chocolate, lots of! Can't go wrong, hey? Still, that's more of an add-on gift…not the main deal.'

'You don't need to do all your Christmas shopping in one day, you know. You have another two weekends before the big day, and you know Hamleys has late night shopping like every other store.' She leans to the left as a woman almost takes her out with a heavily laden backpack and smooths her blonde hair back into place. 'And then there's the internet, that thing where we don't have to trample through the masses to find the perfect gift.'

'Okay, Scrooge, since when have you hated present shopping so much?' I spin back around and almost sideswipe a singing Santa. 'Oops, sorry, Mr C!'

He grins at me as he carries on his happy rendition of 'Jingle Bells' and I sing along, digging in my handbag for my purse. I pull it out, take out a note and stuff it into his collection bucket.

'Merry Christmas, you wonderful man!'

Coco gives a bemused laugh as she digs out her own donation and hurries to catch up.

I send her a look. 'What?'

She shakes her head, her gorgeous hair tumbling about her shoulders, a far more sensible number of bags in her hands as she projects the perfect runway image. 'What *is* going on with you?'

'Nothing. It's Christmas. It's the season to be jolly and merry and bright.'

'There's jolly, merry and bright, and then there's jazz hands on a densely populated street.' She clutches one of my waving arms and drags it down, making me pause and look at her. Her brows are drawn together, her green eyes seeing far too much.

My stomach gives a tiny lurch. 'Nothing's going on with me. I'm just being me.'

I turn on my heel and carry on walking, my eyes on the shop windows, looking for inspiration, distraction, a deflection.

'Not true,' she says, hurrying into step beside me, her eyes not leaving my face. 'You're crazy, wired, talking ten to the dozen. I mean, you've always been a tad manic, but these last few months you're like a battery-powered bunny…and I don't mean the X-rated version.'

No, she wouldn't because, let's face it, I haven't been seen to in that sense since her wedding night… not that she would know that either.

Not only have I not been seen to, I've not been able to forget that night, not for a second.

I laugh to cover up the heat swirling deep within, the sudden sickness that always follows when I remember the next morning and my empty bed.

'You know me, I love this time of year—I *love* Christmas!'

It's the season of giving, of hitting the shops and seeking out the perfect gift, getting merry with family, with friends, being social. Not that Coco and I have done much of that lately, not since her *Married* status. But hey, it *is* the season to be jolly and I will be that in spades, even if it kills me.

'You say that.' She sidesteps a giggling group of women wearing what belongs on a beach in the Caribbean and not London in winter, but I guess the alcohol they've already consumed is doing the work of layers for them. Lucky women. Maybe I ought to try it. Coco touches my arm, drawing my attention back to her and the fact she is still speaking. 'But it was the same last month, and the month before that, and don't even get me started on October. You do remember the chaos you caused at my Halloween party, don't you?'

My cheeks flush a little. 'It wasn't my fault. I told the guy there would be kids present. How was I to know he'd drop his kegs as he serenaded you with Happy Birthday…?' I stifle a real giggle over that. 'You've got to admit it was kind of fun though? A little twist on Marilyn Monroe?'

I know the smile she gives me is a reluctant one and I do feel a pang of guilt because she's right; I should have been more thorough when choosing the entertainment for her surprise birthday party at Halloween. Instead, I'd been too busy keeping myself busy to look into the details properly. It's lucky I've not made a similar mistake at work and launched a PR campaign—an event even—with a similar faux pas. My company would be finished, my career with it, and then I'd have something other than my current celibacy to blame Jackson for.

'Anyway, it was most definitely a surprise all

round,' I continue. 'A surprise on top of a surprise, so to speak.'

Now she laughs, a real laugh, and I feel my shoulders ease. Good deflection.

'It was definitely that. And I'm no Scrooge, by the way.' She crosses her arms. 'I'm just saying I'd rather be sipping mulled wine in a festive bar and finding out what's been going on with you these past few months than traipsing through the shops and getting taken out by rogue shoppers.'

'Tut-tut. If this is what marriage does to you, you can keep it; you are d-u-l-l at the mo.'

She stops walking and my words hit me like a slap in the face. I know I've taken my *I'm all right, Jack* too far and I look back at her, guilt written across my face. 'Just ribbing you.'

'You're not though.'

'I am. I'm just, you know, adjusting to having my best friend married off and losing my wing woman on club night.'

Club night? What club night? My conscience is the one laughing now. *You've not been clubbing in months.*

She switches her bags into one hand and hooks her arm through mine. 'Hey, I'm sorry I've not been around as much. You know that, right?'

I give her an apologetic smile. 'I know. And I'm sorry for accusing you of being dull—you're not, at all. I just miss you; I miss our nights out together. But you and Ash have visited the most amazing places in the world these last few months and you make each other happy. And that makes me happy. Truly it does.'

I squeeze her arm, desperate to convince her. It's not Coco's fault I envy what she has. It's not her fault I succumbed to a night of crazy with Jackson, only to have him run. Well, not quite run. He was stuck in the same wedding party as me for three days, but I might as well not have existed for all he looked at me.

After all we had done—I mean I let him tie me to the bedpost for fuck's sake—we agreed a holiday fling, three nights... Was I really so awful he couldn't face a second?

'Hey, what's wrong?'

I refocus on Coco and the reignited frown she's sending me.

'Nothing.'

I know I don't fool her; her eyes are full of concern as they scan my face.

'Look, let's go out tonight!' she suddenly pipes up, all cheery, and I realise with relief that she's totally misread my sudden pause. 'It'll be just like old times, though not quite...' She gives me a wink and I know what she means. No, we'll never be lovers again, that's a dead cert, but we had fun back when we needed it, and we're still best friends. We should be able to have fun, enjoy one another's company, let our hair down and chill. 'We can go to Blacks, have a few drinks and catch up properly?'

I know my skin instantly pales—*Blacks*. No way. My nails bite into my palms as I clench them into fists and I rack my brain for a get-out. 'You want to go to a sex club to catch up?'

She giggles, her skin flushing pink. 'Hey, at least we can talk there; the music is good and the cocktails can't be beaten. Plus it holds plenty a good memory for me…and for you too.'

I chew the inside of my cheek, fighting back the wave of emotion that comes over me as she elbows me in the side, all light and carefree. 'Come on, it'll be fun—real fun. And Jackson might be there; it'll be good to catch up with him.'

Good? I swallow. It'll be anything but good.

'I'm worried about him,' she continues, seemingly oblivious to the tension she's sparked. 'I think Ash is too, although you know what men are like—they hardly wear their hearts on their sleeves. But he's not been himself for ages. I don't think it helps that Ash still hasn't forgiven him for the cracking hangover he was sporting the day after our wedding either.'

'Hangover?' I say numbly.

'Don't tell me you didn't notice? He barely spoke. He did an amazing job on the day—his Best Man speech was brilliant, had everyone in stitches. The next day he was like a zombie, hardly said a word. Don't get me wrong, he chipped in and everything, helped organise people, but he was just…well, moody. He just wasn't Jackson.'

'Perhaps he was exhausted; it can't be easy being the Best Man.' I don't know why I'm defending him. Maybe it's because of the part I know I played. 'All that responsibility, and the Maid of Honour gets off lightly by comparison.'

'He didn't make my birthday party either, remember? Some last-minute thing cropped up. I think Ash was more annoyed at that in truth. But we've invited him over and those times he has come I've ended up leaving them to it, hoping that with me out of the way he might open up to Ash.'

'No joy?'

'None. So, you see, going to Blacks is perfect. We get to spend time together *and* we get to grill Jackson like only a woman can. We'll have him back to normal again in no time, I'm sure.'

'Yeah, totally.'

'You don't sound convinced.'

'I was thinking a light-hearted night of dancing, maybe some karaoke, not playing agony aunt to a brick shithouse who I'm sure can sort out his own crap.'

'Hey, I thought you'd understand. You've always had a soft spot for him.'

Busted. I give a laugh that I hope isn't as flustered as I think. 'Yeah, in a fit-and-fun kinda way.'

She's quiet. Too quiet. I keep on walking and scan the clothing store to our left. There's a Christmas scene in the window, a mannequin family of four wrapped up all cosy as though they're on their way to a party. The man's tartan scarf has my mind veering sharply to another set of tartan—a certain cravat and kilt—and I immediately look to the woman instead. 'That's nice, don't you think?' I nod at the scarf she wears. 'It would be perfect for Sally. You remember Sally, Joe's wife?'

'Are you changing the subject on me?'

'No.'

She stares at me, probing, and I school my features before looking back to her, resigning myself to the evening ahead.

'I'm not,' I say, pulling her towards the shop entrance. 'We'll go to Blacks; it's fine.'

Her smile lights up her face. 'Excellent, I'll see if Ash can come! We can have a proper get-together!'

'I thought you were meaning just you and me.'

She gives me a sheepish smile. 'Sorry, it's become a bit of a habit. Of course it should be just you and me.'

'Relax. If Ash wants to join us, he can.'

'Nope, we'll have a girly night…then he can be our designated driver.' She gives me a cheeky wink. 'Got to be some perks to being married.'

'Considering how well you look, I'd say there are many, many perks.'

'We just need to find you an eligible bachelor and you can experience it for yourself.'

'I'm quite all right single, thanks.'

She doesn't hear me. I know it by her smile and the sudden faraway look in her eye as I hold the shop door open for her. 'Whatever you're thinking, you can quit it now.'

'I'm not thinking anything,' she says in wide-eyed innocence.

'Liar.'

Her smile builds, her eyes lighting up. 'How about a double date? Ash and me, you and—'

'*Coco!*'

'What? I haven't even said who.'

'I know exactly who you're thinking of and no, just no.'

'But we're not just clients to him, not really; we're friends. And you…' she taps me teasingly on the chest '…*you* could be more.'

'And you're going to find yourself alone in this store if you carry on.'

I head for the accessories department, hearing the hurried clip of her Louboutins as she races to keep up.

'There was a time you would have jumped at the chance to cross that line with him. What's changed?'

I pretend I haven't heard her. The memory alone is enough to stir up an overwhelming cocktail of shame, remorse, longing, disappointment, hurt… Above all, hurt.

'Now I come to think of it, you weren't so hot the day after the wedding either, and the last I saw you, you were on the dance floor with Jackson. Did something happen?'

I stop moving and take a breath. 'I really don't want to talk about it.'

'But this is me, Cait.' She puts her hand on my arm and I turn to look up at her. Her smile is soft, sincere, her worry obvious in the crease between her brows. 'Tell me what's going on.'

If I tell her then maybe she'll understand and agree on going somewhere else for the evening. The idea has merit. And then I realise what it really means is that I'm running scared and, in a weird way, I'd be letting him win.

'You remember we invited you both to dinner last month, and low and behold the day came around and you were both coincidentally sick?'

She's right. We were.

Hell, maybe this has messed him up just as much as me. But I wasn't the one who crept out in the middle of the night and avoided the other's eye the next day.

Maybe it'll be fun to turn up. Maybe it'll be fun to be in the same room as him and watch him squirm. It's the least he deserves. And if I get the opportunity to give him what for while I'm at it, all the better. I even have the perfect plan forming.

'Let's talk about it later, at Blacks, on one condition.' I raise a finger to her, my brows lifting and I'm already grinning at what is to come, because Coco won't say no to me, and this is going to be so...much...fun.

'Hey, boss, can I get you a drink?'

I lift my head from the figures blurring on my laptop screen to see Bates, my head barman, giving me a strange look from the other side of the bar. I say strange, but it's the same look I've witnessed on too many faces lately. They're worrying about me—my staff, the clientele, the few friends I have.

Hell, it's as good a reason as any to pack up my stuff and head into the back office. I may be tucked away in a darkened corner of the bar but I'm still flaunting my misery by sitting here. Problem is, being alone, whether it's in the office or my apartment upstairs, I'm bogged down by my thoughts and I can't stand it.

I need the noise, the hustle and bustle around me. I also need a drink.

'Great idea. Johnnie Walker Blue, straight up.'

'Sure thing.'

I refocus on my screen, on the projections for the proposed club in Berlin. It's a good move. Solid.

I should be buzzing. I'm this close to a new venture, another club in another bustling city, another step in my expansion plans, or my global domination as Ash likes to call it.

But there's a bitter taste in my mouth—*Eliza*.

I've been back from Berlin a week and still she hangs over me. It wasn't like I'd been surprised by her presence out there either. We move in the same circles, run the same kind of business; it's no surprise she and her husband would be interested in the same club I am.

Hell, they're the reason I'm in the business in the first place. They brought me into my first venture, this club. Without them I wouldn't have garnered the skill required to buy them out, and I wouldn't have been able to expand at the rate I have. Something they'll likely regret when I snap up the Berlin property from underneath them.

No, that has nothing to do with the bitter tang. I've lived with them on the periphery of my life for twenty years. This is something else. This comes down to the line I crossed with Caitlin, the line I can't come back from, the line that exists because Eliza made me draw it.

One side safe, platonic, easy. The other dark, twisted and loaded with sin.

There is no middle ground.

And it's worked.

Ever since my fucked-up relationship with Eliza ended, it's worked. I've been content, happy—Christ, according to those that know me, I strut around like I'm the king of the world.

Hence the strange looks now.

The looks that have been getting more and more frequent the longer I go without seeing Cait.

And seeing Eliza again has been a punch to the gut, reminding me why I did what I did, why I left before morning, why I bailed on our holiday fling pact. I bailed because everything I did to Cait was wrong, debased…abusive even. My stomach rolls now as it replays rapidly in my brain every debauched thing I did and I can't deny the similarity, how it parallels Eliza's treatment of me years back. And look at how that fucked *me* over.

How could I do that to Cait? How could I do it and think it would be okay? That *we* would be okay? We're so far from okay we haven't been in the same room since the Highlands.

Hell, we haven't even spoken and I know it's my fault. I left her without a word, no acknowledgement of what happened. No apology. Nothing.

And now it's December, Cait's favourite time of year. She loves Christmas and I hate it. I hate it all the more now it reminds me of her. And it's everywhere. I swear the hype gets earlier every year—the paraphernalia on the shelves, the music playing in bars, on the streets, in the stores. It taunts me with pictures of the perfect family, of being surrounded by loved ones and having mulled-wine-infused fun.

But it was never that way in the Black household growing up. It was just me and Dad, and a clip around the ear if I was lucky enough to warrant attention.

It's the one time of year my mood suits my name— *Black*.

And it's blacker still without Cait.

I find myself pulling up her account, a habit I've formed, and I know what I'll see before it even opens: nothing. No visits, no drinks.

She's cut out not only me, but the club too.

I should be happy she's doing the sensible thing. Happy that she's getting on with her life far away from me. And yet I'm the one asking Ash and Coco how she is. I'm the one avoiding every attempt they've made to host a dinner for the four of us. They first suggested a dinner a few weeks after the wedding. A 'Thank you Dinner' they called it.

An obvious attempt at matchmaking more like. And so far we've avoided any possible meet-up. I should be over it now, moving on too.

But I'm not.

And I only have myself to blame for crossing that bastard line.

Caitlin belonged on the safe side. She was a friend. A friend like Ash and Coco. Just a friend. And I fucked with that.

My punishment is *this*.

To miss her like crazy. To miss talking to her, to miss her presence in the club, her teasing smiles, her sultry looks, all humour and light and so much fun.

I. Miss. Her.

Four months and it feels like a year.

I thought when Eliza and I split my life was over. I was humiliated, broken, and filled with an anger so acute it took years to learn to control it, to trust anyone again.

It felt nothing like this. With Cait. The only anger I feel is at myself for ruining her, for ruining what we had. And I ache inside. I'm hollow, empty; nothing can fill the void she's left.

After Eliza, I filled my life with work and sex. I burned her out of my system. The very idea of doing the same after one night with Cait…

Bates places a glass in front of me just when I need it most. 'Cheers.'

He nods, goes to leave and then turns back. 'You want the bottle?'

'Do I look that bad?'

He gives me a lopsided grin. 'Hate to say it, boss, but you look like shit.'

I rake my hands through my hair and lean back in my stool. 'Glad you can tell me how it is, Bates.'

'You did ask.'

I blow out a breath and lean forward to take up the drink. 'True.'

I throw back a gulp, appreciating the burn.

'You want to talk about it?'

I almost laugh but I know Bates means it. My staff are selected to care about the club's members, to be an ear if that's what they need, or serve up their order and discreetly walk away. And I lead by example.

It's how I treat everyone under this roof, my staff *and* my clientele. Bates is only offering me the same, but I can hardly make sense of this hold Cait continues to have over me, let alone put words to it.

Or I can, but I don't want to, because that means admitting the one thing I swore I would never do again. Fall in love.

I shake my head at him. 'Nah, it's nothing that won't go away eventually.'

Hell, who am I trying to convince?

Him or me?

'No worries.' He leaves the bottle and gets back to work while my head goes back to Cait.

I remember the last time I saw her, stretched out on the four-poster bed, the deep red sheets tangled in her limbs, the moonlight streaking across her bare breasts, the soft smile on her sleeping face, her hair a tangled mass from my hands… My body tightens in an instant, the whip of heat firing through my limbs.

She's not even here and I'm hot for her.

I throw back another gulp, scan the bar and

the couples—threesomes and all-out orgies taking place—and nothing appeals. No one has. Not since her.

Fuck. I throw back another gulp. Four months and not a single lay. And I've tried. I've tried everything, but nothing works.

My fear was that I would ruin her; I warned her, made that clear. What I didn't expect was to be ruined in return.

Liar. You pushed your club rules in her face from day one because you knew—you knew she was different: a tiny bundle of carefree fun which you envied on some level and adored on every other.

I acknowledge the truth of it by draining my glass and pouring another.

From the moment she fell in my lap six years ago, all small and spunky, her laugh melodic, her easy persona a homing beacon to a man like me, so used to the cold, harsh realities of life. She had me.

And now I've lost her.

'Hey, Black, can I get you a drink?'

I turn to see one of my long-standing clients, Max, approach.

'Nah, I'm good, mate.'

'You sure, because I seriously need to do something to thank you for this haven.'

My lips quirk. 'That's what your membership fee is for.'

'I pay that for all-year-round fun, but it doesn't go up in December and it should. This is a bloody oasis compared to the chaos out there.'

'The chaos?'

'It's like Santa's grotto everywhere you go, and I swear to God if I hear *Wham* just one more time…' He makes a throttling action with his hands and I manage a tight laugh. 'You need to add hotel rooms to your offering; you'd make a fortune. I'd camp out here for the whole month.'

'Funny you should say that; I might have just the thing lined up for next year. Berlin suit you?'

'Now you're talking. I'd—'

'Whoa, Mrs C, watch the hat!'

No, it can't be.

But I'd know that voice anywhere and the tinkling giggle that follows it.

I'm not tuned in to Max any more. My eyes are on the blind corner that leads to the entrance, to where Cait's voice is, all light and enticing… God, how I've missed that sound.

Max knows I'm not listening; his head is turning to follow my line of sight and then she's there. She's there and…oh, my—

Jesus H Christ. What the hell is she wearing?

From this distance she's all stripes of white and green and skin—too much skin. White heels, green and white stockings, a green mini-skirt trimmed with white fluff, a wide gold-buckled belt that sits on her hips, her midriff bare… I swear my lungs are too tight to breathe. I drag my eyes up to the tiny corset that thrusts her breasts high, a red and white ribbon lacing it together tight, a halter strap that seems to push them ever tighter together.

She's looking over her shoulder to talk to her companion and hasn't spied me yet. I snap my mouth closed as I look back to Max, but I've no longer got his attention either.

'Forget what I said, Black. If you want to go festive along *those* lines, I'm all for it…'

Not on my watch.

I'm already heading towards her, leaving a chuckling Max behind.

What are you doing? comes the inner growl of reason. *You should be getting into that back office now, your apartment even… Anywhere but here…*

But hell, it's my club. I get to do what I want.

And right now there's an elf looking far too appealing and far too merry to let out of my sight.

Merry fucking Christmas.

CHAPTER SEVEN

'Ash is going to flip.' Coco sweeps the draped hood of her red velvet Sexy Claus number back from her head, its white fluffy trim cascading down her back and almost touching the matching fluffy band that runs along the bottom of the mini-dress.

'You're kidding, right?' I dust off my elf hat after its run-in with the floor and Coco's red boot, and secure it back on my head, shaking out my freshly curled hair from beneath. 'He's going to take one look at you, throw you over his shoulder and take you home caveman style. And don't tell me you're not going to love that!'

'Okay, you have me there.' She laughs as she adjusts her square neckline that's flattering without being too OTT. Me, on the other hand… It's lucky my puppies are small else I would be spilling out. 'Although I can't believe you talked me into this.'

'You're loving it really and, besides, it's the fifth of December, the first Saturday of the month and the perfect time to start celebrating the party season in earnest.'

'You know Jackson hates Christmas, right?'

'Do I?' I say in high innocence, turning away from her as I head for the main bar. 'No, I don't think—'

My voice quits as I come face to face with the Grinch himself. Or, rather, face to very broad, very hard chest. 'Jackson!'

I look up, painting on my most relaxed and happy smile. 'It's been a while. How the devil are you?'

I plant a palm on his chest, ignore the heat that permeates through the thin fabric of his black T and cock my head to the side, daring him to respond.

I know we are not okay.

He knows we are not okay.

But Coco doesn't.

His muscles flex beneath my palm as he folds his arms, his biceps bulging, straining the sleeves of his T and making the lines of his black Celtic tattoo pop. The tattoo that I know runs over the entire side of him. Arm, shoulder, torso, the lot, because I've been all over that and just the exposed section makes me think about the rest. *Not fair.*

'You walk around outside like that?'

'What, this?' I do a slow twirl for good measure, making sure he gets to see every exposed inch before I face him again, and then I grab the bobble that dangles from my elf's hat and tickle his nose with it. 'You like?'

He wrinkles his nose, an action so at odds with his manly presence that I don't need to force a giggle; it comes all by itself, helped along by the mulled wine we consumed while getting ready tonight.

'It's bloody freezing out there, Cait.'

'And who are you—my mother?' I pout up at him and ignore the way the deep timbre of his voice has my body coming alive.

He doesn't smile, doesn't even flinch, and I chase the desire down with anger that he still makes me feel this way after everything he did.

'I had a coat…' I mask my anger with a grin. I have a plan and it means winding him up, full-on tease and flaunt, and acting like I don't care. For now, at least. I'm saving the anger for later. Hence why I walk my fingers up his chest, nice and slow, treasuring every little vibration his body gives. 'Your fancy cloakroom is taking care of it; you know, that place you provided for excess layers that aren't needed inside.'

His mouth twitches. It's a negligible reaction but one that snags my attention and makes me think of that same mouth parting to lick his fingers clean, to lick me from them—*fuck*.

It was months ago and it might as well be happening in front of me for the instant kick to my pulse, the ache in my clit…

Time to move.

'Now, if you'll excuse us, we have a date with your bar…' I turn and loop my arm through Coco's, actively ignoring the way she's watching us both. 'Come on, Coco, let's go and lend some festive cheer to Blacks.' I give him the side-eye. 'Heaven knows it could do with it.'

I see Coco and Jackson exchange a look that I also

purposely ignore as I start to pull her deeper inside, past the unmoving wall that is Jackson.

'It's good to see you again,' Coco murmurs to him. 'Ash is coming by later so maybe the two of you could catch up.'

For Pete's sake, she sounds so worried about him. Like, *really?* He's Jackson. As if he'd be anything but *fine.*

He gives her a gruff response that I don't even try to discern—I'm ignoring him now—one hundred per cent not tuned in to his presence at all, not even one iota…

'What do you think, Coco? Another mulled wine?'

'I don't think—'

'Oh, that's right. Blacks doesn't do festive drinks. Hmm, bet Bates could knock us up a cocktail with a suitably spiced twist.'

I pull her along and feel his eyes on us—okay, so I'm not *entirely* unaware of him. How could I be? I don't possess the same on/off switch he so clearly does. I ignore the fact it only emphasises the difference between us, that I care when he so obviously doesn't, and focus on giving my hips just the right amount of sway, the right amount of confident cheek, and enjoy the burn of what I bet he wishes was X-ray vision.

'You want to tell me what that was all about?' she says as we slip onto a couple of bar stools and I wave down Bates.

'What was what about?' I grin at the approaching

barman. 'Two cocktails with a festive twist, pretty please.'

Bates chuckles. 'You've not been in here for months and you're already veering off menu and making demands?'

'I know, the cheek, hey?' I give him a wink which he laps up and Coco shakes her head.

'You're trouble, Cait.'

'Just what I was thinking.'

Shit. It's Jackson. He's right behind me. And, oh, God, my body thrums with the energy of it, of him.

No. I refuse to be affected, bothered, or in any way forced off course. Tonight I am going to tease him with my presence if it kills me, and I'm going to make sure he knows I'm back to being off-limits. Only this time it's because I say so. Not him.

'You're not invited to this little party, matey—off you go.' I shoo him away and he lifts one brow, his eyes moving to Coco, who gives a helpless shrug.

'It's like that, is it?'

'Yup, girls only,' I answer before Coco can, my attention shifting back to Bates behind the bar as I hook my heels into the stool's footrest and lean over, presenting my bottom with a hint of cheek and suspender straps to Jackson. 'So then Bates, what's it gonna be?'

Bates sends a look over my head and I know he's assessing Jackson's face, which I imagine looks something along the lines of murderous.

'Whatever the lady wants...' Jackson murmurs low and my grin widens.

'That's my boy.' I don't turn, I don't show him any gratitude, and I know I've just sent Coco's curiosity through the roof, but it was worth it. This is fun. Serious wind-up fun. And it beats the way I've felt these past four months avoiding him.

I just have to keep it up and Jackson will be suitably frustrated and, I hope, pissed off. As pissed off as I was when he had the audacity to virtually blank me after that night.

'Two Christmas mojitos coming up, ladies.'

'Perfect! Ain't that right, Mrs C?'

'Jesus, Cait, you need to stop calling me Mrs C. It makes me feel ancient.'

'Nonsense, tonight you are Mrs Claus and I am your *very naughty elf.*'

Okay, so yeah, I do enunciate the last three words and send the retreating Jackson a look over my shoulder, watch him falter mid-stride and give the smallest shake of his head before picking up his pace again. *Bullseye.*

'Right, Cait, drop the act and spill.'

I look at Coco with a little wince. 'Promise not to lose your shit?'

'I'm not promising anything until you're honest with me.'

I settle back into my stool. Where do I even start? The fact I've kept it from her for months is going to sting and it's not easy to recall, let alone talk about.

How does someone go about describing the moment their heart was split in two, for reasons they can't fathom and not through any fault of their own?

Not your heart, your ego, my brain rushes in with its wisdom. He *rejected* you.

It isn't quick enough though and I wish Bates would work faster. I need a drink to douse the queasy unease suddenly ripe in my gut. Is that what this is? Heartbreak? Is that why it hurts so goddamn much? Why I've felt so lost these past four months and gone on a frenzy, trying to forget?

Seeing him again—the anger, the pain; none of it can take away from how he still makes me feel.

I also can't deny how much I've missed him. Missed talking to him. Missed being able to offload. Missed being able to hang out with Ash and Coco and him. Missed him. Just him.

In spite of everything he did.

I could put it down to betrayal, to putting my trust in a friend, to making myself—*my entire body*—vulnerable to him, only to have him renege on our deal.

But this goes deeper, deep enough that I've not looked at another guy since, let alone had sex.

'Seriously, Cait, you need to explain because you've not been yourself for months. No, scrap that, you've been yourself dialled up to one thousand and you've got Ash and me fretting.' She lowers her voice to make sure we can't be overheard by Bates. 'And for the record, Ash never frets, not about you and certainly not about Jackson, yet low and behold he's worrying about the pair of you.'

'Look, I'll tell you, but you have to agree not to be pissed.'

'At who? You?'

'Yes, definitely me.' I lower my voice. 'Hell, you can be pissed at Jackson as much as you want. He deserves it.'

She eyes me and I'd love to say she's sympathetic, concerned, even. Instead she looks worried and I have the distinct impression it's not me she's worrying about.

'Coco?' I raise my brow at her. 'Do I need to remind you how long we've known each other? Before this...' I wave a hand around Blacks '...before Jackson, or Ash, or any of this.'

'No, of course not, but...' She can't even finish her sentence.

'Jackson is a good guy, a nice guy, one of the ones you think you can trust...' I list.

'Yes.'

I scoff, but the truth is that her affirmation chimes with everything I once thought of him too and only makes the question rage louder in my brain: why?

Why leave after such a great night? Why avoid me? Why—just *why*?

'Here we go, ladies.'

I turn to see Bates place two drinks down on the bar. So quick? I raise a brow at the two jars with handles, the orange drink set off by red and white candy cane straws, a slice of orange and a star anise floating around with the ice.

'You had this made up already, didn't you?'

'I may have had some jars at the ready. It is Christmas after all.'

'Ah, you're a good man.' It absolutely is...and,

while I'm intent on giving Jackson a taste of his own medicine, I'm going to enjoy reminding the Grinch of that fact.

'Thank you, Bates.' I take a sip and lift my brows, suitably impressed. The mix of rum, tonic, star anise and '…marmalade, right?'

'Yup, and mandarin juice to go with the slice.'

'It's delicious.'

Coco takes a sip and murmurs her agreement. 'It's perfect.'

He smiles and walks away to serve another client who's waiting. Max, I think, if my memory serves. I give him a wink, which he returns, and I sense Jackson frown as he catches the little interchange.

Not ignoring me any more, are you?

I smile around my straw. At least that part of my plan is coming together. Not so much the heartbreak part or the fact that he takes a seat at the far side of the bar, tucked away but very much still in the room…

What is he doing?

I stop the frown that starts to form. I expected him to run. To go back to his office, or his place upstairs, knowing that I'm here dressed like this and having fun. The kind of fun that Blacks is famous for in our circles, only I'm not because, let's face it, I've not wanted anyone in that way since Mr Grinch himself.

And having him settle in for the *entire* show wasn't part of my plan. But as he opens the lid of a laptop I haven't spied, I realise he's making himself comfy.

'Okay, Naughty Elf, spill!'

I look back to Coco and weigh up the very last barrier: I told Jackson I would keep it a secret. But that was before he broke our pact and blanked me. He doesn't get to make demands of me now.

I'll be making them of him later though. I'm not leaving without an explanation.

And if I have to pin him down to do it, so help me God, I will.

I stare at my screen harder, hovering over the keypad like my work is the most important thing in the world. And all because the person who actually wears that crown is sitting at the other end of the bar and driving me crazy.

I've not touched the whisky I poured. I've consumed the one drink Bates poured and won't dare touch another drop because Cait is drinking enough for the two of us.

The only saving grace is that they haven't left the bar…and I use that term loosely because, although it means Cait is still with Coco and *just* Coco, every time she wants to be served my vantage point treats me to her thrusted cleavage angled over the bar top and I swear to God it's intentional.

She wants to wind me up. She wants to tease. She wants to have me sitting here rock-hard for her. The way she pinches her lower lip with her teeth as she makes her next cheeky request of my bar staff and sends me a grin to match shows she knows exactly what she's doing. And the more I know it, the more I try to resist looking. But hell, I can't.

And I know she's filling Coco in on what went down. I know it. Despite our agreement to keep it between us. Four months she keeps it to herself—I know she has because Ash would have collared me already—and then she comes in here and chooses now to confess.

I want to think Cait's filtering out the worst, but with the drinks she's consumed and the way Coco's green gaze glitters at me too frequently to miss now, I'm not so sure she is. *Fuck.*

I should leave. Now. Nothing worse than a scorned woman, several cocktails under. No, make that a scorned woman with her best mate and they're *both* several cocktails under.

I definitely need to make myself scarce and save the face-to-face for a private showdown because there's no way Coco's going to let me off lightly. I'm surprised Cait hasn't come knocking long before now, just to put me in my place. Hell, maybe that's what worries me most. When I put aside my own feeling of loss, maybe what really has me worried is that confident, outspoken, kick-ass Cait shied away like some wallflower and *I* did that to her.

I roll my head on my shoulders, trying to ease the tension pulling my shoulders together and the dead weight settling in my gut.

Leave.

I can't do it. I deserve whatever I have coming.

And, if I'm honest, after four months of nothing, being in the same room as her is…exhilarating.

Exhilarating and risky.

I may hate Christmas but I have to admit the way the festive duo stand out in the softly lit room with its grey sofas, glass tables and warm wood—no Christmas tree, no baubles, no fairy lights in sight—is eye-catching.

And that's before you take into account the appeal behind the costumes.

Coco, the statuesque blonde with a haughty air that masks the softness inside.

Cait, the petite redhead with enough fire for two and the most amazing, lithe, supple… My groin fires to life anew. *Shit.* I need to get this under control.

She moves again and my eyes lift to her. She's beckoning Bates over, the fingers of one hand trailing up and down the strap that runs around her neck and down to the curve of her breasts. My eyes trace the move, up and down, a slow, teasing caress that has my mouth drying and my cock throbbing. She can't seriously need another drink already…

Bates nods and gets to work. It seems she does.

Someone else approaches the bar and takes them in. Dex, a new client, an investment banker, and slick with it. I don't breathe as I wait, my hands fisting over the keys of my laptop. Is he manoeuvring in, or is he purely there for a drink? He won't have met Coco and Cait before, not unless he knows them outside of Blacks, and either way, he needs to know they're unavailable.

But I have no hold over Cait and I deserve this hell. Dex has a right to fill that role. Me, on the other hand… My eyes go back to Dex just an arm's reach down from Cait, watch him eye her up, and my jaw pulses—

'Boss…' Pippa, one of our waitresses, leans on the bar beside me, her pixie hairdo blocking my view. She's worked for me for years and knows me well enough to give the disapproving frown she's currently directing at me. 'You wanna stop with the death stare, before you scare our customers away.'

I shake my head and take a breath. 'Sorry. Distracted.'

She flicks Cait a look. 'Yeah, that much is obvious. And the way she keeps checking you out, she is too. Girl's got it bad.'

My laugh is harsh. 'Hardly. She's pissed off with me more like.'

Pippa shakes her head. 'What's she got to be pissed off with you for?'

'Where do I start?'

She grimaces and reaches for my untouched drink, slapping it down between us. 'Want my advice? Get that in you, grow a pair, and apologise.'

'Apologise?'

'Yeah, every girl appreciates an apology, so long as it's heartfelt and, knowing you, it will be.'

'It's that simple?' I can't hide my scepticism, or maybe it's more that I know I don't deserve Cait's forgiveness.

She shrugs and gives the festive duo one last glance. 'Damned if I know, but it's gotta be worth a try.'

She gets the attention of the team behind the bar,

effectively leaving me to my messed-up thoughts and I push up out of my seat, closing my laptop lid.

Apologise.

It has to be better than watching Dex as he curves his hand around her bare waist and whispers in her ear.

No, no, no.

I'm across the room in a heartbeat, my arm hooking through hers quicker than she can pull back, and I briefly spy Coco's triumphant grin as I sail past with a fuming Cait in tow. I don't stop until we are in my office, the door slammed shut behind us.

She rounds on me, eyes bright, skin flushed. 'What the hell do you think you're doing?'

I open my mouth, close it again, then open it. What *am* I doing?

She shoves against my chest, backing me into the door, her eyes narrowed and flaming hot, stripping me of any coherent thought. Her breasts thrust as she drags in air.

'Have you seen yourself, Cait?' It's a tight growl.

She pops her hip out, her hands fisted at her sides. 'What? You don't like it?'

'Like?' Christ, I can't even breathe with her this close. Every part of me thrums with the need to reach for her, to crush my lips to hers, to fill the persistent ache of loss that's hounded me these past four months.

'What is it, Jackson? You don't want me but no one else can have me? Is that what this is?'

I shake my head, but hell, she's right, isn't she?

She steps closer, her shoulders back, the move intentional as it thrusts her breasts ever higher and they brush against me. She tilts her chin and looks up at me, her eyes spearing mine.

'Can't stand the idea of someone else touching me?' She wets her lips as her hands lift to my chest, smoothing upwards to my neck. 'Can't stand the idea of someone else getting to taste me?' She raises herself up and, God help me, my head bows to bring her closer, those cherry-red lips glossed and begging to be kissed, to be nipped, to be fucked.

She cups my jaw, her thumb dragging heavily over my lower lip as I play dumb, drunk on her.

'To *fuck* me?'

'Cait…' It chokes out of me, my fists pulsing at my sides as I fight the urge to pull her to me, to take control. I know I can't. I lost the right when I abandoned her. When I walked out on her and betrayed our pact.

And she knows it.

She rubs her lower body against mine, teasing herself over my straining, painfully aching cock, and her smile is slow, sultry, satisfied.

'Well, guess what, Jackson? You lost the option to have this when you fucked me and left. Maybe now you'll understand how it felt.'

And with that she steps away and yanks on the door handle, forcing me to move out of the way and watch her go.

Dumbstruck.

Captivated.

And instead of frowning, I'm grinning. More alive than I've felt in four long, pity-filled months. I adjust my jeans and head straight back out there, ready to fight fire with fire.

I'm halfway, when I stop dead.

Voices carry from the entrance, one voice cutting through all else. The hairs on the back of my neck rise up and my blood runs cold.

Eliza?

She rounds the corner, all confident and at home, her smooth blonde ponytail flicking over one shoulder as she surveys the room. My cock shrivels back as my gut rolls and my eyes flit from her to Cait and back again.

This can't be happening. Cait and Eliza in the same room. No fucking way.

My legs are like lead as I force them to move, but it's not Cait I need to deal with now; it's the unwanted arrival. And the sooner I get her out of here, the better.

She turns to face me, her crystal-blue eyes narrowing as she smiles. The gesture is small, confident, cold. *Very* Eliza.

'Jackson, darling, it's so good to see you again.'

I'm on autopilot as her hands clasp around my arms and she touches her lips to both of my cheeks.

'Eliza.' I'm in no mood for platitudes as I step back and grip her by the elbow. 'Shall we take this to the office?'

But she's not ready to leave. She's too busy watching Cait join Coco back at the bar.

Her lips quirk as she takes them both in and cocks one brow. 'How…fun.'

Her dry remark carries across the room, snagging the festive duo's attention, and Cait averts her gaze, but not before I glimpse her sudden insecurity, her fire all but snuffed out.

'Office,' I say between gritted teeth. 'Now.'

CHAPTER EIGHT

I CAN'T STOP my gaze from going back to Jackson and his *guest* as they walk off into his back office and I hate how inadequate I suddenly feel.

I've gone from feeling empowered, with vengeance and a whole lot more beating hot in my veins, to a very different kind of burn: humiliation. And I know my cheeks flame with it too.

The blonde is stunning. Older than me—twice my age even—but she's a classic beauty. Polished, sophisticated, like an older version of Coco, only colder. It doesn't stop her drawing every eye in the room though. And the way she surveyed the joint and locked onto Jackson, the way her cat-like eyes narrowed, her perfectly glossed mouth lifting into the smallest of smiles…it was so predatory I shudder.

And I don't want to think about the way he let her air kiss both his cheeks, how she leaned into him to make the most of every point of contact.

Or the sardonic lift to her brow and her mocking tone, which only leaves me feeling foolish now.

Compared to her sophisticated black number, her

tasteful black stilettos and haughty air…*argh*. My plan for fun is turning into a great big epic flop.

'I've not seen her in a long time,' Coco murmurs into her drink.

I stiffen. 'You know her?'

'Don't you remember? She used to come in here when we were new. With that guy, the tall, blond chap. Think Daniel Craig with glasses and slightly less muscle.'

Coco's right. I *do* remember.

My brain is already trawling through memories and scenes are coming back to me. Scenes within the club, shaded by the drink and the debauched fun. It doesn't help. Because now all I can imagine is Jackson in those scenes, acting them out with her and, to rub salt in the wound, he's now behind closed doors with the woman. After I drove him to a sexual high and left him hanging.

'Yeah, now you mention it,' I mutter as I stare daggers at the closed door, 'I do remember.'

I feel Coco's eyes on me, and sense her budding concern. 'I'm sure she's just an old friend, or a client seeking the invitation of someone else to the club; there could be many reasons he's taking her through there.'

Her voice is soft with reason and understanding. She knows I'm thinking the worst, but I can't get that predatory smile out of my head. I know in my gut there's something between them—if not now, then before—and I can't bring myself to say it aloud.

'I'm sure it's nothing to worry about,' she adds. 'And it's not like he's taken her up to his apartment.'

I give a forced laugh, trying not to dwell on the possibility.

'Jackson's a free man.' I take a sip of my drink and look back to her. 'He can do what he likes, or *whomever* he likes. A point I just made very clear to him.'

'You did? You weren't in there long… What happened?'

Now I smile, the memory of how hard he was lighting me up inside. You can't fake that. He wanted me.

'Spill, Mrs!'

'He was jealous and he didn't deny it. So I pinned him to his office door and made it very clear that, thanks to his behaviour, I'm very much off the menu.' I even manage a laugh. 'You should have seen him… It definitely gave me the kick I needed.'

'Good for you. But now what?'

'Now, nothing. The idea was to let him stew a little, wind him up, and then I'd have it all out with him later. Now Blondie's turned up, I can't see that happening.'

'You don't know that.'

I throw back my drink and try to stop second-guessing what's happening on the other side of that door. 'It's fine, Coco, we're here to have fun and I intend to have that in spades. Drink up!'

'You don't need to put on a front for me, Cait.'

'I'm not.' But my lie lands flat and I grimace. 'Okay, I am. But Jackson and I agreed a temporary fling, no future; who he sleeps with now shouldn't be any of my business. I still get to be mad as hell at him for hurting me. For bailing without a word after…well, after you know…' Coco knows; she has all the sordid details, thanks to my alcohol-fuelled mouth. 'I thought we were friends, and friends don't just bail on one another without at least saying something…*anything*.'

My mind wanders back to him and Blondie and my throat chokes up, even more so when Coco gives me a sympathetic look that has tears spiking from nowhere. Hell, I'm not going to cry. I've managed to fight the tears off this long…

I take another swig of festive sweetness, but it turns bitter on my tongue and I struggle to swallow.

'I can't pretend to understand why Jackson did what he did, love; it's—'

'It wasn't what he did that was the problem,' I interject. 'It was what he *didn't* do: say goodbye, pull me aside the next day and say something, anything, to acknowledge what happened and make me feel… I don't know, less dejected, rejected, ignored, meaningless…'

I wave a hand around and accidentally catch Bates' attention but, now I have it, another drink isn't a bad idea. And the way Coco is looking at me, she'll benefit from one too.

'What can I get you ladies?' he says, heading our way.

'Surprise us with some more festive fancies. We're enjoying your creations.'

'Coming right up.'

I sigh again. 'Why can't we choose who we want to want?' I grumble into the dregs of my drink.

'Because it would be too easy.' Coco gives me a gentle shoulder nudge. 'The best things in life are worth fighting for, Cait, love included.'

'Love,' I choke out.

'Yes.'

'I'm *not* in love with Jackson.' I wince as I say it far louder than I should have and flick a look in Bates' direction, hoping he hasn't heard. If he has, he shows no sign of it.

Coco stares at me quietly. Stares at me until my brain tells me I'm wrong and I groan. Heartbreak. Love. Jackson.

I'm such a fool. It's been so obvious for so long.

'Hey, chin up. He feels the same; I'm sure of it.'

I force a laugh and shake my head. 'You have no idea what you're talking about.'

I do though. I remember everything he told me that night. I've replayed it verbatim, daily, and confessed much of it to Coco. We didn't even make it past one night. How she can surmise that he feels anything more is beyond me.

'Okay, ladies, get your lips around these.' Bates flips over two square napkins and places martini glasses on top. They're filled with a milky-looking concoction and have a sparkling snow-like finish around the rim.

It looks pretty, but *milk*? I'm no piña colada fan. 'And this is?'

'A White Christmas martini.'

'Strong?'

'Suitably.' He grins. 'You'll love it, trust me.'

Both Coco and I give it a cautious sniff. It smells good. Creamy, vanilla with a hit of sweetness. I place it against my lips, get the instant hit of honey and sugar from the rim and take a sip. *Whoa.* It *is* strong… but it's super-delicious.

'Happy?'

Coco nods at Bates as I take a bigger drink.

'It's perfect.' Perfect to take my mind off whatever's happening deep down inside and beyond that office door.

'Excellent,' Bates says, moving off, happy that we are happy.

'I'm serious, Cait,' Coco says over the rim of her glass, eyes wide with her insistence. 'I think Jackson's in as deep as you are.'

'And I think you've had one too many drinks.'

'No, think about it. He let his guard down too—the things you did together… You don't do that without trust, without a *real* connection.'

I scoff into my glass mid-sip. 'Funny connection.'

'Don't mock it. The things he said to you; they run deep, they make him vulnerable. Maybe you got under his skin far too much and he's running scared?'

I'm looking at her, I'm hearing her, but from the corner of my eye I see the door to Jackson's office and I want to laugh at the very suggestion that Jackson would run scared. He's in there now, fucking Blondie in all likelihood, and Coco wants to convince me he has feelings for me. Real feelings.

A moan to my left pulls my eye and I look to see the intimate arrangement of four in a recessed booth. Two men, two women, and they are deep in the moment, so deep, the passion reaches across the room. They're having fun. They're not bogged down by the ties of jealousy, possession, love. They're enjoying what they can get. Like I used to.

I look back at Coco and she hasn't even looked; she's fixed on me. And she's so loved up with Ash, nothing draws her attention in that way any more. I feel that bloody pang, that longing, and I can't deny I want it too. The biggest realisation to come out of their wedding weekend was just how much I want what they have.

Is that because of Jackson too?

I know the reason there's been no one since Jackson is because he made me feel all that and more. I know it's because I feel more for him than I should. And I know that it's left me like this. Unable to date. Unable to trust. Unable to let go.

Because the truth is, Coco's right. I not only want him, I love him, *I fucking love him*.

And I can't have him because he won't let me in.

He's made it clear that he's not the man for me, and I can't trust him with my heart.

But my heart wants what it wants…

'I say we get Ash to drill him,' Coco pipes up.

My laugh is abrupt. 'What are we, Coco—a couple of kids in the playground, setting up snogs behind the bike shed?'

She giggles softly. 'No, but I think we could do

with a better understanding of the enigma that is Jackson.'

'Yes, but *I'll* be the one drilling him, okay?'

'You're going to have it out with him still?'

'Yes.' Too right I am. Like Coco says, the hardest things are worth fighting for. If he doesn't want me, fine. But the least he can do is explain his actions and, while he's at it, an apology wouldn't go amiss. 'If I can get him free of Blondie, that is.'

Coco grimaces as she looks back to the closed door. 'Reckon we should still ask Ash to do the guy thing...'

'Absolutely not, but speak of the devil...' I gesture to the entrance, where Ash has just appeared. His eyes land on us and his brows hit the roof, his buzz-cut, forbidding frame and mutinous stare enough to send the whole room into hiding. 'Er...sorry, Coco.'

She frowns at me and turns in her seat. I know I don't need to explain my apology now.

'You know that caveman analogy you gave me earlier?' She looks back at me, her green eyes sparkling.

'Yup.'

'You think it's about to happen?'

'Yup.'

I drop off the bar stool and make sure I get to him first.

'Hey, this was all my idea...' I lean up on tiptoe to give him a peck on the cheek 'She was cheering me up.'

'That right?' He grins and gives me an affectionate

squeeze around the waist that lifts me off the floor. 'In that case, I'll thank you later.'

I chuckle as he sets me down and moves past me to take his wife into his arms, the happy aura pulsating around them obvious to all. It makes me smile and cry inside. I'm so happy for Coco, so happy for the two of them, but…

They turn to look at me and I force my grin wide as I climb back onto my stool.

'Drink, Ash?' I beam. 'Coco and I highly recommend the festive collection.'

He frowns. 'Blacks has a festive collection?'

'It does now.' I laugh. 'Bates is conjuring them up to suit our outfits.'

His eyes rake over Coco and the open affection, love and desire alive in his gaze have my heart squeezing tight in my chest.

'Easy, Tiger, you can eat her when you get home.' I lean into him, all sweet and lovely. 'Right now, you have to entertain me. Tell me, do you have a friend just as awesome as you? Lovable, dishy, irresistible…'

He chuckles low in his chest, the blush on his cheeks an alien phenomenon that only makes me love him more. Coco's one lucky lady.

'I don't know. What do you think, Coco?'

'Well, I *thought* you did.'

I don't need to ask who she means as I look to *his* door and see it opening, my pulse jumping. I check my watch. Ten minutes—twenty at most?

Hardly time to talk, let alone…and Blondie looks remarkably serene. Her outfit is smooth with no visible creases. Her smile is fixed, her hair unmoved. My heart's already lighter.

'You've got to be fucking kidding me.'

It's Ash who says it, his eyes set in the same direction as mine, and my heart does a swift U-turn. 'What's up?'

I don't like the anger that sparks in Ash's gaze, worse still the way his eyes follow both Jackson and Blondie as they leave the room.

'Ash?' It's Coco that prompts him. 'What's wrong?'

He refocuses on his wife and shakes his head, his eyes flitting between us as he rubs the back of his head.

'Nothing. I'm sure everything's fine.'

Fine. I have to stop myself from probing. I try to remind myself it's none of my business. 'Okay, back to our prior discussion, my hunky request...'

'What's got you so—'

'Okay, so what have I missed?' Jackson comes up behind Ash, cutting him off, his voice loaded with a forced *nothing to see here* tone.

Well, two can play at that game.

'Not a lot.' I raise my brows at him. 'Did we miss anything, *or anyone*, in particular?'

I see something flicker in his face, something akin to guilt, but hell, based on how he's treated me these past four months, why feel guilt now?

Unless he truly was making out in the back office...

'No, just business.'

'*Just* business?'

No, it's not guilt...panic. It's panic I can see and my insides twist and gripe. *Fuck.*

I grin more and fight it all off as I give him a playful shove in the chest. 'Only joshing with you; it's none of our business anyway. I'm just drilling Ash on whether he has a sexy double hiding out somewhere; I quite fancy me a hunky husband.'

His eyes flare and I think maybe I've gone a step too far, but to hell with it. I want him to know I'm moving on. I'm on the market. And I'm not hanging about.

I slide off the bar stool to emphasise my point and lose my footing in the process, my, *'Oopsie,'* smothered by Ash's chest as he goes to steady me.

I grin up at him as I stand and my head spins just a little. But it's enough to know the alcohol is going straight to my head. The joy of spirits. One minute you're fine and the next minute… I reach out for the bar, my hand closing around something warm, solid… tattooed.

Not the bar.

Jackson.

I look from my hand on his arm to his face and another, 'Oopsie…' hiccups out.

My lashes flutter and my lips part. He's too close and he smells too good. Ah, hell, his concerned smile is setting off thrilling little flutters in my lower belly and I should step away, out of his reassuring warmth.

'You okay, Cait?' Coco asks.

Am I okay?

No.

Do I want her to know I'm not?

No.

'Sure am.'

She gives a little giggle. 'I think that last drink was one too many.'

'You're probably right, but it's been fun.'

'Hey, you sound like you're calling it quits?'

'No.' Not yet I'm not. I had a plan. And it ended with me giving Jackson what-for and demanding an explanation. But the idea doesn't appeal so much now. Not after Blondie's arrival. Not now my outfit feels more ridiculous than fun and I feel about as attractive as Rudolph, only my whole face is blushing, not just my nose.

Maybe I just need to freshen up…

'Why don't you guys grab a table?' I say, 'I'm popping to the ladies'.'

'I'll join you,' Coco's quick to say, hooking her arm through mine and practically dragging me away. I feel a pep talk coming on.

Hell, I could probably do with one of those too.

Ash and I watch as the ladies walk off and I have to keep my teeth glued together to stop myself gawping. Ash is too busy grinning like the cat that got the cream to worry about gawping.

'Take it you approve of the get-up?' I say, turning to the bar and motioning to Bates for two shot glasses and the vodka I favour.

Ash joins me, his elbows leaning on the bar as he cocks his grin to one side. 'Hell, yeah, don't tell me you don't?'

I shake my head. 'Fucking hate Christmas.'

'Yeah, yeah, I know, but when Christmas comes a-knocking like that…' his laugh is a deep rumble '… I'm behind it all the way.'

'You don't mind that your wife is out and about like that?'

He shrugs. 'Hell, no; it's me she comes home with.'

I shake my head and give a nod of gratitude to Bates as he slaps down the bottle and two glasses.

'You're only pissed off because Caitlin's free to do what she likes.'

I pour the drink, all the while giving him the evil eye. 'That isn't funny.'

'I didn't say it was.' He takes up one of the glasses and raises it to me. 'It's the truth though; you have it bad, and the sooner you realise it and do something about it the better.'

A laugh erupts. I fucking did that and look what happened.

His eyes narrow. 'Got something to tell me?'

I ignore the question and clink my glass against his. 'Cheers.'

We knock them back, his eyes not once leaving mine and I go to pour another, anything to avoid his probing stare.

'Not for me.' He covers his glass with his hand. 'Driving.'

'Fair enough.' I still pour myself one and knock it back. It doesn't help. Nothing helps and drinking isn't the answer. If anything, it's only going to make it worse. But seeing Eliza, having her in the same room as Cait…

The woman I wish I could forget, and the woman I wish I could be a better man for...

'So, what did *she* want?' Ash gestures to the exit and I know he means Eliza, his thoughts shifting into the same territory as mine and I grimace.

'She wanted to catch up.'

'Catch up?'

'Yeah. I saw her last week in Berlin. She and Damien were there, checking out the same hotel.'

'The one you're looking at buying?'

'The very same.'

'Seems very coincidental.'

I shrug. 'Not really, not when you consider what a hotspot Berlin is for those wanting some X-rated fun. It's perfect for an enterprise such as this with the added benefit of accommodation... Not that German law requires you to have a bedroom to screw in,' I add lightly, trying to brush the whole conversation off. I don't want to think about Eliza any more than I have to.

'Surely you did enough "*catching up*" then?'

'Did you just do finger quotes at me?' I stare at him, dumbfounded.

'Oh, God, I did, didn't I?'

'Jesus, man.' I laugh, good and proper. 'Is that what marriage does to you, turn you into one of them?'

I gesture to the ladies' room and Ash laughs too.

'Actually, marriage does a *lot* for me. I highly recommend it.'

'It seems Eliza wouldn't agree.' I curse the twist in my thoughts as soon as the words are out.

'What's that supposed to mean?'

I can hardly stay quiet now. 'She wanted to talk without her husband in earshot.'

'What could she possibly want to say without Damien around?'

I pour another shot to wash down the bitter taste in my mouth before remembering my intention to have no more.

'It seems there's trouble in paradise and she wants to reignite what we once had.'

Ash shakes his head. 'You've got to be fucking kidding me. Why on earth would she think you'd be interested?'

I look at him and I'm quiet. I don't know what to say. My history with Eliza is complicated. Messed-up. There was a time when I would have moved heaven and earth to have her.

'I thought you guys were over years ago.'

'We were.'

'So, what's changed?'

'She saw me in Berlin and wanted to test the water.' I give a sardonic laugh as I recall her confident poise, her sultry smile as she walked towards me, intent on seduction.

'You're kidding, right?'

'No.'

'Crazy bitch.' He shakes his head. 'I still don't understand why you didn't pull their membership to this place.'

'I never expected them to use it after I bought them out, not after…'

Ash's eyes dance. 'After you gave Damien a black eye and he couldn't be seen in public for two weeks?'

'He definitely deserved it.' My smile at the memory is dark. 'If I'm honest, so did she, but I'll never raise my fist to a woman.'

'I think labelling her a woman is too kind. What you saw in her in the first place is beyond me.'

I look him in the eye. 'When you're sixteen and a woman twice your age takes a shine to you and shows you the wonders of the world it's a little hard to see clearly.'

He studies me quietly. 'Fair enough. Not that I know the ins and outs of it; you kept a pretty tight lid on it, even after it was over.'

'And it's going to stay that way.' There's no way I'm going to tell him any more now. I don't want to put words to it, ever.

I pour another shot to detract from the churning in my gut and Ash places his glass next to mine.

'Go on,' he says, 'count me in; we can get a car to take us home.'

I know the gesture is bro code for *I've got your back when you need me*, and I grin my appreciation. 'You sure?'

'Positive.'

I load him up and we clink glasses, throwing it back with a vocal wince.

'So come on,' I say, ready for a change in topic, 'how is married life?'

My shoulders ease as Ash fills me in. I'm accustomed to his loved-up state now and I'm happy for him. I'm happy for them both. They deserve it.

'Enough about me though…' He fist bumps my arm. 'Tell me what's going on with you. You've not been yourself these last few months.'

Not a conversation I'm ready for either.

'Cat got your tongue…or Cait, rather?' His eyes sparkle with teasing but whatever he reads in my face has them narrowing sharply. 'Coco's right, isn't she? Something happened between the two of you?'

Hell, are we really that obvious?

'Something's happened and you don't look happy about it, Black. Come on, what gives?'

I blow out a breath. 'You're gonna find out sooner or later.'

'Find out what?'

'It was one night, that's all, never going to happen again.'

'Because you don't want it to, or because she—'

'Because neither of us should want it to. I'm no good for her, Ash.'

He surprises me with a laugh. 'Fuck that, Jackson. You're one of the most decent blokes I know; if anyone deserves that little firecracker it's you. Why do you think Coco's been working so hard to get us all together? Ever since the wedding, it's been her new priority, only you both keep scuppering every plan she puts in place— Hang on! That's when it happened, wasn't it—the wedding?'

I don't answer and I don't need to. He's already piecing it together on his own. 'That's why you were walking around like a bear with a sore head the next day, the rest of the trip even.'

And then he's laughing, a true belly laugh, and I glower at him. 'What's so funny?'

'You! This!'

'I'm failing to see the funny side.'

'No? You once took a pop at me for letting a woman get too close and now look at you! Your entire mood for the last few months makes complete sense now. She's well and truly got hold of you.'

'I'm so glad it amuses you.'

'Oh, come on, man!' He wraps his arm around me and squeezes. 'This is bloody brilliant news; now all we need to do is bang your heads together and you'll both realise it too.'

No, we won't. And if Ash knew the full truth of what went down with Eliza, he'd realise it too. But I can't tell him. I may have given Damien a black eye, but at least that healed. What they did to me, what Eliza and Damien did, there's no cure for. I'm fucked up and if I needed any more evidence of that, Coco and Ash's wedding night delivered it.

I lean out of his embrace. 'You don't know what you're talking about.'

'What who's talking about?'

It's Coco; she's back. *They're* back.

'Nothing, love. Absolutely nothing.' Ash pulls his wife into his side and kisses her cheek, his love for her shining in his gaze, and envy is what I feel. Envy that he can love her so easily, without fear, without restraint.

I look to Cait and she's looking back at me, a strange glint in her eye and so much bubbles up inside, so much that I need to say.

'Can I get you a drink?' I hear myself ask.

'How about your finest champagne…since you're paying.'

Her eyes spark, her sudden smile one of mischief and challenge, and my insides love it; they dance with the flash of character, of her.

The old Cait's back, she's really back, and I don't want her to leave again.

Yes, I'm fucked up. Yes, we cannot be.

But I can't live without her in my life.

CHAPTER NINE

I'M STILL MAD at Jackson and determined to get us alone together so I can have it out with him. Of course, I am. But right now I'm enjoying this.

The four of us, relaxing in one other's company, laughing, drinking, having fun, just like old times. Ash has already given up on driving home and we are going for it. Champagne and giggles.

A ripple of laughter rises up inside me and the three of them turn to look at me as I suppress it and end on a hiccup instead.

'Oopsie!' I smother my mouth as another giggle-hiccup erupts and my hat slips to the side before righting itself as if by magic... *No, not magic.* It's Jackson and he's looking at me like I'm the cutest thing he's ever seen.

No, he's not. That's the drink talking.

But what if he *is* looking at me like I'm the cutest thing he's ever seen?

That's a good thing, right? A really good thing?

'Cait!' I swing my head from Jackson's sweet expression to focus on Coco, who's pulling at my hand. 'We should get going; it's late and—'

'No, this is too much fun. It's been way too long since we've done this.'

Ash pulls Coco up against him, his smouldering look as he eyes his wife telling me exactly why they want to get going and why I should let them, but shit, this was just getting interesting. Jackson definitely looked at me like I was cute, and I want to bask in it a little.

'Don't be party poopers now. Jackson's treating us. I say we drink his bar dry and *then* we go home.' I giggle and lean into him as I say it, but as soon as the heat of his body reaches me I swing away again. I may be merry, but it doesn't mean I've lost all sight of the danger that lies *that way*.

'I'd say two bottles of his most expensive bubbly is enough.' Ash grins. 'Not that it's my drink of choice, but you ladies seem to enjoy it enough.'

'Hey, I can drink whisky with the best of them.' As I say it, my words slur and I realise I'm in over my head. Oh, hell. I haven't been this hammered since… since…who knows.

'Our car's ready and waiting, Princess,' Ash says to Coco, who kisses him back like she could strip him bare any second. They're so cute and I'm smiling like a soppy loon when she looks back to me.

'You coming with us, Cait? We can drop you off on the way.'

I raise my brows. 'You expect me to get in a car

with you two like this?' I wave a finger between them. 'Na-ah.'

'What?' Coco says, but Ash just grins wider.

'Your husband gets my message.'

'Well, we're not leaving without you.'

'I have a *chat* I need to have.' I give an exaggerated wink over the crucial word, reminding her of the little pep talk she gave me in the ladies' and my intent to continue with that plan.

She frowns, probably thinking I've had too many bubbles to do it justice.

'Chill, Coco, I'll be fine. Jackson will sort me out, won't you?'

Jackson's response is to choke on his champagne and I cringe inwardly—how bloody suggestive!

'What I mean is, he'll get me a taxi.'

'Of course.' He nods. 'Taxi. No probs.'

'*See*, all fine. Now, go!'

'Really?' Coco says, looking at me while Ash nuzzles into her neck and I can't help laughing.

'Yes, seriously, go! Before you end up staying here and putting on a performance for the clientele. Unless that's what you're going for...'

'Hell, no!' That wakes Ash up and he's already ushering his Mrs Claus out of the booth.

'Call me, yeah?' Coco says.

'Sure.'

We watch them go, neither of us saying a word, and I cough to clear my throat, to force back the thrumming fizzle of heat that is so determined to ignite around Mr Grinch.

'We should talk,' he says, and I know he's turned to look at me but he's too close like this and I don't trust my body not to climb him like a man mountain.

A man mountain…

I giggle again, sobering when I remember that *talk* is exactly what we should be doing. 'Yes, talk, we must.'

'Okay, Yoda, you sure you want to talk now? Maybe we should leave it for another day.'

'Nope.' I waggle a finger at him. 'You're not running away from this again.'

'I'm not running, Caitlin.' His eyes stare into mine, all warm and yummy and caring. 'I mean when you're not…' He waves a hand at me but all I can think is that those eyes are *definitely* telling me I'm cute, really cute, and the warm fuzzies are getting out of hand. 'Cait?'

'Hmm?'

'Are you…?' He's frowning, definitely frowning, and aw, he gets a little dimple in his cheek when he frowns. How have I not seen that before? Wait, there's two, no…three of them! There's even three Jacksons…

'Are you feeling okay, Cait?'

'The room is kind of spinny…' Ooh, talking is not good. Not good at all, in fact. 'I think… I think I might be sick.'

He curses, or at least I think he does, but it's taking all my effort not to be ill.

'You can't get in a car like this.'

'I'll be…' I swallow '…fine.'

'I'm not leaving you.'

'How novel of you…' I mumble. 'Shame you didn't think that way four months ago.'

I say it super-fast and he tenses up, his mouth a hard line as he rises, but I'm glad I said it. Even if it has made my stomach roll more and I zip my mouth tight as I let him help me out of the booth.

'You can stay at mine tonight.'

My eyes flick to his, wide. 'Hell, no.'

'Hell, yes. I'm not letting you out of my sight.' He sounds angry. Oh, dear. Angry *but* protective, and I like the latter…really, really like it. 'Pippa, can you give me a hand?'

'Pippa?' *Who's Pippa?*

Pippa appears at my side. Ah, yes, Pippa, the pretty waitress. I smile at her. She's so lovely. Really lovely. And she has a nice smile which I think I return.

'Hey, too much festive fun?' She doesn't sound angry, not like Jackson.

I walk with her as I giggle my agreement. 'Maybe just a little.'

'I've got this, boss.'

I look over my shoulder and he's heading to the bar.

Boo. I don't want him to go. I'm still angry. Of course I am. But it doesn't mean I want him to go.

This is my fault. Again.

I hated myself before, but now…

I shouldn't have ordered the second bottle. Hell, I shouldn't have ordered the first.

But I was selfish, wanting to spend some time to-gether, all four of us, just like how it used to be. To have Caitlin, fun and flirty Caitlin, back, even with the unfinished business hanging between us. It was too nice, too warm, too easy.

Yes, I was selfish and stupid. And now Cait would pay the price. Again.

I stuff my hands deeper into my pockets and stare out at the city streets, still bustling despite the late-ness of the hour, and try to lose myself in it. I want to empty my head and ease the heavy weight settling inside me, around me.

'Boss?' I spin on my heel to see Pippa walking to-wards me, her voice whisper-soft. 'She's all settled.'

'Is she okay?'

'She's fine, or at least she will be soon enough.'

I blow out a breath, some of the tension with it. 'Thank you.'

'No problemo.' She gives me a smile that I can't quite return. 'Best to keep an eye on her though. She's not been sick, but she certainly feels it.'

'I will.'

'Here are her things.' She holds out the clothes I hadn't even noticed, the dizzying green and white mix, and a smile tugs at the corners of my mouth as I recall her in them. The smile dies a swift death as I think of her without them now.

'What's she—?'

'I've stuck her in one of your Ts. I figured she'll sleep better, and you wouldn't mind.'

'No, of course not.' Caitlin in one of my shirts…
I'm not sure which is more erotic, naked or—

And you shouldn't be thinking about it either, not
when she's in the state she is, thanks to good old you.

'Do you have a bowl to put on the floor next to
her? I've laid a towel down, but…'

'Sure, I'll sort it; you head off.'

'You gonna be okay?' The way she's now frowning at me suggests she's not referring to the babysit-
ting of a tipsy elf.

'Yeah, I'll be fine.'

'Okay, so long as you're sure… I can stick around
if you want.'

'No, I'm plenty capable of nursing her back to
health.'

She gives a soft laugh as she walks to the door.
'Nurse Jackson. Suits you, boss.'

'Very funny, Pippa. Goodnight.'

She grins. 'G'night.'

She lets herself out and I look to the master bedroom, to the door which she has left ajar, and take
a breath.

On the upside, having Caitlin here gives me the
chance to apologise. Not now, but in the morning. I
didn't fancy my chances when she was merry downstairs, though I fancy my chances even less with her
waking up in my bed sporting a hangover from hell.

I should have let Coco take her home.

And then you'd be running from your mistakes all
over again. You owe her more than that.

I find a bowl and take it into the bedroom, my

feet slow as I near, careful not to make a sound. And though I know she's in my bed, in my shirt even, nothing prepares me for the sight of her. She's heaven and hell in one.

Pippa has left a bedside lamp on low and Cait is turned away from it, her body curled up and facing me. Her hair is swept back from her face, the auburn strands bright against the deep grey of my pillow, her tender lips parted as she breathes softly. Her make-up has been cleaned away and only traces of it exist around her eyes, making them appear darker, more tired, strained, and I blame myself for it.

Blame myself for it all.

I want to stroke her cheek, comb my fingers through her hair, tell her I'm sorry. I want to lie down next to her, offer comfort, support, whatever she may need. I could lose myself in the very idea of it. Fool myself into believing this is the norm—Cait in my bed, a life together. It would be so easy to believe in the fantasy of it. Only I won't.

I dared to believe in a life like that once and was disabused of it, literally laughed out of it even.

I hunch down to place the bowl on top of the towel Pippa's already laid out and allow myself a second to listen to the gentle rhythm of her breathing.

'I'm sorry, Cait.' I say it quietly as I stand, but it's loud in the silence of the room and her eyelids flicker as they open.

'Jackson?' she murmurs.

I crouch back down. 'Yes.'

'Lie with me.'

I'm quiet. I want to, but it doesn't feel right, not when there's so much left unsaid.

'*Please.*'

Her gentle plea breaks me and I climb in behind her, on top of the covers as I spoon her. She reaches for my arm and pulls it across her with all the grace of an elephant and my lips twitch against her hair.

'Jackson?'

'Yes.'

'Who is she?'

I go very still. I know who she means, but I don't want to talk about her, least of all with Cait, and least of all now.

'Who was the blonde?'

I close my eyes and empty my head. 'No one.'

'Don't lie to me.'

She turns, forcing my head to lift as she blinks up at me. Her eyes are damp, her hair sticking to her cheeks, and I tell myself it's the booze, but I know deep down it's not.

My chest aches as I brush away the strands. 'She's no one to me now.'

'But she used to be?'

I nod. 'A long time ago.'

'Did you love her?'

I look away. 'She was married to someone else.'

I say it like it's enough. Enough to condemn me and dismiss Eliza in one.

'But did you love her?'

'I thought I did.'

'Did she break your heart?'

My eyes waver over her face. I take in all that beauty, enchantment and vulnerability, all that my heart truly cares about, and I can't find my voice.

'So you *can* love…' her eyes flicker closed '…you just can't love me.'

She rolls away, her body curling into a ball, and I feel like my heart is being wrenched from my chest. I want to plead with her, make her realise it's because I care that I can't do this with her. I can't let myself love her and be loved in return.

'That's not how it is, Cait. You deserve better.'

'I don't want better…' she murmurs faintly and I know she's drifting off. 'I want you.'

My heart rises in my chest, choking up my throat. *I want you.*

I squeeze my eyes shut against the urge to take what she's offering and use it to suffocate the past. To rid me of the bad so I can be a better man. The kind that can treat her how she deserves.

A thousand things rage through my brain—things I should tell her, things I should confess. But I can't.

I press my lips to her hair, breathe her in one last time and roll away.

I don't deserve her. I'll never deserve her. And if I tell her the truth of my past she'll know it too. I can't even bring myself to do that.

Proof again that I am selfish, undeserving, and she's better off without me.

CHAPTER TEN

I WAKE, BUT I don't want to.

I'm vaguely aware that I don't remember getting into bed, I'm more than vaguely aware that movement sets my stomach off on a sickly roll. I try to squint but even the low light of the room stabs at my brain and sets off another roll.

I moan and close my eyes, staying very still. Something cold and soothing presses against my forehead and chills my eyes that feel like they're on fire.

Thank you, Coco.

I relax into the pillow, letting the peaceful darkness take over.

When I wake again there's the distant sound of music, the smell of…the smell of *bacon*? Someone's cooking. But I live alone.

I remember someone taking care of me. I feel the flannel still pressed against my head, only it's warm now.

I force one eye to open and view my surroundings side on. *Okay*, my brain drawls…not my bedroom, not Coco's…not anywhere I recognise. What the—?

I push up to sitting way too fast and my head spins with it. I press my fingers to my lips and hold my breath.

Someone's slept on the floor next to the bed. A towel and a bowl…for me? I cringe and freak out in an instant. It's not what I see that tells me whose room this is. It's the scent. It's Jackson through and through. *Oh, no.*

I can't be in his bed. In his room. *In his place!*

I try to remember what I can. How I got here. I vaguely remember Pippa. She helped me. But Jackson was with me and then he wasn't. I don't remember anything happening. I don't remember getting out of… My hands clutch my chest as I look down. I'm in his shirt. No remnants of the elf costume, unless you count my thong, which is too negligible and— *what the actual…?*

I look around the room, at the soothing masculinity of it all, and feel like I'm dreaming, just as I did on the dance floor, against the tree, all those months ago.

But, like then, this isn't a dream.

In fact, the hangover pounding through my skull, turning my tummy, is nightmare territory. And the fact I can't remember what happened after the club, I can't remember what was said. *Hell,* I can't remember what happened, not properly, and it's horrifying.

I know I'm safe though. I may hate Jackson for cutting me off, for treating me like he did, but I trust him. And now I think on it, the person I suspected was Coco during the night, tending to the pounding state that was my head, had to have been him.

The realisation messes me up inside. It makes me think of him looking after me, being the Jackson I've known for six years, the one I went to when I had a problem, the one who listened to my rants, my raves. The one I know I've fallen for in spite of all he did.

My gut rolls anew but I know it has more to do with the state of my heart than my head now.

Time to move. To apologise, to clear the air, to move on.

Tentatively, I slip my legs from the bed and touch my toes to the wooden floor. It's warm and inviting—underfloor heating. I should have expected no less from Jackson, with his empire of clubs and his eye for design that clearly extends to his home.

I stand and take a breath. I tug at his T, grateful that my short height means it's almost to my knees, and head for the door.

He looked after me. For that I owe him some gratitude, along with my apology. I can't imagine he wanted to spend his evening looking after a slightly tipsy female—okay, a wrecked female—but he did.

I pad out of the room and follow the scent of bacon down the stark white hallway, squinting against the panoramic paintings that are bold with colour and too much for my hungover head. It leads into an open-plan living space; to the right is the living area, to the left is the kitchen, all of which is surrounded by glass that flaunts the city view beyond. I pull my eyes from the glaring sunlight to the kitchen and the man currently facing away from me as he works at the hob.

I don't make a sound. He doesn't know I'm here

yet and I take full advantage of being able to watch him unobserved. He's wearing a white T, his grey low-slung pants doing something amazing to his behind and making my mouth dry. My hangover-hazed brain's already playing out the little fantasy that he's cooking for us, the morning after the night before.

This is how it should have been four months ago. A night of passion followed by cosy morning comforts. The image lures me in so completely that my eyes prick. My fingers press against my lips as I hide the sob that wants to come out because it isn't real.

Whatever he's doing now he's doing because he feels guilty. He probably pities me. Knowing what a mess I must feel and what a fool I made of myself in my crazy get-up too. I was a bloody elf, for Christ's sake. An elf!

But he wanted me… The evidence of that was very real.

Until Blondie showed up. *Oh, God.* I remember her in all her perfection and my insides shrivel, my nausea swelling with it, and he chooses that exact moment to turn. Of course he does.

'Cait!' He places the pan he's working with down on the side, his eyes wide and cautious as he walks towards me.

'Hi.' I give him a finger flutter of a wave and look away, my legs binding together as I want to shrink in on myself and he stops.

'Sorry for…' I break off. I don't even know what to say.

'Hey, don't apologise,' he says quickly, his voice so

earnest that I have to look at him and the concerned warmth in his gaze makes me want to cry again. It's the hangover. Just the hangover. 'I've made breakfast—come and sit down.'

I sweep my fingers over my eyes as he ushers me to the slick breakfast bar with its black counter-top and cream leather high-backed stools. He pulls one out.

'Sit, please.'

I do as he asks and brush my crazy mass of hair behind my ears as I shuffle in with his aid, my smile shy as I look up at him and he returns it. Time stills. One second. Two. I'd still swear this wasn't real if not for the smell of bacon and the very real effect his proximity is having on my pulse. We don't breathe, we don't move, and then his eyes flit to the steaming pan on the hob.

'Hope you're hungry.' He pulls away and goes back to his cooking. 'I've done eggs, both scrambled and fried, as I wasn't sure which you'd prefer. I also have bacon, sausages, pancakes and the coffee's almost ready. There's milk, cream, sugar—whatever you need.'

He's talking so fast and I realise he's nervous. That fully in control, stoic Jackson is not only nervous, he's also eager to please, to make me happy. And I don't want to soften. I don't want it to douse the anger, the hurt of the last few months. I don't want it to evaporate just because he's able to take care of me when I need it. But still I find myself slipping off the stool and walking towards him.

'Thank you for this. I'm sorry you had to do it. I shouldn't have drunk so much. I was… I was letting my hair down.'

He turns towards me, his head shaking. 'Told you not to apologise.'

I give him a sheepish shrug. 'I feel I need to. Can I help?'

'Absolutely not. Go and sit down; let me do this. And then we can have…well, that talk. Okay?'

That talk… I swallow. I'm not sure I'm strong enough to hear his reasons for rejecting me, not when I'm like this, but I don't want to run from it either. I give him a grim smile and a nod.

'But just because you're doing all this,' I say, and wave a determined finger at the food cooking, 'it doesn't mean I forgive you for four months ago.'

He doesn't look at me as he says, 'I don't expect you to.'

And, instead of reassuring me, it puts me further on edge because it makes me soften more and I curse my own weakness.

I look away from him at the view, squint at the sun that's shining through the fluffy white clouds and the view of London that looks so fresh and clear in spite of my fuzzy brain. I need air and, instead of sitting back down, I walk to the glass and test the handle. It's unlocked and I step out and breathe in deeply. Better.

I've been to the club numerous times over, but I've never been this high up, never been able to appreciate the view over the undulating roofs, the trees that border a small enclosed park and the people taking a walk, enjoying their day. It's calm, peaceful.

'Cait, get in here—you'll freeze.'

I laugh readily at his scolding. He's right. My entire body is covered in goose bumps and as I head back inside I realise it's not just my skin that's prickling up. His eyes darken as they drop to breast level, where my nipples bead against his T, and that look, that fucking look…

I drag in air as my clit pulses, warmth fluttering up through my middle and I press my palm against it. I part my lips to say something, though nothing comes out, but the movement is enough to spur him into action.

He turns away, clears his throat and throws all his focus on dishing food onto the plates like his life depends on it. I'm still rooted, burning up inside from the heat I glimpsed in his eyes. He wanted me. In that second he wanted me, and fuck I would have let him have me. Hangover and hurt be damned.

So much for moving on.

I stride back to the breakfast bar, my head held high against my inner rant, and pin my hands beneath my thighs as I take a seat once more.

I watch him add seasoning to the eggs, taste and add some more. He's proficient, serious about what he's doing…and this is just breakfast.

'You look like you enjoy cooking,' I say, grateful to have something to talk about that's safe. It's not sex and it doesn't touch on old wounds.

'I do.'

'Something you got from your mum and dad?'

He gives a gentle scoff and doesn't turn to look at me. 'Hardly.'

I wince, knowing instinctively that I've put my foot in it and realising as I do that I don't know much about Jackson pre-Blacks. He keeps it all close to his chest. 'Sorry.'

'Nothing to be sorry for.' He gives me a quick smile before turning away to pull two mugs out of a cupboard and places them down in front of me. 'My father brought me up. I don't think he knew a saucepan from a frying pan, let alone how to navigate a kitchen.'

I study his face and look for an edge, a sadness, but there's nothing. 'What happened to your mum?'

'No idea.' He turns back to the hob. 'She left me with my father and vanished when I was a baby.'

My heart squeezes in my chest. I can't imagine it. I have such a big family. A loud, loving, protective—sometimes frustratingly so—family. Did he really have no one but his father?

'I'm so—' He sends me a quick look and my smile finishes the impulsive apology he doesn't want to hear. 'What about grandparents, aunts, uncles?'

'No, it was just me and Dad. Not that he was around much and then he was gone. By the age of eighteen it was just me and the council flat I grew up in.'

'Gone?'

'Dead.'

The goose bumps return to my skin, the coldness

of his simple response washing over me. The need to say *I'm sorry* burns my tongue.

He says it like it's nothing, but how can it be? I want to reach out for him, say something, do something.

'I either learnt to cook or I starved,' he says into the silence as though there's nothing amiss. 'Don't get me wrong, I'm no chef but I can rustle up a mean chilli, even bake bread—not that I do much of that these days. It's therapeutic though. Good for stress, pounding dough.'

I smile a little. 'Yes, I'm with you there. My mum and gran have their own recipe and spend many a Sunday— *Shit!'*

He freezes in his dishing up, his brows raised. 'Sunday shit? Doesn't sound like a tradition I've ever heard of...'

'What time is it?'

He angles the wrist that's supporting the saucepan in his hand and checks his watch. 'Just gone half eleven.'

'Oh, God. I'm supposed to be at my parents'. It's Decorate the Tree Day.'

'Decorate the Tree Day?'

'We all get together. Mum, Dad, Gran, my brothers and their families...' I swallow as emotion chokes up my throat, my mind comparing the Carey brood to his non-existent one.

'You decorate the tree together?'

'Yes, and Mum cooks a roast. It's her dry run for Christmas Day.'

He nods and all I can think is how lonely his Christmases must be. Is that why he hates it so much? I want to ask him. I want to probe even though I know it won't help, that understanding Jackson more will only make me fall deeper and deeper... I press my thighs down harder on my hands and force the thought out.

'Why don't you give your parents a quick call? I can drop you around there as soon as you're ready.'

I frown. 'Really?'

'Absolutely.'

It's a big ask, and yet he's offering it voluntarily. 'Haven't you got better things to be doing with your Sunday?'

'Not at all.'

I swallow, nerves and a far more disturbing emotion turning my voice soft, my insides softer. 'Okay... thank you.'

I slip off the stool and realise I have no idea where my bag and phone are.

He looks up from the plates and smiles. 'They're on the sofa, just over there.'

He nods to the living area and I see them immediately, piled up with the garish white and green of my costume. My cheeks burn as I recall it now and give a quick, 'Thanks.'

I hurry over to them and feel his eyes following me.

'That shirt looks better on you than it does me.'

My stomach flip-flops with pleasure and dangerous delight, and I want to giggle as I tug at the hem of the shirt. 'Thanks for letting me borrow it.'

I bend forward to open up my small sack-style bag and the cool air rushes over my exposed thighs right up to my buttocks. I go to tug the T down again and stop. Somewhere deep inside me is the cheeky elf that ventured out the night before, all confident and determined to drive Jackson crazy.

I pull out my phone and cringe when I see the notifications—several missed calls from Coco, one each from my brothers and another from Mum. I fire off responses to all and tell Mum I'll be with her soon.

As I head back to the kitchen he slides a plate in front of me. As promised, two types of egg, pancakes, bacon, every sauce bottle you could imagine ready for me to use. Juice. And then coffee, a full steaming mug with a small jug of milk, cream and a bag of sugar.

My eyes are wide as I take it all in. 'Thank you.'

'I hope it's okay.'

He finishes serving up his own plate and comes around to sit beside me.

I can't eat though. As I sit there in his T, my body too aware of his beside me, I turn into him just as he does the same.

'Cait, I—'

'Jackson, I—'

We both laugh and I blush.

'Sorry, you first,' he says.

'No, you; it's your house, your food, your hospitality…'

'Nothing happened last night, in case you were, you know, wondering,' he hurries out. 'I'm not sure what you remember but I brought you back here

because I didn't want you alone when you were…
were…'

'Drunk?'

'Yes, that.' He gives me a one-sided grin. 'Pippa
helped bring you up here, got you into bed. I just…'

'You just stayed to make sure I was okay.'

He breathes a sigh of relief. 'Yes. Exactly.'

Oh, God, I want to hug him. I want to hug him and
yet he broke my fucking heart. It's so messed up and
I don't know what to say, what to do.

'What did you want to say?'

I swallow down the swelling need inside. 'I wanted
to say I'm sorry for the state I was in…and thank you,
for looking after me.'

His eyes scan my face; they're all warm and com-
passionate and…so very close. 'I told you; you don't
need to apologise.' His voice is gruff and I can feel
myself leaning into him, or is he leaning into me…?

'I feel like I do.'

He shakes his head and looks to his plate. 'No, you
don't.' His tone brooks no argument and the spell is
broken. 'Now eat. We can talk after. Hopefully, this
will make you feel better and…and then you can say
what you really need to say. I deserve it and more.'

I know he's referring to my anger and I'm so confused, the pounding in my head upping with the mass
of things I want to say, and the crazy things I want to
do even though I shouldn't.

Just eat, like he says. Then worry about clearing
the air. Hopefully, minus the hangover.

'Do you have any painkillers?'

'Oh, shit, sorry, yeah…' He's off into the kitchen faster than I can say thank you, and it's killing off the shred of anger that remains—hell, it's killing off every barrier I've put in place these last four months. 'I meant to leave some with the water on the bed-side table.'

Why, Jackson? I want to scream. *Why do you have to care so much with one breath and push me away with the next?*

I need to understand. If I understand, maybe I have a chance of getting through to him, of making him realise that we could have what Ash and Coco have, we could—

Stop, Cait. Just stop.

I pick up my fork and try to listen to the inner voice that's still capable of talking sense. But as I look at the thoughtfully laden plate and chew over my food I can feel myself continuing to soften, to hope.

'Here you go,' he says, placing the pill packet next to me with a fresh glass of water.

'Thank you.' I smile, popping out two and drink-ing them down. 'I really can't believe you made me both fried *and* scrambled.'

'Please tell me you like one?'

I give a soft laugh. 'I love both.'

I feel the warmth of his grin, I feel it all the way to my toes and I know I'm in trouble.

'Good, I'm glad.'

I'm glad too, and I'm supposed to be mad at you.

He's watching me so intently. He's not eating, he's not anything but watching me.

'What?' I say, lowering my cutlery and eyeing him warily. 'Do I have something on my face?'

'No, considering how rough you must feel, you look remarkably stunning.'

Stunning. I snap my eyes away and stick two sugars in my coffee, stirring vigorously. 'Don't tease me, Jackson.'

'I'm not, Cait.' He leans over, his hand resting beside mine, his energy, his warmth too sincere and inviting. 'I am sorry, you know. For what I did.'

I take a glug of coffee and wince as I scald my mouth. 'Which bit?'

'All of it. I never should have…' He looks away and when his eyes return they have that tortured look I've come to know so well, and I know it's not an act. 'The things I did to you, they're unforgivable.'

I frown and place my mug back down. 'If you mean walking out in the middle of the night and giving me the cold shoulder the next day—yeah, they're pretty unforgivable.'

'No, I mean…what we did together, what I did to you. I shouldn't have.'

I turn in my seat and look at him head-on, too stunned to speak. And when I do it erupts with a laugh. 'You're apologising for the *sex*?'

He recoils, his frown priceless. 'Cait, don't say it like it's nothing.'

'Nothing? Jesus, Jackson! You gave me the best sex of my life and *that's* what you're apologising for!'

He shakes his head. 'You didn't ask for what I did…what I did to you. It was wrong.'

I'm out of my seat faster than I can blink, and I curse my lack of height as I want to tower over him while I put him straight. I settle for poking him in the chest instead.

'I thought I'd disappointed you, freaked you out, put you off, so much so that I sent you running, and now you're telling me you left and you ignored me because *you* thought what we shared was *wrong*?'

He just keeps shaking his head and it's driving me insane. I grab his face in my hands and I stare into his eyes that burn and torment in one.

The truth of the last four months opens up in my heart. Thinking I'd done something to push him away, for him to reject me. Instead he's tortured himself with what he perceives to be some wrong he enacted against me.

'It wasn't wrong, Jackson. It was what I wanted, every kiss, every touch, every fuck!'

'You can't mean it.'

'Of course I mean it. And, what's more, I want you *now*.'

He clutches at my wrists. 'Don't do this, Cait. I don't want to hurt you any more than I already have.'

'Hurting me is ignoring me, hurting me is making me feel like *I* did something wrong.'

'It wasn't you. It could never be you.'

'Then why push me away? Why didn't you let us live out the holiday fling we agreed to at least?'

'Because I'm no good for you; it was better to end it sooner—'

'Bollocks, utter bollocks!' And I kiss him. I kiss

him so hard. I kiss him to punish him for four months of hell and making me believe the worst. I kiss him to make him remember just how good it was and I keep kissing him until his hands fall from my wrists to cup my arse. To urge me closer. His groan is music to my strung-out clit as he lifts me onto the counter, shoving the plates aside, his mouth taking all that I give freely now.

I wrap my legs around him, draw his hardness tight against me, telling him with my body that I want this. Here. Now.

He grips the bottom of the T I'm wearing and pulls it over my head. 'We shouldn't be doing this.'

'We should,' I argue against his lips, too delirious to think straight.

He drags his mouth from mine, his stubble grazing over my jaw as he trails kisses to my neck, his teeth nipping, his hands hot and urgent over my skin.

'I can't give you more though, Cait. *I can't.*'

His movements are as frantic and as brutal as his words, as though he needs to brand me with them, to be sure I understand.

'Stop with the *more*,' I say, gripping his head, tugging at his hair to pull his mouth to mine. I sink my tongue in deep, silencing him, claiming him, before yanking him away so that my eyes sear into his. 'I'm *not* asking for more.'

He studies my face, seeking out the lie, and I launch myself at him before he can see it. Kiss him until he's growling low in his throat before I pull back enough to say, 'Okay?'

'Yes.' His nod is swift, his hands fierce as he yanks my lower body against his clothed cock. 'You killed me last night.'

His eyes are on fire as he leans back to take in my nakedness, my skimpy thong the only thing remaining, and shakes his head. 'That elf get-up... *Christ, Cait*. I wanted to haul your arse out of there and fuck you so hard.'

'You should have.'

'I *hate* Christmas.'

'I know, but that only made it more fun.' I tug at his T-shirt, urging it over his head. 'And, for the record, you should have. You should've dragged me into that back office and fucked me so hard for taunting you like that.'

He grinds against me, his breathing unsteady, his body vibrating with the effort it's taking to keep himself restrained. But fuck his restraint, I want all of him and I rake my nails down his chest, marking him, loving how his pecs ripple, how his sharp inhale hisses through his teeth.

'You should have punished me, Jackson.'

His eyes darken and his jaw pulses.

'Is that what you're afraid of? That I won't enjoy it.'

He grits his teeth. 'I don't want to hurt you.'

I know he means it. I get it even more now, but it only makes this hotter. I lean up to him, suck his bottom lip between my teeth and bite down.

'You could never hurt me in that way.'

'*Cait.*' It's a groan, a warning.

'Fuck me, Jackson.'

It's a demand. Not to make love, but to fuck. I've learned my lesson and my eyes are hard as I lie back and stare up at him, daring him to deny us this. I plant my elbows on the countertop and pinch my bottom lip in my teeth, rolling my hips to caress his clothed cock and he sucks in a breath.

'You really want this?'

I nod.

'This?' He thrusts down his lounge pants, unveils his hard, throbbing length as he fists over it and my body gives an excited little squeeze.

'Hell, yes.' I eye him brazenly, desperate. He works himself with his fist, the tension rippling through his entire body. It's so fucking sexy and I know if he denies me now I'll be reduced to tears. But I know my dirty mouth drives him on and I'm not backing down.

'*Fuck me* like you wanted to last night. *Hard.*'

His eyes flash as his hand slips between my legs. 'Fuck, you're so fucking wet for me.'

I nod and ride his fingers, pleasuring myself on their force as he thrusts three in deep, his thumb rolling over my clit. My insides quiver, my climax coming so quick.

'Now, Jackson.'

He's so quick—one second I'm filled with his fingers, the next he's yanked my thong aside and filled me with his erection. *Yes.* Pleasure streaks through my limbs, the ecstasy of it making my head roll back, my body arching as I plant my hands on the cold kitchen surface and feast on him. He's hard, jagged, his thrusts taking his all to control and I ride him, urging him deeper, harder, with my bare heels pressing into his arse. And then his thumb is back on me, rolling over my clit, nursing every ache, taking me higher and higher.

'Fuck Cait, what are you doing to me?'

I force my head up and look him straight in the eye. 'Fucking you, Jackson, we're fucking...'

The delicious heat is pulling my body taut and my breathy moans are getting louder. I hear the clatter of cutlery hitting the floor, but I can't keep myself in place; it's building too fast, too intensely.

I force my eyes to stay open, to see that he is with me, and watch his climax unfold. He roars with it, the pleasure cording his neck, through his body. It's a sight I want to engrave in my memory, and I stave off my release just long enough to feed on his and then I am gone. The explosion sending my body upright and he pulls me in, holding me tight, whispering things that are far too sweet, far too soft for him to mean, but I'm listening anyway.

'Some breakfast offering,' I whisper when I can finally manage to speak.

'It wasn't what I had in mind.' He presses a kiss to my shoulder. 'I wanted to apologise.'

'And you did. The sex was the icing on the apology.'

He laughs, low in his throat. 'Friends again?'

I nod. 'Friends...*with benefits*?'

He shakes his head as he holds me tighter against him.

'What can I say? I truly am a naughty elf...'

'If you're offering me a private show in that number, friends with benefits it is.'

My heart gives a little leap; my tummy flutters alive. I want to ask if he's serious, but Jackson doesn't just say shit to keep people happy. He means every word that comes out of his mouth.

So why doubt the sweet nothings that came out of his mouth just seconds ago?

I know why. Because to believe them would mean believing in the possibility of more. And he's made it clear. Never. Going. To. Happen.

I don't dare lean back and look up at him for fear of what he'll read in my face. Instead I wriggle in closer, indulging in a second's more intimacy.

'Now let me go,' I say to the ground, my smile too big for my face, 'so I can clean up and eat this amazing spread before it gets cold.'

He laughs softly and does as I ask. 'Luckily, most of it seems to have survived.'

I crouch down for his T. 'Bathroom?'

'Back the way you came, second door on the left.'

'Great.'

I feel his eyes on me all the way and give an extra little wriggle as I pull his T back over my head, feeling his come slick between my thighs. I've never felt so alive. Who'd have thought sex was a miracle hangover cure?

It's not sex with just anyone though. It's with Jackson.

I let myself into the bathroom and close the door, shut my eyes and lean back against it. I take the deepest breath in, seeking calmness, a way to talk down the chaos taking off inside me. The chaos that takes me down a dangerous path to wanting more…the more he's incapable of.

But it's no use. I'm high on adrenaline, on sex, on him. I shiver as I recall how much he wanted me, how much he wanted to punish the naughty elf.

Elf, one.

Blondie, zero.

My smile freezes and my memory stutters to life, flashes of words that were said in the night. In the darkness. Jackson was with me in the bed, curled against me and…

I remember.

The man who won't make love, the man who's made it clear he doesn't do relationships… He loved *her*.

Jackson loved Blondie.

My stomach rolls and I get to the toilet just in time. If only I could throw my heart up and make it hurt less too.

CHAPTER ELEVEN

I GLANCE ACROSS at Cait in the passenger seat, take in her pensive expression as she stares out of the window and I admit I'm worried. Ever since she returned from my bathroom she's been edgy, distant...

Either that or I'm just transposing my inner anxiety onto her.

I know we've made an agreement—friends with benefits—nothing more. It's an arrangement people embark on daily at Blacks and one that beats the last four months of nothing. No Cait, no fun, just...living.

I rub the back of my neck. No, I don't want to go back to that.

But I can't forget our conversation in the dark. And no amount of replaying her declaration that she doesn't want more can wipe out her whispered *'I want you'* or, worse, *'You just can't love me'*.

A good man would still put her first. A good man wouldn't have screwed her over the breakfast bar. A good man would have put her in a taxi and got her the hell away from him.

'Bollocks,' she blurts.

I send her a look. Is she in my head? 'What's up?'

'I forgot the wine I pulled out to bring.'

I remember seeing it on the side in her kitchen but hadn't thought to mention it. I'd been far too busy second-guessing her behaviour.

'No problem. I have a case in the boot; you can grab one of those.'

She laughs and the sound is everything I need to hear. 'Do you *always* travel with one in the boot, just in case?'

I laugh as my shoulders ease, my grip around the steering wheel relaxing. 'It's a new wine I'm stocking at the club. I picked up an extra one for me and haven't unloaded it yet.'

'Now who's playing Santa's Little Helper?' She gives her trademark grin, the one I missed so much during our time apart and which smacks of all things naughty and nice.

'I think the elf outfit suits you far better than it would me.'

She laughs all the more. 'True.' Her eyes stay fixed on me and the atmosphere around us softens into something else. 'You really didn't need to drive me, you know.'

'Driving you here is part of the apology. It's my fault you were in that state in the first place.'

'Whoa, whoa, whoa, Stud.' She waves a hand at me, all alive and vibrant now. 'You may rock my world in the bedroom department, but you don't get to control me out of it, and it was *me* that put away that drink last night. Not you.'

'Whatever, just—'

'Take the next left.'

She gestures to the turning up ahead and I indicate before looking back at her. 'Whatever the case, it was my club, my tab, I should have cut you off.'

'Ooh, are you getting all masterful on me again? Because if you want to pull over and—'

I laugh. I can't help it. She makes me feel lighter, our relationship already easy again. I turn the car down the street and realise it's a private road with several exclusive gated developments.

I give a low whistle. 'Nice.'

'Well, when you've got five kids you need big, not necessarily nice. We're just lucky enough to get both. Though we tease Mum and Dad that they owe their success to us.'

'That so?'

'Yup, if they hadn't had five kids their company wouldn't be the market leader it is. There's nothing they don't know about baby care.'

I frown. 'Your parents are *the* Careys?'

'You hadn't worked that out already?'

'I guess I never really thought about it.'

'Yup, Carey's Baby Care has a ring to it, doesn't it?' She laughs. 'I'm still not convinced Mum didn't load Dad up with whisky the night she got him to agree to the name— *Gah*.'

I wince as I look at her. 'Whisky?'

She nods and presses the button to open the window a little, angling her face to the breeze and breathing in deep. 'It's the next one on the left.'

I almost don't hear her. I'm too hooked on her hair blowing back off her glowing skin and it takes a sudden bump in the road to remind me I'm supposed to be driving.

She picks up her phone. 'I'll just open the gate.'

I slow the car and contemplate dropping her off here. I'm sure she can make the remaining distance in one piece. Instead I turn the car down the drive as the tall iron gates roll back.

Trees line the driveway, fairy lights already twinkling in their bare branches, and as we approach the circular courtyard in front of the double-fronted redbrick house I see icicle lights follow the roofline all the way along. The wraparound porch is littered with decorations too, from light-up reindeer to illuminated topiary bushes and even a swinging seat complete with an elf.

'Take it your parents go all-out at Christmas?'

'Oh, yeah. Proper Mr and Mrs Claus this time of year. Now you know where my elf costume idea came from.'

'Somehow I don't think your parents would approve of that particular get-up.' I pull up in the courtyard but keep the engine running and turn to look at her. I'm still not ready to let her go. This fresh ease we've found is too appealing; *she's* too appealing, even in her sparkly Christmas jumper, jeans and boots. Perfectly modest, super casual and festive. The last should be enough to put me off. Instead, I look at Rudolph's sequinned nose on her chest and think of the colour that creeps into her face when she climaxes.

'What are you thinking about?'

My eyes shoot to her face. 'You don't want to know.'

She leans into me, her fingers combing through my hair at my nape. 'When it puts that fire in your eyes I do…'

She kisses me, her mouth teasing my lips apart and sending the heat rushing south. We had sex not that long ago, and the instant she touches me I'm ready again. She palms my thigh as she leans in further, deepening the kiss, and I release the steering wheel to fork my hand through her hair.

'Why don't I come by your place tonight?' she murmurs against my lips.

'Sounds good.'

'What t—'

'It's about time!'

She freezes in my hold. Hell, I freeze. I don't want to open my eyes and see who's just spoken. Amidst our frantic breaths I can hear approaching footsteps on the gravel outside and risk a peek to see a beaming version of Caitlin many years from now.

'I think it's your mum,' I whisper.

'Oh, God.' Her eyes widen. 'Could be worse though. It could have been one of my brothers.'

I think I take her point. I can just imagine what four older brothers would do to a guy like me, pulling up in his blacked-out Range Rover and making out with their little sister in the front seat. Still, it's better than being caught in the back…

'Caitlin, love! Aren't you going to get out and introduce us to your friend?'

'Hey, Mum.' She gives me an apologetic smile and leans back into her seat to look out of the gap in the window. 'Sorry I'm late.'

'Nonsense.' Her mum pauses beside the car just as a Golden Labrador races up beside her, tail wagging, tongue lolling out. He plonks himself down beside her with a bark and she strokes his head and beams. 'I know, Alfie; I was just thinking the same. If I'd known you were bringing company, love, I would have peeled more potatoes. You are stopping, I hope?' She's looking past Caitlin to me and…and I swallow.

Stopping? Hell, no.

There are more footsteps on the gravel.

'Marlene, did you tell Max to put the tree—' The male voice stops as he comes into view, a tall man, greying hair at the temples, wearing suit trousers with a shirt and jumper even though he's nowhere near an office. Her father, definitely. His eyes narrow as he takes us both in and I immediately feel like a randy teenager caught in the act. And Jesus, if my cheeks don't flush a little.

'Hello, love, who's your friend?' he asks.

'Mum, Dad, this is Jackson.'

'Mr and Mrs Carey.' I duck my head a little as I look to them both with a nod and a smile that I hope is innocent and in no way mortified. 'Nice to meet you.'

'Get yourself out here, lad. No good sitting in the car and keeping us all waiting.' *Lad?* When have I ever been called lad? And what the hell do I do now?

'It's a good job you brought an extra pair of hands,

Cait, love. Think your mum has outdone herself with the new decorations this year.'

You don't have a choice. You're going to get out of the car and join them.

Cait gives me another apologetic look and this time it's a full-on grimace. 'I'm sorry; you don't have to.'

She's letting you off. Take it.

But as I look into her eyes I can't do it; I can't make up a reason to leave. I don't want to. Except we've just been caught snogging in the car, which means there's going to be some explaining to do. *Friends with benefits* isn't going to cut it with her folks. *Shit.*

I clear my throat. 'It's fine; it'll be…*fun?*'

I say it with a mixture of apprehension and humour, and her eyes sparkle back at me, her mouthed 'Thank you' worth every bit of discomfort.

She turns and opens her door. I do the same, the expression *out of the frying pan and into the fire* dancing through my brain.

Time to get my festive on…

Not awkward…not awkward at all.

I'm not sure who's more uncomfortable, me for putting Jackson in this situation and having to masquerade as a bona fide couple. Or Jackson for playing the role perfectly while being assaulted by all that is Christmas. And when I say assaulted, I mean *assaulted*. Right now, Annie, my eight-year-old niece via brother number two, is hanging tinsel around him like he's the tree, while four-year-old Jake climbs on his back so he can hang baubles on the higher branches.

'Annie, you do know that the tree is this way and not—'

'Granny Marlene doesn't want the tinsel in here this year.' She folds her arms and looks up at me as she lays down the Carey law, her blonde ponytail swinging behind her. 'It's only to go on the one in the living room.'

'You have more than one tree?' Jackson looks at me, his cheeks flushed as he angles Jake just so and has his face squished by the boy's palm as Jake uses it as an anchor point to lean further into the tree.

I try not to laugh. 'Yup.'

'We have five, to be precise,' Annie states precociously, and it's all I can do to smile at Jackson and nod.

'And is the plan to decorate them *all* today?'

'Yup.' It's Jake who pipes up now, settling back onto his shoulders. 'Can you pass me the robin now, Jackson?'

'I see now why you have a whole day dedicated to it,' he mumbles, bending down, careful not to dislodge Jake as he digs in the box of unwrapped decorations. 'This one?'

Jake grabs it. 'Thank you.'

As much as I'm uncomfortable, I'm also loving it. In a heart-warming, send-your-soul-to-mush kind of a way. Which I know is bad. Bad for the barriers I need to keep in place around my heart, bad for what the future has in store—just bad. But watching Jackson surrounded by my family, giving him an inkling of what Christmas can be like with a family such as mine, it feels…special. A gift almost.

We may not be a real couple, but we are friends, and I can give him that at least. Although he may not see it in quite the same way. Having spent two hours with us already, he's had a grilling from each of my brothers, had his cheeks pinched by Gran, and been poured a welcome-to-the-family whisky by Dad.

I'll be lucky if our friends-with-benefits arrangement lasts the day.

'You can head off if you need to?' I rush the question out and it has his lips quirking up, his eyes laughing into mine.

'You're kidding, right? I don't dare. I'm sure Marlene has already adjusted the table.'

'Granny Marlene has it sorted,' Annie butts in, pulling out another piece of tinsel and contemplating where she can hang it off Jackson next. 'She made Dad peel more veg.'

'Did she now?' I take hold of Annie's shoulders and turn her towards the living room. 'Why don't you take the tinsel through there, to the right tree, before you have Jackson tied down?'

My cheeks flush as the memory of being tied down for real scores my brain. My eyes flit to Jackson and I know he's thinking the same. I give a quick shake of my head to his deep laugh.

'Right, Captain Jake,' he declares, 'what's next?'

'Are you sure?' I say softly. I don't want him scared off—I don't want him to leave now either, but if it means keeping our fragile arrangement in place I'd rather he went and I saw him later.

But his grin is wide as he looks to me and his eyes shine. 'Yes.'

His happiness doesn't look fake. He looks surprisingly at home and my chest eases, my heart not so much. I want this and I want it for real.

He frowns. 'Hey, are you okay?'

He's asking me and I know the blood has left my face, my throat too tight to speak. I curse Blondie for breaking him, I curse my heart for not playing ball, I curse it all as I swallow and give him a nod. 'Hangover.'

'Right, who's up for eggnog?' Matt, my eldest brother walks in, his heavily pregnant wife, Marie, in his wake.

'Please tell me it's a yes,' she says. 'I certainly can't drink it, not with the amount of rum Granny has put in it.'

'Sorry, love, but she's right, it wouldn't be eggnog without it.' He leans back to give her a kiss to the cheek, their love so obvious, and it stamps all over my bruised heart.

'Thanks, *Matt*.' I roll my eyes playfully. 'You know Jackson has to drive later, right?'

'I can get us a cab,' the driver in question says, like it's nothing. Like staying here and playing happy families with my enormous family is an everyday occurrence for him and I can't prevent the look I send his way. I'm not sure if it's panicked or grateful or soppy or all of the above.

'You sure?'

'Stop worrying,' he whispers in my ear, low enough for me to hear, low enough for its deep resonance to send a tremor of excitement running through my body.

'I sure am.' He lowers Jake from his back and slips his arm around my waist, startling my nerve endings into a dizzying dance. 'Unless you're not up to more alcohol just yet?'

I erupt on a breathless laugh. 'No, I'm ready.'

We join my brother and his wife, scooping up a glass each. 'Cheers.'

We clink them together and drink.

I take in the happy smiles, the perfect moment, and wish so hard I could make it real. I hold Jackson's eye and see everything I want looking back at me…

Why can't you just love me?

I don't know what's happening other than the fact that this feels *nice*; it feels like I belong, which in itself is ridiculous. I don't belong at all. I've never been part of a family. I've never been fussed over, looked after, fed even.

But her family have sucked me into their warm bubble and I can't escape it.

Worse, I'm not ready to escape it.

I tell myself it feels good because it's for her. It's for Cait and it's making her happy. I tell myself it's okay because we're only pretending to be a couple for the sake of her family. That outside of this we are still just friends.

I focus on her and the happiness that glows around the table—the bustling table that's big enough to hold a football team and then some. Her brothers have eased up on me now that a few drinks have been consumed and we're talking football; there's a lot to be said for supporting the same team. As for their wives and her mum, they've eagerly welcomed me in and I get the impression they're just happy that Cait's '*finally*' brought a boyfriend home.

The one person I struggle with is her dad. It's one thing to be polite, friendly, happy with everyone else, but with him… I don't want to pretend. Not about his daughter, who I know is his world. I don't doubt for a second that the Careys love their kids equally, but she is a daddy's girl, the youngest and the one they were holding out for, thanks to the sons that came before.

I know all this because they've actually said it, joked about it even. They're all so free and open and loving. Just as Cait is.

I feel the heavy weight in my gut, the tug on my heart that won't quit, and I have to cough to swallow the dessert wine her father has just poured for me.

'Very nice,' I say, keeping my eye contact brief as I battle with my conscience and the wish that things could be different. 'Thank you.'

'Thank *you* for helping; we'd still be decorating if you hadn't turned up.' He winks at me as he sits back down at the table. 'Not to mention the help with the rabble.'

He gestures to the kids; now fed and watered, all seven have left the table and are once again tearing around like they're on speed, though Cait assures me it's just the excitement of Christmas running in their veins.

'It's been a pleasure.' And it has, in spite of my inner turmoil.

I know I've yet to convince Cait though. I catch the occasional crease between her brows when she's watching me; I'll reassure her as soon as I get her home.

I'll reassure her all the more once I get her in that elf get-up again and do everything I wanted to do last night and more. I'll reassure her when it's back to being about sex. Just sex. Because loving her is too easy when I can mask it in make-believe.

'You know, you could always stay, Cait? You and Jackson are more than welcome, and your old room is all made up.'

She tenses up beside me. I tense too.

'No, thanks, Mum. I have work tomorrow; it's easier if—'

I watch the way the light threatens to flicker out in her mother's face, see her father place his hand over his wife's arm and the latter speaks volumes.

'It's okay, Cait, I can drop you back at yours early enough tomorrow.'

Her head snaps to me, her surprise so evident in her frown. 'Really?'

'Yes…if you'd like to?' I add a nod when I see her continued hesitation.

'Okay.' She shakes her head at me, her smile disbelieving, but there's a glow about her, a happiness, and my chest tightens. It's hardly keeping it about the sex, playing happy families. But seeing her happy, her mother and father too, it makes it feel right.

I don't know what the deal is, whether they don't see Cait much these days and miss her, or whether they're worried about her in general, but I know having her stay is important to them and I can do this.

And what about tomorrow, and the next day and the next, when they expect you to be an item?

She leans over and kisses my cheek. 'Thank you.'

I breathe in her floral scent, her happiness, and smile. 'You're welcome.'

I'm sure we can work our way out of this when we're ready. But for now I'm going to enjoy making Cait happy. I'm going to enjoy being a normal everyday couple, in a normal everyday family…

And maybe, just maybe, Granny's eggnog went to your head hours ago.

I climb out of bed to turn off the light, but as my finger hovers over the switch I turn back to look at him. Jackson. In my bed. My *childhood* bed.

It couldn't be more fantastical if my bedding was still covered in fluffy rabbits and flowers. I've never brought a partner home.

And I haven't now, I remind myself and ignore the twist to my stomach.

He looks at me, the white quilt slung low over his bare chest, one arm hooked behind his head, the other over his front. I trace his tattoo down and my mouth dries. My very own pin-up. Only he's not on my walls, he's in my bed, and he's completely naked. Younger me would definitely squeal.

He cocks one sexy brow. 'You going to stand there all night?'

I wet my lips. 'No, I'm just taking this in for later recall.'

He laughs softly and rolls onto his side, palming the space next to him. 'I'll give you plenty more to remember if you get yourself over here.'

Oh, yes.

Off goes the light and I pad over to him. I can just make out his silhouette in the dark and the excited flutters in my belly feel like they're trying to escape through my throat.

He lifts the covers to welcome me in, letting them fall around me as I join him. His hands are hot on my skin as they smooth beneath my T and pull me closer. I wriggle into him, my hands against his chest, his hardness pressing into my belly as he cradles me to him.

This feels too good, too nice. I blink up at him in the dark. 'Thank you for today.'

He lowers his mouth to mine and kisses me gently. 'You don't need to thank me. I've had a good time.'

I press back off his chest, trying to read his expression even though I can't. 'You have?'

I sense his grin. 'Yes. Why are you so surprised?'

I give a soft laugh. 'Because my family are full-on. Because you met the entire lot in one day and you're not…we're not…' I can't even bring myself to say it and his arms tense around me. 'It's just a lot.'

He's quiet and I wish the lights were back on so I could see his face. All I have to go on is the gentle stroking of his fingers against my skin as he continues to hold me.

'It's okay; you can admit it.' I say softly. 'There aren't many men who can cope with an all-out family affair, even when they *are* in a relationship.'

'I have enjoyed it, Cait. You're lucky to have such a loving family, and they're lucky to have you too.' He presses a kiss to my brow and I breathe it in, the caress, his softness, his words. 'By being here, I know we've made them happy, and that makes it the right thing to do.'

'But it's a lie.'

He tightens his hold around me and swallows my words with a kiss so fierce. 'This isn't a lie.'

He rolls me under him. 'And if it makes your family happy, while we're happy like this…' he rolls his hips into me to emphasise his point and I whimper as I wrap my legs around him and move to meet him '…where's the harm?'

He's right—where *is* the harm? People fall in and out of relationships all the time. And when this is over he'll just be a boyfriend passing through.

It *is* fine.

Or it would be if my heart could let him go as easily. My eyes prick and I squeeze them shut.

'No harm,' I whisper, throwing my focus into the fiery path he's creating with his mouth, along my jaw, down my neck, his kisses no longer fierce. They're soft, teasing, tantalising, as his hard length presses against my knickers and urges my hips to roll.

I lose myself in the sensation of Jackson making love—no, *fucking* me. Though this doesn't feel like 'fucking', not the kind we've done to date. He's gentle, his hands smoothing over my skin as he encourages me to strip off my T.

'You are beautiful, Caitlin,' he murmurs as I rise up and pull it over my head, his hands quick to cover me. 'Your skin is so soft. I've dreamed of you these last four months—the way you taste, the way you feel, the freckles that trail down your front...' His fingers caress the very same path, teasing at the lines of my bra and making me whimper for more. 'I love how responsive you are, I love how your nipples tighten for me...' He tweaks one and kisses me at the same time, swallowing my moan.

'We have neighbours, remember.'

Oh, God. Mum. Dad. Granny!

'You think you can keep quiet?'

'Do you?' I whisper back. He's hardly quiet and the truth is I love how vocal he is; I love his growl that seems to stay deep within his throat, I love his dirty talk.

Enough with the 'love', Cait.

He started it though—his long list of things he 'loves' about me... If only.

A tormented cry rises up within me and I kiss him to trap it, to bury it, to tell myself to take all he is willing to give and be happy. But he's so slow, savouring, unhurried and it feels too gentle, too caring, too confusing.

His hands smooth around my back to release my bra clasp and I shimmy out of it, toss it aside and his fingers commence their slow path over my skin, down my hips, beneath the strap of my knickers as he eases them down my legs and I take over once more, flicking them away with my foot and pulling him back to me.

He laughs softly. 'You're in such a rush.'

I gulp down the emotion. 'I want you.'

'I want you too, baby.'

I nod and our noses brush. I can see his eyes glint in the dark. He's looking right at me, inside me—he must *see* it. My love for him. And if he does, why isn't he running? Why is he running his cock up and down my seam as though he has all the time in the world? Why is he stroking my hair back from my face like he…like he loves me too?

'Jackson?'

'Yes.'

'What are we doing? Really?'

'I don't know.'

'This isn't just sex, is it?'

He drags in a shaky breath and for a second I feel like he's going to withdraw so I wrap my legs around him for insurance and I stroke the tense muscles of his back. I tell him with my body that I don't want this to stop, regardless of whether he can give me what I want or tell me what I need to hear in this moment.

'No.' It's so raw, it's so honest. 'It could never be

just sex with you, Caitlin. I think that's why I avoided it for so long.'

'Why avoid something that feels so right?'

'Because I'm no good for you. I've told you before.'

'But I don't understand.'

He lowers his head and presses his forehead against mine. 'I'm fucked up, Cait. I know nothing of relationships—good relationships, healthy ones.'

'That's not true. Look at Coco and Ash. Look at my entire family; it's bursting with them.'

'*I'm* the issue. Not those around me. Not you.'

'Why? Because you were brought up by your father? Because your mum left you? Because of… because of the blonde?'

He was tense before but now he's cold, his skin prickling with goose bumps, and I know I've fucked up.

'I'm just trying to understand, Jackson.'

His swallow is audible in the dark. 'I know you are.'

'Then tell me…' I keep up the slow stroke of my fingers on his back and I keep my legs wrapped around him. 'Trust me with it.'

'I can't.'

'*Please*, Jackson.'

He kisses me, his lips brushing so softly against mine, and when he lifts his head I swear his eyes are damp in the low light. 'I'd rather make love to you.'

My breath catches, my heart pulses—*make love*. 'But you…'

'*This* I can do…'

My brain finishes the sentence for him.

And it's enough. I think of Jackson four months ago, the one who swore he would never make love… This is something, and for now it's enough.

'Yes,' I whisper, kissing him back, angling my body to meet him and when he enters me I trap my sob in our kiss. I let him fill me, rock into me, and with every thrust I silently tell him that I love him, that I want to keep him, that I want us to work.

If I can just keep hold of him long enough to make him realise this could be real, long enough for him to trust me with his demons and let me in.

I have time. For him, I'll wait for as long as it takes…

CHAPTER TWELVE

I HAVE THIS feeling in my chest I can't describe. It's been two weeks since Cait and I embarked on this affair that's not an affair. Neither of us have voiced what it is, not since the night at her parents' place, and I feel like the clock is ticking. Like I'm slowly suffocating under the pressure of what I feel for her and what I'm keeping locked inside.

She wants the truth of my past and I can't give it to her. The very idea breaks me out in a cold sweat and though I'm sitting alone in my office now I almost retch with it.

I press my fist to my mouth and curse my stupidity. How could I think I could keep all this under control? How could I let it go on so long when every day that passes gives Cait hope that we could be more? I see the look in her eye—I see the love, the belief that I'm fixable, that we can play happy families for real. And every day has those three words clambering further up my throat—*I love you*. Words I cannot confess because Cait will never understand that though I love her I can't have her.

I spin away from my desk and stand to look at the poster on the wall. It's a blow-up of the advert that was issued when the club relaunched under my ownership, when it became Blacks. It's a reminder of how far I've come and what I've left behind. But the scars...nothing can take those away, not even Cait.

And, given enough time, those scars will ruin her too.

It's why I need to end it now. But I told myself that yesterday and the day before and the day before that... Every morning I wake up with her in my arms and in my heart and tell myself the same, but I can't do it.

Which only proves how twisted I am. Twisted and selfish and fucked up.

A rap on the door accompanies my fist to the poster and I take a breath, dropping back down into my seat.

'Come in.' I spin back into my desk, rubbing at my fist and frown at the opening door.

'Hey, bad boy!' Caitlin appears—Caitlin in full-on elf mode. *Holy fuck*.

My heart stutters, the rush of heat down low no less powerful than it was the first time I saw her elfed up. In fact, it's more because now it's filled with everything that's happened between us these last two weeks. It's love, it's desire, it's a wish for so much more, and fuck, fuck. Fuck. How can I stop this?

She smiles at me all sexy and sultry as she flicks the door closed behind her.

'Santa sent me to sort you out... He even gave me a special little stocking just for you.' She saunters up to me all cat-like and sexy, her hips swaying, her midriff bare, her little skirt and stockings showing so much thigh that my cock is already like granite. The blood pounds through my body, between my ears, drowning out my conscience as she swings the stocking in front of her. 'Wait until you see what naughtiness awaits you in this little bundle.'

'Isn't it a little early for presents?'

She sets it down on the desk and leans over me, her hands resting on the arms of my chair as she teases me with her cleavage, her sexy pout and her desire-laden eyes. 'It's never too early for this kind of present and, since Mum's inviting you to stay for Christmas, I wasn't sure when I'd get the chance to give—'

'What?' My chest squeezes tight and my pulse skips a beat. *Wait.* She couldn't have—she wouldn't. I mean Christmas Day. It's one thing to masquerade as a couple and do the odd family dinner together, but Christmas. I don't even like Christmas.

Liar. You liked it well enough these past two weeks when you've been present-buying with Cait, decorating with her, eating festive fancies, drinking mulled wine, Granny's eggnog...

'Hey, it's okay; she knows you don't have family and thought it would be nice for you, for us, to, you know, spend Christmas with them.'

'And you said yes?'

'I said I'd ask you, but—' She shrugs, a frown marring her brow, the spark in her eyes starting to ebb. 'Sorry, Jackson, I didn't realise the idea would upset you so much. I thought after all we've shared these past two weeks, we were kind of in that place.'

In that place. In a relationship. It's confirmation of everything my conscience has been spewing and suddenly my brain is racing, my heart too.

'Cait—'

I break off as the door swings open. 'Jackson, we need to—'

'*Eliza?*'

She freezes in her tracks as Cait scrambles off me, her eyes quick to take in the scene she interrupted.

'*You?*' she blurts, her eyes narrowed and shooting daggers.

'Me?' Cait says, her frown all the more severe and directed wholly at Eliza now.

'So *you're* the reason he's not returning my calls.'

Cait looks from Eliza to me and back again. 'I have no idea what you're talking about, but don't you think it's polite to knock and wait to be invited in before you barge into someone's private office?'

Eliza laughs. 'Oh, girl, I don't wait for anyone.'

Cait doesn't even flinch and I love her for it. I love how her spine straightens and her chin lifts. Doesn't matter that she's all green and white elf, she has all the poise of Eliza in her designer trench coat and polished air. 'No, I don't suppose someone like you would.'

Eliza scowls before looking at me. 'We need to talk. *Alone.*'

She looks pointedly at Cait before coming back

to me and I'm torn. I don't want Cait to feel outdone, but neither do I want her to bear witness to whatever Eliza has come to say.

I stand and take Cait's hand, a gesture that Eliza's beady gaze clocks but I don't care.

'Go upstairs, Cait, and wait for me.' I squeeze her fingers gently.

She sends another look between Eliza and me but nods. 'Okay.'

I watch her go, my entire body hooked on the appeal of her. My heart too.

The second the door closes I round on Eliza. 'What is it now?' My voice vibrates with anger and she gives a high-pitched laugh.

'Calm down, Jackson. You can have your little plaything later, if you find you still want her after what I have to offer you.'

'Want her?'

'Yes.' She smiles. 'I never was the jealous type. I can share. And I have a business proposition for you, one that means you and I can work *and* play together again.'

'You're deluded, Eliza.'

'*I'm* deluded? Seems to me you're the one who's deluded if you think that silly little package can keep you happy.'

'You have no idea what you're talking about.'

'Don't I?' she purrs, strutting towards me, and I know what's coming, I know that look of old and I turn away to head for my desk, sensing the scowl she gives me as she stills. 'Don't turn away from me, Jackson.'

A laugh erupts out of me, stalling my hand as I reach for my whisky. I shake my head and look back at her, not because she asked it of me, no fucking way, but to glare at her. 'Do you honestly think you get to tell me what to do, Eliza?'

Her smile is cold. 'There was a time when you did *everything* I told you. In fact, you'd plead for your next instruction. You remember those days, those nights, don't you?'

I swallow back the bile that rises.

'I wish to God I didn't.'

She laughs. 'You're lying to yourself, Jackson. The things we did, the things you let me do, my sweet, you don't grow out of wanting them.'

I shudder, the words thrumming out of me. 'Get the fuck out, Eliza. Now!'

Her brows quirk, her eyes widen, but whatever's going through her head has her expression changing, colour rising in her cheeks. 'Oh, I get it, it's role reversal. *That's* why you like the candy cane. She lets you do to her the things I used to do to you.'

My gut rolls. Pins and needles fizz all over the surface of my skin and I can't move, I can't breathe. The wedding night comes back to me, the odd night since—the power dynamic, the control.

'But Jackson… I can be just as docile, baby.'

Baby—I call Cait that too. I *say* it just like that.

She steps towards me and my eyes refocus. She's untying the knot in her coat, her head slightly bowed as she watches me from beneath her lashes. 'I can take…just as much as I can give.'

'You *take* one more step and I'll have you thrown out.'

She stalls, her hands pausing in their task as her lips quirk with an uncertainty I've never seen in her before. 'Are you serious?'

'Deadly.' I can't look at her any more. I can't look at her without seeing everything she did to me merging with everything I did to Caitlin. I turn to my desk and take up the whisky bottle, praying she doesn't see the way my hand shakes, the way her words cripple me inside.

'But my business proposition… I want to talk about Berlin, Madrid too. I—'

'Nothing on this earth would make me go back into business with you.'

She gives an anxious chuckle. 'Jackson, be rational for a—'

'I won't ask you again, Eliza.' I focus on pouring the drink. 'Leave or I *will* make you.'

I let myself into Jackson's apartment and try to ignore the unease that's making its way into every part of me. I don't like her, and it's not just jealousy. She looks at him like she owns him, like she's made her mark and no one else can have him.

And I know she broke him. I know it's her that stands between us having a future, that whatever happened, it still affects Jackson now and he won't open up to me.

But seeing her tonight, hot on the back of Jackson's outright panic at my invitation from Mum… My patience is wearing thin. We can't keep doing this. *I* can't.

Either Jackson takes the leap or this has to end. Before I get in any deeper.

Before?

I shake my head, the painful realisation like an arrow through the heart. It's too late for holding back. I love him with all of me and if he turns me away now, if he…

I can't finish the thought. I throw my overnight bag onto the sofa and head to Jackson's fully stocked bar. It's state-of-the-art, all glass and accented lighting. I go straight for the whisky. I need the hit of something strong to offset what's happening deep down inside.

I pour a hefty measure and walk right up to the glass, looking out on the glittering lights below and I see nothing. My head is full of him, of us. I replay all the moments of intimacy, all the signs that things were changing, that he was starting to feel the same. The signs that made me confident he wouldn't turn down Mum's invite…

Not true—you used it as a test, and look where it ended.

I take a swig of the whisky, wince at the burn and take another, wanting it to be more painful than the pinch around my heart.

I shouldn't have left. I should have stayed. Stood my ground.

And then what? End up in a bitch fight over a guy? Never.

And he asked me to leave.

Maybe that hurts more, maybe I wanted to see him throw *her* out, and choose me over her. But he didn't.

My stomach rolls and I lean my forehead against the glass, pressing hard. It's cold and unrelenting. I drag in a breath and my mind replays how he spoke to me, how he asked me to come up here and wait for him. The way his eyes blazed, the gentle squeeze of his fingers around mine, the connection...the very *real* connection that Coco spoke of.

The connection you thought existed when you invited him for Christmas?

I spin away from the glass, squeeze my eyes shut and when I open them again I know this is it. Make or break.

I check my watch, clock the time and wait.

And wait.

I stare at the floor, my hand pressed against the closed door to my apartment, unable to go in. Unable to face what awaits me on the other side.

Caitlin. The woman I love and...and abused. My lungs contract, air rushing out of me as the pain winds me so completely.

Eliza is in my head—her words, her brutal truth—and I can't shake her out of it. She only confirmed everything I already knew. Everything that tells me I have to end this now. Before I go further. Before I break her, like Eliza broke me.

And so I've stalled.

It's late—one a.m. late. I've been gone hours. I've been setting things in motion for the business, finding out through my own channels what Eliza hinted at with regards to Berlin and Madrid. It seems her marriage problems extend to their business and their investors are getting nervous. It's an opportunity. A chance to swoop in and take over, really make Blacks global, and the ultimate revenge for what *she*—what *they*—did.

The calls could have waited though. Eliza and Damien, the club expansion, it all could have waited. I just didn't want to face Cait. The end that has to happen.

I straighten up, square my shoulders and harden my heart.

You're doing it for her...

CHAPTER THIRTEEN

THE CLICK OF the door closing rouses me and I push up to sitting on the sofa, my eyes bleary in the low light of the room. 'Jackson?'

'Yeah…it's me.'

His voice is rough, raw, and I brush the hair away from my eyes to make out his presence in the darkened hallway. I hear his keys hit the dish beside the door. My head's all foggy with sleep and I rub my eyes. I must have been asleep a while.

Was he really with her all this time?

My stomach writhes and I pull the sleeves of my jumper into my palms and bring my knees up to my chest, clutching them to me. I've long since changed out of my costume and into the comfies I packed for tomorrow. I'm so glad of it now.

'What time is it?'

'Late.'

No shit. I know that much.

He's slow to approach and the closer he gets the more I can see. His eyes are bloodshot, his hair is crazed—I swallow, please let it be by his own hand.

The thought zips through me, waking up my brain, clearing the fuzz.

'Has she only just gone?' I feel sick even as the words leave my lips.

He tosses his jacket on the sofa and heads to his bar. He doesn't even look at me. The move speaks volumes. The silence between us stretches, heavy and thick, broken only by the clink of crystal on glass, the release of the stopper in his whisky bottle and the slosh of liquid as he pours.

He knocks back a mouthful, his face, what I can see of it, is drawn tight, grim.

'Jackson?'

He flicks me the briefest of looks, chucks back another swig and heads to the wall of glass, as far away from me as he can. I shiver, the chilling dread building out of my control, and I press my chin into my knees until it hurts.

'She left just after you.'

Hope flickers and my head snaps up. 'Then… where have you been?'

He angles his head to the side so I can make out his profile, but his eyes don't reach me. 'Taking care of business.'

'Business?' I frown. 'What kind of business?'

'She brought something to my attention…something that could benefit Blacks.' He looks back to the glass. 'I've been making calls, putting wheels in motion, it's going to take me abroad for a while.'

He sounds…clinical. I've never heard his voice so

soulless; it takes me another second for his words to actually register and then: abroad? Eliza? Business?

I shake my head. 'I don't understand. What's Eliza got to do with the business? Wasn't she just a client? An...*ex*?' I choke over it. I acknowledge as I say it Jackson's rule never to sleep with the clientele. No need to ask where that rule came from then. I also realise with sickening clarity that he deemed business more important than coming to me.

'She works in the same industry, has her own chain of clubs. She and her...' his shoulders shudder, the move so negligible I wonder if I've imagined it, and then his head lifts '...her husband, Damien, they used to own Blacks...before it became Blacks, before it became mine.'

'You worked together?'

He gives an abrupt laugh and sips at his drink. 'You could call it that.'

'And now...what?'

'Now, nothing.'

'So why was she here? Tonight, and two weeks ago.'

He's silent.

'Jackson?'

His continued silence is damning enough.

'She wants you back?'

He nods.

I swallow down the rising chill. 'And?'

'I made it clear it's never going to happen.'

My body relaxes a little, my voice easing as I say, 'Good. And how——'

'No, not good, Cait.' He suddenly rounds on me, his eyes glittering with so much emotion, so much pain. '*Nothing* about this is good.'

'What—'

'It's over, Cait. *This.* You and me.' He thrusts his glass out and gestures between us, the whisky sloshing over the sides. 'We can't do this any more. *I can't.*'

I'm hearing the words but all I can see is the hurt, the torment, the sadness…all things that our love can take away if he'd just let me in.

He raises a trembling hand to his hair as he sweeps it out of his face and avoids my eye now. 'You can stay here tonight, in the guest room.' Clinical Jackson is back. 'I have a flight out of the country tomorrow. It'll give us the space we need, time to adjust.'

My laugh is harsh, incredulous, and I push myself to my feet. 'Time to *adjust*?'

His eyes flicker in my direction. 'Don't shake your head at me, Cait.'

I don't even realise I'm doing it as I stride towards him, my blood boiling, my heart aching.

'Do you really think it's that simple?' I throw at him when I'm within arm's reach. 'Do you really think *time* will stop me loving you?'

His eyes snap to mine, his pallor severe. 'Don't say that.'

'Say what? That I *love* you, Jackson, that I've likely loved you ever since I fell in your lap six years ago?'

He walks away from me, striding to the bar and pouring another drink, but I'm hot on his tail. 'You can't avoid this conversation, Jackson. You owe me the truth.'

He throws back his drink and gulps it down. 'You don't love me…' His voice is hoarse. 'You can't.'

'Why? Because you don't deserve it?' I fist my hands on my hips and stare at him, eyes wide. 'That's what you keep telling me, right? That you don't want to hurt me, that you want me to be *safe*. Well, news-flash, Jackson, I *am* hurt, and if you want me to walk away from this, from what we have, you need to tell me the truth. All of it…starting with Eliza.'

He has the decency to look at me now, *really* look at me, and my heart is shattering. He's defeated. It's there in his eyes, in the slump of his shoulders, the tremble in his fingers.

'Please, Cait, don't make me tell you.'

'Why? What are you so afraid of?'

He presses his fist to his mouth and drags in air through his nose.

'Jackson, whatever it is—' I soften my tone '—you can trust me with it.'

He eyes me over his fist. The silence stretches and then, finally, he lowers his hand. He is so broken in his surrender that I'm winded. Tears prick the backs of my eyes as I clutch my arms around my middle.

'What did she do to you?' It's a pained whisper and he walks away from me.

He perches on the edge of the sofa and I follow, apprehension weighing me down as I sit beside him. My fingers itch to reach for him and I clench them together, knowing they wouldn't be welcome.

'We had an affair,' he says eventually, 'a long time ago.'

I let out a trapped breath. He's talking. Thank God, he's talking. 'When she owned the club?'

He nods, his eyes glued to his drink, his knuckles white as he grips the glass tight.

'But I met her while I was waiting tables in another bar they owned, in the city. I was young, impressionable and she...'

'She was married?'

Another nod.

'People have affairs all the time, Jackson; it doesn't make you a—'

'I was sixteen, Cait.'

The blood rushes between my ears. My stomach lurches.

'*Sixteen?*' I shake my head. 'No—no, it's not possible. You were a child, not even—'

'It was legal.'

I want to clutch my gut, my mouth, I want to retch, but I daren't. I need to hear this.

'True.' It's quiet, so quiet, because to say it any louder feels like approval and I'm so far from that.

'I felt like the luckiest person alive back then.' His laugh is cold. 'It was hedonistic, intense. She seemed so sure of the world, so confident, and she wanted me... Compared to my home life, to growing up with zero attention...'

'She gave you all of it.'

He nods into his glass. 'I was ready and willing...

and I had a choice. She never made me do anything I didn't want to.'

I shudder, sensing where this is heading and wanting to close my ears and leave them open at the same time. 'What does that mean?'

'She...she had certain...tastes.' His throat bobs. 'Sexually.'

'Like?'

He looks at me and shakes his head, his eyes so pained. 'Don't make me tell you, Cait.'

'If you want this to be over, you have to tell me. You have to make me understand.'

I stare into his eyes and his own tremble back at me.

'Everything and anything,' he whispers. 'It's who she was, who she is. She's a...pro-Dom, and I was her willing submissive.'

Bile rises in my throat, my mind painting the picture of sixteen-year-old Jackson, unloved at home, abused at work. He flinches and looks away; I know he sees the horror in my face, but I can't hide it.

'None of this makes you a bad person, Jackson. Eliza, *yes*. Not you.'

I don't feel like he's listening. His eyes are off me and lost in the past now. 'For years she led me around, took control. I thought she was everything. It didn't matter that she was married, that she was older...'

'You thought you were in love with her.'

'I did,' he scoffs. 'But now I know it was just infatuation. She taught me everything she knew; she brought me into the club to work, invested time and money in me. Gave me the means to start investing in my own interests, gave me the opportunity to buy in to Blacks, to run it with her and Damien.'

'Her husband?' I frown. 'But surely he must have suspected something was going on? You were having an affair under his nose and—'

I break off. I can't make sense of it, but the way Jackson throws back his whisky and stands, turning away from me, I know there's more.

'He knew. He knew from day one...'

'And he let—'

'He watched, Cait.'

'What do you mean, he *watched*?' The blood leaves my face as my hands shoot to the sofa edge, my nails biting into the fabric as I grip it tightly and stare at his rigid back.

'She would set me up in her special room, *our* room she'd call it, and he would...he would watch it through the mirrors.'

'No, no, they...no.' Oh, God, I can't speak. It's playing out like some twisted thriller in my head, only it's no movie. It's Jackson's story, his life, his reality.

He turns to look at me and all I see is the broken teenager he must have been, and I can't bear it any longer. I need to hold him. I need to make him see that none of this is down to him.

'Oh, Jackson.' I push up but he shakes his head, his hand raised, palm out.

'Don't. I can't bear you being close to me, not... not when I'm telling you this.'

I force myself to sink back as the puzzle that is

Jackson falls into place. It's so much worse than I ever could have imagined.

'It's how he got his kicks, how they both did.'

'When...?' My throat closes over and I force myself to swallow, try again. 'When did you find out?'

'Years later...too many years later.' His eyes are back on the glass hanging from his limp fingers. 'The night I proposed and asked her to leave him.'

'You *proposed* to her?'

He nods. 'I told her I loved her, that I wanted to marry her.'

'And what did she say?'

The questions are coming on autopilot now. Questions I need to have the answers to.

He looks at me, his mouth pulling up in one corner. 'She laughed. She asked me how I could possibly think she would want that. That's when she told me the truth—about Damien, about how I fitted so perfectly into *their* marriage, and that things didn't need to change.'

I press my fingers to my lips; they're numb, my whole body is.

'And you,' I whisper. 'What did you say?'

'I was crushed... All that time, I thought she was in love with me, as I was her. She'd played me for a fool, but no more. I told her it was over, that I wanted the club and if she didn't agree I'd sell my story instead. About how she seduced a sixteen-year-old boy, twenty years her junior, an employee, while her forty-year-old husband watched.'

'*Jesus*, Jackson.' It rushes out of me, the picture he

paints too horrific, and I can't stop myself pushing up off the sofa, reaching out for him. But he backs away and I hate that he does so. 'Please, let me—'

'Don't, Cait. I don't deserve your sympathy and I certainly don't want your pity.'

'But don't you see, it wasn't your fault? What she did, what *they* did, it's twisted, wrong.'

'And it made me who I am today. I tried to warn you. I told you I was no good for you. I'm messed up, fucked in the head.'

'No, Jackson, *you're* not. *They* are.'

'That's where you're wrong. The things I've done to you, Ash and Coco's wedding night…' He shakes his head, turning away from me once more. 'What I did to you was no better than what she did to me.'

'You're wrong. There was *nothing* wrong with what we did, what we shared. I wanted that every bit as much as you, and I still want it. I want all of you, Jackson, I want the darkness so I can make it light. I want to show you that you're a better man than you think you are. I want to show you that you are worth loving.'

He turns his head to look at me side on, his eyes pleading, his frown crushing. 'You can't *change* me, Cait. I am what I am.'

I slip my hand around the glass in his hand and take it from him, placing it on the coffee table so that I can lace my fingers in his. Just the simple touch of skin against skin comforts me, warms me, connects us.

I pull him to face me.

'You're not listening to me, Jackson.' My heart pulses in my chest, desperate, needing him to see. 'I don't need to change you; I need you to see yourself as I see you. As our friends see you. I need you to see that you *are* lovable, you are kind, you are honest, you are loyal.'

His eyes glisten and my heart aches so acutely it's a physical pain.

He wets his lips, his voice hushed. 'I'm messed up, Cait.'

'That doesn't make you a bad person...' I cup his face in my palms. 'It means you ought to talk to someone—if not me, a professional. Someone who can help you. But it doesn't mean I can't love you, Jackson. *Please,* just let me love you.'

He squeezes his eyes shut, his hands lifting to cover mine as he drags in a breath and then his hands fall to my wrists, gripping as he forces them down. *No, no, no.* He opens his eyes and I see the steely resolve, the hardness, the decision he's made. My head is shaking before he even speaks.

'I can't. I just can't do it. I can't risk breaking you.'

'You're breaking me now.'

'It's over, Cait. You need to accept it.'

'No, no, Jackson, I won't. I love you. I'm not giving up on what we have, on us...on *you*.'

He releases me and walks away.

'*Please*, Jackson.'

He doesn't even slow his stride as he heads for the door.

'Where are you going?'

'Back to the club.'

'Jackson, don't do this. Don't walk away.'

He keeps going.

'How can you give Eliza the power to ruin your future?' I call out, desperate.

Now he stops, and a tiny spark of hope flickers to life.

'Can't you see,' I plead softly, 'you're letting her dictate your future as well as your past? Can't you see you're letting her win?'

'This isn't some game, Cait. This isn't about Eliza winning. Nobody wins in this. I can't love you like you deserve to be loved.'

'Enough with the deserving, Jackson. I'm sick of it. I wanted you to fuck me, I wanted you to tie me down, I would have begged for it if needed. You didn't *make* me. I'm *not* a naïve teenager and you sure as hell didn't have some twisted fuck watching me unawares…did you?'

'How can you ask me that?'

'See, even you know it's ridiculous.'

He shakes his head at me, and I know it's not sinking in. He's not hearing me.

'Please, Cait, I'm trying to do the right thing.'

'Fuck doing the right thing!' I'm out of words. I can't think what else to say, only that I can't stay here and wait for him to come back again. I grab my overnight bag from the floor and stride past him to the door.

'Where are you going?'

I grip the door handle and turn to stare him down.

'Home. There's nothing left for me to say, nothing else I can do…' I see my heartbreak reflected back at me and still he won't move towards me.

I wet my lips and forge ahead. 'You can do one thing for me, though.'

'What?' he croaks.

'Tell me you don't love me.'

He stares at me, immobilised, pale.

'Tell. Me. You. Don't. Love. Me. Jackson.'

His mouth parts, his eyes flash, but nothing.

'You can't, can you?'

The air shudders out of him. 'I won't lie to you, Cait.'

I give a pained laugh. 'You'll willingly break both our hearts though.'

Anger surges in my blood—anger that he could do this, anger that he could love me and not fight to keep me. 'It's okay, Jackson, I give up. I can't make you accept my love. I can't force you to accept that everything we've done together we've done because we *both* wanted it. And I can't force you into a relationship you don't want to be in.'

I look at the bag in my hand, the glimpse of green and white, the excitement I felt when I came to the club this evening, hyped up on my love for him. My conviction that he would accept Mum's invite, that we would spend Christmas together and what that would mean for us as a couple is long forgotten. I was a fool. But I won't be a fool now.

I straighten up and pierce him with one last stare.

'You can tell yourself whatever you like, Jackson. But screw your past, screw the mistakes, screw what *she* did to you. It's *you* doing this to me now, and if you can't see the love that's staring you in the face, if you can't accept what we have, then…' I lift my chin and hold my ground '…maybe you don't deserve me after all.'

I pull open the door and pause on the threshold.

'You are not Eliza, Jackson,' I say it to the floor. 'It's time you realised that.'

And then I leave. I don't spare him another glance because I know it'll break me. And I won't beg him to let me love him. I won't beg to be loved in return. I won't beg full stop. I was strong enough to go into this with my eyes wide open, the least I can do is leave with the same strength, the same dignity.

And who the hell are you trying to kid?

A sob rises up within me and I stumble on the stairs, righting myself just in time.

I can't stop the tears from falling freely now. I can't stop my heart shattering. I can't stop myself loving him all the more for what he's suffered.

Because I do love him. I love him more now than I did before, knowing what happened, what he's been through, understanding him…

I'm hardly aware of the people manning the exit to Blacks as I brush past them, accidentally shoulder barging one as I struggle to see past the tears. I mutter an apology and keep on going. I don't spy the curious looks being sent my way or acknowledge their concerned remarks.

I just want to get home. Now.

* * *

I stare at the door. Stare and stare until my eyes water.

It's done. She's gone.

It's done. She's gone.

I can't stop the words on repeat in my brain. I know if I do then the other words will rage louder. The ones that repeat her words back at me…

I don't need to change you; I need you to see yourself as I see you. As our friends see you…you are lovable, you are kind, you are honest, you are loyal… let me love you.

And her parting shot: *You are not Eliza…*

She's right. I'm not. I would never, ever do what they did. They abused me.

I was abused.

It's the first time I've labelled it in such a way, and I shudder and shake as my gut writhes with the acceptance.

It doesn't excuse the way I am now. It doesn't take away the things I insist on in bed, the things my twisted mind craves…

But then I think of the night at her parents', the sex in the dark, slow, loving…no need for control, no power dynamic in play. I think of the mornings we've shared, waking up with our bodies entwined. I think of the easy time with her family, the laughter and the fun…even the festive cheer.

I think of Eliza tonight, of how she's incapable of love, but me, *Christ…*

Tell me you don't love me.

Impossible. I *know* I love her.

You'll willingly break both our hearts...

The pain swamps me. Is this how she feels too? This desperate, this alone, this broken? All because of me. And why? Because of some twisted notion that I could be like Eliza. That I am Eliza.

No, it's more than that. It's the loss of control; it's the fear of opening myself up to loving someone and having them walk away, the fear of being broken again.

I drag in a breath and fork my hands through my hair.

She's not the one walking away—you are!

The thought of life without her grips me and I fall forward, my hands clawing at my knees. What the hell have I done? I can't breathe for it.

She loves me. She truly loves me. The first person in my life to ever truly love me and I've pushed her away.

I stumble forward, get to the door and yank it open. 'Cait!'

I'm moving, running, my body and mind focused on one thing—to get to her and tell her the one thing I haven't dared. That I love her.

God, how I love her.

I pound down the stairs, my heart thumping the same beat so loudly in my ears that I can't even take a full breath, can't pause long enough to walk to the next flight, I'm throwing myself down them, but I can't hear her, I can't see her.

How long was I like that for? Hunched over in indecision, paralysed by my own messed-up state?

I reach the pavement outside, scan the street, up and down. She's not there. There are people, there are cars, but there's no her.

I hesitate on the spot and hear the unmistakable skid of a car, a blood-curdling scream just around the corner.

'*Cait!*'

There's a thud, followed by quiet. Deathly quiet.

I know it's her. My head spins, my heart contracts, and I'm stumbling and running.

I break out onto the road, skidding to a halt as my gut rolls. I don't want to see it. I don't.

But no amount of mental talk can take away the image of her lying on the ground, the car headlights highlighting her crumpled state, and my entire world crumples with her.

CHAPTER FOURTEEN

I CAN HEAR VOICES, lots of voices. Or wailing. Or is that a siren?

I try and open my eyes but the light's too bright. I try to move but it hurts too much. I want the blackness back, no pain, no noise...

I'm cold, so cold, and I don't know where I am. I want to open my eyes but my body won't listen. Lights flash behind my eyelids, colours, then white and more white.

I'm moving, being pushed along. What happened? What's going on?

The voices sound worried, panicked. Is that Mum? Mum?

Nothing. The blackness wraps around me, comforts me.

I'm warm now and still, very still. There are hushed voices nearby, but I can't make out what they're saying. I try and lift a hand, but it hurts. My entire body thrums with a strange kind of numbness. I'm fuzzy, out of step with my body.

I try and remember how I got here. Wherever here is.

There's a weird humming, a low buzz, and a clinical smell in the air... *Hospital.* I'm in hospital.

And then I remember the car—the car I didn't see coming because I was crying. Why was I crying?

Jackson. Our argument. I try to push the memory away. I don't want it. I move my head and hear a whimper. Was that me?

Someone takes hold of my hand, someone soft, loving. *Mum?*

I try to open my eyes, but they feel stuck together.

'It's okay baby girl, we're here.'

Mum. It *is* Mum. I rest back into the pillow and feel the tiredness take over. Pushing out the pain, the memory...

I'm dreaming. I know it's a dream because I'm dancing with Jackson again. We're happy, so happy. I look down, expecting to see green silk blending with the navy and green of his kilt and instead I see white.

It's our wedding day. Our wedding day...

Wake up, Cait, don't taunt yourself with this. Wake up!

'Wake up, Cait.' I realise the voice is real. It's Dad.

'Maybe she needs more sleep,' I hear Mum say as someone puffs the pillows beneath me, and the head end of the bed rises up.

'It's been two days.'

Two days?

My lashes flutter open and my hand is taken up as Mum appears a foot away from my face. '*Cait!*'

'Mum?'

I don't sound like me. My voice is raw, scratchy.

'Oh, darling, it's so good to see you!'

I see her eyes well up but it's impossible to focus with her so close.

'Back up a little, love.' My dad places a hand on her shoulder as he leans into view. 'You're sending her boss-eyed.'

'Dad?'

'Hey, kiddo, it's good to see you awake.'

I try to smile but inside I feel like my heart is breaking all over again. My vision blurs as tears well and my mum is back up close again, her hand softly squeezing mine.

'It's okay, love.'

It's not okay. But how can I tell them that? 'What happened?'

'You were…you were hit by a car…' Mum's voice breaks. 'Do you remember?'

I nod and close my eyes then press my head back into the pillow and try to ease the discomfort that seems to throb through my entirety.

'You were lucky, love,' Dad says. 'Not that you'll feel like it right now, but the doctor says you'll make a full recovery. That's the important thing.'

I want to ask what I've done, what injuries I've sustained, but it makes my stomach swim. I look around the room. It's a private room—chairs, table, TV. *Chairs?* I frown as I spy the leather jacket slung over one. Mum and Dad don't own—

'They're having a coffee machine crisis, so I opted for a pot of tea.'

Jackson.

'*Cait?*' His eyes widen and his body freezes, a tray with a teapot and mugs outstretched before him. How is it possible he can look like hell and still I find him so gorgeous that my heart's fluttering wildly in my chest? 'You're awake.'

'Good timing, son.' Dad walks over to him and takes the tray from his unmoving form. 'Come on, Marlene, let's leave these two lovebirds to it.'

'Back soon, love.'

Mum kisses my forehead but I can't respond. My eyes are glued to Jackson. Is he real? Am I still dreaming? Have the drugs done this to me—made me hallucinate? I know I must be on plenty, that the woozy feeling in my gut isn't all down to him.

Mum closes the door and it's just us. He steps towards me and my eyes widen. He's definitely real. So very real and still so very tortured.

And I'm still so in love with him it hurts more than any bruise to my body.

'I'm sorry. I can go. Now that I know you're okay, now you're awake…' His voice is hoarse, his grey eyes bloodshot. When did he last sleep? 'I can leave if that's what you want.' His voice cracks and his eyes water. 'I just had to know you were okay. And to tell you that I came after you. When you left, I came after you to tell you…'

'To tell me what?'

'To tell you I was a fool, to beg your forgiveness,

to tell you that I love you, Cait. God help me, I love you and I've been an idiot, and I'm so—'

'*Stop*.'

I try to push myself up in the bed and wince as the pain grips me. He rushes to my side.

'Don't move.'

'I need… I can't… Did you just say what I think you did?'

Carefully, he takes up my hand, his touch so gentle and a dramatic contrast to the ferocity in his eyes. 'I love you, and I'm so sorry.'

I choke as I try to speak, and a tear runs over one lid. He cups my cheek, brushing it away with the pad of his thumb, his eyes hooked on mine. 'I love you, baby, and if you can forgive me I'll do everything I can to prove it to you.'

'Is this really happening?' The tears are streaming down my face now. I want so much to kiss him, to lean in and take away the tears I see welling in his eyes too, but I can't move.

'Yes.'

'It's not the drugs?'

He gives a soft laugh. 'No, baby, it's all real. Please say you can forgive me?'

I wet my lips. 'Of course I forgive you. I love you, Jackson.'

He bows his head, drags in a breath, and when he looks back at me his head is shaking; the overhead lights glitter in his eyes as they spill over. 'You have no idea how good it feels to hear you say that again.'

I give him a small smile. 'I have a fair idea.'

'I'm a lucky man.' His eyes turn grave as they waver over my face. 'I know I still don't deserve you, but I can't walk away. I'm nothing without you by my side, Cait. The second you walked out I knew it, I knew…and then when I ran after you and…and…'

His voice breaks and my inability to reach for him pulls me apart inside. 'Jackson?'

'Yes?'

'Please shut up and kiss me.'

His mouth quirks up, his damp smile everything. 'I don't want to hurt you.'

'You're hurting me more by not kissing me.'

He chuckles as he leans down, his lips sweeping softly over mine. 'I love you, Caitlin. I love everything about you, right down to your obsession with Christmas.'

'Oh, God.' My eyes fly open. 'Christmas! I'm going to miss it.'

He shakes his head at me, his fingers gentle as he strokes the hair from my face. 'You won't.'

'But what day is it today? It must be the twenty-first…the twenty-second? I'm not—'

'Shh, your mum has it covered.'

'She does?'

'Of course she does. She's Mrs Claus incarnate and has already been on at the staff about what she can get away with.'

'She has?'

'Yes, baby. Christmas will be coming to you, and when you get out of here we'll have another Christmas Day…on a day of our choosing.'

'We will? You and me? But you hate Christmas…'

'That was before I fell in love with Santa's Little Helper.'

I smile and this time it fills my face. I am happy. So very happy. And as I look up into Jackson's eyes I realise he is too.

No more demons. No more torment.

Love. Just love.

'Hey hey, sis! Check you out!'

I look past Jackson to see the door open and a queue as far as my eyes can see…brothers, wives, Granny… I give a soft laugh.

'The Careys are in the house,' Jackson murmurs.

'And now you're one of them,' I say, turning my hand over so I can squeeze his. 'I love you, Jackson Black.'

'Love you too, my naughty elf.'

EPILOGUE

One month later

I OPEN THE door to Jackson's flat and frown. I can hear music—not just any music, but Mariah Carey at her finest: 'All I Want for Christmas is You'.

'Jackson?'

I step inside, pushing the door closed behind me and stop still. Stunned doesn't even cover it. Filling the living area is a Christmas tree, its lights twinkling, its glass baubles in various shades of gold shimmering. It's stunning. Exquisite. But it's the end of January. Where do you even get a tree as late as this?

I sense movement and turn on the spot and—freeze.

No way.

Jackson side-shimmies into the room and starts to mime! Actually mime Mariah Carey! And he's wearing...

'Oh, my God, what are you wearing?'

'You don't like it?'

his Santa hat swinging on his head, his red jacket with white fluffy trim falling open to reveal his tattooed chest, a hint of biceps, and I cover my mouth with my hand, my eyes watering up.

'I thought it would be right up your street.'

He does a roll that has the bare muscles of his chest rippling all the way down to the tight V disappearing into a wide Santa buckle and bright red shorts...

'You do look pretty fine, but you, in a Santa costume?'

I shake my head as he continues his act, extending his little jig my way and I'm torn between salivating over his gorgeous body and giggling at this new festive version of the man I love.

'I told you I owed you a decent Christmas. Just you wait until you see what's in my sack.'

I can't help it, I erupt, my entire body vibrating with all-out laughter and he stops and pouts. 'Right, that does it, time to punish my naughty elf.'

He lunges forward and sweeps me up in his arms. I let out a shriek but there's no stopping his stride for the bedroom.

'Is that...*turkey* I can smell?'

'Yup.'

'And, hey, is that Granny's special eggnog on the side?'

'Yup.'

'Mulled wine?'

'Of course.'

'Do I have a stocking?'

'Why don't you stop asking questions and see for yourself?'

He sets me down in the bedroom and there at the end of the bed is a neat little bundle. I give a squeal and race towards it, lifting it up and giving it a little jiggle. 'Well, it's not Lego.'

He shakes his head at me, his eyes dancing, and I'm hooked on his whole body. He does look delicious as Santa.

'You want to open it or are you going to continue eating me with your eyes?'

I'm so excited. I tip it upside down on the bed and out falls a small square box.

I'm still. I don't think I'm even breathing.

No…it can't be.

The red velvet seems to throb up at me from the deep grey sheet and I… I don't know what to do. I almost daren't open it. I don't want to get my hopes up, I don't…

I look at Jackson and he walks towards me, his eyes sincere.

'Caitlin Carey…' he pauses before me and lowers himself to *one knee* '…will you do this reformed Grinch the honour of becoming his wife?'

'Are you serious?'

He takes up the box from the bed and opens it for me. At its heart is the most exquisite ring, its cluster of diamonds shaped to form a snowflake, and it's beautiful, oh, so beautiful. My vision blurs as I hiccup on a cry.

'I know we've not been together long, but you've

always been the one. From the moment you fell in my lap six years ago, it's been you and only you.'

I'm too stunned to speak. Of all the things I expected, wished for even, this is so much more.

'If you need time, that's fine. I just want you to know how serious I am. And if you'll have me I'll spend the rest of my life making sure you know I love you.'

I stare down into his face and see all his love shining back at me and smile through the tears.

'I will marry you…on one condition.'

His brows lift. 'Anything.'

'You wear this every Christmas. Or a variation thereof. You make the most delicious Santa. I'm quite—'

My words are cut off as he launches to his feet and swings me around, his lips crushing mine.

'You've got it. So long as you return the gesture?'

'Oh, I think that can be arranged.'

He lowers me to my feet and slips the ring out of the box and onto my eagerly awaiting finger.

'Merry Christmas, Elf-to-be.'

'Merry Christmas, Santa.'

* * * * * * *

COMING SOON!

We really hope you enjoyed reading this book.
If you're looking for more romance, be sure to
head to the shops when new books are
available on

Thursday 24th December

To see which titles are coming soon, please visit
millsandboon.co.uk/nextmonth